AN AM

An American Killing

Mary-Ann Tirone Smith

HEADLINE
FEATURE

First published in 1998
by HEADLINE BOOK PUBLISHING

First published in paperback in 1999
by HEADLINE BOOK PUBLISHING

A FEATURE paperback

10 9 8 7 6 5 4 3

ISBN 0 7472 5892 9

Typeset by CBS, Martlesham Heath, Ipswich, Suffolk

Printed and bound in Great Britain by
Clays Ltd, St Ives plc.

HEADLINE BOOK PUBLISHING
A division of Hodder Headline PLC
338 Euston Road
London NW1 3BH

This book is dedicated to Arlene Dippé Manchester and C. Duncan Yetman: inspiring; responsive; passionate. English teachers.

1

The cathedral is still, as cold and silent as the stone it's made of. An uneasiness is settling in, a perceptible worry that the next speaker has forgotten his turn. We peek into our programs to see who the offender is and produce a muffled shuffling. But then a soprano's voice penetrates the vast space, singing the first bars of 'Nearer My God to Thee.' Her tone is like the clean note of a lone piercing flute, sharp, a sound uncapturable on a CD. It's making my chest hurt. I feel Myron's body mass lean against me. He whispers into my ear, 'Denise?'

I lean into him and whisper back, 'What?'

'Who the hell planned all this anyway?'

'The President.'

'No shit.'

'Sh-h-h.'

I thought all morning about avoiding the memorial service, but my mother always said that if you shirk your duty, people will talk. She'd offer me her sage bits of advise just before keeling over, dead drunk. Sometimes her advice was more practical, as in 'If you don't know what to wear, you can't go wrong with a suit.' Then she'd belch. So I have managed to get myself to Dulles, where I picked up Myron, and on to the National Cathedral, where I'm wearing a suit.

Myron and I are in the back third of the pews. The first third is filled with one percent family and ninety-nine percent friends of Congressman Owen Allen Hall, Democrat of Rhode Island. The family, taking up not quite all of the first pew, is a paltry gang of ice-cold blue bloods from across New England who live on purposely bucolic estates with acres of pastureland and nary a cow pie in sight. Owen has no immediate family, no wife or children. He never married.

The friends are Washington's real-life kingmakers and major sellers of influence: smug speechwriters, self-absorbed pollsters, and, his puffy gray head above the rest, our President. My husband, Nick Burke, Bill Clinton's domestic affairs adviser – former academic, now whore – is up there with all the President's men.

The next third of the church holds the in-betweens – prima donna anchormen, talking heads, lobbyists, the constituent bloc gangsters: all the patrons who never socialized with Owen, though he made them feel as if they did, faking them out with brilliant panache.

And then there are the rest: pitifully young aides hanging on by their fingernails, those besotted interns – indentured servants, all – and the vampires of the press corps. Smack in the middle of that band, Myron and me.

I could have been sitting with Nick, but I told him I should guard Myron and keep him from embarrassing anyone. From embarrassing Nick, mostly. Myron only came to the service to take advantage of any passing opportunity to drum up new business; he sees everyone, even Nick, as a potential book deal. His book deal with the congressman is now in an urn back in Owen's hometown, New Caxton, Rhode Island: What remains of Owen is in the family vault.

Myron says, a little more loudly, 'I didn't know dead congressmen got state funerals.'

Again I say, 'Sh-h-h.' But this isn't a state funeral. 'It's a memorial service.'

'Well, it's certainly got all the trappings.'

It only seems like trappings. There has been no lying-in-state, no wake, no paying of respects, no services at graveside. Not in the capitol or anywhere else. There will be no burial at Arlington. My friend Poppy Rice asked me if Owen's family was planning to scatter the ashes. I told her that as far as I was concerned they should be made to eat them, with the citizens of New Caxton forced to serve them up. Poppy agreed.

There is not a single voting, taxpaying constituent of Owen's seated in the cathedral, not even the mayor of New Caxton. They know their place; they are servants, riffraff. I envision the mayor back home on Main Street, passing out cups of Jonestown Kool-Aid, and all the people lining up, welcoming their punishment like the good soldiers they are.

Myron says, 'That singer is sensational, isn't she?'

She is a famous diva, but I am no longer surprised at Myron Harper's provincial exclamations when he's out of his milieu. He's a fiduciary. He thinks he's more than that, as all fiduciaries do. When he's negotiating a contract, he's authoritative, arrogant, a bully. When he's looking to acquire a writer, his charm is such that he'll slide you right into his back pocket without your feeling the maneuver at all. That's how he convinced Owen Hall to consider him when he was ready to produce a book. Now he has to pretend he's mourning the congressman rather than the lost fifteen percent of what could have been a trove.

I introduced them the night Owen showed up in New York at a cocktail party given each year by the Literary Guild for certain publishers, editors, agents, and writers. Everyone in the publishing world who is not invited and, lately, many in the movie business, also uninvited, crash it. It's half invited guests and half crashers. Myron said to Owen, 'Listen, Congressman, Denise here'll tell you – I'm the best.'

When I picked up Myron at the airport, he told me Owen had actually contacted him. He'd signed an agreement with Myron to produce a book about the success of his liberal policies, formerly known as women's issues. At first I thought Owen must have been trying to divert attention from himself, but then I realized it was to direct attention *toward* him, because he would be better protected from controversy if he were in the limelight looking noble – a plan that was imploding as he lay dying.

Myron may be the best, but he doesn't know how to act outside his dissolute world. I said to Poppy once, 'Myron really does need to be socialized.' And she said, 'But if he were, considering all you've said, it means he wouldn't be an effective agent, right?' Absolutely right.

With the hymn sung, the clergyman or bishop or whatever he's called begins going on and on about Owen's untimely death. The man puts great emphasis on the word *untimely*: '. . . cut down in his prime, at the height of triumphs wherein he'd begun to erase the line between the worthy poor and the unworthy poor. This *untimely* tragedy cuts deeply into all of us who care about the invisible but oppressed poor.' He is hinting at government bailouts of corporations like Lockheed after their boards squander all their money and then come crying to Washington. But he is talking about Owen, who cared about poor children, Owen, who glared down at the President but couldn't sway him from signing the Republican welfare bill. Owen asked me at the time, 'So which President do you think supported the original welfare bill? Saw to it that it passed?' I said, 'Johnson.' It was Nixon. Owen said, 'Of course, it was back when the best thing for poor children was for Mom to stay home.' Owen laughed then. Threw his hands up.

The bishop continues with his accolades: how Owen devoted himself to changing the world for the good, and what an *untimely* loss this is to all Americans.

But Owen's death is not untimely, it is unseemly.

They found Owen in a suite at the Willard Hotel, draped with ropes, lying amid broken glass ampules. A Chinese cord was hanging out of his rectum. 'What in God's name is a Chinese cord?' I asked Poppy, who told me these details.

She said, 'Haven't you ever been in a sex shop?' The question was rhetorical. 'See, Denise, it's a kind of rope made out of string, string dyed gold – that's the difference between a cord and a rope, if you're ever a contestant on *Jeopardy*!; cords are gold – and it's maybe a yard long and it's got knots tied along its length every six inches or so depending on individual preference. While you're having sex and the guy is about to ejaculate, he or you gives the cord a yank and out pops the knot and you get to delay his coming – or your coming, if you're the recipient of the cord. From the photos I've seen I'd say girls get to experience the thrill as well, but Jesus, Denise, I mean, it's one thing to have to take time out to stick a diaphragm up your zip, but imagine calling time to cram a rope up your ass? Spare me.'

'Cord.'

'Yeah.'

Poppy was indelicate on purpose; she thought I needed a lack of delicacy in order to see what a fool I've been. To get me back on track. A reality check, as one is wont to say these days.

A woman was in the room with Owen. She didn't die until after the paramedics got her untied and untangled. Congressman Owen Allen Hall, womanizer extraordinaire, and an unidentified call girl killed each other via rough sex. He collapsed on her, wasted, accidentally tightening the rope, not cord, that was around their necks.

Very few people know all the gory details. They think they know them, but the sex paraphernalia was left out of news releases. My husband knows them because he is on the inside, another Yale law pal of the President. And Congressman Hall was a pal of Bill's too, not through Yale. Owen was a Rhodes scholar during Bill Clinton's all-play no-work year at Oxford, the reward for having finished the best schools at the top of their class. As if that bunch saw fit to protest Vietnam. They were far too busy carousing like the Young Turks they were.

My husband filled me in on every detail of Owen's death to punish me. Nick didn't know I'd already heard it all from Poppy. When he came to the part, 'And do you know what a Chinese cord is, Denise?' he didn't hear me when I said, 'Yes.' That's because Nick is an orator. Orators never wait for answers, they proceed to answer their questions themselves. So he told me what Poppy had told me.

But I'd already expressed my remorse for what I'd done the day I'd blurted out my confession. Our affair had been over for months now. It was as if Owen's death triggered a deeper resentment Nick had been able to put aside or at least been careful to hide. Or maybe it finally hit him that when I made my apology I wasn't apologizing for actually having had the affair. At the time, apologizing had just been an attempt to be civilized, the way Nick had taught me. Nick places great importance on acting in a civilized manner and placing your rage elsewhere. Instead of socking someone in the eye who has just done you wrong, you smile with pomposity and go out and shout at an inconsequential staff member that she's an embarrassment to the entire office and if she dares make such a boneheaded mistake again, she's out.

When he finished with the oration, I said, 'More punishment won't make me tell you I'm sorry again. And why would you want to hear it? Do you think forcing me to continue lying to you demeans me further?' He wasn't listening. 'Did he have you do that to him too, Denise?'

Nick saved that question till last, after his description of the leather thongs and the crack pipe in the shape of a penis – a few things Poppy left out. It was the drugs that actually killed Owen, knocked him out, causing his crushing, asphyxiating collapse. I'd sat through Nick's entire tirade, but with that last question I stood up and slapped him across the face. Nick burst into some sort of uncontrollable hysteria, and I didn't know if he was laughing or crying. He was crying. I took him in my arms and he apologized to me. But he sold the beach house. He wouldn't admit he did that to punish me too, but he did. I loved that place. Loved it. I will never forgive him.

When he finally pulled away from me, he started to say something, but he stopped. Before he left the room, I saw in his face that whatever it was had to do with pity. Nick wasn't angry with me, he just wanted me to see how pathetic I was because of what I'd done. Actually, because of who I'd done it with.

A sudden electricity in the cathedral signals a change of players. Ted Kennedy rambles across the chancel to the pulpit and begins his eulogy. Who else but Kennedy? Owen came in a close second to the senator in the ADA ratings. But Kennedy's cracking voice resurrects memories of all the other eulogies he's delivered over the last thirty years – for Bobby, for Dr King, for his father, for his nephew, for his mother.

Right then I want to say to Myron, Let's get out of here. It's been tough enough listening to the bishop finish his tribute, mesmerizing the audience with Owen's genealogy and hearing Myron rasp, 'I figured he must be a descendent of somebody, but not *Ethan Allen*. Shit.' Shit means he could have asked for even more money for the book that is now consigned to ash. One branch of Owen's family went back to the rousing, drunken Green Mountain Boys, and on his mother's side to the Massachusetts Bay Colony, though alas, dear Myron, to one of the more obscure pilgrims, unnamed; not that it matters anymore.

But there is no getting out of here. Not when you share space with the First Family. Nobody moves until directed. Instead, after Senator Kennedy's cracked, scarred speech, I have to sit and submit to Bill Clinton, who cherishes his cohorts, clings to them even, commanding loyalty for his policies while begging affection for himself like an adorable pooch.

And he is adorable. He and his family spent a weekend with us at the beach house in Watch Hill, on the Rhode Island shore just a few miles from the Connecticut line. We played Trivial Pursuit with a special rule initiated by the First Lady – adults couldn't answer until a kid had a crack at the question. My son gave me the eye – imagine that, a mom who showed mercy!

Nick inherited the beach house from his grandfather; his sister took the family farm, the last dairy in Connecticut, which, when she gets tired of catered picnics, will be subdivided, and then a real fortune will come to her. Nick announced to me the day Owen died that he'd sold the house. He sold it for two million dollars. Could have gotten a lot more but he wanted it done with. The property included a mile-long spit of land and acres of marsh full of all sorts of interesting creatures: weasly animals, minks maybe, and masses of red-winged blackbirds, and, very recently, a pair of nesting ospreys. The sale was the result of Nick's latent rage. Our kids loved it there just as much as I did, just as Nick loved it when he was their age, and so he punishes me extra by punishing them too. I want to kill him. But he is a teacher, my teacher, and he is determined to teach me a lesson I'll never forget.

The mass of people stand when President Clinton returns to his seat and then sit down again when a children's choir begins to sing one of those 'I'd Like to Buy the World a Coke' songs. I gaze out over the backs of people's heads. I see Poppy's kinky mass of sandy blond spirals just off the aisle, halfway down. I wish I were with her instead of Myron. I look off to my left and catch another familiar profile: the prosecutor from Rhode Island. She's weeping. She's weeping, not for Owen but because Owen rejected her back when I was beginning the work he had instigated. When I interviewed her, she was hostile at first. But she became intrigued. She liked the idea of appearing in a book written by me. It would be my fifth book, and I'd gained notoriety. A serious writer like me gains notoriety when her books are made into successful movies with A-list stars, the same way non-serious writers gain notoriety.

But there was more. My last book, my O.J. book, was the most successful of all the O.J. books, the one most talked about, most controversial.

The Rhode Island prosecutor agreed to see me for another reason. She figured maybe there'd be a renewed opportunity for contact with Owen and he'd take her back. But as soon as she laid eyes on me, she knew that Owen, at least for the time being, had someone new. So she ended up treating me like a sorority sister. Seeing her now, I know for sure that I do not want to go to the reception following the service. I do not want to stand in a cold, empty White House hall chatting with Owen's associates, including her. I can perform just so much duty, and if my mother turns over in her grave, tough. Nick will have to explain my absence to people. That's his problem. He can use his imagination. He never used to have a shred of imagination, but he certainly has made up for the lack lately.

I press against Myron. 'Listen, would you mind taking me out for a drink after this? I can't go to the reception. I feel sick. Have a drink with me and then you can go yourself. You don't want to be the first one there, anyway.'

Myron's little wheels turn. Flying through the White House gates. Whipping out his entry pass under the portico. Dashing in late. He says, 'Sure, angel.' He was interviewed when Owen's body was discovered. 'Oh, yes, I'm devastated,' he said. 'The congressman and I had wrapped up a solid proposal, and I was just about to show it.' He then cooed about the need for top-notch political writing, and the whole time he is thanking God for the publicity. Fifteen percent of writers' income is peanuts. Access to those celebrities whose books earn him a wad of money is how he stays in business, how they all stay in business. I am a stroke of unanticipated good fortune. The wad I earned him meant he got to move to a corner power office with ceiling-to-floor windows looking all the way to the East River.

The last person to speak is Owen's brother, Charles. As soon as I heard that Owen died, getting himself killed in such a brutal manner, I blamed Charles for driving him to it. Charles clears his throat and reads the Twenty-third psalm. That's it. Can't think of anything to say about a brother in the process of betraying him, congressman or no. I swear Charles makes eye contact with me just after closing the family Bible. I doubt if anyone is staring at him more intensely than I am.

And then it's over. Our pew gets the sign to stand, and when we file out I steer Myron down the far edge of the marble stairs and past the string of limos. We get in a taxi and I tell the driver where we want to go. 'The Willard, please.'

'Yes, mum,' she says. The driver is a huge black woman wrapped in tie-dyed lengths of cloth. African.

Myron turns from gaping out the window and says to me, 'The Willard? But—'

'A fitting place to pay our respects.'

He sighs. 'Jesus, you're a pip, Denise.'

We zigzag through the traffic. The cabbie looks over her shoulder at us and says, 'Now dat dead congressman, he done been some fine man.'

West African. 'Yes, he done been,' I agree.

'Now some fine Democrat.'

'Yes.'

'Someday we go get some udder Kennedy President.'

'Do you think so?'

'Now true. De Kennedys, dem dey breed like *rats*!'

Then she laughs all over herself. Myron says to me, 'What the hell is she saying?'

'Nothing.'

Over a drink, I think maybe I might cry. I haven't as of yet. At the Willard bar, I tell Myron to order me a scotch. He does, and then he says to the bartender, 'I'll have a kir.' I have no idea why I don't burst out laughing. Maybe that's what keeps me from crying, trying to contain laughter: the outrageous memorial service, the outrageous African taxi driver, the outrageous Myron, and his outrageous choice of drink. And his patting me, saying, 'I'm so sorry, Denise. That Owen was a hell of a guy.' All so comical, really.

Owen was a hell of a guy despite everything. But he didn't need drugs to revel in sex. And there is no way he'd cram a goddamn gold cord up his ass, or anyone else's either. But would he do it if he'd intended to fuck himself to death? Even if it required such utter degradation? Maybe.

Later, after I part company with Myron and I'm sitting in my office staring at the wall, Poppy, who comes to see if I'm still in one piece, says, 'Ya know, Denise, men do different things with prostitutes than they do with the women they love.'

That's her idea of comfort.

2

I called in to my office machine from the lobby of the Willard when Myron and I left the bar. Poppy was on it. Her message: *I guess you're there since you're not over here at the mourning party. And if you're not picking up, I'll just assume you're writing. Glad you're feeling inspired. You get inspired at the weirdest times, Denise. I'll be coming over to check on you around five. If you're still there, I'll see you then.*

There were five other messages, but I skipped the first two from Nick and hit the stop button after Poppy's.

In five years' time, I've gone from a shared desk at the *Bridgefield Press* in a chichi town just outside New Haven, where Nick taught a seminar at Yale and didn't have to correct papers, to my present desk in the capitol, where I have an office that overlooks, appropriately, the FBI building where Poppy Rice runs the crime lab.

I met Poppy in Florida at my first trial. She was representing the people. She got a conviction. The murderer was sentenced to die. Poppy told me she was in Gainesville only for as long as she had to be. She'd said, 'Since uncaught killers gravitate to the Sun Belt, Florida especially, that's where I decided to set up shop. 'Course, every other asshole in the world gravitates here too, so believe me I intend to be on the first plane out just as soon as I make my name.'

A serial killer named Sam Litton made her name, along

with a lot of help from me. He's dead now, executed. He's the one I shared the desk with in Bridgefield – him and an old codger named Leo Schatz. The three of us, giggling at the time, designed a plaque for our desk that read LEO, SAM, AND DENISE – WE KICK BUTT. Everyone there at the *Press* laughed, mostly at the irony of it. The three of us together didn't have the nerve to kill a flea. Well, one did, actually, but the cover he'd created for himself was impeccable. We each wrote a weekly column.

Leo wrote dry sarcastic essays on town concerns that translated to diatribes on his own personal pet peeves, such as the travesty of firemen wanting paid paternity leave. Bad enough the *lady* firemen got handouts when they took time off from work to have babies. 'You want to get in on the game, you don't make up new rules. It's a man's game, so act like a man' was his argument. When he'd run out of things to grouse about, he'd nag me about bringing my dog to the office. He held no truck with the excuse that the dog didn't like being home by himself. Leo didn't care about chewed-up rugs or claw marks on the back door.

Sam did the human-interest sports stories to accompany the latest high school varsity losses. Sam was a graduate student in journalism at Southern Connecticut State University in New Haven, and he had a paid apprenticeship at the *Press*, minimum wage. I was always lending him five bucks. He told me he'd worked for a lot of weekly newspapers since college, and with an advanced degree maybe he'd be able to work for a real one. Me, I wrote the food column; I had to start somewhere. When a woman decides to call a halt to full-time wifery/mothering and all she's got is a degree in French literature, she'll take a shot at just about anything.

Writers at the *Bridgefield Press* tended to come and go, but they usually let their departure dates be known so there'd be an excuse for a party. So when Sam just upped and vanished, Leo and I couldn't understand it. We'd had so many laughs together. Our editor called Southern Connecticut State University. No student named Sam Litton was registered. No, he wasn't studying for a master's degree in journalism – they offered no such program, in fact. Sam had procured or forged all the paperwork received by the *Press* requesting his internship. The address of his New Haven apartment turned out to be the Shubert Theatre. Sam had a subtle sense of humor. It wasn't until six months later that we found out where he went. We read about it in *The New York Times*, not the *Bridgefield Press*. Sam Litton had been arrested in Florida, accused of murdering more than thirty young women from one end of the country to the other over a period of five years, beginning when he was twenty-three. That made him twenty-eight. He looked like a kid, looked ten years younger than he was. Sam killed three women in eastern Connecticut, the other end of the state, where everyone was on welfare at the time – this was before the Indians sent a scouting party into the casino industry – a place where no one paid attention to a mother complaining about a missing teenager. Of all the victims he killed, the last five were in Florida.

The *Bridgefield Press* staffers were in shock that such a lovely young man – Well, yes, he was a liar – could be suspected of such a terrible thing. Sam wrote to Leo and me and asked us to come down and testify at his trial as character witnesses. I decided to do it, I was so incensed that poor Sam could be accused of so much as a littering violation. I didn't think of him as a liar. Maybe the school got things mixed up. Leo said bullshit to that. Told me I was a bleeding-heart liberal who figured there was some tragic reason for Sam's lies. I said, 'Maybe Sam accidentally listed the wrong address. After all, he just moved to New Haven when he filled out the forms.' '*Forged* the forms,' Leo reminded me, after which he'd said, 'I rest my case.' All the same, Leo said he would be willing to testify for Sam, but Florida was one of the two states (the other, California) that he swore he'd never set foot in. At the time, guileless as hell, I said, 'Why is that, Leo?'

He snorted. 'If you need to ask, you'll never understand.'

I said, 'I'm from Sacramento.'

He snorted again. 'I'm hardly talking about Sacramento. I'm talking about *California*.'

I took my trusty interview pad along with me to Florida, in case I felt like writing something. I ended up writing a lot: a book, in fact, and the rest, as they say, is history.

I have two desks now instead of a third of a desk: One is for my computer and one is for thinking – it faces a blank wall. I don't go to my computer until I know what I'm going to type onto it. I also have a sitting area with a giant sofa where I sprawl to think even harder, surrounded by notes and notebooks and tattered clippings falling out of folders, pens and paper clips, and Post-Its stuck over all, most of it slipping down and becoming lost between the overstuffed cushions. Just like I'd done in Bridgefield, I'd bring my dog to the office. He always made for good company. He'd sprawl along with me, right on top of everything, and drool all over the Post-Its, diluting the glue and unposting them, which is why they ended up under the cushions, where they stayed. When I wrote my food column for the *Bridgefield Press*, I discovered that as soon as I wrote something down I remembered it. At the same time, I am too insecure to throw anything away, and now my publisher says, 'You must always be prepared for a lawsuit.' Such preparation, to me, means not cleaning up after myself.

I named my dog Buddy. He was christened Black Streak by my children, who have even less imagination than their father, but, sadly for them, he turned out to be a one-man dog, with me fulfilling his need. So at some point I started calling him Buddy.

My friend Poppy's real name is Penelope. She has a key to my office, and I have clearance to hers. How she got me a pass, I don't know. We do keep some things from each other.

I probably would have gone directly home from the Willard to spend some time with my kids before they hit the books and the TV, but when I get Poppy's message, I head for the office to wait for her. The children will appreciate not having to deal with my asking them questions about their school day.

Poppy knocks five minutes after I get to the office. I watch the door open from my sprawl position on the sofa. She peeps in, frizzy hair first, big blue eyes next.

'You okay, sweetie?'

'Yeah.'

She comes in the rest of the way. She always stands in my office, never sits. In court, she takes to pacing when she needs dramatic effect. She wears short skirts, and her legs run all the way up to her ass.

The first time Poppy came to my office, I said, 'Sit down, for God's sake.' She said, 'I wouldn't sit on all those freakin' dog hairs for love or money.'

Poppy's clothes are expensive. She dresses for success. 'If you want to be successful and you've got nice legs, expose them,' she told me. So I do. Previously, my clothes consisted of jeans and sweatshirts, with a few dresses suitable for an occasion along the lines of Di and Charles's wedding, that fancy and that old. Poppy changed my ways.

She usually leans on my desk or file cabinet, or she saunters to the window, where she can gaze out upon her domain.

When Bill Clinton was elected and I learned we'd be coming to Washington, the thought of living in the same town as Poppy is what got me by all the drek: packaging home and hearth, saying good-bye to Leo and my other friends, and listening to two kids who were just coming into association with that distasteful affliction called adolescence. They were excited about what was happening, but their job as twelve- and thirteen-year-olds was to act weary, bored, and jaded, so they sublimated their excitement by torturing me. I told them to just dismantle the Kurt Cobain shrines and start packing boxes. (My daughter even had a votive candle lit for him. It was supposed to be an eternal flame, but I blew it out and blamed Buddy. At the next birthday party we celebrated, she said, 'Nobody gets a piece of cake until *Buddy* blows out the candles.')

Once Poppy made a name for herself prosecuting Sam Litton, winning the conviction, getting the death penalty, she was where she wanted to be – serving justice from the top rung. 'Not exactly the top rung,' she said, when I called her from Bridgefield to congratulate her, 'the top rung just beneath the glass ceiling.' I countered, 'What about Janet Reno?' and she said, 'A politically motivated presidential appointment to attract the feminist vote or to shut up the suits who say, "We'll take a woman but she'd better be a bowwow" – no offence to Buddy boy – is not the same as breaking the glass ceiling.'

She made it clear to me that my book on Sam Litton enhanced her upward charge and she was grateful and, consequently, loyal. My first loyal friend. Her colorful presence in the book hadn't hurt me either, I was quick to point out. At first I thought she'd be the book's hero. After I'd come back from that first trip to Florida, I spent the afternoon, in shell shock, tête-à-tête with Leo at our joint desk, people pussyfooting around us because they had no idea what to say though they were dying to ask me what my visit with a serial killer had been like. I told Leo what Sam had said, what he'd told me through the bulletproof wire-meshed glass.

Sam had asked me, 'Denise, if you testify for me as a character witness, will you tell them I'm incapable of hurting anyone?'

I nodded strenuously but he kept talking, compelled to convince me to do what I was more than happy to do; I didn't need any convincing.

'Believe me, Denise, I didn't hurt any of them.' With those words, his clear eyes took on a demure glisten.

I said, 'Sam, I believe you,' wishing I could hug him.

'They never felt a thing.'

I repeated, 'A thing,' because there came a loud twang from out of my heart muscle.

'Right. Not a thing. I mean . . . well . . . they experienced terror, obviously. You should have seen their faces when they realized! My God! But no pain. I swear to you, Denise. None.'

I put the receiver back in its cradle, but I watched Sam's lips move and his face contort as he went on, trying to make me see the difference, I guess, between killing someone and inflicting pain and killing someone and only inadvertently causing terror. Then I got up and walked out of the room. I don't remember walking out. I just remember finding myself in the corridor outside the visiting room when Poppy Rice, trailed by two assistants, strode past and glanced at me. She slowed. She said, 'Hey. You okay?'

In my daze of low blood pressure, I said, 'I just spoke with Sam Litton. He said he never hurt anyone.'

Her eyes narrowed. 'You're not one of those damned nuns, are you?' She didn't give me a chance to answer. She said, 'Well, if you are, then you should know this: That son of a bitch is the devil himself.' She turned to an assistant and said, 'Tell her about the plaster cast.' She stalked off down the corridor while the assistant looked from her back to my face.

The assistant said, 'Sam Litton kept a plaster cast in the

back of his car. When he spotted someone who looked promising, he'd slide the cast over his arm. Get a young girl feeling all sloppy and sentimental, you know? Like Florence Nightingale. But what she didn't know was that he's also slipped a crowbar up the cast, up along his inner arm.' The assistant shoved two fingers into his cuff to demonstrate. 'First opportunity he had, he'd let the crowbar slide out and smash her face in with it.'

The other assistant nodded. They were both young men, Sam's age. I got out some words asking where the ladies' room was, but I was rooted to the spot and ended up vomiting right there. I splashed their clothes. People came rushing from all over, including Poppy Rice, who helped me to the ladies' room, where I sobbed and sobbed, an unabashed fool. Then she took a breath freshener spray out of her bag and handed it to me.

I didn't tell Leo this last part. I told him what I came to learn about Sam Litton, our pal, a psychopath who wanted to kill every girl who crossed his path, who returned his smile, who threw him a friendly look, who was pretty, who was single. According to the one survivor of his assaults, her jugular intact though her throat was cut ear to ear, Sam had asked, 'You're not married, now, are you?'

Leo said, 'You figure that's why he didn't kill you too? Because you were married?'

'I guess.'

'Don't believe it for a minute. He knew there was a good chance he'd get caught if he killed a Yale professor's wife.'

He took a flask of something out of his bottom drawer and passed it to me. The drawers were all his; Sam and I only came in two or three times a week, whereas Leo lived there. I took a slug and he took one too. I said, 'What the hell is that stuff?'

'Aquavit. Trust the Scandinavians to know how to warm up.'

I realized I was shivering. But once warmed up, I told Leo I had a plan. I wanted to write a book about Sam Litton, about what he'd done. And about how a crazed, murdering wacko could be your good friend without your ever suspecting that he was Jack the Ripper.

Leo said, 'Denise, what a capital idea! After all, you don't *need* to work. Your husband's got enough money to support you while you have a go.'

'Leo,' I said, 'I darn the man's socks.'

'You've got a cleaning woman, Denise, who no doubt throws out any socks with holes.'

'I was speaking metaphorically.'

An eyebrow went up. 'All right, I'll give you that. This is how he'll pay you for services rendered. A subsidy.'

I said, 'Oh, Leo, don't jerk me around. I'm not in the mood.'

'So then do it. Just go ahead and do it. But if you're at all serious, you understand that you are going to have a hero. A crime book can of course be literature, but without a hero it's automatically schlock.'

'It is?'

'Yes, dear. Read a few. Read Shakespeare's crime books, also known as tragedies. Read *Titus Andronicus*. Read them until you know what you're about. The really successful crime books have heroes. Since you have no idea how to write crime, best to learn from the masters.'

'I didn't know how to write a food column either. I guessed.'

'This will probably be a tad more of a challenge.'

'Who's the hero in *Titus Andronicus*?'

'Read it. There are no shortcuts, Denise.'

So I did. The hero was Lavinia, Titus's daughter. She paid for her heroics by being murdered – first raped, tortured, tongue cut out, and hands lopped off and *then* murdered. Leo's idea of a warning.

* * *

I was fortunate. There was a hero in the case of Sam Litton, all right, and it wasn't Poppy Rice, though I thought so at first. The hero turned out to be a short, quiet, pockmarked cop, the center for my story, who would be a counterpoint to the handsome and charming murderer. This cop knew from years before that there was a nut case running around doing these killings; that it was just one particular guy, a guy dumping dead girls in the lakes, rivers, and ponds of the Northwest, the Southwest, the Midwest, New England, and, finally, Florida. A nut who was shrewd enough to get rid of the bodies in spots where he would have an opportunity to clean up before heading back to class in Seattle, back to his apartment in Phoenix, back to his wife in Portland, back to the other wife and his little toddler in Albuquerque, back to his job at the *Bridgefield Press*, back to his last job, managing editor at a Gainesville weekly. The cop knew that someone with such a lust for killing would eventually become less shrewd and make do when no natural washrooms were available.

This cop wanted just one thing, to see the job he'd started through to its finish so he could go back home to his little house in that part of Oregon as far from the Pacific Ocean as you can get without being in Idaho, to an area where the jukeboxes still play Patti Page instead of the northwest bands, and where the coffee is Maxwell House, not latte.

He was a demon, that cop, determined to uncover the truth, to initiate justice. When I asked him what would make Sam Litton do what he did, he said it wasn't in his interest to figure out why. I told him that's what I wanted to do – figure out why. He believed me, though I was performing on my feet and had no idea what I wanted to do right then. I convinced him that my book would be a way to warn people to recognize evil, to be on the lookout for the other Sam Littons lurking.

So he agreed to tell me everything.

As Leo once conceded, 'Denise, you're a world-class bullshitter. So am I. That's why we get along.'

When it was over, when Sam was found guilty, the cop was gone, back to Oregon. Didn't stay for the festivities. Never let anyone thank him.

There in Florida, I found out something Leo hadn't doped out: A hero needs a colorful secondary. In the case of Sam Litton, all the cop's heroics wouldn't have been worth pea soup if Poppy Rice hadn't won the case. The first time Poppy and I got together socially, alone, after my interviews with her, still pretrial, we decided to have a drink and relax. It had been an especially long day, with Sam trying to convince the judge to let him bring in an incest expert. Sam would defend himself. All the actions of serial killers are motivated by the need to manipulate and dominate: the ultimate control freaks. Sam would get to live out the second of his grand fantasies. The first was to control women to the point of snuffing them out, always obliterating their faces to show his superiority, and now he could control a judge and jury to the point of finding him innocent, so he could be on his merry way, off to find yet another sweet young girl. Sam said, in his defense, that his mother had had sex with him from the time she brought him home from the hospital two days after giving birth until he was fifteen years old and ran away from home successfully.

At some point, I think around our third drink, Poppy raised her glass and said, 'Let's toast the dedicated cop from Oregon, shall we?'

'Yes, we shall.'

She said to me, 'So are you dying to get into his pants or what?'

I started to lie, but Poppy and I had bonded. My first bond with my first friend. So instead I said, 'Dying.'

'Me too. He's the pivot in this case. Everything turns on the evidence he's dredged up. But whenever I talk to him I never know what the hell I'm saying, 'cause all I can think of is, I want to fuck this guy for about twenty-four straight hours.'

'He won't do it though, right?'

'Too busy showing me pictures of his kids.'

'Did you try to get him to? After he put the pictures away?'

'Yeah.'

'Did he just say no?'

'Not quite. He said, "No, thanks, Miss Rice, but I appreciate the sentiment." Shit.'

Being tipsy, I said, 'Oh, well, he's probably got one of those little purple two-inch-dart dicks.'

The big blue eyes took me in. Then she threw back her head and hooted.

So did I. And I added, 'But I doubt it.'

'We'll never know, will we?'

So we ended up toasting the cop's mystery dick. Then I told her he was my hero. She said, 'Yeah, well, we've already determined that.'

'No, I mean he's my book's hero.' I explained Leo's theory of a hero as the crucial element of successful crime writing. She seemed to lose interest. So I said, 'Listen, when I put this book together, I'm going to have to go out to Oregon and interview him. Maybe he'll decide to forget about his kids for just one afternoon. Maybe he'll find me irresistible.'

Poppy said, 'Forget it. Heroes don't go around fucking other men's wives.'

3

In my office, three hours after Owen's memorial service, Poppy comforts me once more. 'You'll have to hold up here, Denise. After all, you're the crème de la crème of true crime, and you have your public to consider.'

I say, 'Oh, Poppy. Crème. Right.'

'There are no other crèmes, when you think about it.'

'Truman Capote.'

'I meant alive.'

'Alvin Blanchard.'

'*The Uncharted Passage* was a fluke. The rest of his books suck.'

'Scott Gaffney.'

'His head's up his ass.'

I have to smile. Poppy hates men, all of them. Politicians, writers, lawyers – all the men she works for and all the ones she orders around at work, every last one of them. That's why she's so promiscuous. She keeps trying to like them. First she thinks she might like someone, then she goes to bed with him hoping that maybe even *love* will blossom, and then she ends up full of loathing. I tried once to tell her to wait till she started to feel love blossom *before* making love to someone. She said, 'A fresh idea, Denise. But what if, while I'm waiting for this blossoming between me and the steamfitter checking out the FBI plumbing, I get hit by a Mack truck and miss the greatest fuck of my life?'

I love men. I love women. I love children. I love dogs. I told Poppy women are from Earth, men are from Earth. There are no women on Venus and no men on Mars. We're all here. On Earth. We're all the same – that is, humans. Except dogs. We've got our good sides and our bad sides. Men have virtues, women have virtues. Men have flaws, women have flaws. All comes out in the wash.

Poppy said to that, 'Men are schmucks. They can't be trusted.'

I said, 'Some women can't be trusted.'

She said, 'Denise, we're talking about sex, aren't we?'

I hadn't thought we were. For two bonded people, we're usually in the same church, but never in the same pew.

In my office, she takes a bottle of vodka out of her fine black leather tote. I don't keep liquor around because alcoholism is in my genes and I can't risk becoming a lush. She pours us drinks and I take one, even though I've had that scotch at the Willard with Myron. I try to stick to only one when I'm in a public place or at a party, but when it's in my office with just Poppy, I figure it's okay. Nick has pointed out to me that one drink and I'm adorable, two and I'm calling the pope and Mother Teresa a couple of cocksuckers. And this is true. I referred to someone as a cocksucker when I was with Owen one night, and he said, 'I love aggressive women,' so I asked, 'Why haven't you ever socialized with Poppy Rice then?' and he said, 'Jesus, not that aggressive.'

Poppy and I settle in. We don't talk while we let the vodka slip down into our gullets, enjoying the soothing sensation. Once warm, I say, 'I wish that damned church had heat.'

She says, 'Its spring. Besides, you can't feel heat in a church no matter how high they jack up the thermostat.' Then she says, 'I can't help you on this one, Denise.'

'I'm not asking.'

'I know. But I wish I could offer.'

'I realize you can't. You've made that clear already.' She couldn't. Her job was real important. An important job in general and very important to her, personally. Her life.

'I know you've done crucial things for me,' she said.

'Just one, not counting the Sam Litton book. And there was far less risk.'

'There was plenty of risk. But you went ahead.'

I went to the President. The weekend he was at the beach house. In the middle of a conversation about how the ship was running without him, he brought up the mess going on at the FBI crime lab. I slipped into the conversation a little mention that the only one who wasn't fucking things up at the lab was Poppy Rice. He wrinkled his brow for just an instant, and I could see her image registering with him. I knew it would, since she's blond and beautiful and built like a brick shithouse. I'd given him a gift. Now he could go ahead and can the head of the lab and not have to spend time agonizing over who to replace him with. As soon as he got back to Washington, he canned the guy and replaced him with a woman. Made lots of points. Only thing, Poppy had fucked up plenty just like the rest of them. Things tend to get lax in independent republics tucked away amid bigger countries.

So people waited for Poppy to make a mistake so they could go squalling to the boss. But Poppy would make none. She cleaned house and saw to it that she lived up to my unobtrusive recommendation. If she hadn't, Bill Clinton would have remembered my words and then disappeared Nick.

Now I say to her, 'I never believed for a minute that there was a risk.'

'Denise,' she says, 'I remember when I met you. You were so far out of your league, we all let you sneak in without the smallest qualm. Kind of looked at you like some sort of stray cat with mange that you don't throw out on the street because the guy next to you will think you're a dirtbag, and maybe you want to continue to stay next to him for any number of sound reasons. Being out of the league, you had vision unlike the rest of us, who were just doing our jobs. You saw a big picture in the shit that was piling up all around. We were having fits that Sam Litton was going to defend himself, and then you point out that he'd be doing our jobs for us: the last thing we wanted. It meant we wouldn't get the opportunity to be big shots.

'So right now, you're not seeing the big picture because of Owen. Forget this new book and find another murder. Just chuck it. Owen's dead. You were doing it for him and don't deny it. You don't owe him this. You don't owe Owen a goddamn thing.'

It is true that I had started out doing it for Owen. No, not *for* Owen, *because* of Owen. But I'm doing it for me now. I say, 'It's really taking shape. It's going to be a good book. I'm continuing with it. It's been a long time since this has had anything to do with Owen.'

'Oh, bullshit, Denise. What shape? Since when did you start talking in terms of shape? What happened to "Oh, my books just seem to write themselves"? Now suddenly you're talking *shape*! This is nothing but excuses. You can't let go of him. You—'

'Poppy, this book is going to be more than entertainment. My books don't write themselves, I was just never trained to take credit. I think I'm moving forward here.'

'Forward? Well, then, shall we drink to delusions of grandeur? To the Pulitzer Prize?'

'Thanks a lot.'

'Shit. I'm sorry.'

'You know, I really don't need any garbage from you.'

'I said I was sorry. You know I didn't mean it. I'm just so worried—'

'I never had a real mother, and I sure don't want one now.'

'I know. But—'

'Poppy?'

'Yeah?'

'I got mugged three weeks ago.'

'Say what?'

'I've been meaning to tell you.'

'You've been meaning to tell me? What in God's name are you talking about?'

'I don't know.'

'You don't know?'

'Poppy, stop turning what I say into a question.'

'Then stop giving me this "I don't know" shit.'

'It seemed like it was a dream when it happened. You know how awful it is when people bore you with their dreams. I didn't want to bore you.'

'Denise!'

'Listen, I'd just come back from my trip, and we all realize how traumatic *that* turned out to be. And then Nick sells our beach house, and suddenly Owen dies . . . We were all so nuts. I just wasn't able to tell you. Really.'

Poppy waves her hand so I'll stop blathering, sits down next to me into the dog hairs, and says, 'If you leave out one single solitary detail, Denise, I'll murder you.'

She slugs down another shot of vodka without offering me any.

When I'm working, I follow a pretty firm routine. Every Thursday after lunch, I go to the library way over on K Street near the navy shipyards. Not a hell of a noteworthy neighborhood, but kind of an appropriate place to keep up my ongoing quest for literary crimes. A place where crimes regularly occur. Atmosphere. The K Street library gets daily newspapers from every major city in the United States. Every Thursday I read dozens of them, searching. I could do this on the Internet via a search engine, but there'd be no atmosphere, only a monitor. I hate monitors, formerly known as TV screens. My mother had a TV going twenty-four hours a day. No matter how polluted she was, how seemingly unconscious, if I turned it off she'd sit bolt upright and say, 'Oh my God, Denise, don't!'

Even when I'm already into a book, I try to continue the routine – maybe because this library has an easy chair over in a corner of the reading room that is the most comfortable chair I've ever sat in. It's an orange and loden print, a sixties color combo, a chair from the era Nick waxes nostalgic over. I also love the light at this library. The windows face a branch of the Anacostia River, and what with the water and the sky, the light is ethereal. A nice strong contrast to the disgusting events I read about, searching for a crime where the victims and the murderers are basic folk like the rest of us, me and you, or our friends, so to speak, or even family. Like Sam Litton. My pal. When O.J. was acquitted, I knew the reason all those black people refused to think he did it (besides assuming that the cops planted evidence – what's new?) was because they felt O.J. was basic folk. Their cousin. They'd known him for a long time, ever since he went to college. He'd never done anything bad before. Who can believe your cousin could murder someone? I hadn't believed it of Sam because I'd never known any murderers before. This was the closest I'd come to a murderer, and he was someone I knew and liked a lot. I couldn't – wouldn't – believe he was capable of the acts he'd been accused of until he explained to me that he hadn't hurt anyone. It was hardly his fault that they'd gotten so damn scared.

Sam Litton was convinced he was innocent. Sam believed

the lives of the people he killed weren't significant; it was no loss that they were gone. It didn't really count as *murder*. All sociopaths believe what they choose to believe. What was important for Sam was to make me and his jury understand that he wasn't a bad person. After all, he never hurt anyone. As soon as people understood this, they'd believe him when he said he'd learned his lesson and wouldn't kill anyone else. Promise.

Because of the light, the K Street library is a good place to think as well as to read. I don't write until I've done a lot of reading and thinking.

There's a Metro stop half a block from the library entrance, so when I'm through for the afternoon, I go out the door and I'm back home in Alexandria just about the time the school van discharges Cheech and Chong. I force the kids to have cookies and milk with me, something my mother never did. Some famous feminist said that if you wish someone had done something for you but didn't, quit brooding and do it for yourself. My daughter has pointed out that the idea is for the mom to have been home all day slaving in a hot kitchen, *baking* the cookies. The time she said this, we all three burst out laughing at such an image. My son said, 'Never mind, Ma, nobody's mother makes cookies as good as these' – Pepperidge Farm Nantuckets.

I tell Poppy what happened that day. 'I came out of the library, took a turn on the sidewalk toward the Metro entrance, and then some kind of whirlwind picked me up. I mean, all I was aware of was being efficiently lifted off my feet and rushed into a car. I—'

'Mugged? You were grabbed and put in a car and you're calling it *mugged*?'

'I guess it was beyond mugged. That's what I get for day-dreaming.'

'Don't you dare put any schoolgirl composition spin on this. You weren't daydreaming, you were working. You were thinking about some crime.'

'Thanks, Poppy.' No wonder she's my friend. All my life, I'd heard, Stop daydreaming!

'So what happened?'

'I wish I knew. I was jammed between these two men in the back seat of a big car. Wedged in. I finally said something, something ridiculous, like, "Just what do you people think you're doing?"

'But they didn't speak. In the front, the driver concentrated on maneuvering through the traffic. I demanded they tell me where they were taking me. I tried to convince them they had the wrong person. I told them if they were kidnapping me for a ransom, not to bother, just take me to an ATM and I'd give them everything. I told them my husband was the President's domestic affairs adviser. I even told them I was the one who wrote—'

'Denise, did you ever scream?'

'No.'

'Why not?'

'They looked like the type who would maybe hit me if I did.'

Poppy's lips press together. Her eyes are hard. She will not respond to that.

'Besides, the windows were closed. Who'd have heard me? There's a lot of traffic at that time. But I watched where we were going: Baltimore. We were taking the exact route you take to get to Camden Yards. We were almost there and I heard this noise, and I didn't know what the hell it was at first. It was a cellular phone ringing. The guy driving picked it up off the passenger seat, opened it, and said, Yeah. He listened, and then he said, *You sure?* He listened some more, flipped it shut, and pulled over. He said one more thing: *Let her out.*

'Poppy, I was out of that car so fast, it was just like when they grabbed me. You're kind of aware of this big physical movement, and then you're suddenly in a different place. One minute I was in the car and the next I was standing by the side of the road with all the tourists, gaping like an idiot at them speeding away. So I saw a couple of cabs and flagged one down. It costs a hundred and forty-five dollars to take a cab from Camden Yards to Alexandria, in case we ever want to go to a ball game and we're not in the mood to drive.'

'What day was it?'

'What?'

'What day did it happen?'

'I don't know. Three weeks ago, I told you. I usually go to the library on Thursdays . . . that's where it happened. But I'd been going every day. I think it was a Thursday, though.' I notice that Poppy's hands are trembling. I take one of them. She pulls it away. I say, 'Don't you pull away from me. I'm your friend, remember? I'm sorry I shook you up, but I wasn't actually mugged. I mean physically mugged. Nothing happened. They didn't even take my bag.'

'They took *you*. That's not mugged. That's kidnapped.' She leans back into the sofa and closes her eyes for a moment. Then she says, 'My God, Denise. Jesus. What the hell did Nick say?'

'Didn't tell him either.'

I meant it when I said to Poppy it seemed a dream. 'They must have had the wrong person. I didn't want to upset Nick. You know how crazed I had him already. He's sold the beach house, for Christ's sake.'

Poppy's chest rises. Big deep breath. She slides a thin black notebook from her inside jacket pocket. She has these men's pockets put into her suits. She sticks the bottle of vodka back in the tote. 'What kind of car was it?'

'Don't know. I tried to see the license. It was covered with crud. It was a big car.'

'You've said that already. Doesn't narrow the field much.'

'A luxury car. American. The inside was leather but the trim was fake wood. The leather was that champagne non-color.'

'What else? What stood out?'

'It said something like Executive Series in the corner of the rear window. I'm really good at reading things that are backwards for some reason.'

'Lincoln Continental, 1988. This isn't funny, Denise.'

She goes on. She asks questions, I answer. I am uneasy being on the other end of the questions. But she isn't making any effort to put me at ease the way I do with people who are uneasy. She is deliberately working to make me uneasy.

I describe the men to her, men so nondescript they might have been lawyers. Did they have accents? she wants to know.

'Only the driver talked. He'd said Yeah and *You sure?* unaccented into the cellular phone. And *Let her out* was actually *Letterout*. Maybe a Brooklyn accent, Poppy, except that's how I say it and I'm from Sacramento.'

'Denise, are you so unable to understand the risks here? What will it take—?'

'Listen, the ayatollahs aren't after me. They're after Salman Rushdie, not that I'm comparing myself to him. And don't tell me I'm better than he is, either.'

She snaps her notebook shut. Poppy has great flourishes. Her lips are snapped shut again, too, so she won't say what she would like to say. All her shields are back up. When she'd said My God and Jesus and sunk back into the sofa, hands trembling, the shields had slipped. 'I'm going to look into what happened.'

'Go ahead. But it was some kind of mistake.'

'Denise, there haven't been any kidnappings in a blue moon around here.'

'So maybe they changed their minds about kidnapping someone. It's late. I'm hungry. How about some food.'

She says, 'Sure.'

We go out and head toward Kinkead's, our favorite near-work restaurant. We don't say anything to each other for a while, and then she just stops. I stop a couple of steps ahead of her and turn back. She's glued to the sidewalk.

'Denise, have you considered where you are now?' She stopped so that I would actually have to stop too. Stop and consider where I am now. 'You are living one helluva life. Don't screw it up. Just don't screw it up.'

I experience such a surge of anger toward her that I can't understand how I ever fell for this best-friend business. 'What life, Poppy? Don't you go hanging that particular albatross on me. Like I need you to sound like my mother giving her profound deathbed speech: *You've got a great husband, Denise, great kids, great house, great life.* Right. But the thing is, I don't see Nick anymore. Hardly see the kids. Seems they've grown up without anyone warning me to slow down and take notice. And the house doesn't feel like home. Why should it? When Clinton is out of here, we'll all be out of here. There *is* no great life, as far as I'm concerned. And so what if I'm wrong and there actually is. I'd still have traded it all in a minute if Owen had just said the freaking word.'

That's when I finally cry. And Poppy moves toward me and then I am sobbing into her silk gabardine Armani suit lapel. I say, as I stain it, 'I loved him so much!'

4

I met Owen Hall a year and a half ago at a cocktail party in the Starlight Roof of the Waldorf-Astoria, a tacky old place, too dark and smoky for anyone to notice the faded stars that had been painted across the ceiling seventy-five years ago.

When I go to New York, I take an early train out of Union Station and I write during all those miles and hours, with the rumbling action of the train making for a nice steady din to keep my mind at the task at hand. I like din. In my office, my windows are always open – even in winter, if only a crack – so I get the car, wind, and aircraft din. I was telling that to Nick once and he asked me what was wrong with music, a little light jazz perhaps. I said, 'I don't want to *listen* to the din, just hear it. Like at the library.' He said, 'There's a din at that library?' And I tried to explain, 'More of a hum. A friendly hum. Like at all libraries.'

I don't know how he responded because it occurred to me then that my mother's need to drown out everything with the noise of the TV had been passed along to me, though in another form, like it or not.

When I get to Penn Station, I go walking all over the city, visiting museums or galleries or just looking at the East River. I eat at Jimmy's on York Avenue, where the chalkboard listing the menu was in use when some artisan was painting the night sky on the Starlight Roof's ceiling at the Waldorf. Then I shop until evening, and one of the things I buy is what I'll wear that night. After that, I go to Georgette Klinger's spa, have a shower and a massage, get my hair done, have the guy who does Hillary Clinton's makeup when she's in New York do mine, change into my new clothes, and take a taxi to whatever evening event it is that brings me to New York. Along with that coat, I check a shopping bag full of clothes I wore on the train. I enjoy these glittery New York things, especially when I've been fortified by the food at Jimmy's and a day of wandering, alone, getting pampered, all the while thinking about what I'll be writing the next day.

The Literary Guild throws its party every year in November, and it goes from six to eight. This was the fourth one I'd been to, and though it's mainly a duty call, I enjoy the attention I get as one of a handful of big moneymakers. In addition to the members of the New York publishing world and the crashers, there is an unwritten rule that invited guests may bring a guest of their own if that person is noteworthy. My first time, I brought Nick. He was very uncomfortable with people staring right through him. Yale professors are not considered noteworthy by this crowd unless they've made a couple of gossip columns or won a Nobel Prize. At the next two parties, as Bill Clinton's domestic affairs adviser, he would have been noteworthy, but he had no interest in coming along. Bill works the guys late, and Nick tends to carry a grudge.

At my very first party, after the Sam Litton book had been published, I'd stood in the elevator next to Jeremy Irons, who smiled at me and stared right through Nick. He was wearing a tuxedo, of course, because he's British and doesn't know any better. Publishing people still cling to an intellectual image of themselves and wear natty tweed things that intellectuals stopped wearing eons ago. I was, of course, wearing a suit as my mother would have advised. When I think about it, the only time I ever saw my mother in a suit was when she was in her coffin. My aunt had dug the suit out from somewhere and had it rush-cleaned.

The night I was to meet Owen, I chatted my way through the receiving line – the board of directors of the Literary Guild – everyone falling all over me because of O.J. Then I got a Bloody Mary at the bar and began to scope things out. I would see who I needed to see and who expected to see me while filling up on the Waldorf's famous hors d'oeuvres. Then, duty done, glitter absorbed, I'd be on my way back to the train, back to Alexandria, back to the K Street library, looking for a new crime.

I spotted my publicist across the room through the sea of buzzing, chatting, smiling people, and she waved. I spotted the paperback editor who bought the rights to all my books, and she waved too. And then I spotted another familiar face and I couldn't place him because I was thinking writer, until he grinned at whoever it was he was talking to, and then I recognized the congressman from Rhode Island. Even if I hadn't seen him in person in Washington a few times, Owen Hall's face would still have been recognizable because it was in the papers all the time. He was one of the few bachelors in Congress, and he dated actresses and models and escorted wives of ambassadors plus a lot of other wives to Washington parties. His criterion was glamour. In the tabloids, the word most often used to describe Owen Hall's social life was womanizer.

According to my old friend Leo, the female equivalent of a womanizer is a man-eater. Poppy Rice.

My chief duties at Literary Guild parties are to let my editor brag to anybody standing near him about the extraordinary success of my books – while his arm is draped around me – and to be seen with Myron Harper so all will know that Myron is an agent to be reckoned with. After my first party, when Nick thought he'd be a reigning figure but wasn't, I realized that I was the one who was supposed to reign. So at my second party, I tried to look regal standing in the middle of the room with a champagne glass aloft. Next thing I knew I was chatting with another woman and smiling at a photographer; when we finally introduced ourselves, she was Nora Ephron. She said if I ever wanted to learn how to write screenplays to give her a call and she'd show me. She said it would take about seven minutes. We shook hands on it and I never took her up on the offer, though I've talked up her movies ever since because she was so gracious.

At the third party I spent time talking to Teller of Penn and Teller, the magic act. Teller is the one who doesn't talk, but in person he makes up for it. I'd assumed he was a crasher, but he told me that he and Penn had written a book. He said, 'Actually, it's not literature. It's a pop-up book. The things that pop up tell you the secret behind the magic tricks we do.'

'Isn't that blasphemy?'

'Yes.' Then he rubbed his hands together, and when he stopped there was a hundred-dollar bill lying across his palm. He tucked it in his sleeve and did the trick again in slow motion so I could see how it was done. It didn't spoil things for me though, because I couldn't have done it myself in a million years. He didn't talk during the trick.

I said, 'True crime isn't exactly literature either.'

He said, 'The way you get it on paper, believe me, it is. I know; I used to be an English teacher.'

I thanked him.

There's this camaraderie at the Literary Guild party among the few writers who show up. Most writers can't come because they live in Oshkosh or St Louis and they make about twenty-five hundred dollars a year and no one offers to fly them to

New York free. So at the party after my O.J. book I'd ended up with Richard Condon. He was there with his wife. We got to exchange compliments and compare a few notes, and then his wife asked if I'd really gone to Sam Litton's execution. I said I had.

She said, 'Did he suffer?'

I thought for a minute. 'He experienced terror.'

'No, I mean, did it hurt him?'

'I don't think so.'

'Too bad.'

Richard Condon said, 'My wife is against the death penalty, believe it or not.'

'In theory only, dearest. I'd have liked to pull the switch on that guy.'

'But would you give a lethal injection?' he asked her.

And his wife said, 'Well, I couldn't have done that. Couldn't stick a needle in my worst enemy.' We laughed. Then she said, 'What's in a lethal injection anyway?'

Poppy had answered that same question for me. 'Thallium.'

'Can you get it over the counter?'

'Sure. Just ask for rat poison.'

And then the Condons were looking past me, smiling at someone, and Congressman Hall melded into our group. Richard clapped him on the back. 'Don't tell me you're writing a book, Owen.'

'Not me. Tagged along with some friends.' He was a noteworthy guest.

I was introduced. 'Guess you must know Denise here.' Then Richard scrutinized me. 'Your husband's in Washington, I believe.'

Before I could answer, Owen said, 'As a matter of fact, he's your President's domestic affairs adviser. But Mrs Burke and I have never formally met.'

Owen and I shook hands. I said, 'Denise.'

We took glasses of champagne from a passing tray and placed our empties on it before the waiter could get away. Owen said to me, 'It appears we're both chasing Bloody Marys with champagne.'

'Yes.' I would just sip. I don't think the Condons would have minded if I referred to someone as a cocksucker, but the congressman might.

Owen said to me, 'Richard already knows I've read all his books. I've read yours too. Really good.'

'Thanks. You're really good yourself. I spend summers in Rhode Island. If I lived there full time, I'd vote for you.'

The Condons drank to that, and then Owen said, 'I love to read, you know? Relaxes me.'

I said, 'I love politics. Makes me crazy.'

When their glasses were empty, the Condons began to shuffle a bit. They had plans afoot. 'We're meeting some old friends for dinner.' Richard was glancing down at his watch. 'We'd love for you to join us.' We made our polite declines, and they drifted off. Richard Condon passed away not long after the party, so I cherish the moment.

Owen and I ended up in a corner of the room by one of the bars, sharing it with Kurt Vonnegut, who was in deep discussion with a Cuban waiter.

'Do you really like politics or does it just come with the territory?' Owen asked me, meaning Nick.

'When I was a little girl, my mother – she was a ward chairman in Sacramento – would tie babushkas around our heads. Babushkas are—'

'Where I come from, women still call them that.'

'Oh.'

'That's because they still wear them.'

I laughed. 'I guess I'm glad to hear that. I liked wearing

mine. Well, anyway, we would drive to some social club where there'd be a political meeting going on, and we'd park across the street under a tree so we'd be in the shadows. Then she'd watch as people went into the meeting and she'd dictate their names to me. I had to write them in a little notebook. Print them. I was very young. The first time we did it, I asked her who the people were. She said, Traitors.'

Owen threw his head back and laughed a real laugh, not the pleasant chuckling kind that politicians do. He said, 'So your first writing job was ward politics.'

'Yes.' I didn't tell him about the bottle in the paper bag on the seat between my mother and me, or the spare in the glove compartment. I didn't tell him my father left her for another woman and married the woman without bothering to divorce my mother first. Or his formula for avoiding alimony and child support: Drive your wife to drink and then she'll be in a stupor all the time and unable to go after you. Unable even to stand up.

Just then Louis found us and was kissing the air next to my right cheek. Louis Pedemonti, my editor, is the same kind of Italian that Bart Giamatti was: suave and sleek and a genius. Louis always has a trophy date on his arm, a gorgeous exotic model with spectacularly lush hair. Male model. He introduced us to the one on his arm now, Waltraut, from Berlin.

'His mother was from Tunisia so he can speak French too,' Louis bragged.

Waltraut said '*Enchanté*' with a German accent. Waltraut didn't speak English, alas. Louis said to Owen, 'Have you got a book up your sleeve, Congressman?'

'Afraid I'm not a writer.'

'Well, of course you're not. We've got plenty of those, believe me, to act as coach. You'd get to choose from any number.'

I said, 'Go for the one who did Colin Powell.'

Louis's nostrils gave a little flare of disdain. Owen smiled. 'Thought books by liberals didn't sell.'

'But that's because they keep writing about the environment. Fashions change. Overnight, often.'

And now, drawn to us, an eyebrow raised in my direction, Myron Harper. He eased himself into our circle. 'Hello, Denise, love. And Louis. Always a pleasure.' Louis murmured, 'Always.' Editors couldn't stand Myron. This is another sign of a good agent. I said to Owen, 'This is my agent,' and I introduced them.

'Something going down here that I should know about, Congressman?'

Louis said, 'That's what I'm hoping.'

Owen wasn't interested in agents at the time. As soon as he shook Myron's hand, he placed his palm against my back between my shoulder blades. 'I was just about to ask Denise to have dinner with me. Would you all care to come along?'

Pained expressions came over their faces. Both men had already made dinner commitments, something the congressman had correctly presumed. So regrets were muttered, and as we turned to go, Louis said, 'Call me, Congressman, if the muse whispers in your ear.' They didn't drift off, they kind of backed away, damning themselves for not waiting until the last possible minute to come up with the most advantageous dinner partners. Waltraut tossed his mane and wiggled his fingers at us as he called 'Ciao' over his shoulder.

Owen smiled down at me. He was a head taller, which made him very tall. He said, 'I apologize for being presumptuous here. But if you already have dinner plans—'

'I've been gorging on hors d'oeuvres. I was planning just to head for my train when I finished here.'

'The train? You'll get into Washington in the middle of the night.'

'No. It's the Metroliner that leaves at two a.m. You can board anytime, go to sleep whenever you want.'

'That's the one that's all sleeping compartments?'

'Yes.'

'I've never done it.'

'It's great. I sleep like a rock. You should try it.'

His eyes widened just a little bit. 'Wish I could. Got to be in Brussels for breakfast.'

'I didn't mean tonight.'

'Oh.' He laughed. 'Well. So listen, you could maybe have coffee and dessert while I eat.'

That sounded like a good idea to me. 'Okay. But aren't you with people?'

'I was.'

5

The Waldorf staff person, who seemed to be in charge of maneuvering the latecomers just arriving at the party past the early departures, didn't skip a beat when Owen asked where he could get the best cup of coffee in town. He said, 'Right downstairs, Congressman. At the Bull and Bear.' He touched his cuff link, a gesture of *Ask anything and you'll get the right answer*. 'If you give me your coat checks, I'll see that your things are brought down to the restaurant.'

We thanked him. It never ceases to amaze me how celebrities are treated. Writers may be celebrities, but most are not recognized on the street.

Owen ordered a steak, rare. He said, 'I do this once in a while.'

'What's that?'

'Eat a plate load of red meat. And cover my baked potato with sour cream.'

'I do that all the time.'

'You do? Doesn't show.'

'Thanks. Doesn't show on you either.'

He didn't thank me. He said, 'But do you eat your steak rare?'

'Bleeding.'

I was enjoying the flirty banter with him. Owen had a pleasant laugh. Sincere. He seemed nothing but sincere, his looks, his body language, everything. But I knew he was supposed to look that way. He was a politician.

I said, 'I met this baseball player once who said that back in the sixties, the night before every game, all the players would eat huge rare steaks and then the next day they'd pop salt tablets during batting practice.' The player also spoke about selecting hookers after dinner, but I left that part out. Flirty banter requires censoring or it goes beyond flirty.

'Where'd you meet this ballplayer?'

'Here. Two years ago. He wrote a book.'

'Who'd he get?'

'Dick Schaap.'

'If I thought I could get Dick Schaap, I *would* write a book.'

Owen laughed. I laughed. I was drinking coffee so it was my normal laugh, not my tipsy one, which Poppy says sounds like jingle bells.

The steak came. Bleeding. He offered me a bite. I ate it off his fork. It didn't feel like a foolish thing to do. It felt chummy. I could picture Poppy doing the same thing, only showing a lot of tongue.

'How is it?'

'Wonderful.'

'So what do you do about cholesterol?'

'My doctor told me I don't have any. I swim. Every other day. A half mile.'

'I didn't know swimming gets rid of cholesterol.'

'I didn't either.'

'Maybe I'll try it before those damn new kids on the block take our pool away.'

'But you're a runner,' I said. 'I've seen your picture in the paper.'

'I know. But usually I run indoors. I have a treadmill. It's more fun outside, though. When I can, I head out the door.'

'Do you ever run with the President?'

'He has enough company without me. And it's kind of a slow group, to be honest.'

He put away the rest of his steak in what seemed like three bites and then nibbled on my cookies with me. They'd come with the coffee. I waited for the personal questions, which arrived on schedule, and so I told him about my two kids, their names, how old they were, how they liked school, et cetera, et cetera. He told me he'd never married but that he was close to his cousins' children.

He said, 'Are you afraid of flying?'

'I'm sorry?'

'You're taking the train back to Washington.'

'No, I just really like that train. It's convenient, and it leaves on time.'

'So what happens if you take a plane and you're delayed?'

'I'd get home really late and I wouldn't be able to work the next day. I can't create when I'm tired. I can't afford to lose a day. Some people think writing is like doing macramé. You just pick it up when you've got the time. But it's not.'

'Hey.' He reached over and touched the back of my hand with his fingertips.

'Sorry. I get a little paranoid once in a while.'

'You know, I can understand. I admire your discipline. People who think it's like macramé are just jealous. So is it okay if I share a cab with you and get a look at this train? I can see you off.'

'I was going to walk. It's such a nice night.'

'You swim and you walk too?'

'All over Alexandria.'

'This isn't Alexandria.'

'Owen, there are no roving gangs in midtown Manhattan.'

He leaned forward. 'Denise, you write about murderers. You

interview them. Doesn't that make you nervous?'

'Murderers kill friends and family.'

'That wasn't true of Sam Litton, though.'

'Yes, it was. First he made friends with someone and then he killed her.'

He looked into my eyes. 'I'll just walk with you then, if that's okay. I'll be aware that you don't need protection.'

'That would be nice.'

When we left, the maître d' said, 'Have a nice night, Congressman. You too, madam.'

As soon as we were outside in the cool night, Owen did what I knew he would, something everyone does when they meet me and realize who I am. I was surprised it had taken him so long. I thought it would happen during dinner, but he'd put it off. After exclaiming over the beauty of the evening – and it was beautiful: clear and crisp, mid-fall – Owen said, 'There were these people murdered in Rhode Island. In my hometown, New Caxton. A brutal murder.'

Everyone's got a crime for me. With Owen, I was polite. Probably because he didn't immediately tell me it would make a great book. 'When was that?' I asked, instead of, I have a murder I'm involved with already, thank you. When Poppy's with me, she adds to that comment of mine: 'And she's committed, unlike my present boyfriend.' When Nick's with me, he carefully sidles away. He can't get past seeing what I do as distasteful, which is an improvement over when he saw it as macramé.

Owen went on, 'A little over two years ago. A terrible thing.'

'Was there a conviction?'

'Yes. I thought maybe it would interest you.'

Interest me was still better than it *would make a great book*. Without knowing it, he'd given me an out. I said, 'You know, I start my books with an arrest. When someone is arrested I head out to the scene, and I look into what happened. Then, if things seem promising, I go to the trial. My books mostly come out of trials. But to tell you the truth, I don't remember a murder in Rhode Island. I know about all of them, usually.'

'It didn't get national press.'

That was another strike against his murder's being of any interest to me, but I let him continue.

'It was a triple murder.'

He didn't add on to that, so I asked it if was an open-and-shut case. If the killer was locked up.

'It was. He's serving a life sentence.'

The reading public prefers the death penalty. 'Is there a death penalty in Rhode Island?'

'No, but a couple of state lawmakers tried to introduce legislation to that effect during the trial. Didn't come to anything.'

I looked up at him as we walked. I was holding his arm. He'd offered it. I was actually holding the warmth of his arm against my breast. I felt the warmth of his solid arm right through his suit jacket and my coat. He was looking down at me, and he seemed even beyond sincere. Earnest.

'Owen?'

'Yes?'

'You were close to this crime, weren't you?'

He said, 'Oh, no.' He looked away from me again. 'I mean, yes, I knew of the people killed. And the guy accused of the murders. Both their families. Not personally. But the town of New Caxton is itself a family – one of those towns where everyone knows everyone's name. I think I've never been able to come to grips with what happened because of just that. Because of the closeness the people feel in this town. The guy lived three doors from the people who were killed.'

'It's real small, then?'

'Not that small. But it's very ethnic. Made up of distinct ethnic groups. Three – Polish, Italian, and black. But each group is entirely respectful of the others' ways. The groups are like . . . I don't know . . . cousins. There had been a fourth group – the families of the founding fathers. Cleared out a long time ago. Except me.'

'Not an in place to live.'

'For sure. It's not a pretty place, it's a factory town. But we've always offered people steady work. An equitable day's wage. So there's a strong sense of cohesion even though there are these ethnic differences. The people are generous. They depend on each other. Protect one another. And they're proud of their willingness to do that, of their ability to do that. They brag how no one's kids go around vandalizing mailboxes like everywhere else. So the crime has never made any sense. No sense. Not in New Caxton, Rhode Island.'

Usually, it's not the crime that grabs me, it's the unusual aspects that surround it. So for the moment he had me. And unlike most people with a crime to describe, Owen hadn't jumped right into the gory details. That's what they like to do. Then they can feel free to dwell on the cruel injustice of it all, and how disgusting it was to them, and the enormous hardship in addition to the grief the crime caused the loved ones left behind. And I try to explain that true crime readers want more than all those things, which are quite ordinary.

I said to him, 'Every murder is horrible, though, granted, in varying degrees. But for me to write about a specific murder means that the crime must hold some sort of provocation. The motivation must not make any sense. People want to find some sense in a murder so that we can intellectualize it and then feel safe from it. But we're never safe from it, and that's what I try to pass along to readers – to quit denying that murder happens only to people we don't know and is perpetrated by people who are animals. That's not true. Humans are at the top of the chain; instead of being instinctive predators, they have a propensity toward evil. The rest of the chain isn't evil. It's an unsafe world.'

'You act like you feel safe.'

'Well, I don't. I made friends with this terrific kid. I liked him a lot. A whole lot. I worked with him. I shared a desk with him. He turned out to be a serial killer.'

'So you want to warn people that danger is lurking?'

'How else can danger be subdued if we don't remind ourselves that it's there instead of making believe it isn't?'

'But murderers aren't always evil, are they? I mean, sometimes humans snap. Like a mother killing her baby because it won't stop crying.'

'I think all mothers are capable of smothering their babies. When they're at their wits' end. But being at your wits' end isn't snapping. The mother has to get a pillow. It takes evil to go and *get the pillow*. So I guess I give readers solace because it takes more than exasperation to lose control. It takes other things we *can* control. We can choose between right and wrong and not let our evil side take hold.'

'But what exactly in a crime makes for a good book? What do you look for?'

'Unfathomable motive.'

'Who has that?'

'Susan Smith. She killed her kids because her new boyfriend didn't want the whole package. Now who can believe such a thing? If she hadn't come right out and admitted it, people still wouldn't believe she did it, no matter how much evidence there was.

'And O.J. Who can believe a famous, lovable guy like him, someone who could have any woman he wanted, as the cliché goes, would kill his wife. His ex-wife. Certainly not a jury.'

Then I went into my Leo stuff about the value of a hero. I tend to skip this part when people at a party tell me about a murder, because it elicits glassy stares and everyone suddenly begins popping up with questions like, Have any of you tried that new Kazakhstani restaurant on Dupont Circle? But Owen said, 'A hero?'

'Yes. A cop or a DA or a family member who fights to bring the killer to justice despite huge odds or has to overcome hurdles that cause great personal loss and cost. A hero larger than life. And, most important, larger than fiction.'

'What does that mean?'

'It means your friend Richard Condon. A master. A crime writer needs as big a fellow as the ones that great fiction writers like Richard Condon can conjure up.'

He snuggled my arm a little closer into his. 'You know . . . listen, I hope I'm not being insulting, but a hero . . . Clark Kent is coming to mind.'

I laughed. 'That's exactly who I'm always looking for. Clark Kent. But a Clark Kent who doesn't turn into Superman. It has to be Clark himself, saving the day through his ingenuity and intelligence and determination.'

He made a sound like *whew*. 'Denise, I don't know if there is a Clark Kent connected to this crime, but I wish there were.'

'Why?'

'Because the guy who was convicted didn't do it.'

'He didn't?' I looked up at his profile.

He backpedaled. 'Well, of course I can't know that for sure. But I don't *think* he did it, because— Wait. I shouldn't have said that. I don't know that. I just suspect it.'

'Why?'

'I can't put my finger on it exactly. Something just keeps nagging me. It has to do with the fact that no one is in need of anything in New Caxton, Rhode Island. No one's on welfare. If a person is down on his luck – that's how they'd put it – the town rescues him. A woman can't pay her bills, they somehow get paid. Anonymously.' His walk slowed. He looked down at me again. 'You don't mind if I go on about this, do you? I'm beginning to realize that this has been bothering me for a long time. These people in New Caxton vote for me en masse. I owe it to them to figure out what went wrong here. And I have to confess, when I saw you, Denise – I mean, with the Condons back there at the party – I figured you might just be the one to come up with the answer. There's never been a murder in this town. Ever. Not in all its history. So why did it happen?'

A new wrinkle for me. He didn't want to tell me that his crime would be a good book, he wanted me to solve it. I don't claim to have any knowledge of psychosocial pathology, but I'm a curious person. That's what attracted Nick to me when I was in his class. I was so 'charmingly inquisitive.' I'd ask questions and inspire thoughtful answers. He took it personally, thought I was interested in him, not his answers. But then I became interested in him too.

Now I said to Owen, 'I do love to find things out. I guess that's why I ended up doing what I'm doing. I write answers to why people kill each other. What kind of people would do such a thing to begin with. So what exactly are the details? I am definitely curious about a town where there has never been a murder.'

'A *premeditated* murder.'

'No murder or no premeditated murder?'

'There have been, I guess, crimes of passion. A barroom brawl, maybe, where one guy punches another guy and then they both drop dead of heart attacks. That kind of thing.'

I let it go. 'What's the population of New Caxton?'

'Around fifteen thousand.'

'How long has there been a New Caxton?'

'Chartered in 1688.'

'An old New England town.'

'Very old.'

'And never a . . . premeditated murder.'

'That's right.'

'So tell me about this one. The first.'

'I wouldn't know where to start.'

'With the hard part, Owen.'

'Which part is that?'

'Who the people were who were killed. That's how I start. With a vignette describing the lives of the victims.'

He started straight ahead now. 'The people who were killed . . .' His gaze veered further away from me, into the starry night.

I let him formulate a chronology in his mind. That takes a little more time than explaining some theory that reveals sociological puzzles. People do what he was doing when I interview them. If I ask questions before they have a grip on what they'll say, they get emotional. They have no recipes the way my first subjects did when I wrote a food column.

Owen began with two unfinished thoughts before he settled in. First: 'It was a brutal murder . . .'; then, 'This was such a tragic family to begin with . . .'; and finally he completed his third, 'A sixty-nine-year-old woman, her autistic son, and her seven-year-old grandchild – maybe the child was eight, I forget – they were all stabbed to death.'

'That's terrible.' I responded with the obvious in a voice as sympathetic as I could muster. I'd heard so much worse.

'Yes. And what's so on my mind, what's always been foremost in my mind, is that these three people represent the most vulnerable, most susceptible segments of our society. The elderly. The disabled. Children. The kind of people a town like New Caxton prides itself on protecting. Also the kind of people the rest of the country seems to want to abandon.'

Owen Allen Hall had been fighting for social reform his entire career. The Deadbeat Dads law passed because it was pushed relentlessly by a man who had no children. And when his constituents became Reagan Democrats, Owen's Republican challenger didn't sneak in on Reagan's coattails. Congressman Hall's constituents made an exception and voted for him.

'What else, Owen?'

I watched his profile. So patrician. Gorgeous. 'They were slaughtered on a summer evening, a beautiful night in early August. The humidity had lifted that day after a fairly long heat wave. Everyone was outside. They were murdered two hours or so before it got dark, probably right after they'd eaten dinner. And no one saw anything. Heard anything. It happened on a Friday, but the bodies weren't discovered until midnight Saturday. All that time, and no one seemed to notice they were missing . . .'

'In a town that's family.'

'Yes. Denise, the house where it happened, the street . . . the houses are about three feet apart. Everyone's windows were open. Someone blamed the noise of the air conditioners in bedroom windows. But people in New Caxton, they're frugal people . . . even the ones with air conditioners only have them in their bedrooms, and nobody had gone to bed yet.'

'Wait.'

'What?'

'All these details came out in the trial? I mean, these aren't things you've assumed, are they?'

'I'm just giving you the facts, ma'am.' He smiled at me.

I smiled back. 'Go ahead.'

'Right afterward, people whispered about the terrible things that can happen when they're all asleep . . . when the town lies vulnerable. It took awhile before they allowed the truth to sink in. That murders do not necessarily take place in the dead of night when the hobgoblins are out. These people were not murdered as they slept in their beds but right after dinner. In New Caxton, it's not dinner, it's supper. And supper is served at five-fifteen; fifteen minutes after Dad leaves the factory. They come home in T-shirts on summer nights and they don't change before dinner – supper – unless it's really hot. Then they pull the shirts off and eat bare-chested. The woman's body was found in her kitchen. She and her family were murdered when the dads on the street were reading their newspapers on their front porches before going inside to turn on the Red Sox game, when the moms were washing dishes and all the kids were outside riding their bikes.'

Owen's hand found mine somewhere in the middle of all that. He had calluses. I wondered where they came from. Sailing, I imagined. He said, 'I don't understand how one guy could have kept them from screaming.'

'It was determined that the guy convicted acted alone?'

'Yes.'

'They knew each other?'

'They did know each other. But that would have gotten him in the door. Once he started stabbing these people, how could he have killed all three of them? It would have taken another person, at least, to stop the other two. From screaming. From running out the door. The house is tiny. And the autistic son . . . he was big and strong. He was a vigorous fellow . . . But there's more. There was a girl involved with this guy. Local girl. She was with the guy the night of the murders, seen with him, but she was never arrested. She took the fifth when the prosecutor put her on the stand. It was left to the people of New Caxton to punish her.'

'What did they do to her?'

'Sent her back to the old country.'

'Which one?'

'Poland.'

'Had she come from there?'

'Where?'

'Poland.'

'No. She was fourth-generation.'

'Fourth-generation? And she—?'

'The ties that bind in New Caxton are a few thousand miles long and are stretched across a century.'

'But if they protected her from the law, why didn't they protect him?'

'Now things get complicated.'

Complicated indeed. 'What was the guy's name?'

Owen said, 'Eddie Baines. He was a black guy.'

'Ah-hah. Couldn't send him back to Africa, right?'

'I know this will all sound simplistic, but the black people in New Caxton are not outsiders. I'm talking about racism here. Or rather, the lack of racism.'

'Meaning?'

'When the industrial revolution took hold, the descendants of the original settlers – including my family; we owned all the land along the rivers – imported Italians from broken-down farms and Poles out of the Warsaw slums. But we – they, I mean – also recruited freed slaves and the children of freed slaves. All three groups were mixed together in the factories. They worked together, they earned a wage together, and so there was respect, not racism. Naturally, they have their own neighborhoods, and each group has its own churches, and each group does keep its identity. The Halls never demanded that the groups give up their names or speak English. Become Americanized.'

'You're not talking about the ex-slaves, obviously.'

'Well . . . obviously. The point I'm trying to make is that there is no disdain, let alone racial animosity. But if an Italian girl marries a Polish boy in New Caxton – that's unacceptable, same as if she married a black man.'

I said, 'C'mon, Owen.'

'Denise. This is hard to explain, but I mean it. In New Caxton, there aren't black people and white people. There are Italians, Poles, and Negroes. And us, of course.'

'What do they call *us*?'

'Americans.'

I laughed.

'I believe that if there was no black race, there would still be racism in this country. Except the groups would be called Wops and Polacks. Et cetera. We'd consider each group a separate race.'

'I believe you're right. But we're getting off track, no?'

'We are.'

'Tell me about Eddie. Eddie . . .?'

'Baines.'

'. . . Eddie Baines, specifically.'

'His family lived in New Caxton for four generations, just like everyone else's.'

'Not counting the founding fathers. The Americans.'

'Not counting the Americans. He was a local football player, a great athlete, a smart kid. He took an athletic scholarship to Nebraska, even though he could have gone to any school he chose. The dream for him was football, not scholarship. Sports are very important in this town, another identity that unifies everyone. The street signs are red. Have you ever heard of red street signs?'

'No.'

'In honor of the football team. The New Caxton Red Rockets.'

'Team spirit.'

'Indeed. Anyway, Eddie's arrest was very hard on his mother. His conviction, in fact, killed her. She was a widow. And she was one of those people who is right on your doorstep if there is illness or an accident. Didn't matter if you were Italian or Polish or black.' He smiled. 'Or American. Brought food before anyone else did. Always offering to help. Everyone said to her, "Don't worry, Eddie didn't do it," the underlying sentiment obvious, that his arrest would simply serve to straighten him out. He'd gotten into drugs . . . took his father's death hard. An arrest would throw a little scare into him. They would do right by his widowed mother, since he'd chosen not to. They thought the real killers would be caught and he'd be freed and then he'd get back on the straight and narrow. But then the knowledge that he and the Polish girl had been more than friends gnawed at them. So things got out of hand. In the end, they turned on him. He was led to the slaughter, and she was shipped to Poland.'

'To a nunnery?'

'Wouldn't be surprised.'

'I was joking.'

'So was I.'

'Who did kill these people?'

'I have no idea.'

'But why was this Eddie Bates—'

'Baines.'

'Baines. Why was he arrested for the crime to begin with? There must have been evidence.'

'They found a footprint or something. In the house. Listen, this guy was having a tough time. Ostracized. A failure. Perfect scapegoat. His story was that he'd been lured to the murder scene after the crime was committed so that he would inadvertently leave incriminating evidence.'

'Who lured him?'

'His girlfriend.'

'The one who's in Poland.'

'Yes. He says she told him the family had been killed and evidence had been planted in their house against the two of them. They had to get rid of it.'

'But why would he believe such a thing?'

'That I don't know.'

'You think he did believe her?'

'Yes.'

'Because of the state of mind he was in?'

'Yes.'

'But the bottom line, as far as you're concerned, is that an innocent man has been has been sentenced to a life term for a crime he didn't commit.'

'That's right. The prosecutor said he snorted cocaine, had a psychotic episode, and turned into a raving lunatic. If cocaine did that to people, half the population would all be killing one another in their living rooms. But because this town refused to believe it couldn't take care of its own, they started going along with the state's theory that Eddie Baines went crazy on cocaine and with the brute strength of ten men wiped these people out.'

'Crack.'

'I'm sorry?'

'You go crazy on crack, not cocaine.'

He said something that was half 'hah' and half a laugh. 'Cocaine was the theory. Crack is what people in inner cities take, not one lone wayward young man – not all that young – who was . . . who was down on his luck. Oh, they really beat their chests about failing to take care of him. But the key is, *why* were those people killed? Isn't that what has to be found out? After all, if you find out why, it will lead you to the killer.'

'Who told you that?'

'I read it in an interview with a famous crime writer.' He grinned at me.

I was suitably flattered. 'I thought it sounded familiar. Well, motivation is surely a cop's chief clue. So what was Eddie Baines's motivation?'

'Robbery. Then he went crazy and killed them. Guy never robbed anyone in his life.'

'Listen, Owen, I don't know how to go about writing *The Thin Blue Line*. To be honest, I have no interest in writing a chronology of the life of a wrongfully accused man.'

'A man convicted of murder. Incarcerated.'

'Yes. Incarcerated. That kind of exposé. I'm not doing what I do because I'm trying to right injustice in the world. I write about people whose job it is to do that, but I'm not one of them. I'm curious about what makes people tick. What makes a killer tick. Explain him so that readers can rest assured that no matter how furious they get at their kids or their friends or their lovers, they won't turn around and hit them over the head with the VCR.'

'Okay,' he said. 'I can understand that. But it's interesting anyway, don't you think?'

'Yes, it is interesting. But it's not what *I'm* interested in.'

'A curious antidote to O.J., though, don't you think? He gets off; this guy's in jail. No dream team. Just the public defender.'

'Frankly, I need a change, Owen. From the theme of race.'

'So we'll change the subject.'

I looked up at him. 'We don't have to do that. The terrible

crime that happened in your hometown is troubling you. Perhaps you feel you owe it to the people to straighten things out. I mean, they vote for you. Trouble is, it sounds like maybe they don't want things straightened out. Maybe they're happy that it's all behind them, even if they had to sacrifice one of their own. I mean, after all, he *was* black. Despite all you said about working together . . . times are different from what they were during the industrial revolution, no?'

'Yes.' He sighed.

'What I don't understand is why you don't revive the investigation yourself.'

'Easier said than done. Stirring things up . . . I don't know. It's just a hunch I've got.'

'But enough of a hunch where you're maybe not sleeping nights.'

'I guess.' He stopped and turned toward me. 'Anyway, if you think there might be something in this crime that could interest you – I mean, I wish you'd at least think about it – then call me. I can tell you which rocks to look under. I don't know if it's a book. That's something only you would know. But if it is . . .'

We strolled along. My mind drifted as I took in the lights, the architecture of the city. Owen and I continued holding hands. So far removed from Nick and home and kids. I looked up at him and asked, 'What did you say the name of the family was? The ones who were killed?'

He lifted his chin. Closed his eyes to the night. 'The Montevallos. Connie and Petey. Petey was named after his father. Peter Montevallo, Jr.' He stopped.

'And the child?'

'His name was Timothy.'

In a gesture of comfort, I dropped his hand and slid my arm around his waist. He did the same. I didn't tell him that if his crime came to intrigue me sufficiently, I would know exactly which rocks to look under without his or anyone else's help.

6

I said good-bye to Owen – a little kiss, a brushing of lips that I can still taste – and didn't get much sleep on the train. A taxi ride to Alexandria, and I was home. Nick had already left. I schmoozed with the kids over Froot Loops, looking at them when they weren't looking at me, thinking, Mom has just kissed a man who's not your father. I saw them off to school when the van arrived and then took a shower. Buddy and I went on our morning walk. It wasn't as chilly as it had been in New York. We went down to the river. I gazed into shop windows along King Street and never saw a thing. I had a second cup of coffee on a bench while Buddy sniffed up some friends. I was trying to talk myself out of doing anything impulsive.

I should head out to my office, is what I kept telling myself. Hit the library a few extra times this week. Figure out what kind of crime would be provocative enough to write a book about. Another poisoning, maybe. Poisoners are inherently provocative. My poisoner, the murderer in the book just before O.J., was heartless. To this day I still have to remind myself that she really did have a heart. She was a human being, not a robot. She was simply evil, even though a heart beat in her chest. I thought of her as a robot because there was no way I could see that she would have enjoyed the money she got from her husband's insurance if she hadn't been caught. What made the book successful was not only her motivation – that she'd acted because she needed the money to replace her husband's paycheck (which would be gone when she got rid of him and his annoying behavior) – but also how she was caught.

She put cyanide in her husband's Tylenol capsule just the way she'd seen it done on TV. But the insurance company ruled that his death was from natural causes rather than from murder, which would have paid her triple. His death didn't arouse suspicion because he'd been overweight and smoked heavily. His family doctor decided heart disease had done him in. But the wife had planned the crime to make it look as if her husband had been murdered; she kept suggesting that possibility to the police, the doctor, and anyone who would listen, but everyone pooh-poohed her. I had a good and sarcastic time with that. Someone who dies of cyanide poisoning exhibits some pretty unusual symptoms, none of which are the least bit natural. And no one connected his death to the Tylenol tampering a dozen years before. I had even more of a frolic with that; I got to be especially caustic.

Disgusted, my murderer stopped in at several drugstores and put cyanide in ten more bottles of Tylenol capsules. Within a few days, seven people were dead. It took seven before the police finally took notice. That's because she picked drugstores in poor neighborhoods where those in authority assume that people who die unnaturally are taking illegal drugs, not the ones you get over the counter at your local pharmacy. Then she went and pointed out to her husband's doctor that he'd had the same symptoms as the recent poison victims. When I discussed the case with Poppy, just before I decided to go ahead and write the book, she said to me, 'The woman could have worn a T-shirt to her doctor's office that said IT'S CYANIDE, STUPID, and he still wouldn't have paid attention.'

Eventually, the police could no longer ignore her, and the husband's body was exhumed. The tests they did proved her right. Her husband became Victim No. 8 even though he'd been Victim No. 1.

Of all the dead man's friends and relatives, she was the only one who'd gained anything from his death. Find out why, you'll figure out who. The motive was clear. The only thing that the cops, like me, wondered was what on earth she'd do with her newfound money, the same way we wonder what a car-chasing dog would do if he ever caught the car. (Well, I couldn't have applied that banality to Buddy. If he'd ever caught a car, he'd have thought of something. The sky's the limit.)

They had a tough time with her. No evidence. And they couldn't put a psychiatrist in front of the jury to tell them this was the kind of person who simply desired a large cache of money, because there would be Mrs Sophie Sprain sitting placidly in court in her flowered housedress from K-mart and her black Reeboks with no laces, telling everyone the only interest she had in life was the fish in her tank, her soaps, and *Jenny Jones.*

But then the FBI crime lab found little green specks in some of the tampered capsules. On analysis, the specks turned out to be an algicide. The FBI agent called the homicide detective on the case and asked, 'Does the rich widow have fish?'

The woman had used poor judgement when she chose that brand of algicide for her fish tank. It wasn't the flakes of algicide most fish fanciers use; this algicide was powdered. It hadn't been poor judgment as far as the fish went, since powder is gobbled up more easily than flakes. The woman loved her fish. They were the source of the friction with her husband; he couldn't stand her spending his hard-earned money on them, and she spent quite a bit. Powdered algicide is twice as expensive as flaked. The algicide came in the same kind of container talcum powder does, one with little holes at the top. When she shook it, infinitesimal amounts floated throughout her house. Probably into her bowl of cereal. But definitely into the opened capsules of Tylenol balanced upright in a row on her kitchen counter. In the end, Poppy said to me, 'Ah, Denise, the tyranny of the one-paycheck family. The downside when hubby chooses to be a tyrant.'

In Alexandria, drinking my coffee out in the fall sunshine, I thought, Why spend time searching for a unique kind of crime when I could be spending my time looking into Owen's story, which certainly had unique possibilities? I'd been coming up short on that front. A week earlier, I'd left Chattanooga after three days. The accused had had a change of heart. He decided to confess. He said he regretted shooting his best friend who'd grown up with him, who'd chosen to go to the same college, who'd convinced him to make a pact to be each other's best man, who got married one month after he did, who made another pact to be godfather to each other's first child. The killer said to me, 'I couldn't get him to stop copying me.' The book would have been a 'winner' – that's how Myron would put it – if it had come to trial. Someday, though, maybe the guy will make a good psychological study for Oliver Sacks, who, alas, never comes to Literary Guild cocktail parties.

Maybe I could spend a week or so on Owen's crime. I psyched a message over to Buddy, lying at my feet: *I might have something right under my nose here.* He psyched back, You can always trust your nose.

But I didn't kid myself. If I got to looking into this crime, I'd remain in contact with Owen. I wanted to do that, but I managed to rationalize. Maybe the formula needed some revamping. Maybe a fresh way of approaching a crime was in order. With that, I decided that just checking out this place in Rhode Island was not impulsive at all. And if things proved promising, I couldn't help it if Owen became part of the package.

I went home and dragged out my overnight bag again. I got out the dog crate and watched Buddy's head tilt hopefully. Yes, old boy, we're taking a trip. He went dashing round and round in circles of ecstasy. Nick once said he'd never heard of a dog who loved to fly. Buddy does love to fly, but only insofar as flying might mean his favorite destination: the beach house in Rhode Island. That's where he could nudge the screen door with his nose and be out on the loose whenever he wanted and go wherever he wanted for as long as he wanted.

Him and me both. It would be cold, but I'd get a fire going in the bedroom wood stove, and Buddy would keep me warm too. Then I'd take a little drive to New Caxton the next morning and poke around. I went into Nick's den and got out a map. New Caxton was about a half-hour drive from Watch Hill, where Nick's house is. Was. Everything in Rhode Island is a half hour apart.

I said to Buddy, 'The sea in the fall is purple.'

I left a note for Nick and the kids and stuck it on the fridge with a magnet. The kids would find it, and then when Nick noticed at bedtime that my half of the bed was empty, he'd stick his head in one of their rooms and say, 'Where's Mom?' And either kid would say, 'Didn't you read the note?' Then he'd go and read the note, which said, *Got another hook on the line. In Rhode Island, lucky me. I'll be at the beach house. If you should notice that the dog is off his feed, he's not. I took him along.* I am always needling Nick about his obliviousness so I won't harbor resentment. Nipping resentment in the bud is healthy; besides, Nick is proud of being oblivious and will never change. He doesn't admit to being oblivious; he calls it 'preoccupied.' He says there is no room for the mundane in his life because he's preoccupied with items of import.

In Rhode Island 'in the old days,' as Nick would put it, his family had an arrangement with a fisherman who lived in a shack at the land end of the sandy pit where the house is. He would pick them up whenever their train pulled into Watch Hill. Now there were no more trains, but we kept a car at the beach house – maybe Nick threw it into the two-million-dollar deal – and the original old fisherman, who looked to be a hundred and two, would come over and rev it up once a week or so. When we arrived from Alexandria, he'd have it at the Watch Hill airport, gassed up and ready to go. When we got there, he'd shake Nick's hand and walk off. Once I told him we'd be glad to drive him home. He said, 'I like to walk. Check my bait traps on the way.' And then I looked for him, and sure enough I spotted him fifty feet off the road to the house, standing in a marsh at the edge of a creek, hauling up a mesh basket.

He still used the shack. His daughter told me he was happiest there, where he knew where everything was, and he needed to feel useful even if it meant just starting a car now and then. With a poignant nonchalance, she asked me if I was thinking about getting a new car. Nick had only recently said we should, but I could read her face: She was worried that her father wouldn't be able to start a new model. I told her I wasn't. In hot weather, the old man would open all the windows of the house on the morning we were due to arrive, and when it was off-season, or just chilly, he'd have a fire going in the big river-stone fireplace in the living room. No matter how high you turned up the thermostat in cold weather, the house still felt raw and damp.

The Washington-to-Providence flight was nearly empty, so they let me keep Buddy in the cabin in his crate. The attendant said, 'Even a dog that size is less of a pain than a baby. They need so much more paraphernalia than a dog, don't ask me why.' During the little hop from Providence to Watch Hill, the private-hire pilot let Buddy sprawl across two seats. I have found that the world is divided in two groups, those who can tolerate dog hair and those who can't.

I drove up the long brick-paved drive to the house, and as soon as I opened the car door Buddy lunged out and disappeared from sight. Looking up at the facade of this house was the same as being greeted by my mother – the one I never had but always wished for. The one who would offer me comfort and respite. It was huge and ramshackle with a wrap-around porch, beach-rose vines, now scatter-shot with rosehips, climbing in such obscene thickness over it that the trellises were completely hidden. I couldn't wait to get inside and smell the dampness and must mixed up with the fragrance of salt air.

I parked my bag inside the front door and, right away, put the kettle on and made tea. I took my mug and plopped in front of the fire with a notebook and wrote a list of things to do. That's how I always start, like a housewife planning the day's activities, because if she plans during, instead of before, nothing gets finished. I'd take the car early the next morning and check out this town that Owen had attributed a personality to. I jotted down all he had told me about the crime. I knew it was optimistic to think I could determine in one week whether I should start a book. I just didn't know if I'd be able to write it from a different perspective – after everything was said and done rather than during the saying and doing.

When I finished my list, it was six-thirty. I'd never noticed the day turn to dusk. Pretty cold, too. I jostled the practically dead fire and added some more logs. Then I went out onto the porch and gazed at the fall moon rising. Buddy was chasing its path of light, up and down the sandbar, exposed during one of those especially low, off-season neep tides. The moonlight made the chop appear to quiver. There were a few pinpoints of light on the horizon, ships at sea. I whistled and Buddy stopped in his tracks, turned, and came running. I hustled him into the living room, telling him he'd have all next day to be outside.

I sat on the sofa with more tea, and Buddy lay on the rug, his chin on one of my feet. We watched the fire. His eyes were at half mast; he drooled. If dogs think, he was thinking about drooling. Then I thawed out spaghetti sauce and meatballs that were in the freezer. Nick told me that when he was young he went right to summer camp from school. But he'd get to come to the beach house for two weeks before school started again, while his parents were in Saratoga. The Italian cook would make marinara sauce on damp, overcast days, and when it was simmering, he and his sister would stand on the kitchen chairs, up high where the heat from the stove was, and she'd give them little bowls of sauce and chunks of stale bread and they'd dip the bread into the sauce and gnaw away.

I ate my spaghetti, and Buddy had his kibble, and we watched the news and then a movie on the VCR: *Splash* with Tom Hanks and Darryl Hannah, who doesn't make a better mermaid than Ann Blythe but still a good one all the same. My mother made me watch old movies on TV with her. The Ann Blythe mermaid movie was her favorite. She'd cry all the way through it. She couldn't be a mermaid, she knew, so she drank.

During *Splash*, which I've seen a half-dozen times since we only had three movies at the beach house, I never stopped thinking about an Italian woman named Montevallo and her little family, and why they died. I thought about Owen, too. Then I went upstairs to the bedroom under the eaves and started up the wood stove.

I got a nightgown and a paperback from my bag, changed, and brushed my teeth. The phone rang: my children, jealous. My son wanted me to look in the room where he slept to see if that's where he'd left his Red Sox sweatshirt. It was on the hook behind the door. I'd told him never to hang things on hooks behind doors when you're away from home since that's where they'll stay. My daughter, on the extension, said, 'Explore that, Mom. Then you can write books like Erma Bombeck did.' I told her the world had been allowed only one Bombeck, we didn't deserve more, and I was sorry she had a mother who wrote about murder instead of extra closet space not being as important as you thought it would be once the kids were gone. Then I said, 'Dad home yet?' I got a two-kid chorus of 'Hah!'

The children manage well on their own. When I first started taking to the road, the dear late Mrs Earnshaw came to the house when they got in from school and stayed until Nick arrived home. She was quite elderly, but at the time we needed her we weren't at the stage where we required someone to diaper babies or chase after toddlers. All we wanted was a presence in the house and someone to cook dinner. Mrs Earnshaw taught the children to cook dinner themselves. She made fifties meals – red flannel hash, Welsh rarebit, pigs in a blanket, and desserts like pineapple upside-down cake, the recipe on the back of the Dole can.

On our anniversaries, the kids bring us breakfast in bed, a special dish Mrs Earnshaw recommended for such occasions. One of them bears the casserole pan into the bedroom, the other, a trivet and necessary crockery. The casserole consists of a bottom layer of Wonder bread, crusts removed, a middle layer of crumbled breakfast sausage, and, on top, a mix of beaten eggs and cheddar cheese that bakes into a golden-crusted, lumpy foam. On the evenings of our anniversary we all look forward to eating the leftover casserole cold out of the refrigerator, that's how good it is.

Mrs Earnshaw died while I was in Los Angeles during the O.J. trial. I flew home for a few days. Dominick Dunne would give me copies of all the notes he took at the trial. I'd done the same for him a month earlier, when his son got lost in the Arizona desert and he went out there to help search. When the Dunne son was found, he made all the newspapers, Mrs Earnshaw did not.

After the funeral, the children voted not to have a baby-sitter anymore. They were by then fourteen and fifteen. They pointed out that they had their dad's phone number at the executive office building in case there was an emergency. And if we were both gone at night, they could sleep at their friends' houses. Nick and I checked with the various friends' families and we agreed to their request, especially when Hillary had rung in with, 'I love your kids. They're a riot. Any time.'

I am a great admirer of Hillary Clinton because she is as diligent at being a mom as she was at trying to get health care for everyone. When she visits a Head Start center she's supposed to just pat kids on the head and smile for the camera. Instead, she'll sit down for a game of Chutes and Ladders, a game that very little children love but one that is worse than Chinese water torture. Put that bell on my head and drop water on it forever if it'll get me out of that one. I once expressed my admiration for her fortitude, and she explained to me that when she became pregnant she looked into what would happen besides diapers and feeding. She was prepared for Chutes and Ladders. I told her I had no idea that a person could plan that far ahead for raising a child. So she told me I'd done a good job of steering my own children toward independence and self-reliance. She said they seemed worry-free because they placed restrictions upon themselves that they abide by instead of worrying about meeting mine.

When I got back to Los Angeles, the ever-so-coy Judge Ito said to me, 'I did enjoy my few days of not having you and Mr Dunne distract me with your note-passing.'

* * *

At the Rhode Island beach house, knowing things were moving along at home, I climbed into bed and thought out plans for the following morning, when I would take that drive to New Caxton and get a feel for things, absorbing the local color. I'd nose up and down the streets in my car and observe the people. I would go to the library – I love libraries, the refuge of my childhood – and I'd start reading the daily paper. Put my feet in the shoes of these people by reading what they read each morning as they began their day. That way, if I was really going to get into the murders that occurred there, I'd feel the shock and horror and the confusion they did when their worst nightmare turned out to be real.

In bed, I read for about ten minutes and then turned out the light. Because of all the tea drinking, I'd be getting up around four to pee. But that was okay; I'd toss more wood into the stove then and wake up next morning in a toasty room. Buddy and I usually corked right off. This night, he did, but not me. My brain's planning engine cranked on. And, of course, there was the taste of Owen's kiss.

7

The next morning, I left Buddy outside. I'd be back in around four hours. It was cloudy, but if it rained, Buddy wouldn't mind; he loved rain because it doesn't rain inside a house, which is where he usually had to be. If it thundered, he could nudge the screen, come inside, and hide in the corner of the porch. I'd pulled a chair out from the wall for him to squeeze behind in order to cower comfortably. I dragged out his rug, and put his food and water on the porch, and yelled good-bye to him from the driveway. He was already way down the end of the spit, looking at me over his shoulder. Once he realized he could stay here on his own, he went into his circular dance of delirium.

When we'd had the Clintons as guests during the initial year of Bill's first term, Buddy and the President made friends, probably because Buddy was so gracious about staying outside for three days in deference to Bill Clinton's allergies. We'd all stayed up late because the kids were on school vacation and therefore entitled to watch Letterman. Bill and Hillary just liked to sit and sit at the long table after dinner was over, talking a mile a minute to everyone, and then they'd go out and take long walks by the water while the rest of us hit the sack. I still got up in the morning at six, even at the beach house, because that's when my brain gets me up no matter how late I go to bed. On one of those mornings, I pushed aside the white sheer curtains at my bedroom window to see what kind of day it was going to be, and there was Buddy running madly down the spit with a stick in his mouth. He stopped and waited, and then the President came into view and I watched their little tug-of-war over the stick. When Buddy let him have it, the President threw it as far as he could and the overjoyed dog went charging after it. A dozen secret service men, hunched over against the offshore wind, loomed atop the rises of the sand dunes, miserable in the damp morning chill. I let my curtain drop. The President had enough people watching him. That evening, Bill said to me, 'If we ever get a dog I'm naming him after yours.'

On this morning, I yelled to Buddy, 'You be a good dog!' He yapped.

The drive to New Caxton took exactly half an hour.

I smelled New Caxton before I saw it. Coming into the outskirts along the Scituate River were rows of factories and what was left of long-abandoned factories on rubbled lots. The buildings still in operation were burping up yellow smoke; most of their windows were shattered or cracked. I caught brief glimpses of the river in the narrow spaces between the crumbling brick structures. The immediate question rose: Why doesn't someone take a match to all this? Then I saw that someone had certainly tried. A lot of the grime was actually soot; a lot of the abandoned factories were crumbling because they had been gutted by fire. That's what I was smelling, mixed in with the noxious odor of the yellow fumes. And fire was what had cracked the panes in many of the surviving windows. This broken skeletal skyline, never taller than four stories, ran for miles along the river. And amid this battered, bleak facade were enormous signs stuck up against the sky, one after the other: SPECIALTY PLASTICS, NEW CAXTON CELLULAR PRODUCTS, LARCH SEMI-CONDUCTORS. And there were faded, very old signs still in place, shadows of the businesses now replaced by the minimalist age of high tech. I could just barely make out what they said: ABBOTT MUNITIONS. FOSTER BEARINGS. HALL TOOL AND DIE. Hall. That one had been in Owen's family.

At the end of the line was a dingy body shop and service station that sold a brand of gasoline I'd never heard of. I went inside to get a map of New Caxton. There was a little plaque next to the door that read FRANKIE GEDZENIAK'S CITGO. Inside, a man with F. Gedzeniak stitched onto the breast pocket of his jumpsuit was on the phone. He glanced up at me and said to whoever was on the other end, 'I'll have to get back to you.' At the garage where I take my car, when the mechanic is on the phone he glances at me and not only makes a point to continue his conversation in as leisurely a way as he can, but also tacks on a little last-minute male bonding with some extra chatter about the previous night's ball scores. But I'll take that over the pre-feminism days when there were porn pictures on the walls of your local garage with captions like LICK MY PUSSY.

Frankie Gedzeniak asked if he could help me, and I told him what I wanted. He said, 'Haven't got a map. What're you looking for?' I told him the library, and he said, 'Easy. Left at the next light, library's half a mile down the road on the right.' I'd have to copy a map at the library so I could find my way around the rest of New Caxton.

I thanked him. As I left, I asked, 'How's business?'

He said, 'Business is never good in this town. People bang out their own dents. But I get by.' Then his phone rang. The phone was the only thing in there that was clean. The only object less than twenty years old.

The first traffic light was at the intersection of South Street and Main; I was coming in from South Street. I got to see my first red street signs. They were faded just like everything else. If I took a right, I'd have gone over a bridge to the town of Chester on the other side of the Scituate. I glanced right and saw the sign that said CHESTER. It was green. I took a left onto Main, away from the river.

The businesses lining Main Street were a jumble of diverse but typical small-town enterprises – quite a few, I thought, having moved from a small town myself just a few years back, a suburb of New Haven, before moving to another suburb – of Washington, D.C. There was a coffee shop, a hardware store, a dry cleaner, a drugstore, two shoe stores, two clothing stores, and two banks. No real estate agencies. In Bridgefield, Connecticut, Main Street consisted of real estate agencies and antique shops. I knew there'd be neither here. If New Caxton had a mall nearby, it hadn't affected local business. The street was bustling with people coming and going in and out of the shops, hurrying along in the chilly morning air, wearing sturdy shoes, and dressed in heavy jackets and frumpy wool coats. It wasn't that cold, but there is a segment of American society, to which I once belonged, that views between-season coats as irresponsible. I thought, Of course there's probably a mall nearby, but the people of New Caxton have remained loyal to the local merchants. Owen had set the scene for me well: loyalty for the sake of loyalty.

None of the people were black. Maybe they had their own shopping district in the neighborhood where they'd first settled. I found the New Caxton Public Library. There was only street parking available, and the few cars in front of the library were parked with two wheels on the sidewalk. So I parked that way too, keeping to the pattern, my first move at blending into the environment of the crime. I felt confident because I had a Rhode Island plate and because I was driving the beach car, a ten-year-old Ford Taurus. My own car would not have blended in, parked this way in Alexandria; on the streets of Alexandria, any car with its wheels on the sidewalk is immediately towed away.

The New Caxton library was made of large blocks of dark gray granite, with narrow windows recessed into the blocks, the style, I believe, known as Colonial Revival. Nick taught me things like that. And I'd certainly enjoyed playing Eliza Doolittle to his Professor Higgins and attaining culturization. Colonial Revival, happily, was a revival that didn't last very long. The broad Flemish gables rose up above the roofline – above, I'd guess, every structure in New Caxton except the four-story factories and the three churches I'd seen along Main Street. Three stories plus the gables.

I got out of my car and walked up the sidewalk. I was thinking that, if ever someone held a contest to determine the country's ugliest building, this library would get a lot of consideration. I pulled open the wide, studded, arched door and once inside, in a tiny, dank, makeshift foyer that had been sectioned out of the lobby, jerry-rigged to keep out the cold, I let it go. The heavy clunk and then the loud click of the latch reverberated all around me. I thought maybe sirens and bells would go off, but there was only stillness. The only thing in the lobby was a stand containing three copies of a pamphlet titled 'The Ethan Reynolds Free Library.' Ethan. A cousin of Owen's, perhaps, maybe several times removed, but also a descendant of Ethan Allen. I took one out and read: 'The New Caxton Public Library was erected in 1902 by Ethan Reynolds as a memorial to his younger brother, Henry, who died in an accident at the age of twelve years.'

I tucked the pamphlet into my briefcase. An omen. I was crazy about omens. I would have to look into that particular accident. Owen mentioned the dearth of murders in this town. I wondered if there were, perhaps, an abundance of unexplained deaths. I sighed. The more I do what I do, the more cynical I become.

I liked it that the library wasn't *founded* by Ethan Reynolds but, rather, *erected*. I pictured this older brother mourning the loss of little Henry and just going out and building a library for the town without even bothering to ask if anyone wanted one. I had the feeling that any town-planning organization that existed in New Caxton on that day was no more effective than the town's planning and zoning commission today, if one even existed. My guess was that if the people who lived in the house next door to the library wanted to put up a chicken coop, no one would bat an eyelash.

The door in the foyer to the library proper looked as if it had come from a long-demolished building site. Three different colors of paint showed in the gouges. I pushed it open and entered the lobby. I had to stand for a minute to get my eyes used to the gloom inside. The lobby had, I guessed, thirty-six-foot-high ceilings. No light penetrated the cracked windows because they were filthy, coated with a buildup of the grime and soot that must have settled over the town when all the factories were in full swing and, too, after the arsonists had done their work. The electric lights exuded an eerie yellow color that used to be found in school classrooms before the advent of fluorescence. When I was a kid, I'd feel all cozy when the sky would darken and the teacher would take her ratty cardigan sweater off the back of her chair, place it over her shoulders, and then switch on the lights, creating that oozy yellow atmosphere. I remember chatting about my childhood with Nick once, and him looking up at me over his newspaper and saying, 'What *oozy* yellow atmosphere?'

The man was born oblivious. I'd once thought that trait adorable, his saying 'Excuse me?' when I pointed out a detail of life he hadn't noticed. Back then, when we were besotted with one another, he'd smile and kiss me. I thought it was his way of showing gratitude for my giving him something new. But it had been the kind of kiss you give a child when it's being sweet but boring and its switch needs to be turned off.

Thinking back to the time I spent with Owen, I guess I had a need to have that feeling of besotment again. Some give in to the need, some don't. Poppy has pointed out the downside of besotment: Your reason clouds over and you become an idiot. Those who understand that avoid giving in.

It was colder inside the library than it had been outside, but I could smell the steam heat and, above that, the smell of mold, not something you want in a library. I'd smelled New Caxton as I drove into town, and now I smelled more of it; it was the smell of desperation.

High above me, there were the faint remnants of wide hand-painted borders along the tops of the walls: faded gold stenciling depicting the zodiac and mythological symbols. Post-Victoriana at its best. Or its worst, depending on your perspective. The shelves against the lobby walls were solid white oak, the books in the shelves, a shambles. Loose creased and yellow pages stuck out of them.

There were four pieces of art in the lobby, all doubtless brought in by Ethan Reynolds in 1902, when the erection of the library was completed. Taking up one wall, a gold rococo frame held an enormous reproduction of Rembrandt's depiction of Christ driving the money changers out of the temple. I'd always called that painting 'Pissed-off Jesus.' This reproduction looked as though it had been caught in the middle of a high school cafeteria food fight.

On a stone ledge about six feet above the painting were three sculptures. I had to crane my neck to see what they were. To the left, a bust of Aristotle was askew and faced sideways toward the center of the ledge, possibly nudged out of position by the last person who'd gotten up there to dust. His irisless eyes were staring directly into the breasts of a Venus de Milo. The Venus was exactly the size of Aristotle's head and stood just three inches from him, facing down and away, the way she does, this time with good reason. In full flight on the far right end of the shelf the winged Hermes, the top of his head level with Venus's waist, a little sprinter who had to be thinking, I've got to get out of here. A pathetic but poignant tableau. I also thought, another omen. Why did people like Eddie Baines stay in this place? He'd been a high school hero. Gone to college. Been educated. Where was the Hermes mentality he was certainly entitled to?

The New Caxton Public Library is the only library I have ever been in where I was asked bluntly what I wanted, and the librarian wasn't referring to my research interests. In fact, at the end of this first foray, when I attempted to check out a book – a history of New Caxton that ended in 1860 – with my Rhode Island library card, perfectly valid, though it was issued in Westerly, the librarian told me I couldn't. I asked, 'Why not?' she said, 'How can I be sure you'll bring it back?' It felt appropriate to say, 'Because I promise to bring it back.' Perversely, at that she smiled and said, 'All right.' The smile wasn't because she suddenly trusted an outsider but because of my intuitiveness in coming up with an acceptably straightforward answer.

The librarian was right out of central casting. Potentially beautiful. But her hair was pulled back in a red rubber band, which she'd probably taken out of the little glass custard cup on the counter, filled with more rubber bands mixed in with paper clips. Her hair hadn't been combed before being styled into its pathetic ponytail, just smoothed back with her hands. Beneath the smooth strands were tangles. She had on a pair of glasses that looked as if they came from a free eye clinic. She wore a skirt that may well have been on backwards, the kind of skirt British matrons wear, all tweedy, woolly, lumpy, and shapeless. If the librarians I'd come to know could see this one, they would hold their heads in their hands and have to restrain themselves from issuing a couple of good primal screams.

I said to her, 'I'm interested in the local newspaper accounts of the Montevallo murders.' When I said the name Montevallo aloud, I swear I could hear the sounds of heads swiveling. I glanced back behind me to the reading room just off the lobby, where six people quickly turned back to their books and magazines. I looked back to the librarian. Her eyes searched my face, an eyebrow raised. 'You want the *New Caxton Standard*, not the Providence paper?'

'That's right.'

She called out. 'Anthony!'

A young man, about eighteen, came out of a doorway behind her. As he did, the librarian turned and disappeared through the same door, shutting it. Before the door closed, I glimpsed several women at a table, all looking busy. Probably volunteers gluing pages back into books. Anthony gave me a lopsided smile and said, 'Fiche dates.'

He'd been eavesdropping. 'I need the years between the day of the murders up until the last news accounts of the final appeal.' There were always appeals.

He giggled. He said, 'Fiche dates.' Anthony was retarded. The Montevallo son had some mental illness. Autism, Owen said. Maybe they'd known each other. I thought that, and then saw an image of a scoffing Poppy: *Yeah, Denise, they're both backward so they must have been best friends.*

I tried giving Anthony the year the crime was committed. Still, 'Fiche dates,' with the giggle. I said the year again. He said, 'Fiche dates.'

'From January first until December thirty-first.'

He held up three fingers. 'One box for three months.'

I said, 'All four boxes for that year then.'

He held up two fingers. 'Only two. Rules.'

My plan was to segue into the lives of these people prior to the murder of the Montevallos in hope of experiencing some semblance of what they had experienced before, at the time of, and after the crime. I would begin with the first half of that year, skimming the clips. Then I'd decide about whether to come back – to read on until that one August morning when the town woke up to what must have been a horrific banner headline. The culture of the town would play a large role, and I wanted to be sure of the strength of Owen's description.

I said to Anthony, carefully, 'What I need is the box marked January through March and the next box marked April through June.'

He giggled and came around the counter, then walked to the back wall of the lobby, past Jesus, and through a little door, disappearing up a winding steel staircase. I could hear his feet clumping, the steps becoming more muted the higher he climbed. They obviously kept the rolls of microfiche under the gables.

He was sweating when he emerged. He handed me the two boxes while the six people in the reading room watched intently, no longer concerned with avoiding discourtesy. They were all elderly. Quite elderly and with nothing better to do. They felt free to put down the magazines and just stare. Perhaps that's why their curiosity was blatant. In most places, these people would be housebound or in nursing homes. In New Caxton, the library pitched in so that the town's oldest residents weren't left out, forsaken.

Anthony went back around the counter and through the door he'd first come out of. I caught a glimpse of the librarian at the worktable with the other women, their heads bent to their tasks.

I looked around. One of the patrons crooked her finger at me. I went into the reading room and she pointed at a door between two stacks. A sign hung over the door: REFERENCE ROOM. I whispered, 'Thank you,' and went over and opened it.

The room was small, maybe twelve feet square, but the ceilings soared just as in the lobby. Any zodiac that might have graced the walls of the reference room had been painted over most likely many years earlier; new paint hadn't been applied in a long while.

One wall consisted of narrow floor-to-ceiling windows, the ones I'd seen outside, recessed into the granite, set so far inside the stone that direct sunlight would never penetrate. They were covered with sheets of cloudy, smeared, heavy-duty vinyl affixed with masking tape. The tape was peeling off and corners of the vinyl sheets waved slightly in the breeze. There were waist-high shelves of old encyclopedias lining three of the walls plus an old two-volume edition of *Books in Print*, with most of the entries, I'd guess, now out of print.

Off in the corner, a young woman stood sentry. She started jerking. She had cerebral palsy. I said, 'Hello,' and she came to me and took the boxes out of my hands. The people of New Caxton see that their disabled, as well as their elderly, have a life. Now I figured it wasn't too far-fetched that Anthony and the Montevallo son might have been friends, after all. Maybe he'd worked at the library too.

I followed the girl to a fiche machine that took up an entire corner of the room. It must have been the prototype. It was the size of a toolshed. In a garbled voice, the girl apologized for the fact that, if I made copies, the library would have to charge me thirty cents apiece because the machine hadn't been paid for yet.

She insisted on threading the machine herself. I tried not to laugh. Not at her preposterous efforts, which went on for a long time before she succeeded at her task, but at the entire otherworld scene. I thought maybe someone should consider airlifting the New Caxton Public Library to the Smithsonian. Congressman Hall was on to something.

It took me four hours to get through the first six months of the year three members of the Montevallo family were wiped out. And at the end of those hours, I wondered if I'd have the stomach to read about the crime itself. I was repulsed plenty by January through July. Instances of alcohol-related fights and accidents were rampant. Incredible automobile accidents. Doctors at nearby Providence hospitals were pressing that arrests be made of bar owners who allowed patrons to get drunk and then drive away, only to get stuck on the train tracks that crossed the center of town. A letter from an Amtrak official, copy to the mayor, described the nightmares of train engineers who couldn't avoid hitting cars – or, worse, hitting someone sprawled on the tracks. An editorial asked, 'What happened to the days when wives would escort their inebriated husbands home?'

A lot was laid upon the shoulders of New Caxton wives. The wives who were no longer escorting their inebriated husbands home from the bars were the same wives who were no longer calling the police when their husbands were beating them up and terrorizing their children, since, according to one article, a newly enacted Rhode Island law forced cops to arrest the wife-beaters even if the wives had no intention of pressing charges. So the wives had stopped dialing 911, stopped calling the police to come drag their husbands off them, to help toss them into cold showers, dry them, and put them to bed. Family members weren't supposed to turn other family members in to the cops.

During the months before the Montevallos were killed, there were accounts of two women so severely beaten by their husbands that they spent several weeks in intensive care units. Both husbands disappeared. One came back two months later, a week after the wife finally died of her injuries. He went to his wife's grave and shot himself. That was followed by the editorial calling to task wives who shirk their purpose.

The woman's death might not have qualified as premeditated murder, but it was damn close. Could Owen Hall not have known any of this? Was the state of society here so stratified that 'Americans' were cut off from any knowledge of deranged behavior?

But these articles, along with the regularly appearing column called 'What's Happening Around the World' – which consisted of headlines from the AP – took a back seat to the latest victories and losses of the various New Caxton High School varsity, junior varsity, and freshman teams.

I took notes and I absorbed and I made copies. The machine ground them out with a sound somewhat like a helicopter hovering overhead. It took five minutes to make each copy. I copied an obituary, representative of several:

> *Richard Stanley Wicznewsky, son of Stanley and Wanda Cichowicz Wicznewsky, born May 7th, died of natural causes at an unknown hour five months prior to his expected birth. Calling hours will be between 5 and 7 p.m. this evening at the Boralsky Funeral Home. A Mass of the Angels will be celebrated at St Cyril's Church Tuesday morning at 9 a.m. followed by burial at the Hall-Allen Memorial Cemetery.*

In New Caxton, there were funerals for miscarriages. These were Catholics who put their money where their mouths were.

I went back and made copies of articles that contained the

names of the local politicians, since I would have to interview them if I decided to try a book. I would need more than a name in a notebook, I'd need context. At the end of the second roll of fiche, I stacked up my copies, put them in a folder, rewound the fiche rolls, stuck them back in their boxes, and handed them to the girl. But she backed away, telling me 'Anthony's job.' She pronounced his name *Ant'ny.*

I went out to the desk. No one was there, and then suddenly the librarian came out of the door. There must be a peephole. She tallied up the cost of the copies. 'I'm afraid it comes to nine dollars and sixty cents.' I gave her a ten-dollar bill. The woman smiled to herself – at my extravagance, I imagine. She gave me my change and I asked for a receipt and she wrote on the back of a used catalogue card: *Paid for copies, nine-sixty,* and the date. That's when I asked if there was a history of New Caxton available to check out, and she'd asked me if I intended to bring it back. She went off and came back with the tattered copy of *New Caxton and Its Environs.*

I put the book and my copies in my canvas bag with my notebook, now containing thirty pages of notes. I noticed a stack of maps on the counter, compliments of a New Caxton bank. I took one and put it in the bag, too. I didn't want to. I didn't want to come back. I was uncomfortable. But at the same time, I knew I wouldn't be able to resist. As I left, I took a look over my shoulder at Hermes. He'd never escape. The librarian's gaze shifted from me to where I was looking. And she wouldn't escape either.

As soon as I got back to the house, I took a walk with Buddy and breathed the fresh sea air. But it would take more than the ocean, this time, to feel invigorated. I went to my favorite off-season restaurant in town, a German tavern. I took out a dinner of jaegerschnitzel, potato pancakes, and applesauce with pickled cabbage on the side. There was a fat little loaf of pumpernickel bread, too. And they gave me a bone for Buddy. I needed a hearty dinner because I would stay one more day in Rhode Island; I would go back to that library and take a look at the violence to come during the last six months of the year I'd already found repulsive. As opposed to the violence that lay just beneath the surface of the guileless picture of New Caxton that Owen Hall had drawn.

8

I would have liked to blame the restless night I had on the richness of my German dinner. Or my thinking about some nurse cleaning off a one-inch-long lump of fetus for a Catholic burial. But I tossed and turned because I was questioning where I wanted to go. My editor and I have always acted together, Louis carefully deliberating out loud about how a crime, whether unique or not, might be turned into a unique book and one that would build my audience. That's how Louis talked: 'Denise, yes, this is tantalizing, but is it the direction your audience wants to take?' I think of divas and popes as having audiences so I usually respond with 'It'll make a helluva movie, Louis.' But eventually he has always been able to steer me into a discussion of the merits of one killer over another in terms of the kinds of human behavior that a reader wants to peer into. This would all take place over several phone conversations, and then we'd have a final meeting in New York, over lunch, and we'd make our decision.

We'd lunch at Louis's club. I have come to understand the appeal of 'a club' to men via my relationship with Louis. I understood it when, after lunch, we were on the way out and a butlerlike fellow held my coat out for me. I told him I would carry it over my arm. He said, 'When madam came in, the weather was balmy. But the temperature has since dropped to fifty-two degrees. A new front has approached.' During this explanation, he steered me into one sleeve and then the other. A club is a mom who knows what's best for Sonny, and Sonny knows no argument will be breached. I told Poppy all about it and she said, 'That's exactly what I've been trying to tell you.'

'You have?'

'Yes. About why men suck.'

During these lunches, I would have to concentrate hard to have my own say about which book to write because Louis's virtuoso drinking capabilities so mesmerized me. He would order an aperitif the minute we sat down, then 'a light little wine' with his first course, then 'a solid, meaningful, and hearty red' with his entrée, champagne with dessert, and finally 'a perky liqueur' to help him gear up for the rest of his day. An essence of pears at 100 proof gears me up too, and I would need an entire pot of coffee before attempting to get out of my chair. The first time we had lunch – not at his club but at the Four Seasons, since we were celebrating the success of the Sam Litton book – he started with his Pernod and I ordered a Bloody Mary. I sent it back and told the waiter to remove the vegetable harvest sticking up from it. Louis immediately felt connected to me, as I had the *je ne sais quoi* to send back a cocktail.

Louis never acted the least bit inebriated during our lunches, but the tip of his nose and the tips of his ears would turn red, and then the redness would suffuse his skin until the two blushes merged and his entire face was the color of cranberry sauce. Like the New Caxton street signs, now that I think about it. At the end of lunch, he'd say, 'Denise, we have our formula, and we've matched it up to what is available to us in this particular murder and to this accused killer. I'd say it's a go. What do you think?'

And I'd agree or say I wasn't sure, but in either case I'd go to the town where Louis's preferred killer was in custody and have a peek and soak up the atmosphere. Within a short time I'd know, and then I'd call Louis and say that it was definitely a go or that I was on my way home because it wouldn't work and I had to research a different murder. When it was a go, I'd announce the hero. With the crime I'd just given up on – the Tennessee murderer who decided to confess before the trial started up – the hero would have been his mother; she was the one who convinced him to confess. She'd spent months collecting evidence to present to the police so that her son would be arrested for killing the best friend whose parents had neglected him and who she thought of as a second son. The killer's motivation lay in the hero mother's generous persona, which led to a terrible acting-out of sibling rivalry, the one brother feeling replaced, literally, by a surrogate brother.

When the man confessed, Louis agonized at the loss of such an intriguing theme. I didn't. The confession prevented a huge amount of further suffering all around. I said, 'Louis, you're not particularly humane, are you?'

Louis sighed into the phone. 'The reason you're so good is because you never forget that the product you deal in isn't used cars. I'm afraid that's what books have come to mean to me.' He sighed some more. 'I remember once being on a panel with Norman Mailer. The topic was something like "The State of the Book as We Approach the Twenty-first Century." Why in Heaven's name people come to these God-awful things I wouldn't know, since none of us have any idea what we're talking about. The panel was me; a publisher; another editor besides me, I forget who; a couple of agents, not yours, thank goodness; and Norman. Norman spoke last. While the rest of us had been blathering on, he'd been making us terribly uncomfortable because he kept jotting down these little marks on a piece of paper in front of him. Little sticks. So at the end of the discussion, the moderator said something along the lines of *And we have yet to hear from Mr Mailer*, followed by this irritating nervous chuckle he had, which was all Norman needed to set him off. He stood up and said he'd been tallying the number of times that we'd used the word *product* and the number of times we used the word *book*. He said he lost count of *product* at 117, and in the book column he had a total of zero. He said, 'I have nothing further to say about the state of the book as we approach the twenty-first century.' That's when I admitted that it's all used cars to me, Denise.'

When O.J. was arrested, Louis called me. It was about ten o'clock at night. He'd just left a meeting with the powers that be and had negotiated a huge pile of money to get me to put my life on hold and go to O.J.'s trial. Then I called Myron and he got them to up the ante even more, and then I told my family what was up – that I'd be home only on weekends for what looked like many months. But that I'd be sure my hotel was on the beach and had a great pool besides, so I'd be fun to visit. None of them batted an eyelash. I hadn't even needed to press them with the bribe of great weekends on the West Coast. Mrs Earnshaw offered to move in Monday through Friday.

But now, here I was contemplating my next crime and I'd left Louis out in the cold. Why? Because I didn't want to risk his advising me not to do it, which is what he would advise because of the expectations of my 'audience'. And why wouldn't I accede to his judgment? Because I would lose this thread to Owen. I wanted him. I was looking for an excuse to fall into an affair with Owen, thereby not having to take responsibility for a conscious decision. But I did not like the sound of my voice as I imagined it in a rationalization to Poppy: *God, Poppy, one minute we were discussing this crime of his over coffee, and the next minute I was in his arms. I just don't know how I got there.* The hell with that.

I had to separate this murder in New Caxton from what I intended to do about Owen and figure out whether one could happen without the other. Owen was genuinely upset about the crime, I knew. He wanted me to straighten things out for him. And the oddities of New Caxton had aroused my curiosity, even if I was repelled. I could sense I was at the very edge of zeroing in: finding out exactly what happened there and, most important, *why* it happened. I was not just going to fall into a book about this crime, and I was not just going to fall into Owen's arms either. And so, the next morning, instead of driving back to New Caxton from the beach house to see the other two fiche rolls, I shoveled Buddy into the car and headed into Connecticut, to Bridgefield, the little town outside New Haven where I'd lived from the time I'd married Nick until we followed Bill Clinton to Washington. I had a need to see old Leo Schatz. I needed to talk.

We hadn't kept in touch. If Leo had kept in touch with all the sports and food people who'd come and gone before me and since, he'd have a lot of correspondence. Besides, if he'd wanted to keep in contact, he could have called or written to me. He hadn't. That first year, I did send him a Christmas card from Alexandria and even jotted down *How ya doin'*? but I didn't get a card back. Unless he'd gotten sick or something, or maybe even died – though if that had happened, someone from the *Press* would have let me know – Leo would be there at our desk, sharing space with the sports guy and the food person. There are some people who you are friends with for years and years, and then you don't see them and you forget about them in two minutes, and the thought of looking them up never occurs to you. Then there are people you know just a short time, and ten years go by and you see them again and it's as if no time had gone by at all. I had a feeling that Leo would fall into the second category.

Maybe talking to Leo would help me iron out my thoughts. I hate it when I have trouble sleeping. Reminds me of when my children were infants and I was convinced I was going to die because months of interrupted sleep is a torture that works. The tortured will confess to anything. At least I know I would. Nick wanted to get a nanny when the children were babies, but after having experienced a non-mother, I thought I should be the real McCoy, daffy me. My children were eleven months apart. Even as I lay in my hospital room with my newborn daughter, I was determining to have a second child as soon as possible so she wouldn't be alone the way I had been. I told Nick what I wanted while he was standing over her bassinet, gazing down at her.

He said, 'Denise, she'll have us.'

'What if we're not enough?'

'We'll be good parents.'

I was twenty-two years old, a new college graduate, a new wife, and a new mother, all in the course of a year. 'I really need for her to have a brother or sister.'

He came over to my bed, sat down, and took my hand into both of his. He kissed it. 'I don't know any more about what constitutes a proper childhood than you do. I had a sister, but I remember just tiny moments with her.'

'You were in boarding schools. Different boarding schools.'

'Yes, we were.' He looked back to his daughter and then to me. 'She'll have what we didn't, then. We'll see to it. A little brother or sister. A pal.' The pal was born the next year.

When the children were in school, public school, a short yellow bus ride from our house, I took the job with the *Press* as a favor to a friend. Bridgefield is a suburb to academia, and it's also a suburb to corporate America. So half the population never moves from their eighteenth-century farmhouses where the breadwinner commutes to Yale, and the other half of the population hopscotches every other year from their four-bedroom faux colonials in Connecticut to their faux adobes in Santa Fe to their faux plantations in Atlanta, all compliments of IBM et al. Nick's friends were from group one, and mine from the other, which meant I was constantly making and losing new friends before a bond could set in. One in particular had delivered an ultimatum to her husband that she would never move again, that she loved the Connecticut woods, that she had pulled up stakes for the last goddamned time. And she dusted off her journalism degree and took on the food column for the *Bridgefield Press*. We all knew she meant business, too, since corporate wives don't get jobs; they're too busy selling and buying houses, packing and unpacking. But then, along came an irresistible big promotion that meant a move to San Francisco and the chance of living in an even more gracious manner than they were doing in Connecticut. Also, everyone told her that the offices in San Fran were not going to be downsized, which wasn't the case in her husband's current division. She had to go.

She said to me, 'I need you to step into my *Press* job, Denise. I absolutely promised them I'd stay at least a year. I actually said, "Oh, I'll be here forever!" But they're not idiots like I'm an idiot, and they just keep saying all they hoped was that I could give them a year. I want to offer them a replacement, all trained and ready to go, when I tell them I lied.'

I said, 'You didn't lie, and you're not an idiot.'

She said, 'Yes I am and yes I did. I lied to me. I still haven't faced up to the fact that I'll never be able to take a photograph of my kids down from the wall and realize how much the paint has faded.' Then she burst into tears. So we had cappuccino at the local coffee bar and she said to me, 'You know, Denise, it's really a fun job at the *Press*. I promise you'll like it. They're a real friendly bunch. The only downside is that when you go in to put your stuff in the *Press* computer, you'll have to share a desk with this little homunculus who hates women. Well, he hates everyone.'

I said, 'I could probably handle him.'

She laughed. 'I just bet you could.'

I kept telling her that the real problem with doing her this favor was that I couldn't cook, and even though I got As on all my college papers, my passion was for the subject, not for the writing. She told me that the cooks I interviewed would do the cooking, not me, and all I had to do was tape what they babbled. She said, 'Then, you basically transcribe it, taking out the crapola. Just leave in the interesting stuff, and if they don't say anything interesting, emphasize the decor of the kitchen because that's what people really want to know, if so-and-so has one of those yuppie stoves that costs as much as a car and a restaurant-quality refrigerator that needs a room of its own. A little Martha Stewart kind of stuff, you know?' I didn't.

She also reminded me that since I'd been a literature major I'd probably have some clue as to where commas were supposed to go, and that was all the *Press* really cared about. They had no room in their budget for copy editors. I said, 'I don't know where commas go; I only follow the theory, "When in doubt, leave 'em out."'

She laughed. 'You see? You're a good talker, Denise, you're fun, and you know a lot of people in town because of Nick. Believe me, all these schmoes love getting their names in the paper, telling the public the secret of their hot shrimp dip. And you get to eat the goodies. Some of these people actually can cook, believe it or not.'

This all happened right at the time Nick started making little suggestions about my going back to school. 'To study what?' I'd ask him. His blank expression told me he wasn't thinking in terms of studying; he just couldn't think of anything else for me and he was tired of answering the question *What does you wife do?* with *She's at home*. It seemed that many of his fellow academes got to answer, *My wife is the poet Susan Treadwell-Finch – she just had a little piece of free verse published in the 'Demagogue Review.'* So I ended up saying to my friend, 'What the hell, I'll do it.'

I showed Nick the innocuous tape recorder my friend had passed along to me. He said, 'What will you need that for?' I said, 'For the column.' He couldn't make the connection. 'What column?' he asked, and I told him I'd already told him what column. He waved his hand in the air as if to remove a gnat. Then he revealed to me the latest Yale brouhaha that was keeping him so *preoccupied*; he hadn't really heard me when I'd told him earlier about the Press job.

After practicing with my friend, I began to see that she hadn't been lying to me, either. It *would* be fun. We fell all over ourselves laughing when we role-played and I asked her, in her role as bank president demonstrating barbecuing techniques, 'What do you do when your hot dogs fall off the platter into the grass?' She said, 'My God, Denise, this column is going to have some wit, I can see that.' I told her I hadn't come up with the question for purposes of wit, I was serious. The week before, Nick and I had had a bunch of people over with their kids for a barbecue on the deck, and I tried to balance a huge platter of chicken on the railing and it started to slip, and when I grabbed for it I tipped it and all the chicken slid off and went over the side. The children were sitting on the grass below playing Yahtzee and they all started shouting when the chicken rained down on them, but their parents were gathered around our portable bar, delirious with relief that the kids had found something to do, so they never caught my faux pas. I ran down the deck stairs and had the kids gather up the chicken and rinse it all off with the garden hose. I told them we had a secret to keep. I love the panache of precocious upper-class kids, e.g., during dinner: 'Gee, Mrs Burke, what is this flavor I'm tasting, *mauvaise herbe*?' – which is French for crabgrass.

I bought a couple of pairs of pantyhose, took out my suit, and started interviewing people. After writing a few columns, I found I didn't need the tape recorder. It slowed me down. I took notes instead, and that's when I realized I remembered every single thing that was said by just a glance at the notes. That's why I was a good college student, why I so impressed my teacher, Nick. I have a great short-term memory. But one month after my final exam in Romantic Literature, I never knew Shelley from Keats from Byron from anybody. Nick didn't notice that character flaw until it was too late.

So after my years of carpooling, PTA, Little League, and, finally, court TV as opposed to the soaps of my mother, I found I enjoyed being alone, working on my column in the quiet. And I reveled in feigning grand interest in what secret exclusive ingredient that people threw into the beef stew. 'It's *port* of all things! A glass of port! Can you believe beef stew could taste this marvelous?' After a time, I got up the chutzpah to call the actor Robert Vaughn, whose television show my mother had never missed. He lived in town because he wanted his children to experience a normal life. He gave me that piece of information when I asked why he chose to live in Bridgefield rather than Santa Barbara. I didn't respond by telling him that if your father is the Man from U.N.C.L.E. you won't have a normal life no matter where you live. It'll be far better than normal, was what I was thinking. His son played baseball with my son, and that had been my entrée. One day in the stands I asked him if I could interview him for the food column, and he said 'Sure.'

Robert Vaughn lives in a mansion overlooking Bridgefield Lake. He offered me white wine and invited me to sit in his living room instead of taking me right into the kitchen. He intended to tell me, not show me, how to make perfect scrambled eggs. 'The trick,' he said, 'is to use half-and-half instead of milk – which only makes the eggs runny – or, worse, cream, the way the British do – which makes them taste like custard instead of a breakfast food.'

With that, the interview was over as far as he was concerned, and that was fine with me because I would get to pad the article with all the conversation we went on to have about acting. A lot of the time he talked, I took notes on the decor of his house, which everyone in town speculated over. He used his Emmy as a doorstop. I was about to wrap things up when he poured more white wine into our empty glasses and suggested a fire in the hearth. But it was early fall and the staff hadn't opened his chimney damper yet. He didn't know that when he laid the fire. The room, papered, painted, upholstered, and carpeted in white, filled with smoke. We tried to open the damper, and he cut his finger while managing it. While he went to find a Band-Aid, I opened all the windows and doors. He came back with a strip of paper towel around his finger and a bowl of Wheat Thins for us to snack on. There was blood on the edge of the bowl. Then his wife drove up, came in, and asked what was burning and we both said we had no idea. She looked down at the bowl of Wheat Thins and said, 'Couldn't you have used a clean bowl, Robert?' She thought the blood was dried-on ketchup.

The scrambled eggs column was a huge hit. I didn't include the fireplace/cut finger part, but I did say that when Robert Vaughn threw out the first pitch at last year's Little League opening-day ceremony, he had effused into the squawking mike, 'Ballplayers! It is important to listen to your coach. But it is far, far more important to listen to your mother.'

Right after the column came out, Nick and I went to a large

dinner party and, after thirty seconds of discussing whether or not we'd have invaded Kuwait if the prize had been strawberries rather than oil, the guests fawned all over me, telling me how much they enjoyed the behind-the-scenes action at the house of the Man from U.N.C.L.E. Nick was all ears. Afterwards, he said, 'I guess I'd better start reading your . . .' He was stymied.

'My food column, Nick. Actually, you helped me write that one.'

'I did?'

'Yes. I asked you for a word that describes the way an actor speaks dramatically, and you told me: effuse.'

My stock with Nick went up. And it was a satisfying revelation to realize that I took no pleasure in his pride in my new role as a dinner-party entertainer. Of course my stock bottomed out when people began saying to him, 'Did your wife know this Sam Litton monster?' And he'd say, 'No, she never even ran into him.' He'd been appalled when I told him that Sam Litton was the guy I'd been talking about for a year. 'The sports guy, Nick,' I said to him. 'The one I've been sharing a desk with. I keep trying to tell you – I've been sharing a desk with a serial killer for a year!' When Sam wrote me that letter asking me to come to Florida, Nick forbade me to go. He shouted, 'I absolutely forbid this, Denise. I forbid it!'

The kids came clamoring up from the family room, knocking one another out of each other's way, their eyes bulging. 'Forbid what? Forbid what?' they begged to know. I said, 'Forbid nothing. Dad was just blowing smoke out of his butt.' They retreated back to MTV.

After the long drive from Rhode Island, I pulled into the lot at the *Press* and felt happy to be back. As soon as I walked in there was a groundswell of welcome. My old boss and his secretary and the receptionist and the reporters who were in all gathered around me – lots of hugging and kissing and congratulations and the taking of pictures, which would fill up a page in the 'News of Old Neighbors' in next week's edition.

Leo didn't join in. Buddy, who hated being petted, much less gushed over, made his way directly over to my former cubicle. He was lying there at Leo's feet when I put my head around the corner. Leo the curmudgeon was already dropping peppermint candies to him just the way he used to. Buddy didn't know Leo was hoping he would choke on one. Leo stood, and I went around the desk and hugged him. I felt just a bit of pressure coming from Leo's arms before he quickly backed away. But he did say, 'I have to admit it, Denise, you're a sight for sore eyes.'

I sat in my old chair and we chatted. He congratulated me on rising to the top with my O.J. book. I thanked him. He told me that the half-dozen food column ladies who'd followed me were all a bunch of drips. 'Each and every one of them – dumb as a sack of rocks.' The sports guy after Sam, who I remembered as a refreshing young boy, had decided he was better off going back to college, Leo told me. But the next guy had settled right in. Leo gestured toward one corner of the desk at a pen and paper-clip holder molded into the shape of a Mets cap, bat, and ball. 'He's a retired guy. The only thing we have in common is that we were born in the same decade. He's off at some practice or other. He goes to practices, for Christ's sake. However, all the better for me. I don't have to listen to his drivel. And the latest food lady just drops a disk off every Tuesday. Prefers to work entirely out of her home. God, spare me.'

I said, 'Maybe she's prejudiced against old guys.'

He really looked at me. One corner of his mouth turned up a tiny bit. 'I never thought I'd miss you, but I do. Frankly, I miss Sam too. We had some fun here, didn't we?'

I got a sinking feeling in my stomach. We'd had a lot of fun. I said, 'Yes.'

We hobnobbed some more and then he asked, 'So what is it you want?'

I felt relief. 'I'm so glad you asked. I'd hoped you would. I need your advice, Leo.'

That was the only thing he was interested in hearing from me. He leaned forward just a tiny bit.

First, I told him about the crime, about how a congressman I ran into told me about it. How he had this feeling that the guy who was convicted might not have done it.

Leo said, 'On death row, is he?'

'No death penalty in Rhode Island.'

Then I told him about New Caxton, the backwardness of the people there. 'It's a kind of incest, Leo, like those weirdos in *Deliverance* who lock themselves into some hollow in Appalachia, strum their banjos like that's all they have to do all day, and what they're really doing is taking whatever actions are necessary to keep outsiders out and insiders in.'

He said, 'Well, you know, places like that, like New Caxton, these old industrial towns – Bridgeport, Fall River in Massachusetts – the immigrants who settle there are like the fabled fox with the grapes. They had so little – nothing, really – in the old country, and when there was an opportunity to get out they sailed across the sea and took their chances in American mill towns. So when they find out the new deal ain't what it's cracked up to be, they can't just back out. Where would they go, back to Naples? How? They convince themselves that everything is hunky-dory and they idealize their rotten lives. They feed on each other and they tie down their young. They don't want the next generation to find out the truth, to abandon them. It's a bastardization of the American dream. Most provocative, Denise. But bastardization or not, it's still

America, and that means that the third generation gets an education and expands its horizons. They leave.'

'In this case, nobody leaves. It's more than provocative, isn't it? It doesn't fit the pattern.'

He leaned back, and then farther back, on the two rear legs of his chair. He held my gaze the whole time. 'So now tell me what the problem is. I can see you're enthusiastic. Why not just go for it?'

'Well, this congressman who told me about the crime, Owen Hall—'

'*The* Owen Hall?'

'Yes. He's . . . listen, I don't want a . . . a flirtation to get in the way of my purpose.'

He let the chair slam forward. 'Now there's a crock of shit.'

'C'mon, Leo. I—'

He said, 'Sin.'

'What?'

'Sin. That's what you want to do, so do it. Call it a flirtation if it alleviates guilt. And while you're at it, write the book. This business certainly seems to have more going for it than the other stuff you've done, which has really been mostly fluff, O.J. or not, don't deny it.'

'I never said I could write another *Titus Andronicus*.' He didn't know what I was talking about. He'd forgotten that he'd recommended Shakespeare before I started writing crime. I said, 'Never mind.'

'You only live once, kiddo. And the reason you decided to ask my advice instead of your clergyman's is because you knew what my answer would be. You don't want the clergyman's answer.'

I smiled at him. I love the truth. I needed someone to say it out loud for me. Leo has no morals. He once said, 'We should all be like the people of the South Pacific. They're completely amoral. Who can have morals when you've got the trade winds invigorating your physical needs? I myself decided to emulate the citizens of the islands a long time ago, and I've never regretted it.' Leo had served in the Pacific during WWII. He told me he'd slept with over two thousand women in his life.

'Listen,' he said, 'enjoy yourself, because some day you'll be eighty-two years old and you'll be living on stool softeners. Unless you're already dead.' Then he said, 'Your miserable damn dog is getting on my nerves.' I looked down. Buddy was drooling. Leo looked down, too, and then at me. 'How on earth can you stand him?'

I said, 'I must love him. Otherwise I'd want to pour boiling water over his head.'

He said, 'Do you want to pour boiling water over your husband's head?'

'Yes.'

'So follow the path you've started down. Vengeance is liberating when you're having fun.' He walked me to the door. 'One mope per family is plenty.'

Back in Watch Hill, as soon as I opened the door, Buddy leaped out and galloped into the sea. That's what I felt I was doing, too, when I went in and got out the little piece of paper that had Owen's phone number on it.

9

When Owen's secretary told me she would give him my message and he would get back to me, I told her that I needed to speak to him urgently. There was a very small pause before she asked, 'Is the number you gave me a home phone number?' I said it was. It was the number at the beach house.

'When will the Congressman be likely to reach you, Mrs Burke?'

'Between seven-thirty and nine-thirty.'

'Well, I'm terribly sorry to say that the Congressman begins work at seven and won't be able to return any calls until lunch.'

'I meant in the evening. This evening.' I imagined that married women didn't usually ask Owen to call them at home in the evening.

When I hung up, I knew the die had been cast and so I swore I wouldn't beat up on myself. If I did end up sleeping with Owen, I certainly intended to enjoy it. I would focus on the joy part. Then I went over it all again in my head, only this time, I substituted 'fucking' for 'sleeping with.' Poppy says that if you call a spade a spade right from the start you're less likely to wimp out later. Actually, 'fucking' sounded more joylike than 'sleeping with'. I did try 'making love' but I didn't love Owen. Not then. Maybe Poppy's theories on the chronology of love made sense after all.

The phone rang at nine-thirty on the dot; he just made the deadline.

'Are you about to run out the door?' he asked, after the hellos and how-are-yous.

'No, do I sound rushed?'

'I guess I thought you had to leave for somewhere by nine-thirty.'

I said, 'That's when I go to bed.'

'You do?'

'Well, I read in bed. But don't tell me; you get along on four hours' sleep a night, right?'

'Anyone who makes that claim is lying or sneaks off for after-lunch siestas.'

'So since we're talking politicians – politicians are the ones who always brag about needing only four hours – we're probably talking lying.'

'You're picking on me, right?'

'I'm picking on the liars-slash-snoozers.'

'You sound irritated. Don't you like it in Washington?'

'Not irritated. Cynical. I love Washington.'

'You just needed to get away. Which is what you're doing, I assume. Considering your area code, I take it you're at your beach house.'

'Yes, I am.'

'Alone?'

'No. My dog's with me.'

'Good,' he said, and then he laughed. 'I'm going to be in Rhode Island next week. Maybe we can get together.'

'I'll be back home by then. I'm just staying till the day after tomorrow.' I wanted to say, I'm not playing hard to get; that's my plan.

'Another time, then. When we're in the same place at the same time. So I take it you've given some thought to the people who were killed in New Caxton.'

'Yes. I'm not here to get away. I've already visited the New Caxton library.'

'A museum, isn't it?'

'That's exactly what it is.'

'So what do you think?'

'I have to say I'm tempted. But so far, only that.'

'What tempted you in particular?'

I started to censor what I was about to say, but I stopped myself and said it. I said, 'You tempted me.' But I kept talking, too. I didn't know how to do this properly. 'But I can't really discuss the murders. Not yet.'

'It *is* upsetting, I know.'

'To tell you the truth, I haven't even gotten to the upsetting part.'

'And when do you expect to get to the upsetting part?'

'Next time I go back to the library. In the next few days. But the reason I'm not talking isn't because the crime is upsetting. Most crimes usually are. It's just that if I talk, what comes out in conversation may get lost and then there'll be nothing to put on paper.'

He said, 'I know what you mean. You're still thinking. I find I have to think a lot before I do something. But, Denise, I assumed that's why you were calling. To talk about it.'

'No, to ask specific questions. There are a couple of things I want to know, things that have to do with the character of the town, not the murders.'

'Well, that's okay, but I have to warn you that I don't spend much time there. I went away to school. I'm not exactly an expert on the day-to-day stuff. For that you'd be better off talking to Rosie. But you must have met Rosie. She knows about everything to do with New Caxton.'

'Rosie?'

'Rose Owzciak. The librarian. We were friends when we were kids; she's a few years younger. She was a smart girl. When I'd come home from school, we'd hang around with the same crowd. Whenever I could find the time, anyway.'

'Is she a professional? I mean, did she—?'

He laughed again. 'Rosie has a master's degree in library science from URI.'

'Good. Then she'll probably know the regulations for getting trial transcripts in Rhode Island.'

'What regulations?'

'The rules for gaining access. The cost.'

'They're public record.'

'Only if the public happens to be a lawyer or a DA. The court reporters own the rights to the transcripts. You usually pay them by the page.'

'How come I didn't know that?'

'Professional secret. That's why they're called court reporters now instead of stenographers. They've got a hell of a union. It can be a pretty lucrative job.'

'So what does a layman do who wants to read a court transcript?'

'Calls the courthouse, finds out who the reporter was, talks to her, makes a deal. The state of Texas holds the record for cost: two dollars a page. You can get around it, though. You can pay some law student to tell the reporter he's doing research, and he'll be allowed to Xerox the transcript.'

'There ought to be a law against that.'

'Write your congressman.'

He didn't laugh.

'Sorry. People say that to you a lot, don't they?'

'Not a lot.'

'You don't have to be polite when I'm being schmucky, Owen.'

'You're very hard on yourself, aren't you?'

'I am?'

'Sounds it.'

Well, I thought, fancy that. 'Court reporters are pretty skillful at what they do, get on paper what comes out of several people's mouths all talking ninety miles an hour, and all talking at the same time, besides. The public can see that now, what with televised trials. Anyway, the states can't pay them what they're actually worth. All comes out in the wash.'

'So how many pages of transcripts will a murder trial have? I mean, I know it depends—'

'Depends entirely on the length of the trial. Average is ten thousand, plus appeals. O.J. Simpson, two hundred thousand.'

'Jesus.' Then he said, 'Denise?'

'Yes?'

He fell quiet, not prone to blurting out anything the way I had done. Then: 'Denise, listen, I'm taking up your reading time. Maybe we'll get together when you're in Rhode Island again, if you decide to pursue all this. I'll give you the Cook's tour of New Caxton. Or maybe I can see you in Washington. We can talk about the town. I don't know as much as Rosie, gossip-wise, not that that's meant to insult Rosie. But I do have a perspective that she doesn't. My great-grandfather owned New Caxton. Hers came to New Caxton with not much more than the clothes on his back. So what do you think?'

'I would enjoy the Cook's tour. Or maybe we could have lunch in Washington. Either way.'

'Great. I'll be in touch. Good night.'

'Good night, Owen.'

Buddy followed me upstairs to bed. I lay there staring up into the shadowy ceiling, listening to Buddy's snores from the rug and the waves pounding on the spit of land. It was a windy night. Storm coming, maybe. I love storms. I could use one. Once, when I was offering my sympathies to Poppy concerning her frustration with men, I told her that someday she would meet a man who would cause her to lie awake at night thinking about him. She snorted. She said, 'If I end up in that bad a shape, regressed to adolescent mooning, then he'd better meet my every need. Of course, if he were meeting my every need, I wouldn't be lying in bed thinking about him. I'd be in bed with him, teaching him a few new tricks.'

I rolled over. If I didn't want to leave Nick and if I ended up having an affair with Owen – but didn't want Nick to suspect I was having an affair – I'd have to sleep with both men during the same time period. If I stopped the occasional nights with Nick of we're-both-here-so-we-might-as-well-do-it, Nick would wonder about me. Could I have sex with Nick as a ploy? Once I overheard two women speaking in a rest room. One said to the other that she wasn't with her boyfriend that night because he had to save up some sperm for his wife. I admired the fact that, for this woman, having an affair was like cutting her toenails.

I rolled over again and told myself to stop thinking unpleasant thoughts. Either you're moral or you're not. Make the choice, Denise, and take the consequences like a man, as Leo would put it. The first time he put it that way, I asked him if he ever considered the consequences of the female gender being absent in language. He told me to get over it.

10

In the morning the wind was still howling, but no rain yet. I called in to my office and listened to my messages on my answering machine. Two were from Louis: the first, 'Give me a buzz, my dearest'; the second, 'My God, Denise, don't tell me you're taking a vacation.'

I called him. We exchanged very few pleasantries. He said, 'It's been almost a year since the O.J. book came out.'

'I'm getting choosier. What can I say? We were on to something in Tennessee. Not my fault the guy confessed. Actually, I think I'm on to something else, but I'm not sure.'

'And you've been keeping it a secret?'

'Sort of. At least until—'

'You're worried that I won't like the idea?'

'Yes.'

He framed his words carefully. Editors don't use the same words with writers that they do with other editors, or with agents, or with movie producers. So he had to be sure he was clicked into the right mode. He said, 'Denise, do not stray.'

He meant from the tried-and-true, not my husband.

'I won't. The only difference is that, with this particular crime, the trial and everything are over. I've been trying to figure out a way to tell you that without your—'

'Did you say the trial is over?'

'Yes.'

'You will depend on transcripts?'

'And news accounts. And far more interviews than usual. I'll talk to everyone who participated in the trial – lawyers, witnesses, cops, everyone. Spectators, even. It should be interesting.'

Louis said, 'When a writer uses the word *interesting*, which tells me less than nothing, my palms become clammy. Denise, what murder are we looking at?'

'It took place in Rhode Island.'

'Good Lord.'

'Rhode Island is no less romantic than Tennessee.'

'I beg to differ. Tennessee has—'

'Graceland. I know. Three people were stabbed in Rhode Island.'

'What people were stabbed?'

'A woman, her son, and her grandchild. A couple of years ago.'

'I don't remember it.'

'It didn't make the national press.'

'Excuse me?'

'Things were maybe hushed up. The guy might not have done it.'

'Now *that* intrigues me . . . so positive about O.J., not so positive about whoever this fellow is. My very dear Denise. I have learned to trust you. I thought you were using poor judgment when you didn't show an interest in Susan Smith, but you turned out to be right.'

'I didn't want to write the same book again, that's all.' My second book was about a mom who'd killed her kids. One of those was enough.

When Louis had called me all hysterical over Susan Smith, I told him she did it, so what was the point? Just like our Lorraine. Lorraine Clearwater shot her children because her boyfriend told her that children weren't part of his agenda. Both he and Susan Smith's boyfriend thought it was a nifty way of ending a relationship, since the kids weren't going anywhere. The guys were wrong. The sooner men stop using that excuse to jump ship, the safer children will be.

Louis had called me right after Susan Smith cracked. He said, 'I didn't think she was a Lorraine.'

She wasn't. Not exactly, anyway. Lorraine was a single mom, too, estranged from her husband. But she was harder than Susan Smith. She didn't try to talk people into believing her story. She shot herself in the side instead. 'A man with curly brown hair shot us all,' she kept saying to the police. Didn't play the race card. And she still proclaims her innocence to this day – at least to anyone who will listen – but even Alan Dershowitz has lost interest, so she's got no chance.

I'd said at the time, 'Louis, people who steal cars make sure there are no babies in the back seat. Stealing cars is a business. How cost-effective is it to take a chance of getting the kidnapping police interested in you when all you want to do is make a fast buck?'

He said, 'What happened to maternal instinct, anyway?'

'The concept of instinct is a fallacy. Particularly, maternal instinct. I'm pathologically cynical, I've discovered, so I'm not a believer in that which would be nice to believe.'

'Susan Smith put on a superb act.'

'More superb than any other killer? Than Lorraine, for God's sake? She did hope to get away with it, after all, just like the rest of them. She came up with a plan to avoid getting caught. Crying and pleading and going on about a black guy who stole her car even though her babies were in the back seat. Somebody needs to do a book that debunks maternal instinct. I'll bet you've got a dozen writers up your sleeve who could—'

'Denise—'

'It's a great concept. It can start with the ATF guys who decided to firestorm Waco because they thought maternal instinct would kick in when the guns started blazing, that the moms would scoop up the kiddies and run for it. Right. Or maybe it's just too much country music.' I started to sing "*Stand by your man . . .*"

'Denise, let me finish. *You* have maternal instinct. You stayed home with your children when they were small. You would raise them, no one else.'

'What I saw as responsibility. Based on my having had to raise myself.'

I heard a mumble of voices in the background. 'Denise, hold on a minute.' Louis covered the mouthpiece and spoke to the person in his office. I was glad he'd been interrupted. How could I tell him the murder I was checking out consisted of another black guy accused of stabbing white people? He wouldn't give me time to tell him that this was different from O.J. But there was nothing more for him to say to me. I wouldn't take his advice, and he knew it. He came back. 'Denise, bottom line, you're the writer. You're the one who has to let the chips fall where they may. But promise me something. Please.'

'Sure, Louis.'

'Don't wait too long to abandon the project if it begins to feel a bit sticky. Don't get caught up in something that's not your style. You'll waste a lot of time. You're on a roll, my darling.'

'I really think—'

'It's that congressman, isn't it? The one with you at the Guild party. It's all coming back to me. He's from Rhode Island, true?' I was speechless. Nothing like an editor who comprehends his writers. 'Denise, I am the first to understand the appeal of a pretty face. But none of that is my business. Not that you've ever tried to make your personal life my business the way so many of your confreres do.'

'Louis, trust me. I'll know if I should abandon the whole thing. I haven't disappointed you yet, have I?'

'No, dearest. Forgive my doubting you.'

'I forgive you, Louis. Just don't let it happen again.'

He harrumphed.

I hung up, and the dark sky above the Rhode Island coast finally broke. Sheets of rain smashed against the windows and Buddy came whimpering over to me. I explained to him that he was okay as it wasn't a thunderstorm. We settled in for the duration, Buddy with a couple of Milk Bones, me with the book I'd taken out of the library, *New Caxton and Its Environs.* The book was falling apart in my hands and stank of decay. Maybe I'd suggest dehumidifiers to that Rosie.

I opened the book to its introduction, written over a hundred years ago by the town's mayor. In it, he quoted from a letter sent by a traveler who had visited the area late in the seventeenth century. I pictured him as a young man looking for a place to make his mark. I imagined that he might have been a Hall, grandfather of the one who had married Ethan Allen's daughter and then went about searching for farmland. He wrote:

> *On the ridge southwest of New Caxton riverport, there came a vista upon me of such pulchritude that I was most agreeably startled, compelled to stop my walk and gaze. The Ponaganset, a regal waterway afloat with native craft, lay before me, and an island, like a small green jewel, centers there. And just above New Caxton, the Scituate, rising from an underground fountain, flows down to meet it, meandering through fertile fields and soft-hued copse. There, where the two streams converge, lies the New Caxton outpost, one of the dearest prospects I could ever hope to conjure.*

The traveler did not mention smelling New Caxton before he saw it.

By the end of the second chapter of the book, I learned that settlers had proceeded to follow the route of the traveler, and twelve men were listed who had struck a deal with the Narraganset Indians, buying up land surrounding the outpost and pacing off their farms up and down the two rivers. Three of the twelve were named Hall – my traveler and two brothers, I mused. In chapter three, I read of the dispersal of those same Narragansets. They were marched up into Massachusetts, where they eventually died off in a large tract of space in which there were no regal rivers, just thick New England forestland so stony as to be arid.

The book detailed the activity of the colonial families who created their farms, and the children who enlarged them, and the grandchildren who built new farmhouses and barns, churches and schools, and the next generation, who would erect the grange and the town hall. It was during this generation's time that there came talk of 'the national unrest.' A congressman from New Caxton, a strong supporter of President Lincoln, was called in on all discussions concerning the threats of southern secession. His name was Owen Allen Hall. The book ended a few years before the war broke out.

When I closed the cover, I thought that the first Congressman Hall could never have imagined that his beloved riverside land would be replaced by over a hundred factories, during a time when rivers were not seen as pulchritudinous but rather as convenient sewer systems. Perhaps the Narragansets had left a curse. Readers are wild about curses.

Cover closed, book placed on the table, I began to see the narrative my story would need as I brought readers down a historical path, beginning with the traveler's vista and leading to the terrible murders in a town where there had never been a premeditated murder before (unless you count the Narragansets).

The next day, I left Buddy to his resources and drove to Providence, rather than New Caxton, to learn more history at the main branch of the public library. The librarian there did not question my motives for wanting to look up material and take out books, an armload of which I stashed in my car before driving to Watch Hill and dumping them onto the coffee table at the beach house. Later they would serve to breach the space between the hint of civil war in New Caxton and the murder of the Montevallos. I took a long walk with Buddy, letting him lead, and allowed myself time to think until I realized I was freezing. My feet had gotten wet. Usually that didn't happen, as the sheepdog in Buddy – or perhaps his affection for me – would herd me away from the long combing waves. He must have been distracted by a crab or two.

I called Nick to tell him I'd be in Rhode Island for a few extra days. I left that message on his machine. I left another message on the kids' line to call me for instructions. Then I got out Owen's phone number and talked to his secretary. I told her to tell Owen that I'd be in Rhode Island through the early part of the next week.

In the evening, I went back to my books. I found that New Caxton had not only been subject to unexpected murderous violence, it had been subject to periodic *natural* violence, also unexpected. New Caxton, as the traveler had pointed out, does indeed lie at the confluence of two rivers – powerful ones, in fact, with strong currents, bottomless eddies, and unpredictable whirlpools popping up where boaters least expect them. During fierce spring flooding, particularly after winters that fill Vermont and New Hampshire with tons of snow, the rivers swell, rising suddenly and drastically. But despite dams and retaining walls built over the years, Mother Nature will not be undone. Every fifty years or so, a Caribbean hurricane heading due north is nudged away from the Atlantic coast of Florida by an east-moving front and, a few days later, spares the Carolinas as well. The first body of land it hits is Long Island, where it is held in check for just a bit of time before it regroups over the Sound and plows into the low-lying city of Providence, Rhode Island.

In the nearby town of New Caxton, the Scituate and the Ponaganset rise over their banks and the population flees north before the flood into those forests of Massachusetts where almost every member of the Narraganset nation starved to death.

When the water recedes the next day, the people return to New Caxton to find their houses gone or flattened or badly damaged and full of mud. They come back optimistic, knowing the factories will be waiting for them, the brick and deep concrete foundations still standing like fortresses. And so they are able to rebuild their homes with loans and outright gifts from the families who own the factories, chief among them the Halls.

In August 1955, the last hurricane arrived. People in New Caxton listened to reports of it chugging up the Atlantic, aimed right at them, but were assuaged by weathermen who insisted it was weakening, slowing down, petering out, the waters ahead of it unnaturally cold. By the time it reached Long Island, the winds had died to nothing more than a typical nor' easter. Its eye would pass over Providence at dead low tide. No flooding was anticipated. Unanticipated was that the sluggish forward movement of the storm would allow it to draw in far more water than most hurricanes, and its high-rising water-choked craw would combine with rivers still filled with melt from the record-breaking New England snowfalls of the previous winter. This hurricane did not need strong winds or a high tide for the devastation it was about to wreak.

The residents of New Caxton slept during the predawn deluge, rolling over when they heard the rain coming down, the older townsfolk finding solace in the absence of the whistle and roar of a hurricane-strength blow. But while they rolled over, the Scituate and the Ponaganset filled and overflowed their banks, melding to form a rushing lake that converged on New Caxton in a fluke tsunami.

Even people who lived on the outskirts of town, miles from either river, stepped out on their porches the next morning only to be swept off their feet, carried away by a swift, bulging, ever-widening stream that eventually seemed to have no boundaries at all.

The death toll in New Caxton was over two hundred. Even as the funerals were being held, the descendants of the founding fathers hired engineers to create a plan to hold back the rivers during these great storms. It would be worth the expense; in the fifties, American factories were experiencing a boom. And so a dam was built, creating a vast artificial lake ten miles north of town and enveloping the spring that was the source of the Scituate, where water levels could be raised or lowered, kept in lock-step with rain and flooding.

The dam has yet to be tested, and I couldn't help but wonder if it would work. I figured the people of New Caxton wondered the same thing. And what else did they wonder about? I'd have to ask them. Time to chat up the old folks hanging at the library. And after I got a feel for them and their opinions, I would head back into the reference room and move on to the last half of the year of the Montevallo murders.

11

At the New Caxton library, there they were, still spread out at their tables, as if they'd never left. The half-dozen seniors weren't all huddled together the way teenage friends doing a paper together would be. They'd left plenty of room for hats and coats, canes, and bulging knitting bags. They all had books or magazines in their hands, but they were looking over them at me. Waiting for me, it seemed. I recognized the woman who had directed me to the reference room. She was wearing the same gray felt hat. I had to smile to myself. I was somehow intimate with all these strangers. I was positive they knew what I was doing, and I felt as though we were all keeping a secret together. This other life I live that no one knows anything about except for the end product gives me private little thrills. Nick and Poppy live big public thrills daily. During my childhood, life was about keeping one big secret. I guess I missed that aspect of neglect, the only intimacy I ever had with my mother.

I walked right over to the lady with the gray hat, sitting two seats from another woman, the only two at the table. I said, 'May I join you?'

First they looked to each other and then to me. Then they both nodded.

I said, 'I'm doing some research for a book I'm writing, and I would like to know about the recent history of New Caxton. Do you mind if we talk about your town together?'

The gray hat said, 'You come to the right place, honey.' And with that, the three other ladies and one gentleman sitting at the other tables hoisted themselves up and made their way over. They would be short a chair, so the old man dragged his with him. Then he got another one and held it for me. I thanked him. When he sat down, he said, 'I'm in,' like we were about to start up a poker game.

Ah, the good old days is the refrain for what they wanted to tell me – 'when we would go out and shangri-la.' They used the word *shangri-la* as a verb. And they wanted me to know about the bad times when they were down on their luck, the Depression years: 'We stuck together and came out on top.' Their nostalgia consisted mostly of defending the way they lived, just the way Leo said. I encouraged them to expand on that general drift, since that's where their enthusiasm lay.

I said, 'Your houses are very close together here in New Caxton, aren't they?'

I got: 'My house is a foot and a half from my neighbors on either side. Enough room to get the garbage cans from out back to the street on pickup day'; 'The boys who pick up the garbage don't leave a single scrap of paper behind, they're responsible boys'; 'A foot and a half is enough for the kids to get their bikes through'; 'Our kids don't leave their bikes out on the sidewalk'; 'That's not because they're worried they'd be stolen'; 'They're obedient kids'; 'I have nine grandchildren.'

This last led to a bit of a brouhaha.

'You got ten.'

'Nine.'

'Count 'em.'

The count was ten.

'Shoot me down. Forgot about Lou-Ann's one in the middle.'

I said, 'I noticed that the houses don't have garages.'

They hooted. The old man said, 'A car don't need a house. A chicken needs a house. Remember when we all had chickens way back when?'

They all remembered.

'Remember the Saturday-night dances?'

They all remembered.

'Where were they held?' I asked them.

'At church.'

'At all the churches?'

''Course.'

'See, the Polacks had their polka hops. We had our dances at St Augustine's. And the coloreds had theirs.'

'Did you ever have a dance for everyone?'

They glanced at one another. The gray hat said, 'Why, sure we did. They were held down at the Halls' place, in the schoolhouse.'

I asked, 'The schoolhouse was on the Halls' grounds?'

'They had their own schoolhouse for the servants' and workers' children. They'd clear out the desks and chairs for the town dances. But we'd only dance with our own, naturally.'

'You're pretty much segregated, then?'

They puffed up their chests. The old man said, 'Do we look segregated? We got two Polacks and four guineas setting here. It's just we got different ways.'

One of the women said, 'See, we like our *own* ways, each group. I'd rather dance the polka then eat. But how would I know to dance the tarantella? See?'

Her friend said, 'But some things we mix. We come to like each other's food. I'm a Polack too, but give me a plate of spaghetti any day.' They all nodded in agreement and licked their chops in demonstration. 'We all got our choirs at church, too, and we sing at one another's churches. Well, St Cyril's sings at St Augustine's and vice versa, and the Baptist choir where the coloreds go, they sing at our churches. We can't sing at their church because Catholics ain't allowed to attend Protestant services, only Mass; that's it. But they understand.'

The old man said, 'Thou shalt not place false gods before thee.'

The gray hat said, 'And it ain't none of that prejudice thing that you were getting at. Most of the people at the colored church are out-of-towners now, but they still come sing at our churches. Long as the monsignor says it's okay.'

I asked, 'Why is that?'

The one woman who hadn't said anything yet leaned forward toward me on the table. 'New Caxton ain't good enough for them anymore.'

'For who?'

'Our coloreds. They just about all moved out. They been moving out for a long time. About ten-twelve years ago the Hightowers left. It was the Hightowers, wasn't it?'

The old guy: 'Sure was. Right before Fred Clayton and his bunch. Things started to slide. A couple of the factories went under. They didn't want to stay and keep our factories shored up. Like we did.'

'We?'

'The rest of us.'

I said, 'So the factories began to close, and the black families left to find jobs elsewhere.'

'They didn't have to leave. What they did was they took the easy way out. Now, during the Depression, their grannies and grandpas didn't leave. We all stuck it out together, through the hard times. Then we pulled ourselves back up.'

'See, if they hadn't left, we wouldn't be where we are now.'

'Where is that?'

Gray Hat picked up the book lying next to her hand and plunked it in front of me. The spine was loose and pages stuck out. 'Here. Where we don't have the money to buy new books for our young ones.'

The old gent: 'Your book gonna say that we don't do right by our children, miss?'

I couldn't have them agitated. I nudged my bag off the table, and they all jumped when it hit the terrazzo floor with a thump and jangle of car keys. They all moved to help me. 'I've got it,' I said, and I segued into, 'Do you think that dam will hold if there's another big hurricane?'

More hoots, loud ones. The old man said, 'We get a rain like the one in 'fifty-five, and that lake up Route Nine will be sitting on Main Street and the library will be under a good twenty feet of water.'

One of the women blessed herself – a quick sign of the cross, forehead to heart to each shoulder.

Then I said, 'Do you think Eddie Baines killed the Montevallos?'

No one blinked. They'd been waiting for that question all along. The gray hat was their spokesperson. I think the gesture of the woman next to her, the one who blessed herself inadvertently, gave her a quick answer. She said, 'Only the good Lord knows for sure.'

With that, I told them I had to get back to my work in the research room. The old gent said, 'Work? I thought you was writing a book.'

'I am.'

'That ain't work.'

He held out his hands. They were badly scarred. 'This is from work. In the factory hardening room.' The women all made eye contact with him at once. He put his hands under the table. 'I don't mean to complain. I had it good.'

They were polite with their good-byes. The old man gave me a little smirk and told me not to work too hard, that I was young and should enjoy life. As I stood, one said to another, 'I met my husband at a dance in that schoolhouse,' and so they didn't disperse, they went back to reminiscing about the good old days before their black neighbors saw the handwriting on the wall and bolted. Like Owen's family. Like the Americans had.

Anthony was waiting for me behind the checkout counter. When I placed my New Caxton history book down in front of him, he looked at it, let its presence register, then turned his back and went through the door. The librarian came out. Each time the door swung open, I got that same glimpse of a tableful of women, and now I thought of old-fashioned quilting bees. But quilts had been little grasps at color in colorless lives. These people were faithful to a lack of color.

The librarian said to me, 'You can keep it.'

I guess I just stared at her.

'We've got a couple of copies, and no one ever takes them out.' A hint of the Mona Lisa came to her face, a hint of a hint of a smile, a twinkle in her eye. I couldn't have imagined a twinkle there, since I didn't guess she'd gone to college with a plan to end up supervising disabled library aides, or ladies doing whatever they were doing in the back room. I guessed that giving away books once in a while, disobeying what must be the chief rule of a public library, allowed her a tiny bit of a yank on the chain. I felt a surge of pity. I thought Owen had said her name was Rosie, but I wasn't sure now. I *was* sure that she knew who I was. She'd done a little research. It was the way she looked at me, curious, interested.

'Well, thank you,' I said, and I smiled at her.

'You're welcome. Anthony will get the other boxes of fiche you need.' She turned and opened the door. 'Anthony?' He bopped back out. She said to me, 'Please feel free to call on me if you need anything else. I'm glad to be of help.'

'Thank you again,' I said. 'I will.' She was gone.

Anthony brought the boxes and I took them into the reference room, where the girl with cerebral palsy threaded the first one into the machine and then returned to her position, my own personal sentry. I settled in and scanned the initial several inches of blank film until I found the first line of print, hand-lettered: THE NEW CAXTON STANDARD, JULY 1ST THROUGH SEPTEMBER 30TH.

In July, in New Caxton, the citizens celebrated the Fourth with a parade, fireworks, and a picnic in Hall Park; a heat wave followed for ten long days – there were stories of the heavy humidity and a drought bringing threats of statewide water rationing. The Little League All-Stars made it to the state quarterfinals but lost. The loss was on the front page, headline news. Other stories on that page included an interview with the coach, who was custodian at the high school; a bio of the losing pitcher, who was the coach's son; and plans for the party to honor the team for their outstanding performance despite the loss.

July faded into August with news of company outings, all held at Hall Park; there were accompanying photos of sweaty family groups munching on hot dogs, kids running around. White families. Or, rather, Polish and Italian families. Only one family was black and there were no children or grandchildren in their group. This was the kind of event – an outing – where there'd be a tent set up and there was, but instead of protecting groaning boards of food, a half-dozen men sat inside at a single table, heads bent, as if they were having a private game of Bingo. I couldn't tell what they were doing.

Then I came to an issue with a full page devoted to portraits of uniformed older boys, the Babe Ruth All-Stars arriving on the play-off scene only to fade quite a bit sooner than their younger brothers had. I scrolled back and looked at the two pages of portraits of all the New Caxton Little League teams, from T-Ball to Majors, and didn't see what was prominent in pictures of Bridgefield Little Leaguers – pony tails sticking out of the openings in the back of the caps. New Caxton girls didn't play baseball. I scrolled forward, right on through the first week of August, trying to keep out of my head the fact that something other than the mundane awaited me. And then, on Monday, August 8, came a great glaring four-inch headline: 3 KILLINGS SHOCK NEW CAXTON.

There was very little text on that first page. Four photographs took up almost all the space: a shot of a string of state police cars in the night, parked in front of a little Cape Cod house that was almost washed out by the glare of spotlights; below it, a picture of paramedics carrying a stretcher to an ambulance in the just-forming dawn, the body covered with a sheet; at the bottom of the page in a secondary story, FRIENDS CALL VICTIMS A KIND FAMILY; a ten-year-old photo of Connie Montevallo posed in front of a Christmas tree; and, finally, one of her beaming son holding a grinning toddler.

Before I could begin to read the one full column that began the story of the crime, I became aware of the librarian looming above me. I tilted my face up to her. She said, 'I'm a great fan of your books, and I meant it when I said I'd be glad to help you.' She craned her neck a little to look at the screen. 'I can tell you everything that article says and a good deal more.'

I cleared my throat and told her to pull up a chair.

'Rosie Owzciak.' She put out her hand. I took it. 'I'm really glad to meet you, Mrs Burke.'

'Please. Denise.'

She went for a chair and sat down next to me. 'Denise, then. I've always wondered if a writer would ever come and take a look at this crime.'

'Did you?'

'Yes. Are you intending to get to the bottom of it all?'

'Is there a bottom?'

'One wonders.'

'Well, I haven't decided. I'm going to skim the surface for a while.'

'This crime isn't exactly your modus operandi, is it?'

'No.' I must have raised an eyebrow.

She smiled. 'I've read all your books. You weren't at our trial.'

'I wasn't. But my husband's in Washington, and I happened to meet Congressman Hall. He aroused my curiosity. About this crime.'

'Did he?'

'Yes.'

'I'm surprised. Not about his rousing your curiosity.'

'About what, then?'

'Don't politicians tend to avoid chatting about things like murders in their neighborhoods?'

'I'm not a constituent.'

'What are you?'

Now I know an eyebrow went up. 'An acquaintance. When people meet me, they tend to chat about murder.'

'I guess they would. Sorry for being nosy.'

'Nothing to be sorry about. Comes with the territory.'

Rosie Owzciak put her chin in her hand and looked again at the screen. Her smile slipped away. 'Brenda was the one who discovered the bodies.'

'Brenda?'

'Brenda was also the one who nicknamed me Rosie-Osie.' I looked at her, expecting the little smile to return. It did not. 'She was Connie Montevallo's daughter. She was adopted as an infant, when Petey was five years old and no other babies were turning up for Connie and her husband. But this all really starts with Brenda's son. The child who died. Timmy.'

And via a softly pitched voice, the kind that mesmerizes you with its gentleness, she began unfolding the story.

I turned a page in my notebook and started scribbling, mostly places and names, all I'd need to have in order to verify the information she gave me. Her version of the crime was like an article in *People* magazine, riddled with small asides, titbits never found in straight news articles. She knew every detail, hadn't forgotten one of them. I was sure none of them would need verification. I was as enthralled as the little kids must have been who came in for her story hour every Saturday morning; the tattered notice was above the pamphlet rack in the foyer, hand-lettered like everything else: STORY HOUR, SATURDAY AT NINE. Scribbled in beneath: *Bring along a stuffed animal friend or your favorite doll.*

Rosie said, 'On Friday, August fifth, two years ago, a week after he'd turned eight, Timmy Montevallo pedaled his new bike down the road, away from the apartment he'd been sharing with his mother, Brenda, for the past month. Brenda had moved away when he was less than a year old, and during that time he'd lived with his grandmother. Brenda would appear in New Caxton for a couple of weeks and then go back to wherever it was she'd come from. No one knew where.'

'No one was curious?'

'We were all curious, but "Ignorance is bliss." One of the codes around here.

'Her apartment was a little box above the West End Tavern. Brenda had refused to move back in with Connie, and apparently she couldn't afford anything better. There was gossip that she'd sold jewelry to have the money she did have. Someone heard she'd been in Providence, that she'd taken the jewelry to someone who'd buy it from her. Where she got the jewelry is something else no one wants to know.

'Timmy was on his way over to Connie's house on Winchester Avenue, the last house on the block, about half a mile from here.' Rosie pointed toward the library door. 'Up past the school. Timmy would be able to ride the whole way on the sidewalk except when he had to cross the road in front of the West End. But the tavern was closed during the day, so the road wasn't busy. Timmy was to go to choir practice with Connie and Petey, spend the night with them, and then return home to his mother after dinner following five o'clock mass on Saturday at St Augustine's.'

Soundlessly, the cerebral palsy girl crept over to us and perched on the nearest chair, listening as intently as I.

'When I think of Timmy, I think of one of those Norman Rockwell kids, always grinning from ear to ear, two front teeth missing, freckles across the bridge of his nose. You couldn't help but smile back at him. He was just an exceptionally friendly child, and bright too. His grandmother's friends felt this special pride in Timmy. And sympathy. After all, he was fatherless, didn't have a mother he could rely on, and now he had to live over a gin mill!

'The story is that Brenda never had any idea who Timmy's father was. She'd hung out with a rough out-of-town crowd ever since she was thirteen, when Chick died. That's Pete, senior. There'd been a string of boyfriends. Even then, right after she'd moved into the apartment over the West End, a guy appeared and moved in too. People basically felt bad for Connie; Brenda couldn't be controlled. But that was understandable. She was adopted; she wasn't one of ours.'

I liked the way Rosie put things. What I was doing, besides absorbing, was cataloguing lines for the book just hatching in my brain.

'Connie's friends looked on Timmy as someone who had

survived a curse. A bastard child in this town is a great shame, and Timmy had overcome that shame just the way their grandparents and great-grandparents had overcome the curse of the slums, the emigration, the wars, the Depression, slavery.'

'Floods,' I added, feeling as though we were a pair of Bible thumpers at a revival meeting.

'Yes. Floods. The people Timmy waved to that day on his way to his grandmother's house were the last to see him alive.'

When Rosie said that, I couldn't help but wonder if 'Little Red Riding Hood' might no longer be in the repertoire of story hour.

She sighed. 'It's sad to think about Connie and Petey, and what they suffered that day, the day they were murdered. They must have been waiting for Timmy with great sadness instead of their usual excitement. Because Brenda was intending to leave again. She was going to California, was what she told everyone, and this time she was taking Timmy with her. Connie was crushed. She was the one who'd raised Timmy. Before Brenda had taken off the very first time, she and the baby lived with Connie. After that, she'd come back for visits, a few days, a few weeks at the most. And each time, Connie tried to convince her to stay permanently. This time, when Brenda rented an apartment, Connie got her hopes up. But then Brenda announced she was taking Timmy to California.

'Connie pleaded with her to stay, or at least leave Timmy behind until she got settled, but Brenda wasn't hearing it. Connie went to her priest and to a teacher in town Brenda had taken a liking to, while she was in high school, and asked each of them to try to persuade her to stay. It was hopeless. Brenda just kept saying she had these connections in California and their life there would be filled with sunshine and love. She really was going around saying things like that.

'Poor Petey was miserable, and Connie had her hands full

comforting him, telling him he had to act happy for Timmy's sake. But Petey didn't know how to pretend. He was really wrecked. Connie kept saying they had to be strong for the time being, explaining that they would keep to their habits, and Timmy would continue to sleep over Friday nights and return to his mother after five o'clock mass on Saturday, after supper. And this Friday, they would have a good time the way they always did. They would play Timmy's favorite board games, which were games Petey loved to play, they would have supper, and then they would go out for ice cream after choir practice. They would make believe that this was not going to be their last weekend with Timmy.'

The girl with cerebral palsy interrupted. I couldn't understand what she said. Rosie translated. 'Marie says she heard that Connie kept telling Petey that if he was good, Brenda might change her mind.' Then Rosie whispered to Marie, 'Hush, now.'

Rosie gazed off into space. 'You know, that little boy dreamed of a normal home with a mom and a dad, and maybe even some brothers and sisters. He was excited about going to California. But at the same time he was afraid of leaving his grandmother and his uncle. They were the only family he'd known. He also had a lot of friends here at school. Timmy's principal knew him by name though he had only attended first and second grade. In one of these newspaper articles, he's quoted as saying Timmy was the kid who always called out "Hi, Mr Velucci!" when he passed him in the halls. Besides that, he'd just gotten his new bike. Brenda told him they wouldn't be able to take it with them. Told him they'd get another bike in California. But Timmy didn't want another bike, he wanted the one his grandmother bought him.

'In the end, Timmy wasn't able to hold up. He told Connie he wanted to stay. That he would rather stay with her than go to California with his mother. But Connie had her principles. She believed a child should be with his mother. I think she felt that way because she was convinced she'd failed with Brenda. That if Brenda's real mother had kept her, Brenda wouldn't have gone bad.'

Rosie paused. Marie had been edging her chair closer, and now it was right up against Rosie's. Rosie put her arm around the girl's shoulders and gave her a squeeze. I assumed Marie was anticipating the part of the story about to follow. I certainly was.

'But Timmy was not to be separated from his grandmother and his Uncle Petey, after all, was he, Marie?' The girl shook her head, no. 'That evening, all three would be stabbed to death, right after they'd had supper.' Marie shuddered. 'And more than twenty-four hours would go by before anyone knew what had happened. That was the real shocker.'

I remembered Owen emphasizing that, too.

'The night after they were murdered, Saturday night, late, at just before midnight, Brenda drove to her mother's house from the West End Tavern with the boyfriend. Actually, he seemed to me to be more of an attendant than a boyfriend, followed her around like a puppy. She'd expected Timmy back at around seven. She told everyone later that she'd waited and waited for the sound of bike wheels on the gravel parking lot that encircles the bar. But it was midsummer; it was light out until eight-thirty. Her mother had probably taken Petey and Timmy for ice cream. Even after it did grow dark, she convinced herself that her mother was just angry because of the California plan. As far as Brenda was concerned, that was too damn bad. She was taking Timmy out there with her, and the two of them would start over again. So the possibility that her mother was keeping Timmy for a few extra hours kept her from worrying. Maybe Connie decided to have him sleep over another night.

It made sense, she told herself, even though she knew, deep down, it didn't. Finally, Brenda faced up to the fact that Connie would have called her if she was keeping Timmy an extra night. So she called her mother's house but got no answer.'

I was so mesmerized, I leapt at the sound of a voice, a woman who was calling Rosie from the door. 'Miss Owzciak, someone needs to speak to you on the phone.'

Rosie stood up. She said to me, 'I'll be right back.'

The screen of the fiche machine gave off a garish light. We'd never turned it off. And I stared at it, the glaring photos becoming ingrained in my mind as the roaring machine spewed out copies: the paramedics with their stretchers, the police cars in front of the house, the two pictures of the Montevallos – such a pleasant-looking woman and Petey with a lopsided grin holding the small boy in a striped T-shirt. Timmy. The phrase 'cute as a button' had been invented for this child.

Owen had not said much about Timmy Montevallo's mother, probably knew little about her. But Rosie obviously had a different perspective, one centered on the role she had assumed as keeper of the town's history. I had a feeling that if I told her I was doing a book about hurricanes, she'd know just as many details about the storms that devastated New Caxton as she did about the tragedy of the Montevallos. She was descended from peasants, people who didn't read or write, whose histories came down in an oral tradition. Rosie was a throwback, but she was educated and had taken on the trappings of a librarian, an official keeper of history.

When she returned to settle back into the rest of the story, I really wanted to ask her about herself. To say to her that it wasn't necessary to look the way she did to be a skilled, qualified librarian. But, of course, she knew that.

'At ten o'clock Brenda began calling her mother's house, and at ten-thirty she told the boyfriend she was going over there. He tried to get her to hold off, but at eleven-forty-five she'd had enough waiting. It was almost midnight. Something was wrong. He insisted on being the one to do it. He thought he should go to Connie's alone. He told Brenda she was too freaked out. She probably was.

'So he goes, and when he came back he said no one answered the door and he couldn't get in. Brenda—'

I asked, 'The door was locked?'

'That's what he told her.'

'Owen said something about how no one locked their doors in New Caxton before the crime.'

'Well, Connie's house is the first one you come to when you get off the Route Nine exit.'

Marie chimed in with a slur of words that I could make out. She said Connie had been robbed once.

'Connie had a burglary?'

'Yes. She told people about the robbery, but she never called the police. I mean, the police knew about it, but there was never a formal report.'

I started to say more, but she cut me off – 'I'm coming to that, anyway' – and she gave Marie a little disciplinary look. The girl cast her eyes downward.

'Brenda asked if her mother's porch light had been on, and when he said no she knew something was wrong. If they weren't there, they'd have left the porch light on. If they *were* there, Connie would have answered the door. She insisted that she had to go to her mother's herself. He didn't like it, but he went along.

'When they got there, Connie's front door not only wasn't locked, it was slightly ajar. The boyfriend went a little ballistic, arguing with Brenda that he hadn't lied to her, that it was locked shut ten minutes before. Neighbors heard them arguing. Brenda threw the door open, stormed into the house, and shouted to her boyfriend over her shoulder, "It happened again!" She meant the robbery. The robbery had been an embarrassment to Connie. The less said the better, though she must have told Brenda about it. The reputation that there is no crime in New Caxton is taken very seriously.'

'That poor woman.'

Rosie looked up into my eyes. She said, 'It's the way it is.' Marie's gaze remained directed at the floor.

Intent, Rosie went on. 'When Brenda went inside, she was at the head of the hallway that led to the bathroom in the rear of the house. Front to back, the house is probably twenty-four feet, no more. She was standing in an inch of water. The place had been flooded in an attempt to get rid of evidence.

'She walked by the first door on the right, the one to the living room, and on to the second one, which opened into the kitchen. The two doors opening to the left off the hall were the bedrooms.

'She saw her mother's body lying on the kitchen floor in the water. Hot running water was overflowing the sink, pouring onto the floor. Brenda grabbed the phone on the wall. She dialed nine-one-one and shouted the same message to them that she had to her boyfriend. "It happened again!"

'The cop on dispatch duty managed to get Brenda's name out of her and that she was at her mother's. He sent two officers to Connie's house on Winchester Street.' Rosie came out of her story and said to me, 'The station is right across the street from the library.'

'It is?' I hadn't noticed a police station.

'The station was once somebody's house. Looks like all the rest of the houses on the street. Their sign rotted, and there's only a piece of cardboard nailed next to the door that says POLICE STATION. They're planning to get a new one, but nobody's holding their breath.'

She paused and stretched, moving her shoulders back a little, preparing herself for the rest of the story, the worst part, I knew. She said, 'I don't mean to sound like a tape recording here, it's so horrific. But we've all talked about it so much – the whole town, turning it over and over in our heads – that it's almost like describing a movie.'

I said, 'I know exactly what you mean.'

'I didn't want you to think I'm morbid.'

'I understand.'

She sighed. 'Anyway, Brenda's boyfriend went in, and at the end of the hallway, past the kitchen doorway, he could make out Petey in the bathroom. He was sprawled in the bathtub. It was hard to see. Even though Brenda had switched the hall light on as soon as she got in, the house was full of steam. But he called to her and said, "I think your brother's dead."

'Water was gushing from the bathroom taps too, from the sink and the tub. The boyfriend called out to Brenda again, but she was already running past him. At that point she was thinking about Timmy.'

Marie shivered violently, and the jolting movement had nothing to do with her disability.

'Brenda stepped into her mother's bedroom, just across the hall from the kitchen, and saw a rolled-up quilt lying across the bed. She said she stopped then, because she knew what she was seeing, and what she had to do. She went over to the bed and reached out and touched the bundle. The quilt had eleven slices in it and was drenched with blood. Timmy's killer had wrapped the little boy in a quilt before stabbing him. Brenda unrolled the quilt just as the police were arriving. One officer said he'd never heard such shrieking in his life. The boyfriend was gone. He was out of there. Nobody ever saw him again. His version of what happened earlier came from Brenda.

'Connie had been stabbed nineteen times. She'd put up a huge struggle, but not nearly the struggle Petey had in his effort to get to his nephew. He'd been dragged into the bathroom, pushed in the bathtub to constrain him – he was a big guy, and he was fully clothed – and that's where he'd been stabbed, over and over. He had thirty-five stab wounds. But none of us will ever understand why they stabbed Timmy so many times. I suppose that's how long it took to get him to be still.'

I said, 'They?'

She looked into my eyes. 'Yes. They. One person couldn't have done it. Not all alone. These people weren't asleep. If there was just one killer, Connie or Petey or Timmy even would have run to the door or shouted out the window.'

I tried to picture a single killer stabbing Connie while Petey tried to stop him. The killer holding Timmy by one arm while he killed Connie and then continuing to hold the child while he got Petey to the bathroom and killed him too. Then, into the bedroom with Timmy. Impossible to picture, even if the killer was a huge strong man. Even a huge strong man can't keep three people from screaming. Rosie had said the neighbors heard Brenda and her boyfriend arguing. I asked, 'When Brenda was shrieking, I assume people heard that too.'

'The whole neighborhood.'

I said, 'The night before, one killer couldn't have stabbed them all and held his hand over their mouths, could he?'

Rosie said, 'No.' Marie shook her head, No.

Rosie leaned back and stretched again, this time with her arms over her head. I stretched too and so did the girl, but not very efficiently, accidentally rapping the fiche machine with her arm. She winced, and Rosie patted her and went on.

'After that, the town fell apart. Everything was canceled; parties, weddings, christenings. Mostly, there were recriminations. How could someone not have heard anything?

How could we not have stopped this from happening? We went through the stages of grief: We were in shock, then anguished, and then, of course, indignant. As in: What kind of animals would violate our town like this?' She relaxed in her chair. 'You can imagine what happened at the crime scene; you know about all that. The usual.'

'I would like to hear the usual.'

'They collected evidence. A sneaker print. A watch. They took the bodies out. They looked for the weapon. They hunted for more evidence, outside the house. Basically, they found nothing. Not then.'

Rosie lifted her arms again, but not to stretch. She crossed her forearms over the top of her head. Like a little kid. Her cheap sweater, which was the color of mud, crept up and exposed her white midriff. Her skin seemed to glare. Like the monitor. She wasn't finished with her tale. She was taking a breather. She had more chapters to this horror, I could tell. But her face had suddenly turned to stone, her body stiff. And then I saw why.

Owen, said, 'Hi.' He was leaning against the fiche machine. 'Thought I might find you here.' He put his hand on the librarian's shoulder. 'Hey, Rosie, how are things?'

She tugged her sweater down and eased her shoulder from under his hand. It slid away. She stood up. 'Hello, Owen. Things are fine.'

12

Rosie slipped off, blending into the walls and furniture and books. My sentry, Marie, got herself out of her chair and began inching sideways back toward her post, trembling wildly in the presence of Owen. He reached out for her hand, took it, and pulled her back. 'Aren't you the Ferrigno girl?'

She got out some fumbled words.

'Are you enjoying your job here at the library?'

Now there came a steady, 'Yes, Congressman.' The nervousness faded and a sparkle appeared in her eyes. She was proud of her work.

'That's wonderful. You tell your folks I was asking for them, will you?'

She steeled herself in order to speak clearly. 'Yes, Congressman.' I wanted to hug her. And Rosie Owzciak, too, for instilling this pride.

I was speechless, myself, but Owen was used to leaving people speechless in New Caxton, popping in unexpectedly like this, although Rose had kept her wits about her. She was able to transform herself back into the proprietary librarian in a heartbeat.

He sat in the chair Rosie had vacated. 'Got your message. Turned out I had to fly up to Boston. Take care of some business up there with my brother, some family things. Thought I'd take care of some things here in town too. Well, I just finished my day's business, and if you're about finished with yours' – he smiled – 'maybe even if you're not, how would you like to drive down to Point Judith with me and have dinner at my all-time favorite restaurant?'

'I *am* finished here. And that sounds terrific. I've never been to Point Judith.' I looked over to Marie and said, 'You can turn this off for me now.' She charged over, and I began gathering up my stuff, wondering what my hair looked like. Then I said something about being in jeans and an old sweater. Owen was his usual spiffy self.

'You can wear whatever you want to this restaurant, believe me. One of the reasons it's my favorite.'

'Okay, then.'

'Good,' Owen said. 'I have to stop at my house to pick some things up. Took a chance you'd be in town. Great luck, wasn't it?'

'Yes, it was.'

He helped me gather up my paraphernalia while Marie went to the door and called out, 'Ant'ny.'

Anthony came for the fiche and giggled as Owen asked him how he was doing and gave his regards to the boy's family. In the lobby he said to me, 'Hold on just a minute,' and went into the reading room and shook everyone's hands. Gray Hat got a kiss on the cheek. While he was acting the politician, I left a note for Rosie, who wasn't behind the counter. I thanked her for all the time and help she'd given me, and said I looked forward to seeing her again. I did, too. I wrote, *Maybe we could get together for coffee.*

Outside, we got into a little Saab convertible, the kind of car I associated with celebrating a divorce when your lawyer's seen to it that you're the big winner. I pointed out that my own car was sitting there, half on the sidewalk, and he told me not to worry about it.

'I won't get a ticket?'

'For what? These people are practical-minded. If you park in the ambulance bay at the hospital, *then* you'll get a ticket.'

'I imagine you'd get towed if you did that.'

'Sort of. Someone would get in the car, release the brake, and put the car in neutral, and two security guards would roll it out of the way.'

'What if it's locked?'

'Locked? Denise, the owner would deliberately leave it unlocked in case the ambulance came and it needed to be . . . towed.'

'What if he had a television set on the front seat?'

'Still wouldn't lock the door.'

'Oh, c'mon. Some kid would come along who couldn't resist the temptation, no?'

'He'd resist. Because somehow someone would see him do it. Then his parents would get a call. The punishment would be stiff. All the kids know this.'

'I'm locking my door.'

He laughed at me. I piled my stuff in the back seat and clicked the lock down before shutting the door. We got into Owen's car and I glanced into the rearview mirror. My hair would be officially dirty by seven.

'How far is it to Point Judith?'

'I told you. In Rhode Island, everything is a half hour away.' Then he said, 'Have you seen the house yet?'

'The house?'

'Where the Montevallos were murdered.'

'Oh. I saw a photo of it today. In the newspaper. On fiche.'

'I could take you by.'

'I'm not ready for that yet. I do things in increments.'

He glanced over at me. 'What's the timing on that particular increment? I'm curious about how you work.'

'Usually, I start with a trial. I guess I told you that. I hear the account of the crime from the prosecutor, the lawyers, the witnesses. The whole time I talk to as many people as I can. Along the way, I visit the crime scene. When I feel the urge, sort of. Something compels me to go and see where the murder happened. I sense it. I have to wait for the urge.'

'Want to see *my* house then?'

He was smirking at me. He was damned good looking. I thought about date rape.

Owen laughed at whatever foolish expression I had on my face. 'Really, I have to pick something up. There's a housekeeper there. Or you can wait in the car.'

'I won't wait in the car.'

'Good.'

We went back out on the road I'd driven coming into New Caxton, on past the blackened factories, until we came to an unmarked gravel road. He turned in, and the road began to climb. The house was situated on a hillside next to a small public park bordered by woods. The park, Owen told me, had been the grounds of the original Hall estate; his own house once belonged to a tenant farmer. It was an early nineteenth-century mini-farmhouse with a pretty porch. It had a slate roof covered with moss. He told me that, except for his house, the buildings had been torn down, in compliance with his grandfather's will. The man wanted all his land, including the land where his house had stood, to be a nature preserve, though the townspeople insisted on calling it a park. He told me his brother, Charles, had been the last to live in the main house, had to give it up when both their parents were dead. To comply with the will.

'Couldn't have been too happy about that.'

'No.' Owen pointed toward a mulched garden. 'That's where the big house used to be. Come June, it's all roses. I grow them.'

'You do?'

'Yes, it's a lot of work. I like to do it.'

Explained the calluses. Owen was perhaps meant to carry on the original farming tradition of his forbears. 'I remember my mother once telling someone that if you wanted roses you should move to England.'

He laughed. 'Your mother was handing out gardening advice when she wasn't politicking her ward?'

'You remember that?'

'Why wouldn't I?' Then he said, 'My grandfather's house was magnificent. You drove up under a permanent canopy – a port cochere is what it was called – and walked through the entry into a cantilevered hall that was sixty feet long and two stories high. There was a little organ console in the corner of the hall, and above, in the gallery, hidden behind hanging tapestries – tapestries maybe five hundred years old, maybe older – were ranks of organ pipes. They went all the way around. My grandfather would have receptions there. A musician would arrive at some point, sit at the console practically hidden in a corner, and then, suddenly, you were in a cathedral. I remember when I was young I'd go up into the gallery and play in the pipes. Make believe they were forts. Hide from my brother.'

'Why'd you have to hide from him?'

'Oh, we'd fight, you know? Like all brothers. I had to deal with his feelings that he was a stand-in for my father, who was quite elderly when I was a kid.'

Owen gestured toward the woods. 'A street from the other side of town goes up the back side of the hill. There's a cemetery over there, where all my ancestors are buried. I'll take you another time. It's a very beautiful place. At one time, cemeteries were meant to be public places. People used to come and picnic next to their family graves.'

'The Hall-Allen Memorial Cemetery?'

'Yes.'

'I read a few obituaries in the paper.' I looked toward the woods, but they were an impenetrable New England forest.

We went into the house. Owen sat me down on a little bench in his own reception hall, a tiny foyer with small contemporary tapestries hanging on either side of the door, tribute to the more exalted tapestries his grandfather had owned. I wondered what had become of the originals and at the same time I found such expression of sentiment alluring. He went off to get what he'd come for.

The housekeeper was polite, no doubt polite to all the ladies Owen brought around. She offered me a cup of tea and I nodded, feeling a pang of jealousy, thinking of all Owen's ladies taking tea there before me and of the ones who would come after. She led me into Owen's living room and, a few minutes later, brought out a tray with a pot of tea and two cups. Owen would join me. He came back carrying a folder and sat down across from me. I poured our tea into the two cups. 'Lemon?' I asked. There was a small bowl of lemon wedges.

'Please.'

Our eyes met and we laughed. He said, 'I'll squeeze my own.'

'Let me.' I picked up a wedge and squeezed the juice into the cup without getting any seeds into it. I passed it to him. Our eyes met again and held. What a great way, I thought, to prime ourselves for what lay ahead.

He said, 'I don't really live here. It's no more than a comfortable kind of pit stop for me.'

'DC's home?'

'Yes. Has been for a long time.'

So we talked politics all the way to Point Judith; he never mentioned the Montevallos once, nor did I. He told me he and Nick were working closely together on something –

something to do with sustained development in rural areas. Talking about Nick to this man soothed me, allowed me to see clearly that this was no fantasy. I was married. He knew it, and I knew it.

At Point Judith, there was no restaurant. There were docks, and tied to one was Owen's very white, very speedy-looking ChrisCraft. 'I've got a sailboat, too. For summer.' He nodded toward a looming schooner nearby. The calluses came from sailing, too. My glib guess proved accurate. 'You could go around the world in it, but it requires a production to get moving, including a crew of more than two.'

'I imagine.'

'The restaurant's on Block Island, actually.' He pointed to the little knob of land barely breaking the line of the southern horizon. I looked from where he was pointing to his gaze, which was on me, not on the island. He waited.

I said, 'I've always wanted to go to Block Island, but I was so happy in Nick's summer house that I never got past it. Haven't even been to Newport.'

'We'll do Newport another time.'

We barely did Block Island. The first time I made love to Owen was when we were anchored a hundred yards offshore – in matter of fact, the minute the anchor found purchase. I'd never made love on a boat. The claustrophobia I felt in the cabin made sex all the more forceful. I was moving when I wasn't moving, the swells rocking us when we weren't rocking each other. I kept bumping my head without knowing it, without caring what the noise was. The first time, we were starving and we acted starving. The second time was after we'd eaten dinner at the first restaurant we came to. Docked the boat and it was fifty steps away. Owen said, 'All the restaurants here are my favorite; they all understand how to steam a lobster.' The second time we were sated and heavy with the lobsters we'd polished off, and the clam chowder and corn bread and Indian pudding and God knows what else. A platter of steamers. Shrimp. We rode the waves instead of against them. First passionate flinging around, and then a steady peace. The mix was delicious.

He took me back to my car in New Caxton just before dawn, a preposterous gesture of discretion. The next time I went to the library, the librarian and everyone else, for that matter, would know what I'd done. But if Owen didn't care, why should I? The people of New Caxton were the kind who were conditioned to believe that those above them, their President, for example, had some sort of dispensation from the course of conduct they expected from each other. In college, I'd been screwing my professor in a supply closet. Everyone knew then, too. At first I didn't realize everyone knew. When I began to see the sly glances and take in the double meanings, I was upset. Nick wasn't. He said, 'Of course everyone knows. So what. Adds to the cachet.' Then he explained to me the ramifications of my repressed working-class background. And so I flaunted our affair and, lo and behold, people treated me with respect – and envy too. I wouldn't flaunt it now, but I wouldn't pretend to be innocent. Let New Caxton see I was no hypocrite.

When I got back to the beach house, I apologized to Buddy with some prosciutto from the deli, our favorite treat. Then I let him sprawl across me as I went through the copies I'd made from the *New Caxton Standard*. I stopped at the photo of the little house on Winchester Street, drenched in the flaring spotlights of the police cars. I would take a ride there in due time, drive by, get my bearings. Alone.

13

We didn't make love on the boat again. That was just to dazzle me. We made love in Owen's house in Washington. Every week. There was a schedule. Sometimes, Owen was able to see me an extra time each week; he'd call me at my office and I'd see a taxi waiting outside my window. He surprised me once, knocked on my office door, and when he came in, Buddy gave us both such a look of disdain that we just laughed while we hugged, and then I hugged Buddy, and Owen and I went out for coffee. One week we managed to see each other three times.

Owen lived on the best street in Foggy Bottom, a couple of blocks from the Watergate: one of those nineteenth-century mews homes made of brick – insular and romantic – one upon the other just like London. One upon the other just like New Caxton. Also, just like New Caxton, no garages, though the reasons for not having them were wildly different. Unlike New Caxton, at Owen's Washington address each house had a huge amount of property in back with vine-covered fences protecting the inhabitants with an intimate privacy that didn't feel artificial. There were Mercedes-Benzes and BMWs parked on the streets, but I never once saw a soul. All workaholics, and I visited Owen when most people worked. He insisted I take a cab rather than drive because newspeople would begin to notice, to recognize my car.

I said, 'I can take the Metro.'

He found that charming 'No one from my neighborhood takes the Metro. It's a long walk from the station.'

It wasn't, but I didn't protest further.

He'd attempt to reimburse me for the taxi fares, and I'd say, 'Don't you know the rules? Buy me diamonds and furs instead.' I was acting like a nincompoop and I didn't care. I was having fun.

The garden behind Owen's house was an oasis. It had a plinking fountain that you could hear, but it was too enveloped in carefully tended flowering fall plants and perfect shrubs to see unless you looked very closely. He said, 'In June, all this is roses.'

We'd sit out there afterward, for a few minutes, before I had to go and he had to go. I didn't feel like a mistress. I felt none of what I was doing had a name. The way any adulterer feels when she's fallen in love.

Once I told him on the phone that I wouldn't come because I'd just gotten my period and felt really crummy, and he said, 'Then what better time for you to be here with me? I'll have a hot water bottle waiting,' and that time we didn't go to bed, we just sat out in the garden talking, and that's when I went from falling in love to being in love with him: when he brought me the hot water bottle, placed it against my tummy, and asked if I felt better. A new experience for me. Fussed over. Like his rose gardens. Not bad.

The first time Owen and I made love in that house, we lolled around for a good while afterward. I kept waiting for him to say that he had to get back to the Hill, but he didn't. He let me lead. And when I said that I had to go, he said, 'Are you sure?'

And I said, 'No.'

He kissed me and I stayed.

I couldn't help comparing him to Nick. I didn't want to,

but it was just something that was there. Sex with Nick meant that he and I would take turns lying spread-eagled on the bed, letting one bring the other to gratification. It could be quite thrilling, usually was, but the old concept of afterglow couldn't happen because it was always the other person's turn to perform. And then the performer would be all energized again while the other one was swimming to dreamland. Owen and I just lay in each other's arms blathering on and on about nothing pertinent until – miraculously, it seemed – we'd find ourselves making love again.

After officially cheating on my husband that time on Owen's boat I tried to make it up to Nick. I felt no guilt. I just felt sorry for him. He didn't know how to relax, didn't know how to drop everything and allow an impulse to take over. Everything was treated as an emergency. He'd missed a lot. So I went right back home and planned his favorite dinner, osso bucco. I made it with the telephone, but I did set the table myself, on nice china and with wineglasses I'd bought in one of the antiques stores on the waterfront. Then I called the restaurant back again and asked if they could also send over those long spoons that you need to get to the marrow. I told them I'd have them back the next day and the manager said 'Take your time,' even though, it turned out, they were sterling.

I told the kids they could watch Letterman – Yes, kids, I know it's a school night – in exchange for eating dinner at ten o'clock with their father and me. Nick usually pulled in just before ten to say good night to them. I told them, too, that they could still have their real dinner at six when they were starving, and then they could just play around with the osso bucco while they answered Nick's questions about their lives. We hadn't all had dinner together for months.

It was a success. We enjoyed ourselves. We had to put up with the children's descriptions of the bone marrow, my son winning out with 'the placentas Snowball ate after each kitten was born.' Snowball had to stay in Connecticut when we moved to Alexandria. She liked to roam at night, which was fine on our woodsy cul-de-sac in Connecticut. She'd have been killed by a car in Alexandria in a minute. She was adopted by my daughter's best friend, and the children get to visit with her when they go back to Connecticut to see their pals.

When the kids tuned in Dave, Nick said to me, 'So where are you?' He meant what stage I'd reached in production. He saw me like that now, a producer of a popular product.

I told him about the murders in New Caxton and then explained that I'd be spending a lot of time at the beach house working on it, returning there, in fact, tomorrow, to visit the crime scene, which was a lie.

He asked, 'When's the trial start?'

I began clearing the table. 'It's over. I'm trying something a little different this time. Instead of a trial, I'll depend on the transcripts and probably do a lot more interviewing than I've ever had to before.'

He had no more questions. I knew he wouldn't. So as I was clearing the table and he was eating his favorite dessert, Ben and Jerry's Cherry Garcia, I said, 'Owen Hall was the one who told me about this crime.' Then I swept into the kitchen so that the next thing I said was, 'What, honey? I didn't hear you?' And he'd called back, 'Nothing, never mind.'

So that part of it was over – getting a feel for lying. Far easier than contemplating what a divorce might mean: for me, for him, and for the gangling Letterman fans in the next room, faking having fun because they were exhausted and should have been in bed.

14

The complications in doing a book on the Montevallo murders, what with the trial over and the accused convicted and incarcerated, were not nearly as daunting as the complications I'd faced in Florida when I jumped in feet first, not even knowing if there was water in the pool. Back then, I was on the periphery, trying to elbow my way in every minute. I paid close attention to what was going on. When the DA visited a crime scene, I followed. It was easy. I got into my rental car and trailed the group to the deserted stretch of road near a marshy wasteland where Sam had taken his second-to-last victim, who also happened to be his oldest: She was twenty-four. His final victim had been his youngest, twelve. I learned from Poppy that serial killers expand their envelope, get less and less persnickety about who to choose because their lust becomes increasingly insatiable. If Sam hadn't been caught, she told me, he'd have continued to become less and less a purist. Up until his last two victims, in fact, it had been strictly college girls or girls of college age.

Poppy said, 'He'd have graduated to older women, black women, any women, and, of course, hookers, and more little kids, too, since they're the easiest to get to.' She looked at me. 'And married women, eventually, would fit in that mix. Naturally.'

That day in the marsh, I parked behind all the other vehicles and got out and watched the proceedings from the rear of a group of a dozen or so people. I'd expected to be asked to leave. I wasn't. Poppy noticed me. She was striding at the head of the pack, and then she turned toward where I was ambling along the shoulder of the rutted track attempting to be invisible and said, 'You're the woman who upchucked in the hallway.' I gave a little wave, didn't make eye contact, and fell in behind two reporters and a photographer. And then someone spoke to Poppy, distracting her.

Whenever anything went on concerning Sam, I made sure I found out what was happening and where it was happening. I watched carefully, asking questions all the time, quiet little questions of anyone who was standing around. If an eyebrow raised, I just said, 'I'm writing a book.' I didn't meet a single person who questioned my credentials. And no one said, *Listen, I don't want my name in your book,* which was what I was afraid of almost as much as being asked to leave. Instead, people would say, 'No kidding,' and they would spell their names for me. Soon I became known as the newspaper woman from Connecticut who upchucked in the hall and was writing a book. A guy from a Florida newspaper helped me apply for a press card. I told him I had a Connecticut press card but I had to get one from Florida authorities. I made that up, but he wanted to be helpful. He got me one even after I admitted that, damn it, I couldn't find the Connecticut card. But no one ever asked to see a press card. This was before the days when publishers would send an established crime writer to the crime site to write a book, all expenses paid, which is what happens to me now.

At one point during a court proceeding, when I was off having a flat tire, the judge asked aloud where I was. No one knew. When I arrived all out of breath, the Florida reporter told me, 'All of a sudden, the judge stops in his tracks and says, "Where's that woman from Connecticut? The one writing the book."' At first I thought, Even the judge wants to be in the book. But I found out that with a crime investigation, a coterie of groupies forms, and when one of them is missing, things seem askew and the proceedings don't move forward efficiently. The day is always canceled early.

Sam was to be tried for the murders of the three sorority girls because Poppy had the most evidence available on those killings to indict him. When we all went to the crime scene at the University of Florida, I kind of hung out after everyone had left, getting the feel of the sorority house, picking up details the way I did when I went to someone's house as a food columnist: colors, and pictures on the wall, the condition of the furniture, whether the ceilings needed painting. It turned out Poppy was hanging around too, picking up details important to *her*. She wanted to do it alone, when people weren't around jabbering at her. We saw each other in the lounge where the girls watched TV when they needed a break from studying, where they could bring guests. Sam Litton had been a guest there and scoped the place out carefully for his own purposes. He learned how to get in at night, when the doors were locked.

Poppy said, 'Who exactly are you, anyway?' I told her some of the truth, that I'd once worked with Sam at a small newspaper and I'd decided to quit my job and come and chronicle his trial. End up, hopefully, with a publishable book. I didn't tell her, not then anyway, that I'd come initially to act as character witness. She folded her arms across her chest and said, 'In other words, you're nobody.' Without pausing, I said, 'Yes.'

She threw her head back and laughed. Then she whapped me on the back and said, 'Believe it or not, all I was asking was your name. What the hell is it?' I told her. She said, 'Well, good luck, sugar.' At the end of the day, I went up to her and invited her to dinner. 'Pick a place,' I said. 'I don't know Gainesville.' She said, 'Count your blessings.'

We had a good time. I'd been lonely. It was the first time I socialized with anyone since I'd gotten to Florida, except for the reporter who'd helped me with the press card and who was on the make and stopped being helpful once he realized I didn't find him irresistible. I discussed aspects of the crime with Poppy. I was in awe of so much. I said, 'Sam Litton can't remember all the crime scenes. He killed so many women, he's forgotten where he disposed of some of the bodies.' Poppy said, 'Yeah. Ain't it a bitch?' She was not in awe of anything.

Six months after Sam was executed – the key evidence against him, the bite marks on the shoulder of one of the sorority girls, which matched his own teeth – Poppy called me. I hadn't heard from her since Sam had been sentenced. She chose not to witness his execution. 'Not part of my job, thank you,' is what she told me when I heard she wouldn't be there. She was calling to tell me she'd read the book and found it so curious that the details that made for the emotional pull of the story were ones she hadn't cared about. Like the significance of the ages of the last two victims. She said it never struck her until she read my book how appalling it was that, except for those last two – who represented Sam's growing out-of-control insatiability, the end of his persnickety inclinations – these were all girls on a threshold. The threshold just prior to really living. College was the last step before independence, self-reliance. He struck them down before the struggles of childhood and adolescence paid off. He took away the reward. 'The reward we all look forward to, Denise. No more parents, no more teachers. Just us. In charge.'

'What *did* you think of them as?'

'As the empty shells they'd become.'

'But, Poppy,' I said, 'I saw real clean rooms at that sorority house. You saw the rooms when they were full of blood.'

'Hey, *I saw* the blood, but at the time, to me, the blood had poured out of shells, not out of real young women struck dead when they were on the cusp of life. I looked at the blood, and what was in my mind was finding out what broke open the dam that released the blood. I didn't put together that it was a crime that turned three college women into empty shells, that the shells used to be women almost set to fly. I'm glad your book made me consider a different perspective. Your perspective. Makes me realize I'm doing something for real people here. People who shouldn't be shells. People who should be struggling through their chem class. A good book, Denise. Congratulations.'

I thanked her. She told me to keep in touch, and I did.

I wasn't affected by any of the crime scenes where Sam Litton had killed. They were simply dark parking lots, wooded ground, lonely roads. And in the sorority house where he had gone on a murderous spree, killing three girls in their beds, their rooms had been transformed from crime scenes back to college living quarters by the time I arrived. I saw these places in daylight, not in the dead of night two hours after Sam had left. While I wrote, I felt I was making up the terrible things he'd done. That's because I could never picture Sam doing any of it. But it was very different with my second book, about the woman who had shot her three children to impress her boyfriend, the boyfriend who'd readily admitted having kissed her off with the line, 'If you didn't have those kids, honey, you and me would make it.' There was only one crime scene. She'd shot the children in the family station wagon. I can't even imagine a family station wagon at night. It's a daytime image. So in broad daylight I peered into that car and stared at upholstery completely saturated with blood.

The blood was all over the back seat, all over the front

passenger seat, and was even covering the driver's seat where Lorraine had sat, because she'd shot herself too, to make her story more believable. More imaginative than Susan Smith, but the same basic story. This story had some guy holding a gun who just leaned in through the window and started shooting. Not a black guy, but a guy with curly brown hair. Some sort of hippie is the persona Lorraine chose. But the police found an anatomy book on top of the television set in her home. She'd studied it and then shot herself through her left side in a spot just below her ribs where she'd be sure to miss the big organs. Only she nicked a fairly large vein. Lorraine was not only willing to kill her kids to show Mr Right she was now free – had given him what he'd asked for – she risked killing herself.

There were blood spatters all over the ceiling of the car and the insides of the doors and the windows, all over everything that the bigger splotches of blood hadn't obliterated. I steeled myself, then, and was proud that I didn't flinch when I spotted the doll between the two front seats and the Legos all over the floor. I'd been warned by the DA at how horrifying the kids' toys would be, splattered with their blood. But I was okay. Shaky, teeth clenched, but okay. Then I saw the Seattle Seahawks jacket rolled up in a ball on the floor. A tiny jacket that would fit a three-year-old.

When I would take my kids somewhere in the car, they'd be playing happily in back and then one of them would suddenly announce, 'I'm hot,' and strip off his or her jacket, roll it in a ball, and throw it on the floor. Kids viscerally taking out their discomfort on their offending jackets. I was looking at a regular station wagon with regular kids' detritus strewn about, and everything was laid over with blood – except the little jacket down on the floor. Just a few brownish-red dots, as if the kid had scratched a mosquito bite. I started to tremble. The DA got me over to his car and poured me a shot of something. He poured a shot for himself, too.

The Seattle Seahawks jacket belonged to the youngest, the one who'd bled to death before the emergency room attendants could get him out of the car and into the hospital. His mother had planned to wait a bit before driving to the hospital, so her children could not be resuscitated. But she couldn't wait; she needed to save herself. She intended to accommodate her boyfriend – please him – not punish him by committing suicide. The doctors and nurses, through monumental efforts, were able to save two of the three dying children. The medical staff served as my secondaries. The DA in that case turned out to be my hero. He went on to adopt the two maimed children, who'd barely survived their mother's attack and were left severely disabled.

After that, I decided, no more murdered kids. So I'd been rationalizing the fact that one of the New Caxton victims was just a little boy by telling myself that the crime scene would be like the Florida sorority house. Cleaned up. New people in the rooms where the murders happened. There would be no tiny jacket belonging to Timmy Montevallo dotted with blood, lying on the floor of his grandmother's kitchen. I knew there would be pictures, but there were pictures of murdered people on the front pages of the *Star* every day at the grocery store checkout.

Not long after my trip to Block Island, I was sitting in my office petting Buddy with one hand and holding a photocopy of Connie Montevallo's house in the other – the little Cape Cod that was so shrunken by the glare of police lights. I remembered houses like that, built in the fifties all in their rows, tiny boxy facsimiles of an architect's scheme of coziness. In Bridgefield, I lived in the Reagan era's style of Cape Cod, as removed from the original design as Connie's. Where hers was as scaled down as possible, mine was ostentatious.

In Bridgefield, my house had a lovely, romantic, freshly painted front door, centered always in fall with the latest designer wreath, wild grape vines or bittersweet or dried eucalyptus, replaced after Thanksgiving with fir and pine cones and big red and green plaid bows. In summer, no wreath, but a basket hanging from a brass hook off to the side of the door overflowing with some mutant, incessantly proliferating geranium.

A Cape Cod house in the town that had been home to me for a dozen years, from the time I married Nick until we left for Washington, meant huge double-hung windows and handcrafted shutters, perfect pruned shrubs amid pachysandra, and a brick walk bordering all. It meant a full dormer in the roof so there were four oversized bedrooms upstairs for children and guests, and two bathrooms as well, so the two groups wouldn't cross paths.

Downstairs, a back-to-front living room wallpapered in William Morris reproduction and, dividing the living room from the majestic wainscoted dining room, a huge open foyer with a wide staircase finished off with white newel posts. An up-to-the-minute kitchen in back with an extra wing containing the family room and another bath. And somewhere, somehow, through an etched crystal-paned door, a master bedroom, a suite with a dressing room and another bath with Jacuzzi, a bathroom large enough to hold a dance. And a den, too, hidden, amid all those rooms with a cozy fire burning and leather wing chairs to sink into so that one could read, all alone, lost in the atmosphere of a personal private library.

I studied the photocopy in my hand: The image was unbearably harsh, swathed in floodlights blinding me to any details. Pictures of my house in Bridgefield showed it bathed in sunlight filtering through maples creating a play of shadow and brightness and reflecting domestic bliss. There was no wreath on Connie's door, no shutters, no boughs of maple trees, no sweep of finely clipped grass. Just scraggly, sparse shrubs and a tiny lawn dipping down a steep short bank to the street. No dormers, either. Probably an attic space not high enough to allow for standing room. No extra wing. No chimney, no cozy fireplace. Four rooms: kitchen, living room, two bedrooms, and, squeezed in, a minuscule bathroom.

In the darkness outlined in the aurora of the spotlight, I could make out an identical house next door, just a few feet away. I looked at my road map. Winchester Street. On the near side of Connie's house was a void. On my map, I could see that a short, narrow road ran along her property line. I looked up its name – Forster Street. On the other side of Forster, now showing up in the news photo, a cemetery called, ironically enough, the Cemetery of the Three Martyrs. I would have to find out which three martyrs the Catholic church had chosen to honor the dead buried there.

I was ready to have a look at the white Cape Cod house that Connie Montevallo had moved into upon her marriage, where she had raised her family, and where she had died. Just drive by and take it in, before I would get into blueprints and photographs of the chalk lines marking the sites where the bodies were found, before the call to whoever lived there now to offer them cash to let me walk around in their house, taking notes and photos. The people murdered were becoming real to me, and I was beginning to imagine the house I saw on the microfiche. In my mind, it was an extinct thing, no life to it, no movement within. But three people had died there, and I would know them better by seeing where they'd lived.

I looked at my watch and put the map and the photocopy back in my bag. I called the airline and reserved a seat on the plane to Providence. Before I left for the airport, I gazed out the window at my view of the FBI building, but I didn't see it. Instead, I was seeing a cemetery, one packed tightly with large marble vaults, rows of crosses, elaborate stone angels. Framed oval portraits of the dead set into granite. Shrubs carefully tended, little American flags marking the graves of veterans.

I left Buddy home. I wanted to concentrate. I didn't want to have to think about getting him fed. In the plane, I leafed through my stacks of copied articles. According to one, two items of note had turned up in the cemetery amid the headstones: a bloody pink polo shirt – Eddie's – and a cracked bowl that belonged to Connie. No knife, though. No weapon had ever turned up. Nothing else *whatsoever* had turned up.

I drove along the highway past the usual exit that would have let me off just before the line of factories beginning their parade along the Scituate. I got off at the next one, which came out right near Connie's house, the route the conjured-up strangers in the night followed before the court made the decision that there were no strangers after all, just a neighbor named Eddie Baines out to steal from his neighbors and kill them. Between the two exits, the highway was elevated, and I got a view of the entire town. The factories hiding the two rivers seemed even sootier, darker, and more menacing than when I'd first seen them closer up. The spires of the two Catholic churches, St Augustine's and St Cyril's, both were too skinny, too sharply pointed. They seemed like needles, not spires. I turned off at Exit Twelve.

The homes were tiny; they had multiplied across the hillsides as more and more workers were imported and as those workers then went on to have children who, in turn, grew up and needed homes of their own. The houses were one on top of the next, in varying degrees of disrepair reflecting the recession that had hit all the country's mill and factory towns, after the Reagan years when nothing trickled down.

I parked just off the bottom of the exit. Directly in front of me was the Cemetery of the Three Martyrs, a cemetery in miniature and no bigger than the lots that the houses stood on, an eighth of an acre if that. There weren't any marble vaults or carved angels. Instead, tiny tipped headstones stuck out of weedy grass. It must have been the first Catholic cemetery in town, easily a hundred years old, long past containing any room to include recent remains.

The little white Cape Cod stood on top of an embankment, as did all the other houses on the street. The houses were painted sixties colors: barn red, olive green, gold. Only Connie's was white. The three houses that separated the Montevallos from the Baineses took up little space, so very little space, between the victims and the neighbor who was convicted of murdering them. I kept thinking that murder was too big for such lilliputian buildings.

Connie's house faced the end of Winchester Street at the corner of Forster. Forster Street was only the length of two houses, the Montevallos' and the house backed up to it. Beyond that house was a bluff too steep to build on. How anyone in the two houses bordering Connie's hadn't felt the catastrophe going on, even if they didn't hear it, I couldn't understand. The houses were so close, so flimsy.

On the corner of Winchester and Forster, something else caught my eye. At first I didn't know what it was that diverted me, but then I looked at the pole on the corner. There were two street signs, one a beat-up rusty red that read WINCHESTER STREET. The Forster sign had been replaced. The little street called Forster had been renamed. There were a lot of letters, and at first I had trouble making out the name. When I did, tears sprang to my eyes. MONTEVALLO COURT. The sign was shiny and red. Blood red.

I shifted my car into drive and headed down the far side of the cemetery to look for a spot to turn around and get back onto the highway so I could get the hell out of there. Suddenly, I didn't want to be in a place where people wore ugly sturdy shoes and parked on sidewalks, and where libraries had budgets that didn't allow cracked windowpanes to be replaced.

I drove. But the road was narrow and twisted, and there was no place to turn around. I saw another street sign ahead. I would turn there. But when I reached it, I realized I was on the road that Timmy Montevallo traveled almost every day from his mother's apartment over the tavern to his grandmother's little Cape Cod, the last time riding his new bike. And I was back in Bridgefield, running alongside my son's new bike, holding on to the back of the seat, then letting go and watching him sail off into his first solo flight. When I got to the West End Tavern, I had to pull over and control myself.

I found some shredded Kleenex at the bottom of my purse and blew my nose. I wiped my tears on the cuff of my coat. I could see Timmy riding that bike, his Uncle Petey the one racing along beside, gripping the back of the seat till Timmy held steady enough for him to let him go. And, of course, Timmy's grandmother, beaming with pride, watching her son and her grandson from her front steps.

Timmy Montevallo should still be riding that bike, I thought. He shouldn't have been turned into a shell in the eyes of these people in this town. Had someone who killed a little kid gotten away with it? Were there strangers in the night after all? My side trip into grief fled, and at that moment I became bent on finding out. I had separated Owen out. There was the crime; there was Owen.

15

I thought I'd call Owen when I got home again. But I didn't; the person I wanted to speak to was Rosie. I reached her at the library.

'Have you got a couple of minutes?'

She said, 'Sure.'

'I wanted to ask you a few questions.'

'Shoot.' One word. Flip.

'I appreciate your time.' She didn't respond. 'At what point did people actually start asking the hard questions?'

'Which?'

I had anticipated the possibility of just such frostiness. I'd gone off with Owen Hall leaving my car parked in front of her library, and she didn't like it. Tough.

I said, 'Rosie, have you changed your mind about wanting to help me? Was that just something you were trained to offer everyone?'

'Look . . . No, I mean it. Ask away.'

'Exactly why was it that no one heard Connie or her family screaming for help?' I waited. Nothing. 'You mentioned the shock it was for everyone to learn that they had lain dead for twenty-four hours without anyone checking on them. Why didn't the choir members call Connie when she and Petey didn't show up for practice?' No response. 'How could Brenda have waited so long before checking on Timmy?' Nothing.

'Listen, if you've had a change of heart—'

'I haven't. The last is easiest. She was a bad mother, quote, unquote. That's how they first started rationalizing all of it. You take in an outsider, she'll turn on you. These are shallow, miserable – never mind. The rest of your questions, those first couple of questions – well, honest answers would reflect the fact that small-town God-fearing America is not what it's cracked up to be. If you hear yelling from a neighbor's house, mind your own business. It's probably just old Fred getting a little drunk, yelling at the kids, smacking his wife, kicking the dog. And if someone's schedule got thrown off – well, we've all got our problems, let's not cross the line and interfere with other people's lives. That's how it is.'

'That's not the reputation of New Caxton, according to someone I've spoken to.'

'Who, Owen Hall?'

'Yes.'

'Well, here's the question the editor of our local rag asked, and this was good; I give him credit. He asked, "If those helpless people can be wiped out so mercilessly, who is safe?" His question hid the real issue here, the one no one will ever face, not the congressman, not anyone else. If a crime like this can happen in our town, then what are we? What have we become? Or, maybe, what have we been all along?'

I said, 'Your questions answer mine, don't they?'

'I guess they do.'

'This crime happened quite a while ago. You know so many details. You're still dwelling on it, aren't you?'

'We all are. And it happened a little over two years ago. Not so long. All of us know the details, every little one. Just like the people in Holbrook, Kansas, know all the details. Still. And the Clutters were killed over thirty years ago.'

'I guess you're right.'

'Remember my telling you about the earlier break-in at the Montevallos?' she said, picking up the story right where she'd left off that day in the library. 'Because of that earlier break-in, Connie kept her doors locked, wouldn't open her door to a stranger. But there was no evidence of a forced entry. In fact, Connie would still have opened her door to a stranger. Sort of. She'd have opened the door, stood behind her unlocked screen, and asked whoever was at her door what they needed. If they chose, they could just yank the door open and push her aside.

'We all ate up those little bits of information that the cops began to leak. Gossip passed along from neighbor to neighbor. Not only was everyone shocked that the murders had happened twenty-four hours before the bodies were found, they heard there was hot water coming out from under the front door when the cops arrived.' She changed her voice to a mocking falsetto: *'I heard there was hot water coming out the front door, of all things! The killers returned the next night! They were in there when Brenda's boyfriend went to look for Timmy. They'd come back to clean up the mess! Get rid of their fingerprints. They had to get rid of the evidence!'*

'Rosie, is that true? The killers came back?'

Her own voice returned. 'The water was hot. It couldn't have been running for twenty-four hours. Between the time the boyfriend went to the house and then came back with Brenda, we figured the killers had fled, in too much of a hurry to bother turning the water off. Or maybe they left it on on purpose to create a flood that would remove anything they'd missed. You have to ask the police about that. What actually happened – well, no one knows what actually happened. There's Eddie's version and there's the version of the cops who responded to Brenda's call. Ask them – well, you can ask one of them. He's now our chief of police, Jerry Weinecke. The other cop quit. Figured being a cop in New Caxton was supposed to mean wearing mirrored glasses and chasing speeders, not coming upon murder victims. He was just a kid.'

'I'll speak to your police chief. So what next?'

'The buzz kept up. Nobody remembers seeing or hearing a car racing past their house that night. But if the killers fled on foot, there isn't so much as a tree in those yards on Winchester Street where they could have hidden. It dawned on us that whoever killed the Montevallos, they weren't afraid of being seen in the area.' Back came the mocking voice. *'Nobody's dog barked either.'* She paused. 'It sank in. The killers were not strangers. They were *us*.'

'Is that what you believe?'

'I don't know as I believed it then. I really didn't know what to believe. You know, it was all so horrible. Once in a while it comes back to me, how horrible it was.'

'Listen, I can go back up there and read all this. I can ask your cop—'

'I'm almost finished. I want to finish. Weinecke will give you the official story. But I want you to understand our shock. Why, in the end, I don't feel that justice was served. I need you to know.'

'Okay, Rosie.'

'Another bomb dropped that made us all sick. So sick that back we went to the theory of mad dogs arriving in the night, bent on killing. The coroner's report was made public. It turned out that the bottoms of Timmy's feet were covered with his grandmother's blood. He had been in the kitchen during or after Connie's murder. He had, in fact, not been killed in his sleep and then wrapped in a quilt as everyone had first heard. He had witnessed the attack on his grandmother and was then killed for it. They'd heard something about a quilt, but now they learned that the killer had actually wrapped Timmy in a quilt that Connie had made and then stabbed the child eleven times. Apparently, these killers couldn't quite stomach killing Timmy until he'd been wrapped up and hidden from their eyes.'

For a few minutes I lost the sound of her. Now I recalled a drug hit in New York, a houseful of people wiped out, the children first wrapped in blankets before being killed. I had looked into that crime. It's like the Mafia when they send you a fish. Wrapping children before killing them is a signal that the worst punishment has to be dealt their parents for the worst crime in the drug world – betrayal. Killing the children is the ultimate revenge. The Montevallo child had a parent: Brenda.

Rosie said, 'Denise,' in a sharp voice. That's what she must do with the story-hour kids who become distracted: pull them right back.

'Yes. I'm taking it in.'

She said, 'I'll tell you, everyone in this town imagined their own kids screaming and crying, struggling as a quilt was wrapped around them, and then the first plunge of the knife, then the second, and then nine more. Timmy Montevallo died a tortured death and no one heard, let alone responded to what should have been horrendous screams of terror and cries for help. No one heard them. No one heard Timmy or Connie or Petey because they didn't make any noise. They'd been subdued. By more than one person. Two. Maybe three.'

'Was Eddie Baines one of them?'

She was silent. I could just make out her breathing. Then she said, 'I've been hoping your interest in all this stemmed from the possibility that Eddie didn't commit the crime.'

'Some of my interest arose from that, yes. But now I'm wondering what you think. What about Eddie Baines? Was Eddie's version of the story true?'

'I take it Owen told you Eddie's version.'

'All he told me was that he wasn't sure Eddie did it.'

'He didn't. I'm convinced of it.'

'So, Rosie, who framed him?'

'Framed him?'

'Yes. Who framed Eddie Baines?'

'You tell us.'

We were invited, Nick and I, to a state dinner welcoming the Crown Prince of Japan to the United States upon the signing of a new trade agreement. It was a simple surrender, no trade involved: The Japanese agreed to stop charging its citizens an exorbitant tax if they chose to buy American cars. The previous administration had threatened to tax Japanese cars in an equivalent manner, meaning that a Nissan Sentra would cost around $70,000. The Japanese laughed it off, knowing the American people would say bullshit to that. So Bill Clinton went over there and told them to remove the levy, because if they didn't he'd resort to the peace treaty signed by Hirohito in 1945, which said, in diplomatic language, that their import-export arm would be broken into pieces, thereby eliminating any imbalance of trade favoring Japan. Our President pointed out, 'If I decide to enforce that provision – and I can – you'll all be fucked.' That's how he said it, according to Nick, who'd been along on the trip, ostensibly to learn about sustainable rural development in Japan. Bill just wanted an old pal to relax with after sticking it to the Japanese carmakers.

So the Japanese agreed to a 'compromise', and they sent the Emperor's son over for some face-saving, and Nick and I were invited to the dinner not just because Nick was in on the original trip but because the entertainment would be Kool and the Gang, the future emperor's all-time favorite group. Also mine and Nick's. The President's way of thanking Nick for dropping everything and schlepping off to Japan with him.

Owen, it turned out, would be there too.

I called him. I told him I would be uneasy. He said, 'Then I'll do my best to keep my distance.' I thanked him for understanding.

In the receiving line, Bill Clinton said to me, 'Whatcha workin' on now, Denise?'

I said, 'A triple murder, Mr President.'

'Which one?'

'Happened in Rhode Island, so no one's ever heard about it. Trying something a little different.'

'Hey, that's great. Listen, I put my old friends together tonight. You'll be sitting with Owen Hall. You can do a little research for yourself while we wait for Kool and, hey . . .'

'Yes, Mr President.'

'Give that dog of yours a pat on the head for me, okay?'

He passed me down the line. Hillary said, 'Are you letting your daughter go to that damn dance? I mean, they're only tenth-graders.'

'Sure. Good practice at suffering so she'll be ready for the torture of the real dance.'

'The real dance?'

'The heinous junior prom.'

She laughed. She said, 'My junior prom was the most miserable night of my life.' Then she sighed and laughed again. 'How good it feels to admit that.' We hugged, and I moved along the line.

Then I spotted Owen, and he was unaccompanied. I fell in love with him all over again. I told myself he hadn't brought a date so as to spare me discomfort. But when we were seated, I was not seeing chivalry. Owen was the one who was uneasy. He couldn't look at me. He was on the other side of the table, directly opposite, and he never once made eye contact during the entire dinner. Even when the lights dimmed, while Kool sang, he didn't look my way, and when the band took their bows, he mumbled something to all of us at the table and then he was gone. I thought, This must be the real thing here. But then I stopped kidding myself. I'd looked forward to the sexiness inherent in socializing with someone I was sleeping with in front of a lot of people, exchanging glances. He hadn't been uneasy over my feeling embarrassed, what with Nick right there. It was something else.

The next day, I had a message from Owen on my office machine asking me to call him at home that evening. I did. He said, 'I have something I have to say to you, Denise. I need to see you. Sooner than we'd planned.' He never mentioned the previous night's dinner.

It couldn't wait three days? Such a statement tends to turn a person's stomach over, mine no exception. It's unfair. Owen could have said, I miss you. Can we meet tomorrow for lunch? I can't wait three days. So I would not say to him, What is it, Owen? which is what he expected. I responded in a way that he wouldn't expect, to throw him off his next line, which would have been, We'll talk about it at lunch. I said, 'I do love you, Owen.'

The silence was pathetic. Then he said, 'And I, you.'

Now he wasn't ready for the question, and I sprang it. 'So tell me, cutie. What's up?'

I think he started to go back to the preprogrammed response, but he stopped himself. He said, 'I'm sorry I sounded so melodramatic. I need to be touching you when I say what I have to say. If you decide to leave me, I want the opportunity to hold on to you.'

When I arrived at his house, there was no move toward his bedroom. Instead, we sat in the garden, where it was too cold. He knew that, and he'd brought two big mugs of coffee. 'Have you been to the Montevallo house?' he asked, cutting to the chase.

'Yes.'

'How'd it go?'

'Badly.'

'I'm sorry.'

I thanked him.

'What's next?'

'Someone official. Someone on the scene. A police officer.'

'That would be a mistake.'

'Excuse me?'

'I need you to know certain things.'

'What things?'

He put his coffee cup to his lips.

'Owen, what do you want me to know?'

He played with my fingers. 'Listen, Denise, I have to tell you something and I don't know how you'll take it, but, believe me, it has nothing to do with betrayal, I swear to God.'

I waited. He waited too. 'I'm all ears, Owen. Believe me, you've got my attention.'

'Eddie Baines did it.'

'He did?'

'For sure.'

'How do you know that?'

'I found out certain things.'

'These certain things are what you wanted to tell me about?' I took a Kleenex out of my purse and blew my nose. 'I think I'm catching a cold.' He didn't say, Let's go inside.

'Denise.'

'What?'

'There's no book for you if he did it. You've wasted—'

'Of course there is. And if you found out certain things convincing you that he's guilty, maybe the book will be even more interesting. But there are no "certain things," are there?'

He took my hands. 'I'm lying to you.'

'No shit.'

'As if I could lie to you,'

'Owen, why? Why did you suddenly want me to think Eddie Baines was the killer after all?'

'Because I don't want you to do the book.'

His gaze into my eyes seemed almost desperate. He wanted me to say, For you – all right, I won't.

I said, 'Why?'

'Because I should be the one to find out the truth, not you. I should go to the police, not you. I've been a coward. My town decided to punish Eddie for screwing up, for ruining what was left of his family. Let him get arrested. He needs a scare. But then, when things started to get out of hand, go wrong . . . that was when I should have seen—'

'We've been through this. Once he came to trial, it was too late for anyone to say, Hey, we just wanted to throw a scare into this fellow. And because of some bizarre false sense of pride, they couldn't backtrack. Frankly, I don't know how you could have believed such a thing. But I didn't question it because of the god-damned stars in my eyes. I'm beginning to notice some space between the stars, Owen.'

'The stars are finally clearing from my eyes too, thanks to you. But there was so much more than people fooling themselves. Another thing was that everyone began to feel good with the sham – I'm sure you can understand this, Denise – because they also began to see the advantage of feeling safe in their beds at night again. Otherwise, if Eddie hadn't done it, back to square one. Who did? And where would he strike next? And the thing is, Eddie did leave evidence and they all began to cling to that. I'm ashamed to say, so did I.'

'Explain this evidence to me?'

'There was the footprint. It proved to come from a sneaker that belonged to him. There was this watch, too, found at the scene. Eddie's watch. I mean, it was assumed to be Eddie's watch since a hair was caught in it. His hair.'

'Why assumed? If it had his hair in it?'

'During the trial there was some question as to whose watch it was.'

'What are you saying?'

'It may have been Petey's watch. It was found on the floor. It was never established as to whose watch it was. The watch business was what got me to wondering. I've done a lot of wondering since, and I've reached the conclusion that Eddie and his girlfriend were supposed to be found at the scene by the police. I learned that, ten minutes after the police got the call from Brenda, the dispatcher had another call. An anonymous call that there was trouble at the Montevallos. Even though Connie never reported the earlier burglary to the police, the cops were aware of it and the caller knew they'd dash over there. If Brenda hadn't decided to go to her mother's when she did, and if Eddie hadn't been scared off, the police would have found Eddie in Connie's house. But of course, the call was ignored since the police already knew there was trouble at the Montevallos.'

'So you're saying that whoever got Eddie and the girlfriend over there intended to see that they were found there by the police.'

'I'm sure of it.'

'You know, Owen, I'm having a tough time here. You believe that there was someone who got the girlfriend to convince Eddie to go there.'

'Yes.'

'Who?'

'The actual killers. I doubt he believed what she was saying to him, that the Montevallos were murdered. He had to mollify her, humor her. I don't know, maybe he figured she was having some psychotic drug episode. When he got there, he just did what the girl said. Clean off any fingerprints. She'd brought buckets—'

'Stop right there.'

He closed his eyes. 'I know it seems—'

'Far-fetched.'

'Eddie did as he was told because he had no choice. Getting arrested for this crime would be the end for him, as low as he could sink. When he saw what he saw in that house, he believed her. That someone had killed these people and planted evidence against him and his girlfriend in order to get away with it. To be arrested for such a horrible crime, to sink that low . . . He couldn't be arrested for killing those people – for drug money? They were his neighbors, for God's sake. He couldn't let his mother, his sister, his community think he'd become some kind of animal. His dead father, too. There was no way out for him except to do what she said he had to do. And she was willing to *help* him. I think that gave him the strength he needed: her loyalty. Essentially, they flooded the house, just flooded it. When Brenda's boyfriend arrived, they ran.'

'In other words, Eddie Baines could have done anything to save his skin.'

'Who knows what we're capable of if we're trapped in the kind of place he was in.'

'So what happened next?'

'A few days later, the girlfriend told him she didn't want to see him again. She wouldn't meet him, wouldn't answer his calls, or take the messages he sent through their friends. He stalked her, begging her at every opportunity to at least talk to him. She wouldn't. He became suicidal. He tried to do it, too.'

'Do what?'

'Kill himself. Delayed reaction, maybe. I mean, after what he'd seen and all. Almost managed. Then he was arrested. Based on the evidence found at the scene – the footprint and the watch. The girl wasn't. Nothing was found to trace the girl to the scene.'

'Owen, I can't understand why you never spoke to the police about all this.'

'About all what? The police know everything I know. But now I'll go to them because I just can't stop deconstructing things. The pieces aren't fitting together. I have spoken to my brother, and he—'

'Your brother?'

'The head of our family. He—'

'Why aren't you the head of the family? I should think prestige takes priority over age.'

'You're getting agitated, Denise.'

'Damn right I'm agitated. You're saying—'

'The trial had been over for a long time. Eddie was already in jail. My brother convinced me, initially, that the real murderers would turn up and be arrested and the case would be reopened. Eddie would be freed. I believed all of them. I thought—'

'Who's *all of them*? We were talking about your brother.'

'I mean all the people there. All the people who live in the town.' He let go of my hand. He reached up and brushed my cheek with his fingertips. Then he said, 'I told you I was a coward. I am. And now I'm feeling very guilty about what I've done to you. I couldn't keep up this lie any longer. So I had to explain to you.'

I lost his thread. I looked into his face for what seemed a long time, though it probably was a tiny moment. He was trying to have me understand something beyond his tumble of words. The touch of his finger on my cheek brought me back to the intimacy I shared with him, and I saw.

I said it in a whisper. 'You set me up.'

'That's not how I'd put it.'

I got to my feet and knocked my cup over. It rolled off the table, fell to the bricks, and smashed. I said, 'How could you?' I couldn't believe myself, sounding like some idiot out of Jane Austen.

He stood up, too, and grabbed both my hands and held fast. 'I spotted you across the room in New York. I knew your husband. I had an in. I suddenly got some stupid notion that I could interest this famous crime writer in writing the story of the Montevallo murders. You'd set the record straight. It was a fantasy. And I had no idea I'd fall in love with the famous crime writer. But I have, so I came to know I must tell you the truth. If Eddie didn't do it, there *is* another killer out there, and that means I've put you in grave danger.' He eased his way around the table to me, still gripping my hands. 'Please, Denise, abandon this project. I can only hope that you won't abandon me.'

'Why should I abandon my book? It's getting more interesting every minute.'

'I told you. Because the real killer is out there.'

'Maybe he is, maybe he isn't. Maybe I'll come to discover Eddie really did it after all.'

'Denise, can't you understand the jeopardy here? I keep trying to tell you—'

'I'll buy a gun.'

'For God's sake, be serious.'

'Owen, my husband is Bill Clinton's good friend. He's his—'

'I know what he is. I don't mean to sound paranoid.'

'Fine. Don't sound that way.'

Owen's eyes were damp. Politicians have a way of shining

down on people. He'd waited until I'd gotten in too deep to get out. He'd planned for that too, as well as dredging up a few tears. I yanked my hands out of his. He said, 'I'm scared for you. I love you. I'll find the means—'

I looked into his eyes, now filled to the brimming. Love, my ass. There was none. I knew what love looked like. I saw it whenever I looked in the mirror when I was thinking of him. Which was most of the time. I sat back down. 'What were you doing at that party in New York?'

He sat too, relieved. 'I told you, I was with friends.'

'How did you come to be with these friends?'

'Denise, I don't know what that has to do with anything.'

'You didn't spot me from across the room. You planned it, chose a place to see me where I wouldn't be with anyone we both knew. Where running into me would truly seem a coincidence. You love me? Then admit it. Admit that this has all been a deliberate sequence of events.'

His face became set. 'It wasn't at first. I was simply at a dinner one night, and people were talking about Nick Burke's wife. The crime writer. It triggered something. What if a crime writer were to look into these murders? Do what I was impotent to do? Then I found out about the publishing party in New York. So I—'

'How did you find out about it?'

'I made some calls. I—'

'Forget it. I don't want to hear the details. I'd rather hear about Eddie Baines.'

He seemed confused. 'Denise, don't you see? I'm trying to make you understand that I intend to take action myself now. There is no longer any need for you to walk in my shoes.'

He was beginning to sound like Nick. He hadn't heard anything I'd said. So *I* took *his* hand. I said, 'I want you to tell me about these failures of Eddie Baines. I want to understand how he could have gotten into such a mess and how in God's name he found the wherewithal to go into a house where his neighbors had been brutally stabbed to death to look for planted evidence that would incriminate him. How he could bring himself to wipe up all that blood just in case someone, say, stole his sneaker, dipped it in the blood, and made a footprint on the floor. I assume he didn't leave the sneaker print while he was cleaning up blood. He went to college. He wasn't stupid. I'm just curious, Owen, that's all. Tell me.'

He was boxed into a corner. He had no choice but to continue the charade. I settled in to listen, gnawing at the inside of my bottom lip so I wouldn't speak the words I was feeling: *Stop. Take it all back. Be in love with me again the way I thought you'd been.*

He said, 'I should start with his father.'

'Whatever.'

'His name was Big Jim Baines.' His gaze drifted past me. 'Blacks in New Caxton have nicknames like Big Jim or Fast Mike. Italians and Poles have nicknames that come from their ethnic roots, Yutch or Pishy. Mr Montevallo's nickname was Chick.'

'So what about Eddie's father?'

He came back from his tangent. 'He was very popular. And so was his closest friend, Chick Montevallo. They'd been childhood playmates. As teenagers they were the heart of the front line of the undefeated New Caxton High football team of 1951. The New England championship team. In those days they'd have a big tournament in Boston patterned on college bowl games. Not anymore. Kids have been determined to be too fragile to compete for such high stakes.' He stopped. I smiled at him, acting as if I were all better so he'd continue. I could see the relief in him at my smile, his relief in thinking I was back in the palm of his hand.

'They served in the army, asked to be stationed together. When they returned and married, they bought houses practically next door. And they would have lived right next door if side-by-side houses had been available.'

'A black man and a white man.'

'A black man and an Italian man. New Caxton men.'

'Yes.'

'The two of them headed up this round table at Stoshu's. That's kind of a coffee shop, a news store. Every Saturday six guys would go there for breakfast. They'd all played football together. And they all had sons, sons all born within a few years' time. Big Jim's son, Eddie, was . . . blessed. That's how they'd put it in New Caxton if a child had the potential to be a talented athlete. Eddie's athletic career, in fact, would be unsurpassed. He became the town's dream. He was a black quarterback.' Owen stopped. 'What that means—'

'I know what that means.'

'Eddie Baines led the Red Rockets to their first state championship since Big Jim and Chick played. Eddie wasn't the size of his father, took after his mother's side, tall, willowy. He also captained the basketball team that winter, something more suited to his temperament, people said. But basketball wasn't football. In New Caxton, basketball is nothing.

'When Pete Jr. was born, Chick held high athletic aspirations for his boy, but unlike the dreams of his friend – of Big Jim Baines for his own boy – his were not to be. Chick's son was strange, quote, unquote. Peculiar. And then *peculiar* became *autistic*. I remember all this. I remember it well. It was tough. Always is, I guess. But Petey did become special, you know? Special is a good term for people like Petey. He was bonded to his parents in that kind of protected way that only handicapped children are.

'Big James Baines was the founder of NASCA – my family put up the money – the New Caxton Association for Special Children and Adults. He started up the group as soon as it was confirmed that his friend Chick's boy was going to need help. Big Jim had the insight to know that Petey would need assistance all his life, not just while he was a child. Through NASCA, and our money, and the devotion of his mother, I'd have to say, Petey's talents were developed. He was a musical savant. He could sing any score, no matter how complicated, after he'd heard it once. His voice was beautiful. He was in the school chorus, got to leave his special ed classes to practice and perform. And as an adult, he became a soloist for St Augustine's choir. He sang the national anthem at the football game when Eddie Baines threw the lone touchdown to win a championship, a forty-yard pass to the end zone, timing and placement perfect.'

'You were there?'

'We were all there. The New Caxton High field is bigger than a lot of college stadiums. After that, Petey performed nationally in singing competitions. He auditioned to sing the anthem at the 1986 Special Olympics. He won the audition.'

'Did you ask Ted Kennedy to help with that one?'

He stared at me. Then he laughed. 'Yeah, I did.' I made an attempt to laugh too. He went on. 'Chick Montevallo never missed a single one of Eddie's games, even traveled with Big Jim and their cronies to watch him play at college, at Nebraska, where Eddie won a scholarship. And Big Jim Baines, though not a Catholic obviously, attended St Augustine's every Christmas Eve. He went to Midnight Mass to hear his neighbor's son sing his solo. "O Holy Night." It became a tradition at the church.' He paused. 'Don't ask. Yes, I've been. Every Christmas Eve until he was killed.'

'He was really good?'

'He was beautiful. Probably would have won the audition even if Ted Kennedy didn't put in a call to his sister.

'Petey's father died suddenly. It was almost twenty years ago. Heart attack. His buddies held a wake at their table at Stoshu's. Italian and Polish men and a black man too, Big Jim Baines. They were completely distraught. Petey was inconsolable. The men promised to do all they could for Connie and Petey, and for the daughter, Brenda, who'd been giving her parents a hell of a lot of trouble all her life.

'A couple of years after that, when Big Jim Baines dropped dead of a heart attack just as Pete had, the round table broke up. Big Jim's son, Eddie, was as inconsolable as Petey had been. Jim's widow, like Connie Montevallo, was a strong woman, and she had a daughter too, but one who was a good girl. This daughter was determined to help her brother through his grief. She couldn't though.

'Neither of the men lived to see the insinuation of drugs into their families, or maybe Eddie and Brenda turned to drugs because they died, who knows? Eddie was able to function again after his father's death only with the help of cocaine.'

'And why didn't the Halls and the good people of New Caxton help him?'

'The good people of New Caxton wouldn't accept what was happening to him. They whispered about it, but they didn't come out and do something because of the shame of it. In a way, they were helping his mother save face by not speaking of it. As for Brenda Montevallo, she had advanced, apparently, to become a dealer before she took off. There wasn't going to be any help for her either. And the upshot of all this is a guy who isn't a killer is in prison for the rest of his life. These are my people, Denise. I have to do something about this. I've used poor judgment up until now. I'm ashamed. Now I will take charge.'

Again, I smiled. Let him think what he wanted. But *I* would remain in charge.

16

I parked in my usual spot, two wheels up on the sidewalk in front of the New Caxton library. I crossed the street and went up the dilapidated front porch of the police department, a two-story frame house with asphalt shingles. The hand-lettered sign hung where there had once been a doorbell. The entry door, though, was steel, heavy and strong, standard police issue in big cities not in small towns.

I went in. The house had been gutted, and reception was behind heavy glass. I went to the sliding window in front of the uniformed dispatcher. A little plaque on his desk read that all conversation was being taped. I stood for a moment and then, when he ignored me, pressed the buzzer. He looked up, and I put my mouth to a round microphone set into the glass.

'I have an appointment with the Chief. Denise Burke.'

The officer looked me over. 'ID.'

I showed him my driver's license and he buzzed me in. Behind the glass there was a clean and polished order, three people at desks filling out reports, busy, their heads bent over their tasks. They were all in uniform, neat and pressed. This was not like any police station I'd ever been in; they were normally full of commotion and comings and goings. The first police station I'd encountered was in Harlem, the 26th precinct. I'd gone with a classmate my freshman year at Yale to visit his cousin at CCNY. After the visit, my friend was going to show me New York. We'd chatted with his cousin in the library. The cousin was very proud of my friend, told me he was a genius. He said, 'But I guess you're all geniuses at Yale or why else would you be there?' I'd put my coat on a chair at the table next to me. When it was time for the cousin to go off to class, my coat was gone. It was a leather coat. It was the only thing I owned worth anything. My mother and my aunt gave it to me as send-off present. They must have sold something to do it, but I couldn't imagine what either of them had that could have gotten them enough money to buy it.

My friend took me to the police station a dozen blocks away. Some of the homeless we stepped over seemed dead, not asleep. Inside the station, the peeling walls were covered with grime and the space was full of old wooden tables where the officers sat. They sat on the tables because there weren't any chairs. Only one man was in uniform. There were handcuffed prisoners on benches, and women in holding cells that looked like cages at the zoo. The women reminded me of my mother except they had on a lot of makeup. It was just like television. Someone asked if he could help us. His name was Detective Detulio. I told him about my coat. He said, 'Welcome to the Big Apple.' He gave my friend and me cups of coffee, and then he went about his business. My friend felt bad, but I told him that having coffee at the 26th Precinct police station made up for the coat.

In New Caxton, I was led to Chief Weinecke's office. He opened the door just as the officer raised his knuckles to knock.

'Please come in, Mrs Burke.'

His cheeks were ruddy, his face round as a moon, his small eyes sky blue. He looked like a working farmhand who'd just left a hot field, taken a shower, and stepped into a brand-new police uniform. He had a mustache like Lech Walesa's.

'My name is Jerzy Weinecke. Here, people call me Jerry.

Please do the same. I am happy to meet a writer. An honor.' He had an accent; people were still emigrating to New Caxton from Poland.

'Thank you. Please call me Denise.'

'With great pleasure. Please sit down.' I did, and so did he.

I took out a notebook and fiddled with my pen so he would continue speaking. Instead, he gazed at me, his face empty. So I said, 'I'm interested in speaking to you both in your capacity as the present police chief and because you were the first person to arrive at the Montevallo crime scene.'

'The first person to arrive after Miss Montevallo.'

'I meant the first officer of the law to arrive.'

'Yes, I see. This town has been traumatized by the deaths of the Montevallos and by the conviction of Mr Baines.'

'Are you convinced that justice was served?'

'He was given a fair trial and was found guilty based on the evidence against him.'

He spoke in a stilted manner. His English was learned at school in Poland, not on the streets of New Caxton. If his inflection was stilted, it was also syntactically correct. He'd been educated. I found myself mimicking his speech. 'What you say does not answer my question.'

'I believe Mr Baines killed them. He was under the influence of drugs. In my mind, he was what is called a bad seed.'

'You're also certain he acted alone?'

'He was an athlete, tall and strong.'

'I didn't mean to ask whether you thought he could have committed the crime alone, but rather whether you feel he could have had an accomplice.'

'Not an accomplice. I understand what you are getting at. You want to know if I believe his girlfriend was with him when he killed the Montevallos. There was nothing at the scene to allow the police to place her there.'

I flipped a page in my notebook. 'Can you describe what you saw at the Montevallos' house when you got there?'

'Gladly. I entered a fog. The house was filled with a steam cloud. There was an inch of water on the floor, and it was hot water. That is the reason we were convinced at first that the crime had taken place that evening.

'The bodies of Mrs Montevallo and her son, Peter, were white. There was no blood left in their bodies. The blood had been washed away by the running water. Only the bed where the child's body lay was red. It was saturated with blood.'

'It must have been horrible.'

'It was far worse than horrible.'

'What did you think? What did you think happened?'

'At first I thought only of the possibility that perhaps the child still lived. But that was not so. Then I thought to calm down Miss Montevallo. However, what you are asking is what my theory was as to who killed them. My initial theory, correct?'

'Yes.'

'There was no father in the family. Mrs Montevallo was a widow and the child's father was unknown. So I knew it wasn't a domestic crime.'

'Your first thought was to eliminate the likeliest possibility.'

'Yes.'

'If there had been a husband or a father, you would have suspected him?'

'Yes.'

I flipped a page. 'What did you think next?'

He swiveled his chair away from me. He looked out the window. His view was the back of the house behind the police station. He put his fingertips together and recited what he'd prepared.

'A hypothetical scenario developed in my mind based on hearsay and tidbits of gossip. Based on that first robbery of

Mrs Montevallo's house. The home is the first on the road where Exit Twelve comes off Route Nine. It is also the last exit before the turnoff to the Providence connector. When traffic is heavy, motorists get off at that exit, hoping to find a back road to Providence. Some even stop in front of Connie's house and go knock on her door, asking for directions to Providence. If there exists a back road. So of course, a couple of crack-crazed demons on the way to Providence to buy drugs got off at the last available exit, not to find a shortcut but to burglarize the first house they saw, which would certainly be what happened during the previous burglary there. We don't know.'

'No evidence?'

He stopped his window gazing. 'As I recall, the only thing taken was cash. The event was never officially reported here. A small amount of cash that Mrs Montevallo had in a cookie jar on her refrigerator was missing. People who rob in order to buy drugs only take cash unless they know, specifically, that they can sell other items – certain makes of televisions, perhaps – to someone who will hand them cash in return. Usually, they don't take the trouble.'

'Are you implying something?'

'Yes.'

'That Eddie Baines was the one who had robbed Connie Montevallo earlier?'

'Yes. In hindsight that is what I have concluded, but not at the time of his arrest. After the bodies of the Montevallos were found, we set up roadblocks on Route Nine, and we asked drivers if they had driven the area on Saturday night and whether they had seen anything unusual. We were grasping at straws, trying to capture a band of nonexistent creatures who had invaded New Caxton like a virus. We would not believe, even the police, that one of our own citizens could have committed this terrible crime. Then we were forced to face reality, you see. The state coroner's report stated that the deaths had occurred twenty-four to thirty hours before the bodies were found, within two hours of their last meal. So it turned out they hadn't been killed late Saturday night during a time when marauders roam. They had been killed early Friday evening right after supper. They had lain dead a whole night and a whole day and then on till midnight while the good people of New Caxton—'

He swiveled back to me. I finished his sentence. 'Were minding their own business.'

'I am afraid so.'

'And then Eddie Baines came to be a suspect.'

'Yes.'

'Why?'

'Tips.'

'What tips?'

'He was seen near the Montevallo house on Friday night.'

'He lived three doors away.'

He went directly to his big gun. 'He wore sneakers like the sneaker that left a print in blood at the crime scene.'

'Where was the print found? I mean, wouldn't the water have . . .?'

'On the wall of the bedroom.'

'The wall?'

'He must have braced himself while he subdued Petey.'

The buzzer on his intercom was jarring. Weinecke pressed a button. 'Yes?'

A voice responded. 'Excuse me, sir, we've got something, that information you needed.'

'I will be right there.' He stood up. 'I will be happy to continue our interview at another time, but I have urgent business to attend to.'

I stood too. 'Chief Weinecke, were you promoted to your

present position based on the work you did on the Montevallo case?'

'Yes, in addition to my other accomplishments.'

'When did you emigrate to this country?'

'When I was eighteen.'

'When was that?'

'Nine years ago. Excuse me, I must leave.'

He took his cap from his desk and carried it carefully in his hand as he came around to escort me out.

I said, 'Seniority didn't figure into the equation?'

'It was considered, naturally. There were, naturally, other officers. But my work was exemplary.'

I congratulated him on his achievements and didn't ask what his work had entailed – aside from the Montevallo killing – in a town with no crime, just unreported domestic beatings and a couple of cocaine users. He asked me to call to make my next appointment. He was too busy to 'notify his calendar at the moment.' It was the first time he had misused a word.

As he shook my hand I asked, 'Did Eddie's girlfriend help him kill them?'

'No.'

I decided to try his patience. 'Was she on the scene?'

'I've already answered that question.' He pulled his hat firmly onto his head.

I called the young cop who had gone to the crime scene with Weinecke. He was at home. He lived with his parents. He told me he was still unemployed. He told me he didn't want to talk about the crime. He said he was finally not having so many nightmares. I asked him whether he thought Eddie's girlfriend helped him kill the Montevallos. He said, 'Eddie didn't kill anybody. Neither did she. They went there afterward. We gave her a lie detector test.'

'She was given a lie detector test?'

'Yeah.'

'How'd she do?'

'She passed the part about not killing anybody. But she lied so bad on the questions about being on the scene that we thought she was going to blow the doors off the thing.'

Back in Alexandria, I began to shape the information I had into an elaborate outline, making order out of the chaos of material I'd gathered, since there was no hope of making order out of the chaos of my life. I told Owen I needed to lie low so I could think. I would let him believe I was thinking of him instead of my book. My anger allowed me not to miss him too much. He'd used me to do what he obviously needed to do himself. Now, while I was unforgiving, I would use him. His name would save me the trouble of explaining to people why I needed to interview them. I would use his name where he hadn't laid the groundwork, though I worried he'd be a step ahead of me, calling all the people he'd asked to help me and tell them not to, after all. Even if he didn't, he'd no doubt get wind of my trail. Owen would learn I was going on with the book. Then maybe he'd tell me his *real* reason for wanting me to stop. His speech about his burning conscience didn't cut it.

A stack of mail was collecting in my office. I can only deal with one thing at a time, so I'd let it pile up. If there was anything really important, I'd get a telephone call from whoever hadn't gotten their letter answered. Once, I'd tried to organize backed-up mail, creating a file I labeled PENDING – GET TO WITHIN A WEEK. I didn't get to the file for three years, and when I finally did the world was still spinning on its axis.

But the letter on top of the newest mail I added to the pile bore a name I was so familiar with it that it didn't seem a surprise to hear from him. I'd never met or spoken to Mike

Longman, but his byline was on all the articles in the *New Caxton Standard.* He'd covered the Montevallo murders and the trial of Eddie Baines.

I had intended to contact Longman myself when the time arrived to gain a fresh perspective on things. His name was pretty far down my checklist – below Dan Gorman, Eddie's public defender, and Gretchen Loeb, the prosecutor, below the police officers, the witnesses, et al. His letter came on the stationery of the *Providence Journal-Bulletin.* He'd moved on from the *New Caxton Standard,* but obviously he still had connections in town or he wouldn't have known about me.

His letter began, *I understand you're doing a book.*

He wanted to speak with me. He asked me to call him. I went to the phone right then. He was at his desk. We chatted a bit, and then he told me he had some information that might be useful to me. I'd assumed he would, he'd been in on everything. Then he asked whether I'd been ordered to give a command performance by Charles Hall yet.

'That's the congressman's brother?'

'Sure is.'

'No, I haven't heard from him.'

I didn't ask him what he meant by 'command performance.' I just waited. Nick has taught me the value of creating the discomforting pause.

Finally, he said, 'Maybe you'd like to know what's in store for you when you're summoned.'

'I would.'

'The relationship between Owen and his brother is more paternal than fraternal. Charles is fifteen years older than Owen. Owen was one of those menopause babies. Charles Hall knows things about the murders that Owen doesn't.'

'I'm listening.'

'And I'm talking. But not on the phone.'

'What's your schedule like?'

'You name the time. You're the famous writer.'

Mike Longman was a bit jealous.

I told him to choose a restaurant and I'd be in Providence for lunch the next day. I enjoyed his surprise. He said, 'You'll fly up here tomorrow?'

'Of course.'

He wanted famous, he'd get famous.

He was, naturally, young. I'd met so many like him, getting their start on a regional weekly like the *Bridgefield Press*, moving on to a small-town daily and then, hopefully, to a city newspaper. Mike Longman had made his two steps past the weekly – first the *New Caxton Standard* and now the Providence paper. Ambitious and optimistic. Maybe he'd go even farther. I had once lumped Sam Litton in with that group, except Sam hadn't wanted a journalist's career. He just wanted a cover. He'd been bright, eager, and determined. So much so that he was quite brilliant at the persona he created for the time he spent in each geographical area of the country. He was a charlatan for all seasons, making me believe it was actually possible for a person to pretend to be a doctor, perform surgery successfully, and have patients insist on remaining his patients even after it's revealed that the good doctor never got through eighth grade.

The restaurant Mike Longman chose was in Little Italy, just a short walk from his newspaper. I got there first and waited inside the door so I could guess which man coming in was the reporter. I guessed right. He was unassuming but walked with the kind of confidence that accompanies determination. He had on a red sweater with a layer of pills built up at the elbows. A cheap sweater, but it was red. He had something to say.

The maître d' said, 'The table you requested is ready for

you, Mr Longman.' He'd reserved a table next to a wall with a built-in bookcase. When we were seated, he said, 'There was a big hit in this restaurant, bullets flying all over the place. Took a lot of plastering and paint to cover the holes. But look at this.' He pulled a book out of the bookcase and handed it to me: *Jane Eyre*. There was a bullet hole straight through it, in the front cover and out the back.

'I can't believe it.'

He took the book from me, put it back, and pulled out another. He handed it to me also: *Valley of the Dolls*. I said, 'Somebody around here has rather eclectic taste.'

Just like *Jane Eyre*, there was a bullet hole in the cover. I turned it over. No exit hole.

He said, 'Bullet's still in there.'

I opened the book a crack. The metal glinted in the light of the lamp hanging above the table. I looked up at Mike Longman, my jaw probably touching my collarbone. He had an ear-to-ear grin across his face.

'Don't tell.'

'My God.' I handed it to him. 'How did you know?'

'Took a guess based on what I'd seen just after it happened. We heard the shots over at the office and I run fastest of all the staff, so I got the story. I'm waiting for the right moment to say there's still a bullet in a book on the shelf.'

He was cute. 'Who exactly got shot?' I asked him.

'The mob shot one of its own.'

'So is the food good?'

He laughed. 'Of course. The mob knows how to eat.'

So did he. And drink. He told me he ordered food based on the wine he liked. Today, Montepulciano. He ordered a veal specialty with pasta on the side. I got pasta too, but with a made-on-the-premises sausage that Mike recommended and said he'd eat if I didn't like it. The name sounded like koota-ging. The taste was spicy and strong, the texture heavenly because it was full of large chunks of creamy fat. Up crept an urge to grab my notebook, head for the kitchen, and ask the sausage maker how the fat could have the consistency of butter – what animal it came from. The wine was outstanding. I would have to recommend it to Louis.

I said to Mike Longman, 'I've read your articles on the murders. I haven't gotten to the trial pieces yet.'

'Colorless, weren't they? I mean, aside from the topic.'

'Shouldn't they be? I mean, in news reporting—'

'No. They should have style. Mine.'

'That'll come.'

His head tilts. There's a little frown.

'Sorry.'

'That's okay. You're entitled to be condescending. I intend to be condescending myself someday.'

'I said I was sorry.'

'Okay. So am I. Anyway, my style was there. But at the newspaper in New Caxton, my style was quashed, along with a lot of facts. They'd keep reminding me that I wasn't an investigative reporter. Everything I wrote was pared to the bare bones.'

'I'm surprised. Usually those small-town editors want the articles to reflect the writer's wits.'

'Not when it came to *that* crime. The editor's goal was to make the murders mundane. The word everywhere was "low key." The person who engineered that town did not want things sensationalized, or the outside world would come prying. I can't tell you how many times I was told that I shouldn't be arousing curiosity. "The town has suffered enough without attracting outsiders" was what they kept giving me. The trial was to start on a Tuesday, I forget the phony reason they gave for skipping Monday. Then, at the last minute, they changed it back to Monday. Turns out that the one reporter beside me, a guy from my paper – I mean my paper now – missed that day. So he didn't know what the hell was going on, couldn't quite catch up with things, and the *Journal* ended up giving the trial short shrift.' He speared a piece of veal.

'Who was this orchestrater? This *engineer*, I think is what you called him.'

'Charles Hall. He orchestrates everything in that town. He has a sustaining goal: to protect his brother.'

'From what?'

'From losing his congressional seat. A security blanket for Charles.'

'To comfort him about what?'

'His fear of being found out.'

'What's he up to?'

'He's involved in illegal activities. I'm not saying what they are. I have no proof yet. But I'm getting closer.'

'But what would Charles do if the people decided they didn't want Owen in office anymore?'

'Won't happen. He'll see to it that they'll never want any such thing. Without Charles Hall, there *is* no New Caxton. He owns it. So he has to assure them that Owen is entitled to his foibles. Sort of like the Prince of Wales. I'm talking about Victoria's son here, not the reigning Elizabeth's. Owen had an affair with Brenda Montevallo awhile back. It really wouldn't have looked very good if—'

'What?'

'*What* what?'

'Nothing.' I grabbed my glass of water and took a long drink.

'You didn't find that out yet? About Owen and Brenda?'

I shoveled a forkful of pasta into my mouth, which gave me a chance to look down and shake my head, no. I looked back up, somehow chewed and swallowed, and asked, 'How did you know about that? I mean, not being an insider.'

'I dated a town daughter. Till her father told me to take a hike. See, although Owen loves 'em and leaves 'em, he sees that they're pacified when he moves on. Brenda was paid off. Kept her in drug money. Connie went to Charles. Help my daughter. She asked, he granted. Kind of medieval – the peons come and ask favors. Those subjects deemed worthy have their wishes granted. Connie hadn't a clue that his benevolence had to do with keeping Brenda under wraps. Charles got Brenda fixed up somewhere – job, place to live, whatever. And he protected her from the investigation into the death of her family. Right after the funeral, she was gone.'

I took another long sip of water. Maybe I was trying to drown myself. 'Why would she have been investigated?' If Louis could hear me, he'd say, I thought you were the one who always suspected the mother.

'Because she was a drug addict. She'd been away for all those years. No one knew where. I think she came home to hide. Maybe she had an abusive sugar daddy out there and decided the sporting life wasn't worth it. Or maybe the sugar daddy was a pimp. I don't know. But my feeling was that she was in New Caxton because she knew she'd be protected no matter how much she hated it there. An umbrella of safety, sort of. But the umbrella had holes in it, didn't it? There was someone out there even bigger than King Charles.'

'What exactly are you saying?'

'I think the murder of Brenda's family was a hit. Whoever did it, did it to warn Brenda to get her tail back into line. It threw a real scare into Charles. If he wanted to remain head of his little fiefdom, he had to protect Brenda.'

I put my glass of water down onto the edge of my spoon, and it fell over.

The waiter helped mop up. Mopping up allowed me to

regain my bearings. 'Mike, this is a fantasy, isn't it? You're talking in terms of *fiefdoms*. You want to write a book too, right? You're upset that I beat you to the punch.'

'Previous apologies not withstanding, condescension is apparently difficult to suppress.'

He was grinning when he said that, teasing me, not angry. I wondered if the guy ever got angry. 'I'm going to try to fix that particular flaw, I promise.'

'A deal. And believe me, I'm going to write a book, all right. But not your book. A book about the Halls. One that will take Charles down like a house of cards and the entire goddamn town of New Caxton with him. Charles is up to no good. He's doing things that would put him in deep shit if he were ever found out. And I won't just take him down, I'll take his phony-ass brother too.' He could get angry.

'You a Republican?'

'Yes, but that's—'

'I'm joking. See, Mike, I'm having a little trouble taking this all in. There hasn't been a hint anywhere that—'

'You won't find any hints, for sure. But here it is in a nutshell. Eddie Baines got set up. Owen supported his brother in that particular endeavor. Charles's reasons had to do with protecting Brenda, and he got Owen to believe he was protecting the town. Owen, like everyone else, never thought Eddie would end up paying for a crime he didn't commit. Owen maybe turns out to have some kind of conscience hidden under his massive ego, but I doubt it. More likely there's something else going on I haven't doped out yet. Something Owen found out that he wasn't supposed to find out. Something that pissed him off. So my feeling is that he asked you to look into the murders because he couldn't risk his brother's wrath if he did it himself. Did he approach you about this story?'

I felt myself flush up to my hairline.

He said, 'That's Rosie's theory, actually. Rosie-Osie. You've met her. You've been hanging out at her library.'

'You two are friends, I take it?'

'The only one I had down there, not counting my short-term relationship with the town daughter. She says Owen doesn't know how to be honest because he's never really aware of what the hell's going on. He never knows exactly what the truth is. But he knew about Eddie getting set up. So suddenly, maybe, he's got a conscience and keeping quiet while some innocent guy is sent to prison for life just to make his brother happy finally got to him.'

'Hold on. Are you saying that Owen knew Eddie was innocent *before* he was sentenced?'

'That's what I'm saying. So now he wants somehow to right things for Eddie, but at the same time he wants to keep his distance. That's where you came in, and now that that's out in the open, brother Charles will come courting, you can bet on it.'

Mike didn't know that Owen had done a 180-degree. That I'd been called off. But I wasn't about to tell him that, nor that I wasn't about to let Owen pull any more of my strings. Let him find it out for himself, and then I'd ask him *where* he found it out.

Mike leaned back. His plate was clean. I reached over and took it. I exchanged it with mine. I'd eaten one bite of pasta and two of koota-ging. Mike Longman dug in.

I said, 'You talk and eat at the same time quite well.'

'Yeah, I do.'

'Owen didn't exactly approach me. We happened to be invited to the same party. Everyone I meet at parties tells me about a murder or two.'

He eyed me. I believe he was about to contradict me, but instead he said, 'I don't even care about that. All I care about is the fact that Owen is crazed. The Congressman has struck out on his own. Through you. I only wish I knew what little tidbit came to him, and who saw that it reached him. But that's not what I'm about. That's what you're about, and I wanted to give you that lead. And I wanted to warn you of something.'

'I'm listening.'

'Owen will drop you like a hot potato when he's finished using you.'

'Well, screw you, Mr Longman.'

One eyebrow went up. 'Sorry. God. Condescension is contagious.'

'I think we're talking jealousy here.'

'You know, we are. I'm jealous that you're on the inside. At the same time, you must have done the work to get there. Someone like you knows what she's getting into.'

'Who is *someone like me*?'

'Someone who has the power.'

Powerful but a fool. 'Owen has finished using me. Now I'll be using him.'

He shrugged. 'Well, good for you, but I told you, I don't care about any of that.'

'What do you care about?'

'The story I'm going to break. I'm going to time it for when your book comes out.'

I laughed. 'I gather you're not going to tell me the gist of this exposé.'

'That's right. But I'll tell you about the capture of Eddie Baines, how's that?'

'The capture? What *capture*?'

'There wasn't a shootout, if that's the image I just gave you, but there was a capture. All you'll find in the paper, though, is that he was arrested: time, place, date, but not the circumstances. Some of it came out in the trial. Not all – just what the doctor said, the one who demanded to be allowed to testify.'

'The doctor.'

'Yeah. From the emergency room in Providence where they took Eddie. The surgeon who witnessed the arrest and who Charles Hall didn't dare shut up.'

I picked a piece of bread out of the basket, smeared it with butter, and ate it. The circumstances of a murderer's capture and arrest are normally the quietest part of the unfolding chain of events that begins with a crime and ends with either acquittal or punishment. In the case of Sam Litton, two Florida homicide detectives accompanied by the cop from Oregon – invited along as a professional courtesy – walked into the newspaper offices where Sam had risen to the position of managing editor, told him he was under arrest for the murders of the three sorority girls, handcuffed him, read him his rights, and led him away. His coworkers thought he'd staged a joke. They applauded the performers as the group made its exit, Sam waving and smiling over his shoulder.

There really are no 'captures' of the sort we expect, based on our exposure to the melodrama of the movies and television. A suspect usually isn't hiding in a closet ready to leap out with guns blazing. The mom who shot her kids was arrested in a surviving child's hospital room during her daily visit.

Police forces simply determine when they have accumulated enough evidence to authorize an arrest, get a warrant, and then go to wherever the suspect tends to be at that time of day. Usually at work. My Tylenol poisoner was home watching TV. She complained incessantly thereafter that she didn't get to see the rest of Sally Jessy.

But *capture* was the appropriate word in the case of Eddie Baines. Mike Longman described the circumstances while he ate my meal.

'Eddie Baines's arrest was the result of a bizarre episode at a time when he was seriously injured. He was arrested because of the words he blurted out to a police officer, not because of the hair in the watch. They hadn't even discovered that yet. His words were interpreted in such a way as to incriminate him.'

'What words?'

'I'm about to tell you that.'

'Interpreted by whom?'

'By the cop who heard them, according to the report he wrote. Eddie Baines hadn't been a suspect in the Montevallo murders anymore than anyone else in New Caxton had been suspects. A pair of Providence cops accidentally stumbled into arresting him.'

Mike Longman was a taskmaster at chewing, waving his fork, and talking. As spellbinding as Rosie Owzciak, but with a different style, the style that didn't come out in the *New Caxton Standard*. Now he aimed his fork into my face.

'Exactly ten days after the murder, the Providence police, at eleven p.m., get this call from some hysterical woman who says she'd been kidnapped at gunpoint, but was able to escape. Within a couple of minutes, a police cruiser pulls up to the sidewalk, where she's standing huddled in a public phone booth. The woman says that she and a girlfriend were in a bar where they were threatened by a gunman and forced to go outside and get into the friend's car. He ordered them to drive all over the city, which they did for a good hour. The woman says eventually she was able to leap out of the car but so did the kidnapper, intent, she said, on killing her. The cop asks her where the girlfriend is and she says her friend took off in the car, deserted her. But a passerby came along – a passerby long gone by this point – and scared off the kidnapper, who'd run into a nearby house. The woman points to a house across the street. She tells the cop that the man's in there.

'The officer calls for help and a backup cop arrives on the scene with a dog. The dog's turned loose into the house, which was empty, the owners not home, the front door unlocked, and when the cop – the handler – joins up with his canine partner, the dog is in the pantry, his jaws clamped shut around the ankle of Eddie Baines, who happens to be slumped in a corner conscious but covered with blood. There's a butcher knife sticking out of his chest.

'So the officer asks Eddie to identify himself and to give his residence, which he does, and he recognizes Eddie's name. He knows the story of the dissolution of the most promising athlete ever to come out of Rhode Island. But he also recognizes the street address as the same as the site of the Montevallo murders. First the officer says, "Mr Baines, you're dying." Then he asks, "Mr Baines, did you kill those three people in New Caxton on Winchester Street?" So Eddie, grievously wounded, in huge pain, and drunk besides, says, "I did it." The cop whips out his notebook and writes the words "Dying declaration." Well, at the time he probably wrote—'

'Deathbed confession.'

'Something like that. Spiffed it up for the record. There were no witnesses to this scene. The original cop was back outside with the woman in the street.'

Mike took a long drink of water, then a sip of wine. I picked up the last piece of bread. Now I was starving. He never noticed me signaling to the waiter, pointing to the empty bread basket and the empty wine bottle.

'At the trial, the public defender said Eddie Baines claimed never to have heard the officer's question. He claimed he did hear the cop tell him he was dying, but then the officer asked him something else but he couldn't understand the question. He said he didn't want the officer to think his girlfriend stabbed him so when he said *I did it*, he was saying that he had stabbed *himself*.'

'Wait a minute. Why would the cop think his girlfriend had stabbed him?'

'The woman out on the street was none other than Patty Olschefski.'

'Who?'

'His girlfriend.'

'You're kidding.'

'Nope.'

'You know, I don't think I've ever heard her name before.'

'Her name wasn't printed in the paper, my editor saw to that, and besides, she was one of those people you find in any town. She goes through her life stepping in potholes. Digs the potholes herself before she falls into them. Can't get anything right. So people keep their distance so they don't go down with her. Patty hooked up with Eddie because there was no one else to hook up with.

'That night, she'd managed to escape her parents' guard and sneak out of the house, knowing instinctively that she'd really be in deep shit if she went near Eddie. So she and a woman she worked with – she was a waitress – went bar-hopping in Providence. Trouble is, Eddie knew her haunts. He found her and got to her. There was no gun. She'd made that up to be sure to get a cop to come. Something to tell her family, too: *He forced me to go with him*. And beside that, she'd be fulfilling her earlier assignment.'

'What's that?'

'Get him arrested.'

'You believe that?'

'Yes.'

'So what happened to Eddie?'

'For starters, he was never read his rights. No Miranda for

Eddie. The cop said he didn't read Eddie his rights because he wasn't arresting him and – let's see, how did he put it? – *I considered him to be in the last moments of his life.* Memorized that line at a later date, I'd say, to produce at the trial. This cop would have said, "I was sure he'd bought it."

'So then another cop arrives – a bigger cheese – along with an ambulance, and this guy starts questioning Eddie. Still Eddie isn't read his rights. But they get him into the ambulance and, halfway to the hospital, according to the cops, Eddie realizes he's not dying and recants. Says later that the "confession" the cops kept referring to was something they made up. Before he slipped into unconsciousness, he realized the cops were accusing him of killing the Montevallos. And all he could say was, *Ask Patty*. Patty would tell them he didn't do it. Ask Patty meant she could give him an alibi; they'd been together the night the Montevallos were murdered, doing their usual thing, hanging out, and others had been with them. The cops said he was attempting to incriminate her. That she was his accomplice.'

The young reporter sat back in his chair. He was finished eating. We ordered some coffee. I got a piece of an Italian rendition of cheesecake. I said, 'So how could there have been a trial with no Miranda?'

'Oh, they fit it in just before Eddie was wheeled into the OR. Reading him his rights put off his treatment for several minutes, which really pissed off the surgeon. He kept telling the cops that he couldn't save the injured man's life if they kept on. But the police continued to question Eddie until they arrested him just before the nurses closed the operating room doors in their faces.

'They filed their report several days later. Said Eddie told them he and Patty were sitting in the cemetery across Forster Street from the Montevallos' house on the night of Friday, August fifth, snorting cocaine. They usually went there to have sex. *Supposedly* that's what Eddie told them. And he also told them – supposedly – that Patty had never done drugs before, but allowed him to inject her with cocaine. "Inject her with cocaine" was a phrase right from the report.

'The report segued from *snort* to *inject* in one paragraph. Within a few minutes, she went crazy, ran across the street into the Montevallos' house and began stabbing Connie, Petey, and the little boy. According to the cops, Eddie said he couldn't stop her. The next night, since no one had discovered the bodies, they both went back to clean off any fingerprints they might have left. While they were cleaning up the crime scene, they were interrupted by Brenda's boyfriend knocking on the door and took off as soon as he'd driven away. So the officer's report said that both had taken part in the murders, but that Eddie was attempting to pin the blame on Patty.

'But the doctor wrote a report too, which was not allowed into evidence at Eddie's trial; please don't ask me why because I don't know. Ask the judges. The doctor said he was never able to make out a single thing that Eddie was saying, to the police or to him. It was all babble. He said that when Eddie plunged the knife into his chest, he meant business. The thrust broke his sternum. We have sternums to hold our rib cages together and to protect our hearts. It protected Eddie's heart, all right, but according to the doctor, a broken sternum is one of the most painful injuries there is. The patient, the doctor insisted, was never coherent until forty-eight hours after surgery, when he finally spoke with his mother. With the police present. Ask me if there was a lawyer present.'

'I take it there wasn't.'

'That's right. With just his mother there, he told the police he was in the Montevallo house the night *after* the slayings, and he was there to clean up because Patty told him someone had planted evidence against them. Obviously, she convinced him of it. But he insisted they'd never killed anybody. So now the police reported that, after surgery, Eddie kept changing his story in an attempt to show he was innocent. He—'

I interrupted. 'Not an uncommon thing for a killer to do.'

'Yeah. But Eddie was adding details, not changing his story. But so what. Fifteen years after the death of his father, a death he never got past, Eddie Baines was indicted for the stabbing deaths of his neighbors: his father's friend's widow, their son, and their grandchild. The main evidence against him was his "dying declaration." Then there was this bloody footprint—'

'On the wall.'

'Strange, right? I thought so too. But besides that, there was a watch with negroid hairs in it, which, by the way, got lost. The hairs, not the watch. On the way to the lab. To be tested for DNA. So yes, there were negroid hairs, but not necessarily Eddie's. And then, at the trial, things got really screwed up about this watch. The prosecutor was told it was Eddie's watch, only it wasn't, it was Petey's. I'm convinced Patty took it off Petey's wrist and stuck the hairs in the band. She was supposed to make it look as though Eddie had stolen Petey's watch, got his own hair into the band. Maybe she was supposed to drop it somewhere. The cemetery probably. She screwed up there; she lost it. In the kitchen. The police found it next to Connie's body. So at the trial, the argument went on and on about whose watch it was—'

'Wait a minute. Why do you think that about Patty? I mean, it's really incredible that she could have been—'

'I'll tell you, when she walked to that stand her knees kept buckling. She was a wreck and she was on some kind of tranquilizer. I just had this instinct that she was given the job to set up Eddie. A job she did pretty well, considering. The prosecutor, though, nearly blew it when she assumed, or was misinformed, that the watch was Eddie's. Or maybe it was mislabeled. An official screwup even worse than Patty's.'

'I still don't get it. Why would Patty want to set up her boyfriend?'

'She didn't *want* to. She was ordered to. She had no choice. The threats overwhelmed her. She was told there was evidence planted against both of them. She had to get rid of whatever they told her was there – her fingerprints, I'd bet – and make sure it looked like Eddie did it, or else.'

'Or else what?'

'Who knows? I'd ask her if I could find her. No one'll find her. This entire thing was carefully constructed by someone who knew exactly what to do.

'There were two other pieces of evidence. A cereal bowl was found in the cemetery. It matched Connie's dishes. Patty told the police she didn't know where it came from. Said Eddie found it there one night and used it to hold his cocaine.'

'She took it from the house and then had the wherewithal to get it to that cemetery?'

'She had no wherewithal. Someone else planted it there. Took it from Connie's house and put it there. Took it, I think, during that first robbery and then told Patty what to say.'

'The first robbery was part of all this?'

'That's my guess. And then there was a shirt found in the cemetery. Supposedly Eddie's. It had a few spots of Eddie's blood on it. But it wasn't his shirt.'

'How'd his blood get on it?'

'Your job.'

'What did Patty say about the bowl at the trial? About the watch?'

'Say to who? She was never arrested. No evidence placing her at the scene of the crime was ever found. The bargain with her had been made and carried out. It was only Eddie's word.'

'What about at the trial? When she was called?'

'I'll tell you, I couldn't wait till the trial, when she'd be asked why Eddie Baines kept his cocaine in a cereal bowl and not a closed container. Or a plastic Baggie would be nice. But she didn't have to answer those questions. Prosecution called her and asked one question: Did you witness the killing of Connie Montevallo, Peter Montevallo, Jr., and Timothy Montevallo? She took the fifth. Man, if ever a witness could have incriminated herself, it would have been Patty Olschefski. Defense didn't call her at all – too risky. She could well incriminate Eddie further. She was whisked in and out of the courtroom in less than two minutes, wobbly knees and all. But there isn't a single member of the State Police investigation unit or the New Caxton Police Department who doesn't believe that Patty was in the Montevallo house either during the crime or afterward.'

Outside the restaurant, I offered Mike Longman a ride to his paper.

'Nah, it's around the corner.' Then he said, 'Don't use the bullet in *Valley of the Dolls*, okay?'

'It's all yours.'

He gave me a peck on the cheek and bounded off, turned once, and waved. I waved back. Kind of guy I hoped my daughter would marry.

17

I went home and spent the following days strolling with Buddy amid the joggers and in-line skaters and bikers along the cobblestone streets by the Potomac, trying to weave the fact that Owen and Brenda had been lovers into all I'd come to know. The web I wove in my head did not have the pure symmetrical lines of a real web. My book would, though.

One afternoon, Poppy was able to meet me for espresso. She'd been away for months, in New York, working on a case for the archdiocese there. 'Someone's been helping themselves to the collection plate,' she said. 'Major pilfering going on. Many millions missing. That's also known as grand larceny. Plus it's an obvious inside job, so call in the FBI. The cardinal is ready to kill and he's treating me like I'm a slave. Can't understand that I have to sleep at night.'

The little bookstore and coffee bar on the waterside in Alexandria never objected to Buddy lying down for a rest just inside their door, pretending to guard it while I browsed or sipped coffee, so I brought him along. When Poppy walked in, the first thing she said was, 'Is *he* here?'

For a moment, I thought she meant Owen. That she knew. But then she pointed at Buddy.

'Love me, love my dog.'

'Listen, Denise,' she said as she sat, 'the sound of a dog

licking his balls may not be a nuisance, but it distracts from my enjoyment of life.'

'He's not licking his balls, he's chewing a piece of rawhide.'

'But then he'll remember he could be licking his balls instead. And he will.'

'He actually makes less noise doing that than when he's chewing his rawhide.'

'Forget it. I'll slurp my coffee real loud. So what's up?'

The conference we were about to have would normally happen between Louis and me, but I needed to talk about more than story direction. I needed to confide. 'Poppy, I've got this murder.'

I told her about the crime. I told her I'd met Owen Hall at a party and he'd put me on to it, but I didn't tell her I'd been sleeping with him. I kept talking so she couldn't mention how gorgeous Owen was. I told her about my lunch with the reporter who'd covered the Montevallo murders for the New Caxton paper, but I didn't tell her about the bullet-in-the-book part, either. She wouldn't be able to keep her hands off that. When I finished, she said, 'He was cute, right?'

'Who?'

'This Longman fellow, who else?'

I said, 'He was young.'

'Dear Denise,' she said. 'Obviously, I'd gathered that or I wouldn't have asked if he was cute. I'd have asked if he were provocative.'

'Actually, he was kind of cute and very provocative.'

'Well?'

'Well?'

'Did he make a move?'

'No.'

'Oh, of course he did.'

'Poppy, whether or not I recognize moves, I told you – he's *young*.'

'And?'

'My God. I'm just not interested.'

'Why not?'

I sighed. 'Poppy, we have different theories of sexual attraction.'

'You don't know what you're missing.'

'Yes, I do. I slept with young men when I was young.'

'But now you'd get to *lead*.'

'Poppy, I invited you here because I need to confide. I have to tell you what Mike Longman told me, and then I have to tell you about Rosie, this librarian who's been helping me. Now are we going to talk or shit around?'

'Sorry. Shoot.'

And so I filled her in on all that Mike had revealed to me. She asked me where he got his information. I told her that reporters didn't divulge their sources and then I didn't let her interrupt until I got to the part about Mike telling me that Owen was using me. I couldn't prevent her from interrupting then.

'What do you mean, using you?'

'Poppy, Owen Hall planned to be at the party in New York. He intended to hook me on this crime. Con me, sort of, because the guy in jail was falsely accused, and Owen – at the time – didn't want to get involved. I mean—'

'Whoa. Does this Longman character think Owen Hall's a hypnotist? Did you tell him he was full of shit?'

'It's true.'

'Of course it isn't true. How could you believe such a thing? Are you sure you didn't sleep with this guy?'

'Poppy, Owen admitted it.'

'Owen Hall admitted such a thing to a *reporter*?'

'No. To me. And it went beyond using me. He set me up.'

'Owen Hall has actually *told* you—'

There was no holding off. 'I've been sleeping with Owen for three months.'

When Poppy's blue eyes widen, they widen. 'Oh my God. Are you crazy?'

'Yes.'

'But . . . Oh my God.'

'I'm telling you this because it's over. It was over for me when he admitted what Mike Longman only guessed at – what I was too gaga to see. But Owen doesn't know it's over. And I wish it weren't, I'll tell you that. God did I fall in love with him. But I'm not a fool. I'll get over him, the son of a bitch.'

'I need another coffee.' She called the waiter. Buddy came over. 'Not you, for Christ's sake. Go back to your door.'

Buddy plopped down next to her chair.

'This dog smells.'

'No he doesn't.'

'All dogs smell, face it. Denise?'

'Yeah?'

'What in hell does Owen want from you?'

'I don't know. But I need to tell you the rest of what Mike Longman told me, and then maybe we can put two and two together.'

'And I wonder what makes me think it won't add up to four.'

'Just listen to me.' I told her the rest.

'Now let me get a hold on this. Longman thinks there's a connection between Charles Hall and his nefarious activities – whatever they might be – and the Montevallo murders?'

'Yes.'

'But he doesn't know what it is?'

'That's right.'

'So his book is actually an investigation?'

'Books *are* investigations.'

'Denise?'

'Yeah?'

'You want me to check out Owen's brother?'

'Yes.'

She drained her second cup of coffee. 'You know, when you've got a brother who's a congressman you are depending on as a safety net . . . well, there's not going to be anything to find unless this Charles is really stupid. And he couldn't possibly be really stupid or he'd have been caught already at whatever it is he's supposed to be doing.'

'But Longman thinks—'

'Longman is young, remember?'

'Well, the librarian I told you about who gave me all the crime stuff. She's not young. I'm going to ask her about it.'

'Ruby somebody?'

'Rosie.'

'You'll ask Rosie if her congressman is in cahoots with his brother to go around framing a guy for murder?'

'Don't get testy. I'm not saying any such thing and you know it. But she trusts me. The trouble is, Rosie assumes I'm having an affair with Owen. I don't know how that's affecting her.'

'Be truthful. Tell her you're not. And you're not since it's over, remember?'

'I guess.'

'How's about we back up? So how come it's over? Wasn't he any good?' She was leaning over the table toward me.

'Get your rocks off on your own, best friend.'

This tremendous hurt came over her face. And then she smirked. And then she banged the table and laughed. And then, 'Can you at least tell me why? Why'd you do it?'

'He's comforting.'

'Ah-hah! Something Mom never was. And certainly not a virtue Mr Academe-turned-politico has ever demonstrated.'

'Poppy, whatever works. Gloria Steinem said—'

'You've already told me all the things Gloria Steinem ever said. But there's a course that Owen no doubt passed with flying colors that Gloria never took, since only men sign up.'

'And that is?'

'Ingratiating Behavior One-oh-one. Pass it, and you've learned there's a lot more to winning a girl's heart than candy and flowers.'

I thought about the hot water bottle. 'Poppy, you don't trust that someone just wants to be nice?'

'Nice? What the hell is that? The key is, did you get to lead, Denise?'

'No. But I was happy.'

'Not surprised. Every call girl worth her salt knows that men in power need a break and like to be led in the bedroom. That's why Dick Morris got off on getting down on all fours with a dog leash around his neck. So with Owen, you were the real thing or he'd have said, Okay, honey, make me happy. Put a bowl of kibble on the floor and kick me while I'm eating it. Instead, he fell in love with you, just the way you did with him. Now he's kicking himself. Hah!'

More Poppy-style words of comfort.

The next day I went back to New Caxton to face a foot of snow on the ground. Rhode Island had had a good blizzard, with a freak thaw following immediately on its heels. The temperature wasn't cold enough to sustain the snow, so it was wet and sticky and there were puddles forming everywhere. The temperature inside the New Caxton library was just a little bit warmer than outside, maybe forty-five degrees tops, I guessed. As soon as Rosie came out of the back room in her three layers – turtleneck, pullover, and a big cardigan over all – I was pretty sure I wouldn't be able to do what I'd come to do. My fingers would fall off if I attempted to scroll fiche. Once, Nick said to me, 'May I ask why you don't hire staff to do that sort of thing for you?' I told him I'd think about it. After I'd thought, during which time he'd forgotten having asked the question, I told him that the reason I didn't hire people to research for me was because then I'd be able to work faster. He tried to focus but couldn't figure out what I was talking about. I said, 'Nick, if I work faster, I might miss something. I need to go slowly, and doing things like making copies slows me down.'

Then he remembered the conversation I was referring to. He said, 'Perhaps there are advantages to efficiency that you aren't considering.'

I said, 'When I'm slowed down, I have a time frame that is conducive to the thinking I have to do.'

'But the time you'd save by hiring a research assistant would give you a clear block of time to think in a more productive manner.'

I said, 'If I had a clear block of time, I'd use it to redecorate our ugly dining room.'

'It isn't ugly.'

'Yes it is. You refuse to notice things like that because it would cut into what *you* prefer to think about. It is my responsibility as the housewife to keep dining rooms in my head, dining rooms being a metaphor representing all the responsibilities of a housewife.'

Nick didn't respond. He has already told me it is impossible for him to understand what is outside his personal experience, and my dining room talk, he has made clear, is outside his frame of reference. So then I reminded him that whatever it was he was referring to as inefficiency had been working for me quite nicely. My daughter was eavesdropping at the time. She stuck her head in the living room doorway and said, 'Whatever floats your boat, Dad.' She has, appropriately, learned diplomacy in Washington. A few years earlier she'd have said to Dad, 'You're such a know-it-all-meister.'

Rosie was alone in the library. The furnace, she told me, kept shutting down. She'd sent Anthony and Marie home, and the relatives of her elderly clients had seen to it that they were picked up and taken somewhere warmer. I said, 'Then close the library till the heat works. We'll go get some hot chocolate or something. I only came to pick your brain anyway.'

She smiled. She said, 'I just want you to know I could have shut down if I chose to. But I had nothing better to do than putter around,' and she gestured back toward her workroom. 'Hot chocolate sounds wonderful.'

While she got her coat, I thought about what life would be like if I had nothing to do but be miserably cold while puttering around in one of the sorriest excuses for a public library that I'd ever dreamed could be possible. Why on earth did I feel an affinity toward someone who could lead that sort of non-life? But then again, whatever floats your boat.

We had our hot chocolate at a table in the back of Stoshu's, where Chick Montevallo and Big Jim Baines held forth at their Saturday morning breakfasts. I'd pictured a coffee shop with people sitting on a row of stools at a long counter, eating and reading the morning newspaper, a coffee shop full of cozy little tables with everyone gabbing away. Again, my mind-set was Bridgefield. But there was no counter at Stoshu's and only three tables. The place seemed to serve mainly as a news store and tobacco shop.

I watched a stream of old men coming in for cheap cigars, or tobacco for their pipes, and younger ones for packs of Marlboros. Young men in New Caxton still smoked and they still smoked Marlboros. All of them grabbed little items, too, like *TV Guide* or Life Savers. And every single one of them picked up a racing form and stood flipping through it. Before leaving, they'd pass little pieces of paper to the proprietor. The man had a pencil behind his ear, and he'd jot things down. Stoshu's was the local bookie joint; the proprietor was Rosie's uncle.

Rosie said, 'My father is Stoshu. But he was injured a few years ago. They had a propane explosion. Nothing's up to code in this town. The tank didn't have a proper valve.'

I wondered if Rosie's father had been a bookie too. 'Is he all right?'

'He is except for his leg. He's got a cane. He spends every minute of the day telling my mother what to do.'

'He doesn't do anything?'

'He does the books. For this place.'

'And you live with your parents?'

She laughed. I thought she was going to say, You must be kidding. But she said, 'Of course. In New Caxton it would be unnatural and suspect behavior for offspring who aren't married to live anywhere but with their parents.

'Well, I imagine your mother must need help. I mean, besides money, what with your dad—'

'My mother's beyond help.'

At the back of the shop, behind the three tables, was a curtain and Rosie had me sit down while she went through it into a little kitchen. There wasn't room for the two of us in the space between the stove and the refrigerator, so I stayed put. At lunchtime, she informed me, her aunt would be in there making sandwiches and soup for the customers. Rosie left the curtain open and I watched her pour milk into a pan and heap some spoonfuls of Nestlé's Quik into a couple of mugs. The uncle kept glancing at us.

She came and sat down while the milk heated. I said, 'I just can't understand how a jury could find Eddie Baines guilty with so little evidence and so much question as to the confession and all.' I was attempting to see if she'd take Owen's tack – that the police, the town, and the jury all took the notion of throwing a scare into Eddie a little too seriously, and suddenly a judge was sentencing him to life in prison.

She said, 'He didn't have a jury.'

'What?'

'Hold on a minute.' She got up and checked the milk.

I couldn't hold on. 'Did I hear you say he didn't have a trial?'

'Denise, is there a napkin holder on any of those tables?'

'No.'

Now I caught the uncle staring at us. I stared back and his eyes went down.

Rosie came out with napkins. 'He had a trial, all right. But he waived the right to a jury.'

I was confused. 'How do you waive the right to a jury and still have a trial?'

She looked a bit stern as she gazed down at me. 'I take it you've never covered a trial by a panel of judges.'

'A panel?'

'Yes, a panel. A bench trial.'

'Wait. I know what a bench trial is. But it's just one judge, isn't it?'

'Not in Rhode Island. In a case of this sort, three judges sit on the bench. Three criminal court justices. You can do that, you know, if circumstances warrant it.'

'Like what circumstances?'

'Eddie's public defender was convinced that if a jury saw the videotape of the crime scene, they'd have found anyone guilty just for the sake of their need to strike back. Also, professionals would understand that you can't convict someone when you have no evidence. Judges wouldn't be swayed by emotion. They know the law. When lawyers are convinced their man is innocent, convinced there is nothing to show that he's guilty, convinced that legal procedures carried out or not carried out could throw the case right out of court, they go to a trial by justices. Bad choice, it turned out.'

Every day I find out how little I know about anything. Poppy says that's why my books are a dream. They seem written by a common slob and every revelation holds stunning shock value since I am, personally, so easily shocked myself. *Stunning*, she had said, which got me past *common slob.* She also said, 'You know, Denise, I'll be reading along and I'll stop and think, *Holy cow!* Then I say to myself, What are you, stupid? You knew that! Denise old pal, you have a charmed perspective, both as a human being and as a writer.'

'What you're talking about is called my narrative point of view,' I'd said, trying to show her there were some things she didn't know.

She said, 'Whatever.'

Now, I looked up at Rosie and, though I tried to stop acting like a dolt, I asked her another dumb question. 'How does one go about waiving the right to a jury trial?'

'You don't. Your lawyer does. At the indictment, the public defender said that the details of the crime were gruesome, and that because the coroner had taken a ninety-minute video of the crime scene, a jury of Eddie's peers would become quickly biased . . . prejudiced . . . would want to find someone guilty. Anyone, whether he'd done it or not.'

'So then what happened?'

The milk boiled over. She dashed back to the stove and grabbed the pan off the burner. She poured the scalded milk into the mugs and stirred. Then she went to the refrigerator. She took out a can of Reddi Wip.

She came back with two clunky mugs, once white, now gray and pitted with age, steam escaping from around two large piles of whipped cream, and sat down. 'The state selected the panel, and three justices acted as judge and jury.'

'No judge presides?'

'One of the three presides.'

A book about a trial by legal professionals instead of one's peers. I was perking up. 'Isn't there a conflict of interest here?'

'Sure as hell is. They get to decide what can be allowed in as evidence and what can't. If you think of them as judges, that's not shocking. If you think of them as the jury—'

'This is amazing.'

'Am I going to get an acknowledgment here?'

'Sure.'

She smirked and shook her head.

'Now wait, Rosie. The very people trying the defendant can withhold evidence that might show he's innocent?'

'One would hope they wouldn't do that.' She stirred her cocoa, pushing the whipped cream below the surface with the back of her spoon. The blob slowly dissolved into tiny white bobbing balls. I sipped mine. Divine. 'But this panel of judges did. I watched it happen. The public defender seemed to be in a state of chronic shock. His name was Gorman. He explained to the panel right off the bat that his client was surely innocent as there was no weapon found, no witnesses had come forward except those who placed Eddie elsewhere during the crime, no fingerprints other than the Montevallos' on the scene. And, of course, Eddie hadn't been read his Miranda rights until after his questioning. He never had a chance to call a lawyer, either. Was never given the opportunity. Dan Gorman was really sure of himself on the first day. Then things began deteriorating right under his nose, and he was totally unable to stem the tide. He became – I don't know – impotent. He kept challenging and challenging, making one objection after the other, and the judges kept overruling them.'

'Which judge gets to overrule or sustain a motion?'

'Any of them.'

'Does it happen that one says sustained while another is saying overruled at the same time?'

'Not in this case. None of them ever sustained one single motion by the defense. Before you knew it, the whole thing was over. Four days.'

I was now slurping my cocoa. There was some special ingredient in there, not just Nestlé's.

'What's your hot chocolate secret, Rosie?'

'There was a Milky Way on the counter. I broke off a piece of it and put it into the pan of milk. Big piece. Half a bar.' She laughed. 'I have to have *some* excess in my life, Denise. Wait'll you spoon up the dregs.' Then she took off her glasses. They were steamed up. She had another sip of her drink. Her eyelashes lay against her cheeks. They were thick and long. She looked up at me; her myopic eyes were hazel, almond-shaped. Bedroom eyes.

'I suppose you know you've got Bette Davis eyes.'

'I didn't know.'

'Baloney. And you know you've chosen ugly glasses to hide them. Librarians don't do that anymore. Never did, as a matter of fact. Only happens in the movies. So what's the story?'

'How I look is my business, isn't it?' She put the glasses back on.

'Sorry.'

'Forget it. Want to get back to business?'

'I do.'

'Next question.'

'Okay, these judges. From what you're saying, the public defender assumed they had probably formed opinions before the trial started, based on professional knowledge. That there was no question but that they'd find Eddie innocent. The public defender – what was his name?'

'Dan Gorman.'

'Gorman figured they'd have to find Eddie innocent since they knew the rules. Makes sense. This is what they do for a living. Juries of plain folk don't know the rules or they forget them as soon as they're instructed. That was his thinking, right?'

'Exactly right. And another factor Gorman saw as an advantage for him is that the verdict in a bench trial doesn't have to be based on a unanimous ruling. So even if one judge got up on the wrong side of the bed, Eddie would still be found innocent. That surely backfired. What's the matter?'

'You're kidding.'

'About what?'

'They can send a man to the electric chair even if one of them says he isn't guilty?'

'In states that have electric chairs. We don't. But he probably wouldn't be sentenced to die anywhere under those circumstances. Mitigating circumstances. They can sentence him to life though. They did in this case. Even though one justice did vote for acquittal.'

'Which one?'

She smiled at me. 'Only their hairdressers know for sure.'

'Rosie, you're serious, aren't you? A man was sentenced to life imprisonment by a two-out-of-three vote?'

'I had a hard time believing such a thing, too. We all did. At first, everyone in town went around saying, *How can he go to jail? One of those guys says he didn't do it.* They wanted Eddie to be taught a thing or two, never actually convicted. Then, *He's going to jail? Well, at least this will be a lesson to these kids today.*

My father, actually, was the one who said that. Never mind that Eddie Baines was a grown man, thirty-six years old. Then, within a week, they all washed their hands of it; they knew their place. End of story. Poor Gorman. He'd never expected less than having all the charges dropped.'

'Do you think Eddie would have gotten the death penalty if there was one?'

'There was some movement in Providence during the trial to pass a death penalty bill. It faded away. In Connecticut and New Hampshire – those are the only New England states that have a death penalty – there'll never be an execution. There can be no mitigating factors at all. And there are always mitigating factors in a murder, right?'

'Almost always. My Tylenol poisoner didn't have any. I don't know if you read—'

'I read all your books. Yes, she did. She was fat and ugly. She didn't have a life.'

'She could have turned down a few plates of lasagna. Rosie, I appreciate your cynicism, believe me. But we're talking about Eddie.'

She sighed. 'We are. I'll never forget the day Eddie was convicted. One of the judges stood up and said, *By a vote of two to one, we find Edward Baines guilty of three counts of first-degree murder.* There was this horrible silence. Then Mrs Baines stood up and screamed, *No-o-o!* She dragged the word out forever, and as the sound slowed and became softer, she went down with it. She was on the floor and everyone was trying to help her. Eddie, too. They had to drag him away.

'People wept for Eddie's mother, but not for long. The tears stopped when they realized that the police weren't looking for the real killers. That Eddie was going to stay in jail. They started rationalizing. And pretty soon they didn't talk about killers, plural – *real* killers. They talked about *the* killer, singular. And finally, *the killer* became *Eddie Baines*.'

'Rosie?'

'What?'

'Were you at all the trial dates?'

'I was. The appeal too. Eddie lost again. I had about ten years of vacation time built up. I took some of it.'

'The appeal was based on . . .?'

'Judicial misconduct.'

'You're kidding.'

'No, I'm not. And rest assured Dan Gorman will never be more than a public defender, I'll tell you that.'

That morning, in the coffee shop/newsstand/bookie joint, in the equivalent of a schoolgirl's essay, 'What I Did on My Vacation,' I listened to two hours of Rosie describing the details of the trial while I made her backtrack over and over again to clarify Eddie Baines's destruction. And his mother's, as it turned out. She died three months after the failed appeal.

We started with motive. 'Robbery,' she said. 'Brenda was the one who told the police that her mother kept a few dollars from her cashed social security check in her cookie jar on the refrigerator. Money was gone. Police decided that Eddie had robbed the house first time around, too. Connie's most recent social security check had been deposited into her bank account. She'd taken only twenty-five dollars of it in cash. The money she kept in her house or in her wallet would not have amounted to more than that much. That's the most money women are allowed to carry on them in this town.' She laughed at what wasn't a joke. She told me, too, that Eddie had been paid his salary the day of the murders. He didn't have to steal what was less than twenty-five dollars from anyone.

I ate up the dregs at the bottom of my hot cocoa, the warm and sludgy Milky Way. I said, 'In New York, a black businessman was accused of killing a doctor he'd supposedly swindled. The doctor went to his house and demanded his money back. His body was found the next day in a ditch just down the road. Some philanthropic group hired William Kunstler, may he rest in peace, to represent the defendant. Eddie Baines was a star athlete. He worked hard to get an education. He was from a good family. How come no one sprung for *any* lawyer, let alone a good one? Like the Halls, for example.'

'Why don't you ask Owen why they didn't?'

'Because I'm asking you.'

She cupped her chin in her hand. 'Maybe the town would have felt betrayed. There's no interfering with the earth's movement here. Or maybe because the trial was put off for so long while Eddie healed from his knife wound, and then happened so fast – the days around Thanksgiving yet – that everything just got out of control. Like when you drop something and you're watching it fall to the floor and you know it's going to smash, but you can't do anything to stop it. It's hard to believe that about a murder trial, but that's how it was.'

'You know what I think?'

'No, I don't, to tell you the truth.'

'I think the town was glad to see Eddie punished, but not for the murders and certainly not to set an example for their children.'

'What then?'

'For being a black man.'

'No, that isn't so. The only thing we've got going for us in this town is that racism passed us by. We—'

'Nothing to do with racism. It was to do with resentment. Hurt pride.'

She squinted from behind her glasses and leaned toward me. 'I don't understand.'

'Eddie represented reason. The brand of reason the black people in this town demonstrated when they deserted a sinking ship. When they moved on to make their lives and their children's lives viable. If all the Polish Americans had left, the Italians and the black people would have felt the same toward them. Resentment.'

She did not protest.

'Rosie?'

'Yes?'

'What the fuck are you doing here?'

'Having a cup of hot chocolate.'

'C'mon.'

She looked into my eyes. 'I hate it here.'

'Yeah, well, no kidding. That's why I ask.'

'I'm enjoying hating things. And hating people, too. Granting forgiveness is supposed to free you. I haven't found that. Because no one around here is interested in repentance. They aren't entitled to forgiveness. When you're raised a Catholic, you're taught that your sins will not be forgiven unless you're sorry for having committed them. No one's sorry. I've found that letting myself hate everybody is liberating. It's wonderful.'

I said, 'I don't think the pope would understand that, but I certainly do.'

'Yeah. Seems funny to be understood, Denise. Do you want to hear the rest of what I saw? At the trial?'

'Yes.'

She finished her dregs. 'By then, Eddie understood that Patty Olschefski would not testify for him. There was talk of her turning state's evidence in exchange for a light sentence, but she was never arrested in the first place. Gorman didn't have her subpoenaed because he figured she might say something that could incriminate Eddie. He was right. Talk about an unreliable witness. Her head wasn't screwed on right, I'll tell you. She'd rebelled, and you don't do that in this town. Simple. Gorman knew Patty could get up on that stand and, without batting an eyelash, say she saw Eddie kill the Montevallos. Forget unreliable. She'd perjure herself in a minute. God only knows the threats she was under. Well, I know. House arrest in Poland. And that's what she got anyway.'

'She's really in Poland?'

'Yeah.'

'Where?'

'Who knows? Someone in Poland with the same last name as her great-grandfather probably handled it . . .

'So Gorman called all the people who saw Eddie the night of the murder: his mother, his sister, his friends. During cross-examination of the defense witnesses, the prosecutor kept saying to each of them, *But you were Eddie's friend, isn't that right?* The implication being that they'd testify for him no matter what. She treated them as if they were character witnesses, not people who swore they were with him, or talked to him, or saw him at different times during the evening that he was supposed to be murdering the Montevallos. And then Gorman got around to calling his actual character witnesses: more of Eddie's friends, his neighbors, his coworkers, his former teachers and teammates. None of them believed Eddie Baines capable of murder, not even if he were under the influence of drugs, and it was determined his was a five-dollar-a-day cocaine habit. A cigarette-after-dinner kind of habit. He was not known to use other drugs.

'The prosecutor kept trying to get one of those people to say what she wanted, that Eddie was a walking, ticking time bomb just waiting to go off. But all they said was that he was a quiet respectful fellow who minded his own business and had never exhibited any aggressive behavior in his entire life. I did too.'

'You took the stand?'

'Sure. I baby-sat for Eddie Baines, once upon a time. And his sister too.'

'How'd your testimony go?'

'It was simple. I just said he was always a nice kid. Took me one minute. Gorman saved his best witness for last: Eddie's football coach from high school. Coach took the job here in 1958. Before that he'd played pro ball for the Cleveland Browns. Had to stop when he was injured. He took the job at a starting salary three times what the high school principal made. The coach never even finished high school. No one thought of that as incongruous. Made perfect sense.

'He'd just retired that year . . . the year of the murders. He was around seventy and he wasn't well. He had Alzheimer's, the early stages. Now he's in some nursing home. He took the oath and he looked up at the judges and—'

Rosie stopped. She looked down and started biting on a hangnail.

'You okay?'

'Yeah.'

'What did he say?'

She sniffed before she finished. 'The coach was supposed to state his name. Instead he said, *"Once upon a time, Eddie Baines was a champion"*.'

She grabbed a napkin and held it to her lips to stop their trembling. She put it down.

Then she said, 'I'll tell you, Denise, there were a lot of people shuffling their feet while he was on the stand. No one could look him in the eye. The coach was a god, now wounded, and no one could go to his aid. Bring him food. Take him out walking . . . for a ride . . . whatever. The coach started rambling about how he should have encouraged Eddie to concentrate on basketball. Then Eddie would still be a champion today. He said Eddie wasn't mean enough to play football. Wasn't ruthless. Gorman didn't have to try hard to show the judges that Eddie wasn't a sociopath. Without any prompting they had this broken coach telling him how Eddie was so gentle he shouldn't have even been playing football. He went on and on about Eddie's last game, how he gave his heart for the school, for his father, for the town. Not for himself. Not for glory. He didn't care about glory. He was just a good kid.

'During the cross, the judges couldn't get him to answer the prosecutor's questions. He'd respond to them with whatever it was he was thinking about Eddie. She'd say, "How long did you actually know Mr Baines?" and he'd say, "Once I let him take my car – only player I ever let borrow my car." So finally the prosecutor cut to the quick. She reminded the coach that he hadn't had Eddie on his team for years and years. Gorman kept objecting, the judges kept saying, Overruled. I remember at that point, she looked over at Gorman and then she said to the coach, "You haven't had any contact with Eddie since he graduated from high school, have you?"

'Coach said, "Yes I did." She asked him when. He kind of fidgeted and she practically shouted, "When?" He answered, "When I did." She gave up. She told the judges that the coach's recollections of Eddie's character were no longer germane. That those recollections probably weren't accurate anyway, since he'd coached hundreds of New Caxton High athletes since.

'Then she walked from the witness stand, where she'd been right in his face, to the prosecution table. She walked very slowly, as if she were finished. Then she kind of whirled around and she really did raise her voice. From her table, she shouted at the coach, "*Do you remember who the President was that last year Mr Baines played football for you? The year he won your championship for you?*"'

Rosie leaned forward. 'Now get this, Denise. The old man

straightened up his spine and put his shoulders back. He was insulted at her shouting the question at him. He wasn't deaf, he was just forgetting how to go about hearing. He lifted his chin and his voice became deep and strong, the way it had been when he was coaching his team. He said, "*No I don't. But I remember who won the Heisman Trophy*.'"

18

On the plane back to DC, I updated the list of names I'd been building since I began probing the murders. It's part of my way of working, this list-making. Once, Nick and I were traveling together, and he watched me going through my list and asked me what I was doing. I told him. He didn't ask me about the list, where the names came from, who the people were, how a list helped me. He said, 'Why don't you have a laptop, Denise?'

I told him I'd tried that once.

'And?'

'And when I went to scan my list, I could only see a screen's worth of names. I need to see all the names at once. I need to be able to spread out my lists so I can get to look at the whole picture, so to speak.' I didn't get into crossed-off names with him. On the laptop, I had deleted names I thought I wouldn't need and then realized that crossed-off names triggered little details I might usefully stick into chapter seventeen.

He asked, 'Are all writers neurotic?'

I began to say something about Ernest Hemingway lining up pencils and needing a six-toed cat in his lap, but then I stopped dead. Instead, I turned to him. His eyes were riveted to his own laptop screen at the time.

'Nick?'

'Hmmm?'

'I do believe you just used the word *writer*. And I was in the group you were referring to.'

He turned to me. He smiled. He said, 'I'd never have thought such a thing was a possibility once upon a time. There was a part of you I knew nothing about, that you kept hidden, that I believe you weren't even aware of yourself. But I should have known you were meant to be someone of significance. After all, you're able to read three pages of lists at one glance. A computer screen isn't big enough for you. But I worry that—' He stopped.

'That what?'

'That *I'm* not big enough for you.'

I reached out and touched him. I said, 'Nick, when do you suppose we stopped telling each other things we worry about?'

'When we came to fear disdain.'

'I didn't know I was ever disdainful of you.'

'You were. And you are. But you do it to get even with me. Though I can't help my own disdain. It's like a nervous tic. And it doesn't mean anything. However, you're a very sensitive individual, and it's too bad you can reflect my character flaws back at me with such panache.'

'Nick?'

'What?'

'Did you ever consider attempting not to be disdainful toward me since I'm a sensitive individual?'

He thought. 'No.'

He went back to his laptop and I went back to my lists. I wondered, Just when was it that Nick and I stopped finishing conversations? Retreated from them with feelings of great relief to see them end?

On the cab ride to Alexandria, I drew a line through Eddie's mother and his high school football coach. I scanned back to the top of the list, headed by Owen's name. I crossed him off in my head.

Back at the bottom of the list, I added a new name: Charles Hall. Who, according to Mike Longman, would be calling me. If Mike was wrong, I'd be doing the calling.

Mike Longman was right. In my office, I played my machine. Charles Hall's voice was stronger than Owen's, more serious, more evenly paced. But in tone it was identical. The tone was charming coming from Owen, but from Charles it had the resonance of an especially colorless businessman delivering a lecture to his management team, a businessman obviously distracted by other things. He said, 'I understand you are planning a book about the murder of the Montevallo family.' He said *planning*, not *writing*, negating any possible existence of words already on paper. He said he would like to talk to me about the Montevallos, that he had knowledge of certain elements that might give me pause. He said, 'I do hope you'll see me. Please call, and my secretary will make arrangements.' Then he left his Boston office number. I dialed.

'A half hour should do it,' his secretary informed me. 'Monday or Tuesday, the week after next. He has twelve o'clock Monday, or twelve-thirty Tuesday.' I would be put into one of the blank spaces people leave to squeeze in the riffraff before dashing off to lunch. She added. 'Of course, Mr Hall will be paying your travel expenses.'

I said, 'I'll be in Boston next week, not the week after. I have some free time Friday at around one. And, of course, my publisher will pay my expenses.'

She coughed. 'I'm afraid that day would be unacceptable.'

So I told her, 'When you get back to Mr Hall, tell him that the only time I have available is Friday at one. Tell him I have *many* people to see. I'm sure he'll manage it.'

Another cough. 'Why don't you give me some future dates and I'll see what I can do for you?'

I said, 'I can never plan very far ahead. Just offer Charles that Friday, and perhaps he can cancel something. But get back to me soon. My schedule is filling fast.'

That's the way Nick talks to people. The way he talks works well because people are always in a rush to sneak out from under intimidation. The secretary called back an hour later. 'Would Friday at two be all right?'

Well, I wouldn't force him to cancel his lunch, but I'd make him rush through it.

He gestured toward a large leather wing chair. It was a chair he put people in who were under five feet ten, which, of course, included just about all women. Even I would have to sit forward or my feet wouldn't touch the floor. I acted as if I didn't notice the wave of his hand and sat in another chair that I had to drag up to his desk. It was his secretary's chair. I crossed my legs in such a way that my pantyhose made a little rustle. His secretary didn't have legs worth crossing.

Behind him, in the frame of the huge window, the Prudential building rose above the Boston skyline. On the adjoining wall was a magnificent tapestry, very old, with fine stitching. One that had been used to hide organ pipes in his grandfather's reception hall, which, in turn, had hidden his little brother. I uncrossed and recrossed my legs. I smiled. 'You wanted to speak to me about the Montevallos. About the book I'm writing.'

The man was tall and perfectly proportioned, his hair snow-white. Owen had his squareness of jaw, but not the rest. Owen was soft.

He said, 'Congressman Hall has, for some inexplicable reason, developed a little cause for himself. Apparently, making laws isn't cause enough. And so he saw in you an opportunity to—'

I interrupted. 'Owen did, in fact, mention that cause to me. He saw an injustice. He would like it set to rights.'

He laughed. Not Owen's laugh. A non-laugh, loud, the way humorless people laugh. 'Mrs Burke, there is something about Congressman Hall I imagine you don't know, and frankly you should. Congressman Hall is guilt-ridden. He and Brenda Montevallo had an affair . . .' He waited in order to enjoy my reaction. When he realized I already knew he went on. 'Congressman Hall knew the family personally. His feelings aren't unlike our own refusal to believe that one tiny speck of dirt the likes of Lee Harvey Oswald was all it took to eliminate President Kennedy. To believe that an inconsequential nobody could cause so much destruction shatters our collective ego. Owen can't believe one small fellow – this Baines – could have wiped out Brenda's family. That incident shattered Owen's ego.'

'Then Owen cared for Brenda? As opposed to having had a fling?'

'No, he never cared for her. Her family, the Montevallos, were his constituents. All his constituents are loyal to him. He lives by his commitment to compensate such loyalty.'

He leaned back, the chair fitted perfectly to the contours of his body, loving him, holding him. He was waiting for me to play my card. But I was practicing Nick's ploy once again. True to form, Charles shifted in his chair once, twice, and filled in the silence. And when he did, he ripped the rug out from under me so forcefully that I felt suspended in midair, just on the verge of falling into an abyss. He played his trump. He said, 'But there is something else. Something I don't want Owen to find out. Timmy Montevallo was his child.'

When I was a little girl I slipped from the top rung of the monkey bars in my school playground. I'd decided to try hanging by my heels, since hanging by bent knees was so easy. I remember feeling not as if I was falling but as if I were in a state of suspended animation and objects – big heavy objects – were slamming against me one after the other. The sensation lasted forever, the feeling of getting pounded all over by heavy hard things. I picked myself up off the asphalt, but I couldn't walk.

Charles Hall was standing over me with a glass of water. I hadn't fallen off the monkey bars, or out of my chair, which is what I was afraid had happened as I focused on the water. I was flushed. When I took the glass from him, he said, 'Would you prefer something stronger than water?'

I shook my head, and drank.

'I was able to protect him from this, and I intend to go on protecting him. He will never know the child was his. Unless, of course, you tell him. I'm sure you agree that it wouldn't do you any good to reveal such information.'

I drained the glass.

'It would have been too great a distraction for him to know. When Brenda Montevallo realized she was pregnant, she sent her mother to me, presumably to soften me. I was vague, but I told her I would help her daughter. Then Brenda came, intimating blackmail. She approached *me*. Me, not Congressman Hall. She is not a stupid woman, though a very foolish one. I saw to it that Brenda was removed for a while with the understanding that the name of the baby's father was to remain a secret.'

Finally, I could speak again. 'I assume having an abortion was out of the question.'

He smiled. 'The people in New Caxton bring issues of morality to heights the rest of us will never understand. To have an abortion is not simply a case of murdering an innocent. It's as if the act will bring a curse upon the . . . peasantry, shall we say? She would never have done it.

'She came back when the baby was six months old. The infant was convincingly small enough for Brenda to claim that he was born only three months earlier. Brenda slept with everyone and anyone. So people accepted that she conceived during a time when Congressman Hall was having a much-publicized affair with a movie actress, during the time when Brenda herself was away. Brenda came to see me again. She was an adept blackmailer. She wanted to be more than a cocktail waitress, which was the best she'd been able to do on her own. I asked if she'd like to see what life was like in the Southwest. In Tucson. I have business dealings there. The plan was that, through my connections, I would set her up as far away from New Caxton as she could get. Give her a start: money and a position. I did. It was easy. Brenda Montevallo is an exceptionally beautiful woman.

'I asked her how she'd like to live in a little house just outside of Tucson at the base of a lovely mountain range, a house where she could swim in her own pool. How she'd like to drive . . . now, what was it? Oh. An Acura Legend.

'She agreed. And I made it clear that she would be destroyed, financially, her reputation – whatever – if the truth were ever made known. She agreed to the bargain. I knew what she had in mind. She was going to leave the child with her mother. And her mother would be glad of it. Before Brenda left, Connie Montevallo came back to me too, and actually asked me to document the particulars of the child's heritage. She told me the child would want to know who its father was. So I told Connie we'd fix up a biography. The child's father was from Chicago, I think is how our story went. In the army. Died in Panama during the intervention. I was surprised to find out that Brenda had put her up to it. Brenda had some interest in doing the right thing by her son, something that had not been done for her. Brenda has no idea who her own father was. Who her mother was, for that matter. She wanted her child to know or, rather, to have a story he could believe. They would have liked me to come up with a false marriage license, but I didn't want the child to act on his curiosity. Brenda would be satisfied that her son would know that a father did at one point exist and the son would not ask more questions than there were answers to. In New Caxton, a child does not go around saying he had parents who weren't married. But at least he'd be able to talk about his father when his friends talked about theirs.'

I don't think I've ever felt so violent a dislike for anyone as I did for this man. I asked, 'What do you do?'

His brows lifted for a moment and then he said, 'I'm from the old school, Mrs Burke. I'm a product of a time when it was deemed rude to make such an inquiry. Usually, my answer to that question is, "Do about what?" But I think you're probably getting at something here.'

'I am. The old school you speak of didn't do anything at all. Having accountants keep track of one's money isn't work. It isn't anything. And that's what you do, isn't it? Nothing. You live vicariously through your brother don't you? You would own Brenda Montevallo in your own way.'

He stood. 'I'm not interested in what you have to say. I have another meeting in a few minutes. I hope you'll consider how your . . . book . . . will affect a man's career. Congressman Hall has flaws, but men of his ilk do. With power comes strong sexual drives. His constituents would prefer him not be embarrassed.'

I stood too. 'You could have said all this to me over the phone, Mr Hall. We've both wasted a lot of time.'

'Well, obviously I thought I'd have a greater chance of convincing you in person. I've told you all this because I'd hoped you could see that the Congressman owes Brenda nothing. I will make him see that it is ridiculous for him to feel guilty about his . . . fling. He doesn't know that Timmy was his child, and I expect you will keep our secret from him.'

I smiled at him. 'Oh, but I would guess Owen knows our secret already. It explains a lot.' A little wrinkle appeared between his eyebrows. 'Owen doesn't know the meaning of guilt. Someone must have told him.'

'No one else knew. Brenda wouldn't have dared.'

'Then someone unknown managed to find out and passed the information to him. And whoever told him may well have told others. You think about that, Mr Hall, and not make a fool of yourself with anyone else. Whether or not I write this book will have no bearing on Owen's actions. In fact, he's apologized to me for trying to get me to do what he should have done himself. How about that? And you know what I'm thinking? I'm thinking you didn't want Owen to know Brenda had his child because his feelings of loyalty might have pushed him to make her an honest woman. Marrying a promiscuous drug addict would not have proven beneficial to his political career.'

He glared at me.

'But there came to be another reason you wanted to keep him from knowing that Timmy Montevallo was his child, wasn't there? The child was killed, and if Owen knew his child had been murdered, he would want revenge. He would want the child's killer found and brought to justice. So I have to ask myself, What's wrong with that? What *is* wrong with that, Mr Hall? Why wouldn't you – why wouldn't any human being – want a child's killer brought to justice?'

'Eddie Baines is the killer.'

'Your brother doesn't think so. He's figured you lied to him. But you don't want him turning over a single stone. You don't want me to upset an applecart. Why? What will happen if this case is reopened? What's the downside for *you*?'

He smacked his fist into the desk. 'How dare you suggest any such thing. How dare you?'

I leaned over the desk into his face. 'Your cart has already turned over, hasn't it? The apples are hitting the ground as we speak.' His skin flushed just as mine had. I turned on my heel and was out of there.

After I left Charles Hall, I returned to my childhood refuge, where I went when I needed a mother, when mine was sitting on the couch with an empty bottle in her hand, crying. The nearest library. In Boston, that meant the main branch of the public library system. I had a fleeting thought when I walked in the entrance that it made no sense for Rosie Owzciak to be working in her library rather than this one. I hoped she'd soon tire of hate for hate's sake.

I looked up Charles Hall's company. Financial consultants. He'd incorporated five years ago. I found out what he'd done previously. Hall Enterprises, main office located in New Caxton, Rhode Island. Maintaining his factories. Then finding tax breaks for himself as, one by one, the factories closed. A hundred factories that once kept the US war machine going over the course of several wars, manufacturing ball bearings and tank parts and ammunition, now reduced to a half dozen making cellular products.

I closed the reference book and gazed into the large space big-city libraries make available to you when you settle into one of their big oak chairs in front of an expanse of heavy table. My comfort was an empty sight line and always would be. It was why I loved Nick's beach house so much. The buzz of a library, the lapping of waves, no ceiling close to my head – all I needed to rejuvenate myself. I was supposed to go right back to Washington after I saw Charles Hall. But I had to think, plan how I would now approach Owen. I was feeling huge pity for him; he'd found out a murdered child was his child. I didn't want to do anything foolish. It was easy to see why he'd been triggered to do something about Eddie Baines's conviction, not that he cared two hoots about Eddie. He had a personal stake in seeking retribution, a stake that was worth risking his job for. But he wouldn't lose his job. New Caxton would see him as that much more noble, gaining revenge for his son. He would rescue them from their own guilt, too. They may have talked themselves into believing that Eddie murdered the Montevallos, but they could just as easily talk themselves out of it.

So what made Owen call me off? Why did he want to take matters into his own hands? Either way, I would find out that Timmy Montevallo was his son.

I drove to Providence and went to the offices of the *Journal-Bulletin*. I needed to have another chat with Michael Longman. I wanted to ask him if he knew who Timmy Montevallo's father was. At the paper's reception desk, I asked for him. The receptionist gaped at me. She looked down and began shuffling some papers, fiddling with things, pushing buttons, coughing. When she looked up again, she said, 'Are you an acquaintance?'

'Yes, I am. But—'

'I'm sorry. I'm terribly sorry. Mr Longman passed away' – she glanced at her calendar – 'three weeks ago Wednesday.' She turned her face from me, then rose and hurried toward the door behind her. She was crying, but I could understand the words she struggled to get out. 'Please excuse me. He was well thought of here.'

He'd been killed in an auto accident. Presumed to have fallen asleep at the wheel of his car, which rolled down an embankment on Route 9. At the library, I read the article about the accident and then his obituary. He'd graduated from

Gettysburg College in Pennsylvania, had stayed on to work for a weekly paper. From there, the *New Caxton Standard*, and then the *Providence Journal-Bulletin*. In the article, his mother was quoted as saying, 'I can't believe my son fell asleep while driving his car. None of us ever knew Michael to be tired. Ever.'

So when I got back to Alexandria, I called Poppy.

'You feel so bad, honey, I can tell.'

'Worse.'

'I wish I could do something. But I'm psyching you a million hugs.'

'I know you are. But there is something you can do. You can maybe make a few calls for me.'

I told her what Mike Longman's mother told the Providence newspaper.

She asked, 'You want me to look for the fall-asleep-at-the-wheel pattern?'

'I didn't know there was a pattern.'

'There's a pattern for everything. If there weren't, my guys'd never figure out a damn thing. So what's this about, Denise?'

'I don't know. I'm—'

'Yes you do.'

'I'm suspicious, that's all.'

'That he didn't fall asleep at the wheel?'

'Yes.'

'Why?'

'Can you just have a look?'

She made a sound something like *hmph*. Then, 'No problem, sugar.'

'Thanks, Poppy.'

And it wasn't a problem for her. She had someone call the Rhode Island State Police to get copies of pictures of Michael Longman's vehicle. The police called back to say that the pictures weren't in the file and they couldn't locate them. Poppy told them to go take new photos, from every possible angle. They said the car had already been towed to the yard that crushes cars. Michael Longman's Geo Prizm was now in the form of a bale of hay. In my office, Poppy related that part and I said, 'Damn it all anyway.' But she was an investigator. She hadn't stopped there. She told the police to fax her the order to get rid of the car and 'wonder of wonders, Denise,' she got another call saying the order had been voided. The day before the car was to be sent to the yard, Michael Longman's mother contacted them and arranged to have the car towed to her home in Pennsylvania, just outside Harrisburg. The cop said to Poppy, 'we tried to tell her that the frame was bent and there was nothing she could do to get it running again, but she wanted the car. What do you say to a mother who's just buried her kid, right? I let her have it.' Poppy assured him that he'd done the right thing.

Poppy said to me from her favorite position just inside my office door, as far from Buddy's hairs as she could get, 'I called her. She has the car in her garage. I asked her if I could have someone come and take pictures of it. Jesus, Denise, you won't believe this one.'

'What?'

'The woman said to me, "It's not necessary. I can see the dents on the driver's side." She told me that her son's car had rolled over five or six times but that the dents on the passenger side were not the same kind of dents as on the driver's side. She told me she could see little bits of green paint in those dents.'

'And the car was . . .?'

'Red. She knew about patterns. She deduced them, Denise, because she's a loving parent. I'll tell you something here. When I interview potential employees, I find out if they're parents. I ask them how they'd feel if I put them on a special case that meant they'd have to work until midnight for three straight months. When they say they wouldn't be too thrilled since they've got family to consider, that's it. They're hired.'

'What if they say the job comes first?'

'I schlep them right out the door.'

'You won't ever have kids, will you, Poppy?'

'Nope. You want to hear about Mike Longman's mother now?'

'Yes.'

'She's scared. She wants to find out who killed her son, and her first thought was that she would die trying if necessary. She didn't care. Until her two other children caught her eye. One's still in high school, totally crazed over his brother's death. They need her. I told her I intended to see that her son's accident would be investigated thoroughly without any connection made to her. That I would find out who ran him off the road. Then I told her we'd need the car.'

'What did she say?'

'She said to come and get it. We did. Denise, Michael Longman was run off the road, all right. No two ways about that.'

'Are the Providence police stupid?'

'I shouldn't think so. Someone was able to deep six any consideration of a possible manslaughter, I'd say. Whoever it was didn't figure on some low-level cop feeling bad for a distraught mother. So we're looking around. For a four-year-old Chevy Nova. Evergreen is the name of the paint color Louisa Longman saw in the dents of her son's car. But call her. Go talk to her. Tell her he was a friend of yours.'

'He was, Poppy. You'd have liked him a lot, too.'

'I know, baby. Don't cry. Whatever you're on to here, maybe she'll be able to help. Wouldn't be surprised, in fact. Then maybe you'll fill me in on what the hell you're up to. Obviously you feel the need to hide things, and I won't beg you to tell me what or why. But when you're ready, I'll listen. I promise.'

I thought of Eddie Baines's mother, who wasn't able to help me, and who I know would have.

'And Denise, be goddamn careful here. Maybe whoever bumped Mike off the road was only in a big hurry. But all the same—'

'Poppy?'

'What?'

'Timmy Montevallo was Owen's child.'

She said, 'Oh, joy.' Then she came and put her arm around my shoulders. 'Sorry, sweetie.'

19

Louisa Longman's graciousness in the face of her agony tied my stomach in knots.

Her home was lovely; it was her art form. All the colors were soft, all the edges rounded, a home that was welcoming, a style as elegant as she. There was a family portrait standing on the piano in the living room. Mike's tie was a bit askew. He was the middle child – an older sister, a baby brother.

We had tea on a sunporch where all was bright and clear and green with plants lovingly tended. Not a curling yellow leaf in sight. The cookies she'd made were large round lemon-filled wafers. She placed a wafer on my cup and one on hers. The cookies warmed and the filling became just short of oozy, and we nibbled and sipped. She said she wished her husband could have been there with us. He'd wanted to meet me. I believed that, but I imagined he couldn't bring himself to do it.

I also knew Mrs Longman couldn't keep up the front, and I waited while she listed a rehearsed litany of the details of her son's accident and how she came to know he was run off the road by another vehicle. I felt as if I were listening to a book on tape, the words read by a competent actor, the rhythm precise. Then she said the phrase 'perhaps deliberately . . . to frighten him' and those words contained a tremor. And when she followed that with 'but I am thinking the worst . . . that . . .'

the words bobbled and she broke.

I put down my cup of tea and went to her. She suddenly seemed so helpless and small. I sat beside her and took her into my arms. After the first tiny attempt at resistance, she let herself collapse. She wept and wept. I said nothing, just held her and kept my cheek pressed against the top of her head.

And then, of course, when it was over, she kept apologizing and telling me she felt such a fool. I protested, following her into the kitchen, where she patted her face with a cloth while I refreshed our tea. Now we took it to the kitchen table; I didn't go back for my notebook, still in the sunporch, until an hour later, when it was time to leave.

She said, 'I went to Rhode Island to claim his body. My daughter and I made arrangements to fly him home. At first, we thought we'd go back again after the funeral to go through his things and take care of all that. But then we thought better of it and decided to collect his things then, because he wouldn't have had very much, and besides, he'd have to have clothes, you know, for . . .'

I said, 'I know.'

'Michael never was one to own things. He just wanted to hang around in old clothes writing. All I need, he'd say, is a room, paper, and pencil, and then later he'd add, "and my computer."' She smiled a little at the image she was having of him. 'His life was his writing; he was interested in little else. A girl, once.' Again, there was that wistful smile. 'Two weeks before he died, he shipped a box of disks to me, asked me to keep them in his old bedroom because there wasn't much room in his apartment. While we were out there in Rhode Island, on the way to his place, it dawned on me that his not having room for such a small box seemed strange.

'The apartment had been ransacked. And he really *didn't* have very much, as I knew he wouldn't. Just a few pieces of furniture, a little television. The computer wasn't there, it had been stolen, and what little else Michael owned was thrown all around. Underwear had been pulled out of drawers, clothes were tossed on the floor everywhere. The mattress was cut open. I told the police. They were nice to us. They said that people . . . burglars . . . read the obituaries and then . . .'

That was all Mike Longman's mother could manage. I think it helped her that I was teary-eyed, too. And so she ended up comforting me. She kept saying she knew how it must be for me to have lost a friend. She said, 'I want to show you something that I know will make you feel better. It was something that must have meant a lot to Michael.'

She got up and left the room and came back with a framed photo and sat back down. 'This was all that hung on his wall. In his little apartment. Just this and a calendar.' She handed me the photo. The matting and frame were professionally done. She said, 'This was Michael's hero.'

It was a photo of a grave, a neatly clipped, perfectly square plot with little shrubs and flowers forming the border. In the background, huge towering maples were in full leaf. In the center of the plot was a small plain tombstone. The other tombstones outside the carefully tended plot were ancient; this was a new stone in the middle of an old New England graveyard. The tombstone read CORNELIUS RYAN, REPORTER. No dates, just that.

Louisa Longman said, 'His hero. We're putting "reporter" after Michael's name on his stone. I don't think Mr Ryan would have minded.'

'He certainly wouldn't have.'

Before I left, she gave me her son's box of disks. I asked her for the calendar she mentioned. And then it occurred to her that Michael's notebook calendar, the one he always kept in his back pocket, hadn't been found in the car wreckage. We held one another's gaze after she told me that. And then she said, 'I need you to walk in my shoes, Denise.'

I sat in front of my computer for hours on end, going through what was Michael's own book. There were a ton of notes, an elaborate outline, and three drafts. Michael Longman, reporter, was in the process of exposing the illegal activities of Congressman Owen Allen Hall's brother, Charles.

Over the last three decades, he had watched his assets dribble away as the factories closed, one after another. Charles made feeble attempts to keep them going, but when he could not, he donated all the land they were on to the town of New Caxton. He helped develop plans for riverside parks to be built along the two rivers. Holdings within the town were to be converted to senior centers, teen recreation areas, and to the library, the plans just about to be put into effect. Then, divestiture notwithstanding, the Hall finances suddenly began to improve, suddenly and substantially.

People in New Caxton who'd been unemployed began listing their occupations as 'clerk' or 'bookkeeper,' and on their income tax forms their employer was Charles Hall Enterprises. The only problem was that there were no enterprises beyond the suite in the office building where I'd met Charles.

Michael Longman noticed that. He went on to do a lot of research and began formulating theories on what Charles was up to. I'd been dead wrong accusing Charles Hall of doing nothing for a living. He was doing plenty.

The New England branch of the Gambino crime family, headquartered in Providence, controlled all illegal gambling in New England, a business that brought in billions of dollars a year until the Feds pulled the plug, timing it to the biggest wedding the New England contingent ever had, whereby a dozen or so guests never made it from the church to the reception. This gang of outlaws was indicted, tried, convicted, and sent to prison and their physical plant evaporated. Back rooms in bars all over the city of Providence were emptied out and cleaned up. And so, none other than Charles Hall slipped in and filled the vacancy, took over the entire operation, and moved the plant to a little town in Rhode Island. Charles Hall turned New Caxton into one big wire room, the heart of a multimillion-dollar conglomerate. Instead of the back rooms of bars, business was carried out in living rooms or, more often, kitchens. Michael Longman wrote, 'The wives tend to be good with numbers.'

He had a list of names of the people who worked for Charles. Over a hundred names, almost all residents of New Caxton. There were Montevallos on the list, and there were Owzciaks, including Rosemary, who had an asterisk. I found Michael's asterisk reference. He hadn't worked it all out yet, but the few asterisked names were managers reporting directly to Charles. The ladies in the back room of Rosie's library weren't mending books. They were consolidating lines from bookies. Each geographical area in New England had a manager who called in to the library to get morning lines in general and, specifically, worked with the ladies to balance the bets the bookies were taking – if a bookie in one area found that a football team was getting heavy play, he'd work through the library to trade off bets with a bookie who was receiving overly heavy betting on the opposing team. I thought, Not unlike shipping brokers.

There was a Brenda Montevallo listed with a Tucson address. She had an *L* next to her name. I checked the references. She was connected to the 'launderer.' Mike had even found out who laundered Charles's money, a Mexican national who also lived in Tucson. I added his name to my own list, the kind of name that keeps a reader in his seat: Maximo Sostre. His address was the same as Brenda's.

None of the material Mike had gathered showed that he saw any connection between what he'd discovered and the deaths of the Montevallos. He would have had to know who Timmy Montevallo's father was in order to believe that there was a connection and to pursue it. He hadn't known, but he was coming close to finding out. And someone knew he was about to find out.

When I finished reading everything Mike had written, the big question to me was: Who was Mike's Deep Throat? I wondered if it had been Rosie. But why would she spill the beans? And then, of course, the real question arose: Was there a connection between the person who killed Mike and whoever it was that wiped out Brenda's family? My first instinct, always my first instinct, was to get to Poppy. But I wanted to know more before I did that. Substantiate a few things. I would go see Rosie.

In the end, Rosie was my second stop. I reconsidered and decided my first was going to be Charles Hall. I flew back to Boston, rented a car, and headed straight to his office building.

I stood in front of the receptionist's desk and said, 'I need to see Charles for a minute.'

She was flustered because I had referred to the boss by his first name, something I expect no one else did. It was hard to imagine his *mother* doing it, although I had a hard time imagining that he ever had a mother. The door opened behind the receptionist's desk. He stood framed in the doorway, a stanchion. He said, 'Come in, Mrs Burke. Did we leave a loose end?'

I didn't go in. 'Yes, we did. If Owen goes ahead and gets a new trial for Eddie Baines, you will be exposed, won't you?' I watched his lips part slightly. He ran his tongue over them. I said, 'Owen doesn't care, I'll bet. And I've just figured out why. Because he's found out that you knew all along about

Timmy being his child, and he's furious.'

He drew himself up, tall and slim and as hard as a telephone pole. 'Get out of my office.'

'You kept Owen's constituents in the chips, and he saw to it that what you do stayed under wraps. But now he's in a rage, isn't he? Not thinking rationally. Wants to betray you the way you betrayed him. Little brother rebelling against big brother at last.'

He shouted, 'Get out of my office!' The receptionist was twisted around in her chair, gawking at us.

'A new trial with a real lawyer and a real jury will bring out information you don't want brought out. The information Mike Longman was about to reveal.'

He said, 'Miss Flynn, call security. Tell them we have . . .'

I didn't hear the rest. I was gone.

I sent Poppy Mike Longman's disks. Within a very short time, the FBI was doing what they do; Poppy couldn't say how long it would take to verify what Mike had uncovered.

Rosie wasn't Mike Longman's Deep Throat. Owen was. He wasn't just angry at his brother, he was hell-bent on getting even. Owen had been operating on two fronts, Mike and me. One of us was dead. That was why Owen wanted me to stop. He knew what his brother was capable of. As I drove out of Boston, I had a fleeting image of Louisa Longman. I passed into a stage she had arrived at not long before she welcomed me into her home: fear. I had two children who, like all children, like Timmy Montevallo and like the grown child of Louisa Longman, as it turned out, were vulnerable.

I called a security group. I hired them to watch my children, surreptitiously, so no one would notice. To keep a surveillance on my house when they were home since Buddy was useless as a watchdog, and on their school when they were there, and wherever else they might be. I said, 'I don't want my son to tell me there's a strange guy hanging around the schoolyard either.'

The fellow I spoke with said, 'If there is, we'll spot him before your son does, believe me.'

20

I remember a time when I was a fairly young kid and my mother took me aside, all cozy and compassionate. She told me I should feel free to have my little girlfriends from school come over to the house. Anytime I wanted.

'You could walk home together,' she said. 'Isn't that how it works?' She wasn't quite sure. I didn't answer her. My stomach was churning at the thought of such a humiliation. She then instructed me in the importance of close friends rather than belonging to a group in the schoolyard, 'though that is certainly important too, Denise. You need a *best* friend so you'll have someone you can really talk to.' I suppose she was getting tired of me talking to the neighbor's cat. It must have taken a lot for her to give me advice as coherent as that. Almost immediately, I came to know that it had; her parenting moment took so much out of her that she passed out that night, bottle in hand, right at the kitchen table. Her usual habit was to get through a few bites of 'dinner' and manage to climb into bed before collapsing. I had to slip the bottle out of her hand, for once grateful for her condition since it meant she might forget the one-sided conversation we'd had. I poured the little that was left in it down the drain. The next morning she was furious with me, as I knew she would be. She'd disciplined herself to save a mouthful to give her the boost she needed to get out of bed in order to start her day's work – journeying to various parts of town to different package stores to get in the supply of bottles she'd need till the next morning. She figured that was how you went about hiding the fact you were a drunk. The distraction of finding that her first-thing-in-the-morning fortification was gone ensured that she'd forget the idea that I bring a friend home from school.

It took me three decades to learn that if a friend knew a secret about me, she wouldn't look at me as if I had two heads. A secret wouldn't cause a friend to make fun of me. A real friend would not run around blabbing my secret to everyone. And I learned that when you reveal a secret, a true friend will reveal one of her own. So, after all those years, I finally took my mother's advice: After Poppy phoned to tell me she liked my Sam Litton book, I invited her to my home.

She came to Connecticut, arriving at the door like a whirlwind, flirting a little with Nick, making my children feel cool. Then she and I had a great time. We'd started out just planning to go to the coffee shop, drink coffee all afternoon, and catch up. We did that, but we weren't finished catching up when the coffee shop closed at three. So I mentioned the antiques stores that lined Main Street and she said she was looking for a Hoosier and I thought she meant an old-fashioned vacuum cleaner and we had a laugh, one of many. We strolled along in and out of the shops, pointing at pieces of furniture and at knickknacks we remembered as being in our own homes, growing up.

She'd say, 'My grandfather had a table like that next to his chair. He died of a coronary sitting in that chair. His last words were, "Oh, shit," and then he keeled over and his cigar fell out of his mouth onto the table. It was exactly like that table, except it had a big burn mark.'

I saw a pair of painted cast-iron bookends. One bookend was an Amish farmer and the other was an Amish farmer's wife. My mother had a row of books on a shelf, and she'd keep a bottle hidden behind them. We had those same bookends; my father had brought them home from one of his trips. I hated those Amish people for hiding my mother's bottles.

We didn't find a Hoosier and we didn't buy anything. Neither of us were compulsive shoppers, another thing we had in common. Shopping was just an excuse to hang out together. My kids were always telling me they were going to go and meet friends and hang. I was so happy for them that they got to do that without one of the friends saying, 'Did your mother get out of bed today?' So now, finally, I got to hang too.

Once Nick and I moved to Alexandria, I let Poppy know she could feel free to drop in on me any time. She does that, too, but mostly at my office. She's told me she's not that interested in being friends with Nick and his gang. Neither was I. She always calls me first.

Now it was time, I decided, to make another friend, the second in my life. Rosie. I'd given Rosie my phone number, but she'd never called. I continued to call her, though, and we'd chatted about various details of the Montevallo killings. Now I called her and asked her point-blank about Charles Hall. I asked her what connection he still had to New Caxton. She said, 'Without Charles, this whole town would have gone sliding into the rivers.' I said, 'And with him?' She asked me what I meant. I told her, 'Seems you'll still end up in the river, no?'

She paused but decided to act as though I were speaking in general terms. 'Maybe. But he's bought us the time we needed to be something else. He pays for everything. Once this town is back on its feet, we'll move on. The old generation is dying off.'

'How are you back on your feet – how will you move on – if you're all doing time?'

And then she knew I knew. There was no end to her pause, and I had to speak. I told her to come visit me for a few days and we'd talk. 'Our guest bedroom looks out over the Potomac from the front window, and you can see the Washington Monument out the other.' I said, 'I'm your friend, Rosie.'

'I don't have friends.'

'Tell me about it. I knew we had that in common not too long after I met you. Actually, I have one friend. My first one ever. I turned thirty before I made my best friend. I want you to meet her.'

She didn't know what the hell to do. She hemmed and hawed. So I told her I just wouldn't take no for an answer and gave her some information on the best flight to Washington from Providence. I told her I was a hop, skip, and a jump from Dulles Airport and it would be no problem picking her up. She said she didn't want to be so much trouble. I said, 'How does that sound like trouble?' And then she blurted out, 'Yes, I'll do it. I need to talk to someone. To you. Thank you.'

I told Nick I'd be having company. He asked, 'Who's going to man the library while she's here?'

I said, 'Now why would you ask me that after I left *Codependent No More* on your nightstand? She'll have to cope.'

He laughed.

Rosie arrived carrying a brand-new suitcase full of brand-new clothes. She wasn't wearing her hair in a ponytail held back by one of the rubber bands in the little glass custard cup on the library checkout counter. When I picked her up at the airport, the first thing I saw was that she'd had a haircut. Not exactly a *style*, just hair that had been cut off at jaw level. The sides hung straight down and the top was anchored off her face with a straight barrette, the kind my mother used to put in my hair, either gold or silver, though the gold or silver paint would start chipping off days after she bought them. Rosie's haircut was the kind that exposes the fresh clear face of a child. On an adult, it was a haircut that could only emphasize a grown woman's flaws. But Rosie's face had perfect bone structure; she had beautiful skin, and each feature was in symmetry with the others. She was standing there, ugly glasses off, cleaning them with the corner of her new shirt, which she'd just pulled out of her skirt for that purpose. I wondered just why and when Rosie had made the decision to be unattractive, to keep hidden. She spotted me, tilted her chin up, put the glasses back on, and tucked her shirt back in.

Rosie's visit caused a turn in my relationship with Owen. When she decided to come, I had to change a date with him. I felt a huge relief that I didn't have to see him. I still couldn't face him, couldn't allow myself to say, 'I know about Timmy.' But I wasn't ready to end things officially. So impossible to act rationally when you're in love with someone. I'd said to Poppy, 'It takes a lot to kill love, doesn't it?'

She said, 'For me, very little. Then there's you and Nick. God knows how the two of you still manage it.'

'I don't think I love Nick.'

'Of course you do. You're just pissed at him. You married him because you took care of an adult all during your childhood, and you wanted a turn at being taken care of too. Now you just have to teach him that you've had enough of it.'

'Why would he have married someone just to take care of her?'

'Go ask a shrink, Denise. I'm rambling. Who knows why people get married? Who knows what passes for love?'

I said, 'Poppy, can you love two people?'

I was sure she started to say *Of course you can*, but then she said. 'No. You can't. You have to choose.'

I left a message with Owen's secretary asking him to call me.

When he got back to me, I told him I was sorry I couldn't meet him that week. I was sorry, despite all. Yes, I told him, I knew we'd been away from each other for a while. Yes, I knew we had things to straighten out. Yes, I knew he loved me very much. Yes. When he was finished, I told him about my impulse to invite Rosie to spend a few days with me and how she'd just taken me up on it.

The I-need-you tone of his voice disappeared. He said, 'Why?'

'Why did I invite her or why did she agree to come?'

'I'm serious, Denise.'

'You know, Owen, with every book I write, I seem to find one person who is able to give me behind-the-scenes insight.' Then I couldn't resist. 'Sort of like Deep Throat.' I nattered on about how intelligent Rosie was, how observant, how this, how that. I stopped because I realized I was filling in all my pauses. I said, 'Still with me, Owen?'

Incredibly, he said, 'I thought I was Deep Throat here.'

I laughed. He didn't.

'Denise, she told you, didn't she? That's the real reason you're not seeing me.'

He was talking about Brenda. About Timmy. I didn't know why he'd think Rosie would tell me that. 'Told me what, Owen?' I tried to sound genuinely puzzled.

'Told you . . . never mind. Listen, I love you, Denise. Very much.'

I needed to clear my throat. 'I know.'

'Nothing in all my life has been as painful as what I've been living with. It snowballed. You can't fool with fate a little bit and then try to stop what you started. You get trapped. The more trapped in this ruse I became, the harder it was to set things straight. That's because I didn't want to lose you. I *am* losing you, aren't I?'

'Owen, I need to think.'

'Think aloud. To me. Talk to me. Please.'

'Owen, Rosie leaves on Thursday. I'll see you then.'

'I just want you to hear what I have to say.'

'All right, Owen.'

'Promise me.'

'Of course I promise.'

I hung up, feeling a bit of a rush. Living a lie can tie you in knots. Being tied in knots can be a thrill. I would let Owen tell me that he was Timmy's father and give me his excuses as to why he hadn't told me sooner. Then, I would announce that it wasn't Rosie who'd told me, it was his brother. I wondered exactly what kind of rise that would get out of him, damn him.

Poppy hit it off with Rosie. I knew she would. Both have chosen lives of isolation, each in her own way. They were soulmates. Poppy and I weren't soulmates, we just liked each other a lot. We trusted each other. But we didn't really understand each other, didn't have some esoteric quality in common that drew us together in an emotionally intimate way.

The three of us went out to a West African restaurant and ate food so hot and spicy we were high as kites. Didn't even need to drink, although we did. There was one dish we loved. It was a cooked spinachy kind of thing, green and stringy. Rosie said she'd had it several times. I said, 'You have?'

Poppy said, 'What did you do? Go on a cruise to Nigeria?'

She said, 'I've had it in New Caxton.' She told us it must have been from a recipe prepared by African slaves and passed on to their descendants who ended up living in New Caxton. We asked the waiter what it was called and he said, '*Njama-njama*,' just barely pronouncing the n's, making a new consonant sound none of us could reproduce. We asked Rosie what it was called in New Caxton. She smiled. 'You won't believe it.'

Poppy said, 'We believe everything, that's our problem.'

'*Jemma*.'

'C'mon.'

'Honest to God.'

We washed down our *njama-njama/jemma* with Star beer imported from Cameroon.

A little band started playing high-life music and we ended up dancing the night away with a bunch of Ghanaian students, six of them, two each. Rosie never hung back. She got into the beat and learned the steps. Rosie was capable of living. The question still remained, Why had she decided not to? Back at the table when the band took a break, I asked her. She told me it was because she was raised to be a martyr. To take her punishment like all the women in New Caxton took their punishment.

'Punishment for what?' I asked her.

'For where I went wrong.'

'Where'd you go wrong?'

She didn't answer. Poppy said, 'Bet it had something to do with sex.'

Rosie raised her eyes from her glass of beer to Poppy.

Poppy said, 'In which case, Rosie, it's a matter of having to follow rules that aren't possible to keep. The church traps us in its cycle: We sin because it's impossible not to, repent, promise never to sin again, and then, because it's impossible, go out and sin some more. If everyone who sinned against the rules of sex were punished physically for these transgressions instead of psychologically, there wouldn't be anyone walking around without a shirt made of hair.'

Rosie said, 'We all make choices, don't we? I made mine.'

'Perhaps you made a choice based on some Catholic thing.

Like thinking that accepting undeserved punishment is noble.'

I kicked Poppy under the table, but Rosie could take it. She said, 'Sometimes promiscuous sex is a form of undeserved self-punishment.'

Poppy looked at me. She said, 'Shit, Denise, have you been telling secrets about me?'

Rosie said, 'It's no secret.'

'It isn't?'

I said, 'Yeah, Poppy. You let those students keep their hands on your butt while you danced.'

She said, 'I did? God, I didn't even feel their hands on my butt. I'm so used to it, I guess. Didn't they have their hands on your butts?' She was looking at me.

I said, 'Yes, and I moved them back up.'

Rosie said, 'So did I. I told them we didn't do that in America. And the guy I was dancing with said, "What is your friend, then?"'

Poppy said, 'What did you say?'

'I said you were Canadian.'

Poppy and I pretty much became hysterical with laughter.

It was while we were driving home, weaving our way to my house where Poppy would drop us off, that the inevitable happened. It was just a matter of when.

Poppy said, 'If a cop stops me, Denise, trade places with me. You'll only lose your license. I'll be dead.'

Rosie said, 'What's the matter? Have you gotten that many tickets?'

I was the one who actually let fly. 'She means she'll have trouble at the office. Poppy's an FBI agent.'

I think I felt Rosie's shudder. I turned and looked at her. She was staring at me. I looked away.

21

'Before I say anything else,' Owen said with profound solemnity, 'I want to tell you about Eddie Baines. Someone who isn't a murderer.'

This was going to be my second time with Owen that we didn't make love first and talk later, my second time where we skipped the first part, which always made for such a nice second part. He kissed my cheek and led me into his living room. He did break out a bottle of great wine. So I sipped, knowing I'd refuse a second glass, and listened to his explanation for why Eddie needed to be rescued. By him, not me. 'A truly gifted athlete,' was the phrase he began with.

He went on a bit about what that meant, one cliché after another. 'Eddie's father died during his last year at college and Eddie fell apart. He was injured. He quit football. They let him keep his scholarship. He came home from college intent on helping his mother. He had a younger sister. He would teach school and hoped to work his way into coaching the high school team as assistant to the head coach, a man he worshiped. But this was during a time when there was an overabundance of teachers and no jobs available.'

'Local boy makes good, then suffers a tragedy but still graduates from college. How come nobody helped him out?'

'You can't manufacture a teaching job.'

I let it go.

Owen said, 'I think maybe Eddie didn't try hard enough to follow through on his plans. He'd been pampered. He didn't know how to really go after something.'

'I should think he'd be good at that – going after something. Touch-downs, right? When you described *gifted*, Owen, you left out drive. Has to be there, no?'

'Well, yes, I guess it does. But when he came home he really just took the first job that came along. The owner of the factory where his father had been employed told him he could work for them until something turned up.'

'And he did?'

'Yes.'

'So how is that pampered? I'd say if he was willing to take whatever job was available, willing to work at anything while he looked for the job he wanted – well, that says a lot for his character.'

Owen sighed. 'Look, Denise, I know the situation. You weren't there. Please let me finish what I have to say.'

I did. As Owen told it, Eddie's problem was that he was accustomed to being taken care of. He'd had all his needs catered to from the moment he'd first exhibited his athletic talents. So when care was no longer available, he was stymied. Owen actually added, 'People like Eddie Baines are often content to be in jail – their meals are cooked and served to them; they're told when to go to bed, when to get up, what to do. They have no responsibilities. Just like members of an athletic team, an inmate leads a totally structured life. I convinced myself to let things be.'

Instead of telling Owen he was full of shit, I said, 'Sort of like nuns in a convent.' I was tempted to add *Like slaves on the plantation*, but I needed to keep him off balance, distracted from the line of nonsense he had prepared. I had to know what was going on.

'Denise, someone killed my flesh and blood.' Really big pause. I kept a blank impression on my face. 'I didn't know it until recently. Brenda and I . . . Timmy Montevallo was my child!'

I put my hand up, palm facing him. 'I know.'

He slammed his fist into the palm of his hand. I jumped.

'She did tell you then, didn't she?'

'I'm sorry?'

'How long ago did she tell you, Denise? I'm curious.'

'Who?'

'Rosie, goddamn it. Who else?'

'Rosie wasn't the one who told me. And how the hell would Rosie have that information, anyway?'

'I wish I knew.' He waved his hand in the air. 'It doesn't matter.' He thought I was protecting her. 'What's important is that you know what went on.'

'I know what went on.'

'I'm not talking about the little dalliance I had with Brenda Montevallo. A weekend of . . . of nothing. Listen, Denise, after the crime, my only intention was to protect Brenda. I felt sorry for her. I'd taken advantage of her. So I felt I owed it to her. I didn't want her to be arrested. She didn't have anything to do with the crime but she was involved with drugs, so there were some suspicions. She didn't deserve to be suspected of an event that nearly killed her too. She could have *been there* – been there when it happened. Her family may have been murdered because the people who did it were looking for *her*.'

He wasn't talking about Brenda's grief when he said that the crime nearly killed her. His words were literal.

'Denise, Eddie would be the perfect fall guy while we got Brenda started again. Somewhere else—'

'By *we*, you mean you and your brother?'

'Well, yes. My family. But then, later, when I found out about the boy – that he was what had come of that weekend with Brenda – I didn't know . . . I had a child! And someone killed my child. Stabbed him to death! So I needed my brother. I still need him. He's got a lot of power. He can—'

'Owen, you're a congressman.'

'Denise, I want the real killers found. I've been a coward, I admit it. Now I will go about finding out who killed my son. I'll do it myself. I've used you. I'm sorry. I'm truly sorry. At that point, I guess I was still in shock. But I've also fallen in love with you, and for that, believe me, I'm not sorry. I beg you to forgive me.'

He was protesting too much. He took both my hands in his. 'I know how diabolical it sounds. I did go to that party in New York with some intangible notion that I could get you to do the job I was agonizing over. I didn't sit around planning it like some mad scientist, it was all blurred. I told you before – a fantasy. And then everything just seemed to fall into place. When I told you about the murder, when we were walking after dinner, at that point I wasn't thinking that you could do what I didn't know how to do. The way I had when I spotted you. Do you know what I really wanted? Sympathy. Empathy. I couldn't cope. But I got far more, didn't I? Love. Our love for each other strengthened me. Looking back, yes, I used you. But it wasn't the way it . . . it wasn't . . .' He took my hands to his lips. 'Let's drop everything. Let's start again.'

I said, 'I don't believe you,' and pulled my hands away.

'Denise, you found out about Brenda and me and you've lost your trust. I don't blame you. But please let me—'

'There was no blur at that party. You did calculate. You positioned yourself to take advantage of me. I am not an idiot, Owen.'

He said, 'Well, I am. I'm tangled in this web. I can't get out of it. I love you. Help me. Please, please help me.'

Help him. How could I love this hypocrite? This liar? How could I when I wanted to strangle him? 'Owen, you don't give a shit about Eddie Baines. Never have. Can you at least admit that?'

'Eddie Baines? Of course I do. I know I may sound self—'

'I'm curious. Exactly when did you find out that Timmy was your child?'

'A short time before we met.'

'Why hadn't Brenda told you? I mean, when she found out she was pregnant.'

'I would have insisted that she get an abortion. Given her money. But my child was her ticket out. So she went to my family. She knew they'd take care of her. That's how things are done in New Caxton. Go to Charles for intercession. If she'd told me, she'd have never gotten what she could get from Charles.'

All of a sudden, fury bubbled up in me. 'Who are the rest of your family?'

'What do you mean?'

'How many others are there?'

'None. Neither of us ever married. And that's why—'

'Charles isn't a family. He's your warden. But you know, Owen, if by some chance you ever go to jail, you'll be real happy there. Just like now, you won't have any responsibilities and things will be taken care of for you the way you're used to. You'll have your life structured and your goddamn meals served to you just like Eddie Baines. But what about sex, Owen? Or will Charles be able to get you women in there?'

'God damn it, Denise—'

'Just tell me this. Who told you that Timmy Montevallo was your child?'

Confusion came into his eyes. I could see things in his eyes now when before I could only see blue. 'Denise, I learned the same way you did. Rosie was close to Eddie Baines and his family. She couldn't tolerate his being in jail. He was innocent.' He shrugged. 'She said to me, "You want my vote, Owen, get him out." I explained to her that things had just skyrocketed out of control. I told her I believed no one would ever find out who did it because it was a professional job. So cleverly plotted that an innocent man was framed and convicted. I told her I was afraid for Brenda Montevallo. If she had, in some way, been connected to the people who did it without her being aware of it – if she dealt drugs for them – the knowledge of such a thing would kill her. She was already practically off the deep end. That Eddie was probably better off where he was.'

'And that's when she told you?'

'Right after she slapped my face. Gave me the jolt I needed. This is no longer about Eddie Baines. Timmy was my flesh and blood, and I will find out who killed him.'

'When did Rosie tell you that Charles knew from the time Brenda was pregnant that Timmy was yours?' He didn't answer. 'About the time you made your confession to me? Announced to me that you'd been a coward and you would take on the job you'd connived for me to do?' I could see his fists clench, but he still didn't speak. 'Okay, Owen, so you're saying that first your goal was to protect Brenda, just as you'd protect anyone you'd used. You owed her that. Then you found out Timmy was your child so you had to gain revenge for Timmy, your son, but without your brother knowing about it. You would do it even if – and this is what I think you're saying – even though Brenda might have *known* the killers. But Brenda can go to hell, right? If the case gets reopened and Brenda is dragged through the mud, tough. Timmy has superseded her. But Timmy's dead. Owen, Eddie's incarceration killed his mother. Who's going to take revenge for her?'

'She was not my flesh and blood.'

He sounded deranged. I kept it up. 'With things stirred up, Brenda suffers, and in the end, if Eddie didn't do it, if someone else did – who's to say they'd ever be found? Especially if they're pros. It's probably too late, Owen. Too late to find the killers. But it's not too late to get Eddie a new trial. And that's my goal. And now it's become your goal because you've decided to stop hiding from Charles. If there's another trial, another investigation, and he's suddenly in deep shit, too bad for him.'

'What are you talking about?'

'There was a reporter at the Providence newspaper about to expose him. He died under suspicious circumstances.'

His face set. He looked at me in a new way. Disdain, I thought. He said, 'Now, although family is paramount, don't think—'

'You have no family! You have one calculating, criminal brother. Owen, Rosie didn't tell me.'

He actually said, 'Yes, she did.'

'Rosie did not tell me you were Timmy's father.' And again, he insisted she did. I stood to leave. He stood too. 'If you don't want to know who did tell me, that's okay. What do I care?'

He grabbed my upper arms in his hands. My first touch from him that wasn't loving. But his face didn't match his grip. His face seemed about to crack. He said, 'Who?'

I waited for him to let go of me. He did. 'Your *family*. Your brother, Charles, told me so I'd stop loving you. Didn't work. But I'm out of your life all the same, Owen.'

He let me leave. He never heard the love part.

I stuck to my guns. I didn't return his calls. I wouldn't see him. His messages went from stock statements of repentance to artificial hurt, to angry recriminations, to pitiable pleas. I wrote him a note offering no pity. It was over. Done with. I said in the note that I intended to visit Eddie Baines in prison and would let him know how happy Eddie was there, rather than outside where he would have to, God forbid, cook his own meals.

I told it all to Poppy. On the phone. She was back and forth to New York again. She said, 'Fury is good.'

I called Rosie and told her. She said, 'It's all nuts, isn't it? Now I know why I'm sporting a black eye.'

When she said that, I don't know what I did, but the funny noise I heard came from me. Maybe it was some kind of gasp. Then I tried to make words but couldn't.

She said, 'It isn't a bad one, though. Once I heard the accusation, I thought it would be worse.'

I found I was able to speak. 'What accusation?'

'That I told you Owen's little secret.'

'Who did it?'

'Who told my father? Owen, I guess. Before he found out from you that he was wrong about where your information came from.'

'Jesus Christ, Rosie. I'm asking you who hit you.'

'Hit me? My father, who else? I don't have a husband, remember? That's why it wasn't so bad. He's old. Not as strong as he used to be. I didn't deny that I was the one who told you about Timmy. Let him think that, what's the difference? Anyway, I announced – and this came right off the top of my head – that I'd invited you to dinner whether he liked it or not. That now I'd have to postpone your visit for a week till after the bruise faded. He had apoplexy. I told him to sit down before he had a stroke. So will you come?'

'Will I ever.'

'Good. I'll give him the new date.'

'Rosie, I don't understand how you knew Timmy was Owen's child.'

'Digging around is not only my profession, it's my hobby. Denise?'

'Yes?'

'Gonna bring the FBI this time?'

'No. Listen—'

'Forget it.'

Rosie could take punishment. It was what she was trained to do.

One wall of the Owzciaks' dining room was paneled, floor to ceiling, with strips of mirrors shot through with gold fissures. On the wall opposite the mirrors hung a huge gilt framed print of the Last Supper. While you ate, you got to look at it directly or at its reflection in the crackled mirrors. The dining room table held twenty people, and it was full.

Rosie had spent the first several minutes after my arrival making the introductions. 'Denise, I'd like you to meet Mr and Mrs Kowalski. Mrs Kowalski is my chief assistant at the library; I don't know what I'd do without her. This is Denise Burke, she's writing the book about the Montevallo murders.' Then, 'And this is my aunt and uncle, Mr and Mrs Pluta. I never formally introduced you to my uncle, but I'm sure you remember him.' Mr Pluta was the guy now running Stoshu's – the coffee shop. And then, 'Mr and Mrs Olschefski.' Eddie's girlfriend's parents. 'Chief and Mrs Weinecke.' The chief gave me a nod and I nodded back. 'Chief Weinecke and I have met.' Mrs Weinecke wore thick pancake makeup. It couldn't hide the port-wine birthmark that covered three-quarters of her face.

I'd seen the ladies before, all of them, glimpsed them in the back room with Rosie at the library. Now she had everyone in the palm of her hand, even her parents. Her father could take a swing at her whenever he liked. It would do him no good. She was in charge.

Rosie had somehow taken over and they couldn't fight her power. Maybe they thought if they went along with her she was somehow going to save them from the slide into the river. Except, that is, for the police chief, who saw himself as above it all. He didn't look scared to death, as the rest of the men did, their women mortified.

Rosie's mother was hospitable even though she was shaking in her boots. Her husband looked as if he were still having apoplexy. His face was red. Maybe he would have a stroke. All these people's livelihoods were at stake. Like Rosie, I showed them no mercy. I told them I didn't think Eddie had done it. That my book might lead to exactly who killed those poor Montevallos. I looked at the Olschefskis. 'Perhaps your daughter could lead the way to the real killers. I understand she's abroad?' Neither knew what they should say. The husband nodded, followed by the wife.

We sat down to dinner. We had blood sausage and dried mushrooms 'sent from the old country.' I turned to the Olschefskis. 'Did your daughter send these?' Mr Olschefski choked out a yes. We had *galumpkes* and kishka and grilled kielbasa that didn't taste like any kind of kielbasa I'd ever tasted. Delicious. I asked what the secret was. Rosie's mother said it was just kielbasa, but it hadn't been smoked. It was fresh.

There was also a huge platter of homemade gnocchi with a sauce full of chunks of veal. And on the side were two vegetables, two bowls of cooked greens and they both looked like spinach. One was *njama-njama*. Whatever the other one was, it was flavored with some kind of rendered fat. I asked Rosie's mother what the dish was called.

She said, 'Collards.'

The three ethnic groups that made up New Caxton had indeed accepted one another. They accepted one another's food, learning how to cook it and enjoy it. It was in the kitchens of New Caxton, I decided as I surveyed the table, where Poland, Italy, and Africa ended and America began.

* * *

I headed for the beach house. If I'd arrived, it would have been the last time I spent the night there. But five minutes out of New Caxton, I heard a thud and felt jarred. The high beams of a pair of headlights were right up against my back window. Whoever was driving behind me had given my car a bump. And then I got hit again, a little harder, and I heard a scraping sound. The headlights slid left out of my rearview mirror. The driver was coming up alongside me. I veered toward the right, away, and saw the sharp dropoff at the shoulder of the road. I veered back and pressed the accelerator to the floor. The Taurus V-8 engine thrust the car forward. The other car's headlights slipped back a few feet behind me and then they were dead center in my mirror again, blinding me.

My mother said, when I was a teenager and learning to drive – something she knew would make her life a lot easier – 'Denise, if another driver is so rude as to follow you too closely, just brake the car a bit and give him a scare.'

I let the headlights close in on me once again. When his bumper had to be almost touching mine, I braced myself and slammed on the brakes.

The car plowed into me. A ten-year-old Taurus with an eight-cylinder engine is not only powerful, it's damn sturdy. All I did was bump my chin on the steering wheel, not hard. Again, I jammed the accelerator to the floor, shot forward, did a U-turn on two wheels, and took a good look at the other car as I sped by. The driver was tangled in his air bag, struggling to peel it off his face. It was a small car, dark, the front end accordioned, its headlights throwing one beam straight up, the other off to the side of the road. I couldn't see the plate.

I headed for Providence and checked into a big hotel. I lay awake at the edge of the kingsize bed, going over and over it in my head: Who did it? Who killed Mike Longman, and who tried to kill me? Who knew I would be at Rosie's house this night? Everyone. I just couldn't imagine Charles Hall crashing his car into people. Who was his flunky? I fell asleep around four, once I'd told myself that I'd need a big breakfast to think it all through. Fury is more than good, it makes you strong.

In the morning, after my bacon and eggs and home fries and a stack of toast, I assessed the damage to the car. There wasn't a whole lot – the taillight casings were smashed but the bulbs still worked. The bumper was disfigured and the trunk was dented. I noted the color of the little chips of paint in the trunk dent. Dark blue. Definitely not green.

I drove to the beach house, gathered up my stuff, got back in the car, and went over to the old fisherman's daughter's house, asked if she could take me to the Westerly airport, and then asked her, sheepishly, if she could have my car fixed and have the bill sent to me personally, at my office. She had no problem with that. She winked.

22

That night I was home again, sitting with Nick, him looking at some papers, me trying to concentrate on my book – settle myself back down – reading about the first wave of immigrants that arrived from Poland and Italy on US shores in the nineteenth century, people who had been expressly imported for the purpose of providing cheap labor. Our children were off visiting Nick's sister and their cousins in Connecticut for a few days. I was reading, but I wasn't seeing the words. I was thinking, How can it be over? Yes, Owen had lied to me. But he'd had no choice but to lie. Well, not at first. Maybe he did love me. I was rationalizing. But I felt empty. I wanted to be filled up again. I mumbled something aloud. I was rebuking myself silently, but 'It's over,' came out of my mouth. I knew I said those words aloud because Buddy's ears pricked up and he looked at me.

Nick was looking at me too, over the tops of his reading glasses, which were identical to Bill Clinton's and looked just as cute. He had an expression on his face, not one of puzzlement but still the kind that was about to transmute into the question, *Did you say something, Denise?* But other words came out of him.

He said, 'Don't be silly, Denise. Things are just tough. I'm working hard, and you've got a new book bogging you down . . . we just haven't had time for each other.'

I found what he said so ludicrous that laughing seemed appropriate. He thought I was talking about our marriage. We didn't have a marriage. We had a judicious arrangement.

I said, 'I'm not telling you that our marriage is over. I thought you already knew that. I'm telling you that the affair I've been having is over. Things aren't tough for me because I'm in the middle of a book. That's when I'm happiest, as a matter of fact. Right now, I'm miserable. I'm sorry to have to tell you this, Nick. But I want you to know I haven't seen him in a while, haven't talked to him—'

Nick interrupted me, even though I was trying to keep babbling forever so I wouldn't have to get to whatever the next step tends to be in such a conversation. The next step turned out to be Nick saying, 'Our marriage is hardly over. I've known about your affair, Denise. I've been waiting for it to burn out. I'd guessed it had. And I was right.'

His face was completely calm. I wanted to hit it.

'No, you didn't know anything about it. I took great care—'

'How could I not? You were acting joyful.'

'Since when do you notice how I act?'

'I don't. I'm sorry. But that's because I'm used to you. The way you were acting was unnatural for you. So I guessed. Admittedly, this was all happening to me – my taking notice – on a subconscious level.'

I felt my stomach turning over. 'Nick, hadn't it ever *bothered* you that I never acted joyful? Didn't you want to give me joy? When did you stop wanting to do that?'

'I told you, this has all been unconscious on my part. I've known, but at the same time I couldn't come to terms with it. I've been in denial.'

'Aren't you angry?'

'No. Anger will probably come.'

Was there no end to this man's indifference? Depraved indifference? I said, 'Does Owen know you know?'

'Who?' he said. Then, loudly, 'What?'

He'd said *Who?* in a voice that was almost normal. When he said *What?*, his tone was up ten decibels. When he said, *What?*, Buddy headed for the hills, slinking out of the room, hugging the wall. Nick, the master of misdirection, was suddenly the victim of misdirection, even if my misdirection hadn't been intentional. He may have discerned that I was unnaturally joyful, but he hadn't thought the lover in question was someone of any significance. Nick assumed he was the significant one in my life, even if I had a lover. Now he was on his feet, his papers fluttering to the floor. The anger had come. 'What the hell did you just say?'

I didn't speak. I was enjoying observing as the revelation sank in. I could actually see it sinking in, deeper and deeper. He stepped toward me. 'Are you saying you've been fucking Owen Hall?'

Sink away.

His face was red, but then he stiffened his spine. The imperious academic aura returned as the red faded to pink, then to his usual light tan, but then to white. He said, 'You are ill-bred.'

Fury is good, says Poppy. I stood up too, and we were face-to-face. 'You're telling me, Nick, that if I were *well*-bred I would have been fucking the mailman? Is that it? Is that the scenario you were imagining? Kind of an adorable little tragicomedy where I would come running to you, confess, and then beg your forgiveness?'

He said, 'Why don't you just shut up?'

'Shut up? You mean "disappear," don't you? You go nuts when you find out I'm having an affair with someone who is your equal? Excuse me, make that *better than you*.'

He turned and strode from the room. I shouted after him. 'You're an asshole, Nick! A pompous asshole! You want ill-bred, believe me, I can give you ill-bred.'

I sat back down and put my face in my hands and cried. Because I missed Owen. Who was an even bigger schmuck than Nick.

Nick came back into the room. I felt him return though I didn't hear his footfalls. He sat down next to me. He said, 'So what were you wanting to say to me before I interrupted you with my ego?'

I lifted my face. 'I know this is really good and corny, but we've led separate lives. I want a joint life.' Trouble was, not with him.

He heaved a mighty sigh. 'Denise, since the day we met, we have been busy people. We've worked hard. I was never interested in living someone else's life. I believed that to be true of you as well. We complemented each other. When your first book came out, people kept asking me if it was my support that allowed your breakthrough. Could have knocked me over with a feather. I took great pride in the fact that I didn't even know what you were up to. I bragged that I'd had no idea. I've had no qualms about saying, She gets full credit. She worked her way up. She had to write a food column, for Christ's sake.

'My God, Denise, it's been fun watching you move mountains. We've never needed *attention* from one another. That's why we're both successful. We don't interfere with one another. We just make our own brand of contribution so that the merger works. Until you took on that blessed *food column*, they were traditional roles, I know. I know that. I produced money, and you used it to produce a home and family life. We wanted what we assumed to be normal, since what the two of us had when we grew up was anything but. I don't think either of us thought the other was doing anything except what we'd intended. I'd hold up my end of things; you'd hold up yours. We've never derided each other about anything, but then again, we've never bothered to praise, have we?'

'You derided me, Nick, because you felt there was nothing to praise me for. There is no praise for a woman who's a wife and mother. *You* get praise for crossing the street. Yes, we made a choice, but mine wasn't a particularly viable one. Because no one ever whapped me on the back and said, Well done. And you never thanked me. In fact, when the children were both in school you started dropping hints that I should—'

'You never thanked me either.'

'Okay, fine, thanks should have been understood. Except for the shove I gave you that got you here. I deserved thanks for that, because it was something you couldn't have done alone.'

'What shove?'

'To call Bill Clinton.'

'I only called to congratulate him. Then he hinted at—'

'Bullshit. You called because I shored you up and you found the wherewithal to risk being rejected. What the hell did you know about politics? Nothing. If we weren't such screwed-up people we would have *discussed* such an opportunity. But I was beneath you. You couldn't discuss it with me because you would not have considered the reasons I might offer for your rejoining Bill's circle. You'd have defended whatever excuse you'd make to yourself not to take such a risk. Because—'

'Denise—'

'I'm not finished. Because if you failed, you couldn't be what you felt you had to be in my eyes. The great provider and protector. What an extraordinary burden you've been under since the day we goddamn met.'

At that moment, I knew why I'd spoken my thoughts out loud to begin with, when the two of us were sitting, reading. I needed to tell him, to get it over with. 'Nick, I made a confession to you because I want an official end to my time as your student. I want to get that straight with you. Who the hell has room in married life for going around falling in love with other people? Not me. It's not what I want. I thought it was when it was happening, but no thanks. I'll get over him. I want to get over him. I intend to.'

He had a resigned look on his face. 'It's always more trouble than it's worth.'

I think I whispered '*Jesus*,' the way I'd whispered '*It's over*,' but maybe not. In any case, he didn't respond to it. He said, 'We have everything now, Denise. You have what you want, I have the same.'

While I pictured Nick in bed with every woman we've ever known, I said, 'On a professional level.' Then I smiled because I was picturing him in bed with Poppy. God, she'd have chewed him up and spit him out. 'On a gracious-living level.'

'Yes.' He smiled too. Then he said, 'I lied. I've been in denial. I wasn't so independent, so removed, as I like to think. I was jealous of that actor.'

'What actor?'

'Robert Vaughn. The one you interviewed who made the scrambled eggs. Don't laugh. I was jealous of his making a move on my wife.'

'He did not make a move.'

'He obviously liked you.'

'Liking someone is not a move, Nick. He was a gentleman.'

'Yes. Of course he was. But I was more jealous than I felt just a minute ago. And then, when you dashed off to Florida, I couldn't figure out what on God's earth you were doing, but I was damn jealous yet again. But after I searched my soul as to why I felt that jealousy – it was obviously because you don't need any help in moving those mountains of yours – I started to become very proud of you. And I don't mean that to sound condescending. Honestly. You know my pride. I was proud when I knew what you were able to escape from at eighteen. A magnificent escape. I was proud of your academic excellence, I was proud of how you took charge of raising a family with no experience in the correct way to do it. And now—'

He reached over and touched my wrist. That's what his first touch had been. Years ago, when I was in his class. After class. A touch on the wrist. But this time, I didn't wait for his second touch: running his fingers up my arm, lightly, like a moth. Instead, I took his hand, turned it over, and unbuttoned his cuff. I slid my hand up his sleeve, and my touch was not a moth's. I climbed over on top of him, kissing him while my hand was up past his elbow. The stitches of his shirt sleeve started popping. Then he was on me, rolling me under him. The sofa is blue silk damask and even the children intuitively know not to put their feet on it. We grabbed at the cushions as well as our clothes because we didn't know which was which. At some point, half undressed, we slipped off the edge of the sofa and down onto the floor, rolling over one another, bumping into furniture. The carpet is white. A fleeting thought of what I would say to the carpet cleaner the next day came and, mercifully, went. Married sex.

When he was inside me and just before he was going to come, I whispered, 'Say something.'

He did. He said, 'I love you,' of all damned things. Then he started to come; I knew he was starting to come because he pressed his face into my neck. I gripped his shoulders and pushed him back above me. I held his eyes with mine. While he ejaculated, I watched his face contort, a moment of vulnerability he had never let me see, not me and not other women, either, whoever they might have been. I was sure of that. His twisting expression turned me on. I started to come without having to concentrate. Still, I held him up. I made him watch me too. And finally, I turned to just skin and flesh, no muscles and bones, and let him collapse on me, and I was crushed by his weight.

That's the way Owen liked to do it: Watch me. I would teach that kind of intimacy to Nick if it killed me. Because if I didn't, if I allowed him to remain the calculating professor, he would lose me, and I wasn't sure yet if I wanted to lose him.

We went upstairs to bed. In our bedroom he was getting out his pajamas. I said, 'Nick.' He started to ask me what. 'I want to talk to you, only naked.'

That's why people have sex, so they can talk naked. We got under the covers and entwined ourselves in each other's arms. He said, 'I'm sorry, Denise, but please believe me – I wasn't avoiding you deliberately. I was thinking that if you left me, then I'd have thrown my life away like a pair of old shoes.' He pulled me up so that I was lying on top of him, looking down into his eyes in the bit of light coming from the crack in the closed draperies. He said, 'You wouldn't leave me for the mailman, I knew that. But you'd leave me for Owen Hall. That's why I freaked out. I'm incredibly flattered that you didn't. And, of course, very grateful. Denise, I'm sorry.'

I said, 'So am I.'

We made love again.

23

A month before Owen died, I began a new list incorporating all the research I'd done that would be the core of the book, a list, as it turned out, of negatives.

No weapon
No Miranda
No lawyer

Then I made sub-lists headed by categories.

Under WITNESSES:

No witnesses to the crime
No witnesses who saw Eddie wearing bloodstained clothes
No witnesses who saw Eddie ditch bloodstained clothes
No witnesses who saw Eddie ditch a weapon
No witnesses who saw Eddie acting suspicious

And under EVIDENCE:

No fingerprints
No knife injuries to Eddie (not even a little cut like O.J.'s)
No struggle injuries to the victims (no skin under their nails)

I began writing brief essays about what little the prosecutor did have. First was the sneaker print of blood found on the wall of the bathroom. The wall? Where else can you leave a print of a sneaker in a room with an inch of water on the floor? The sneaker print was Eddie's size. A sneaker was found in Eddie's home that fit the print. A local podiatrist testified that the sneaker conformed to Eddie's foot, to his particular gait, and that it could only be Eddie's sneaker and no one else's. This podiatrist's name came up several times in Michael Longman's notes. He was a 'manager' in Charles Hall Enterprises.

The sneaker entered in evidence was clean as a whistle. People said that was because Eddie was a neat fellow, knew how to take care of his things. And there were also little murmurings that a mother can make anything clean when no one else can. But even the most fastidious housewife in the world cannot get rid of all the gore that would accumulate on a sneaker after the wearer knifed three people to death.

There was the lavender Ralph Lauren polo shirt – not pink, as the newspaper report had it – found spotted with blood in the cemetery. Several friends testified that they'd never seen Eddie in such a shirt, and it was a color he would never wear. The blood was Eddie's. The DNA matched. But if Eddie went to the trouble of hiding the weapon so successfully and the rest of his clothes as well, went to the trouble of cleaning his sneakers until they looked brand-new, why toss his blood-spotted shirt in the cemetery? The shirt hadn't even been found until several weeks after the crime. The cemetery had been searched with a fine-tooth comb before that, many times, during the hunt for a weapon.

I dug around a little more. And I called Rosie. She said, 'The shirt belonged to Eddie's sister's boyfriend. She always liked wearing oversized men's polos. It was in the backseat of her car when Eddie cut himself opening a flip-top can – a *Coke* can. She and her boyfriend were on the way to Fenway Park. Eddie had gone along. He was in the back seat. She told Eddie to use the shirt on the floor while she rummaged around for a Band-Aid in her bag. The boyfriend told him not to worry, he was sick of the shirt. She was using it for a rag.'

'How did the shirt end up in the cemetery?'

'His sister has no idea what happened to the shirt.'

'Is that what she said when she testified?'

'She didn't testify. She told people.'

'How come she didn't testify?'

'She wasn't called. Ask Gorman about that. Ask her.'

The shirt went on a list of things to ask Dan Gorman, Eddie's public defender.

I said to Rosie, 'How could this Gorman guy not have gotten Eddie off? I feel as though *I* could have gotten him off.'

'He miscalculated, Denise. Simple. Him and Marcia Clark, both of them, screwed up. He in his way, she in hers.'

Public defenders are always overburdened; they take meals on the run, they work long hours into the night. But still. The time had definitely come to visit Dan Gorman.

Owen had told me, when the time arrived to make an appointment with Gorman, to mention his name and things would move quickly. Things did. Obviously, Owen hadn't called him to say, I've had a change of heart. Don't see her. Gorman's secretary put me through then and there. I told him what I was about, but he already knew. Could I have an interview with him? He said, 'Sure, why not?' I told him I'd like to see him as soon as possible. He said, 'Squeeze you in tomorrow, if you like. Before things get rolling. Nine o'clock.'

I headed for the airport, first apologizing to Buddy, explaining that I wasn't going to the beach house. His eyelids lowered to half mast, and he gazed dramatically off into the distance. 'Next time,' I promised. I gave him a slice of baloney, the least favorite of his snacks but all I had on hand.

I arrived at the Providence Superior Court building at ten of nine. The fanciful front doors on Main Street were locked. The locks were rusted, the mantra, no doubt, budget cuts. I had to elbow my way through all the people standing in front of the side entrance to the court. There were three groups: young hoodlums in jeans; traffic violators in going-to-work clothes; and suited, cocky, high-end petty criminals. Cigarette smoke drifted up from all three groups. At one minute to nine, there was a mass movement, dropped and squashed butts as the lawyers arrived, a dozen of them at the very last minute, car wheels squealing before they leapt out, self-important, hauling bulging briefcases. The lawyers and their clients found each other and entered the building.

I went in and immediately passed Courtroom A on the left, the courtroom where Eddie Baines had been tried and found guilty of murder in four days. I passed Courtrooms B, C, and D; at the end of the corridor was a door with a brass plate that read OFFICE OF THE PUBLIC DEFENDER. A long list of names to the side of the door included Daniel X. Gorman. Most Irishmen with the middle name Xavier are named Francis. Maybe the guy would be a little different from the harried stereotype I was imagining.

Inside was a tiny waiting room about six by eight feet with a bench against one wall. A young man sat on the bench, staring at his feet. He looked Arabic. Directly opposite the door, a chest-high wall was topped with a glass partition. There was a partially opened sliding window in the glass, the kind you see in a doctor's office, and a thin gray-haired secretary stood attempting to communicate with a young woman facing her. The woman's arms were wrapped around a struggling one-year-old slung onto her hip. She had spiked purple-black hair, ripped jeans, and a row of gold studs edging the perimeter of each ear. She was shouting at the woman behind the glass.

'I'm gonna fight the charge!'

'And what was the charge again?'

'A loud party.'

'The charge was disturbing the peace?'

'Yeah.'

'That's a misdemeanor. You just pay the fine. You don't need a public defender.'

'It ain't no misdemeanor to me. I'm telling you, I need a lawyer but I got no money. That's what this guy is for, right?' She jabbed her finger through the inch of space in the window.

'If you want to fight a charge, you need to fill out a form with the police department in the jurisdiction where you were charged. Then you will be notified of a court date in the mail. A lawyer will be assigned.'

The young woman slung the baby around to the other hip. 'As a matter of fact, I just changed my fuckin' mind. I don't want to fight the charge. I want to *sue* my *fuckin' neighbor* for calling the cops! I don't call the cops when *he* throws a party!'

The secretary behind the glass began explaining the difference between a criminal suit and a civil suit. She went on and on, even after the baby had set up a hearty howl and had managed to pull one arm free. He grabbed hold of a chunk of his mother's hair and began yanking away. With her head pulled down almost to her shoulder, she interrupted the secretary's calm instructions by turning on her heel and striding past me to the door. She shouted over her shoulder, 'I'll be back, let me tell you!'

A man walked in, surveyed the scene, gave a shrug of disgust, and walked out. I said to the Arab, 'Did you want to go next?'

He ignored me. He was stoned. I moved up to the window. The secretary looked at me, turned, and walked off out of sight.

I waited for her to return, but after a few minutes I knocked on the glass, pushed the sliding window open the rest of the way, and called out, 'Anybody in there?'

A man's muffled voice called back, 'Hold on,' and then I heard him mumble, 'Shit.'

Daniel Gorman emerged from a door at the end of a short corridor and stood there. He was red-haired and freckle-faced and had a head too big for his body. People with big heads give off an aura of being overbearing, and he did, but his face had humanity in it. Reminded me, actually, of Buddy. He asked me, 'Where's my secretary?'

I said, 'She disappeared. She took one look at me and left. I'm Denise Burke and I have an appointment with you, I believe.'

'You do. Sorry. Come in.'

But I couldn't get in. The door to the inner office was locked. I went back to the window. 'This door's locked, Mr Gorman.'

'Dan. Hold on.'

He came down the corridor, opened the door, and led me back to his office. The string of red lights on his intercom were all blinking. They continued blinking throughout our interview. He gestured me to one of two chairs in front of his desk. We both sat down. I did not cross my legs. I told him I wanted to spend just a few minutes describing what I knew of the crime and asked him to correct me if I was wrong.

He interrupted my first sentence with the panache of someone who is interviewed by writers all the time. Harried, but not the stereotype. My first sentence was, 'I understand that Eddie Baines never admitted guilt to the crime.' Before I could ask him if that was so, Gorman said, 'I'd rather start with the basic situation, okay?'

'And what would that be?'

'Eddie Baines was in clinical depression when the crime

occurred. He was losing his girlfriend just the way he'd lost everything else. After he learned of the crime he was upset and sad about it, like the rest of the people in town. The crime only added to his misery. He started drinking heavily.'

'His state of mind, I take it, didn't help matters when he was arrested?'

'That's exactly right. In the days between the discovery of the bodies and his arrest, the family of his girlfriend, Patty Olschefski, wouldn't let her see him. He tried but failed. He had failed at everything; that was his outlook. A week or so after the murders, he heard that Patty had escaped from her house arrest; he knew where she'd go, to this bar they liked in Providence. When he found her, she told him to take a hike; because of him she was in a shitload of trouble – her expression, according to Eddie – and couldn't see him again. But she relented a little because she thought he might have what she was most interested in. Asked him if he had any cocaine for her and her girlfriend. He didn't. He'd been drinking all day, though, so he was fortified; he lied, told her he knew where they could get some, and they left the bar and got in the friend's car.

'They drove awhile and they argued. When the friend realized Eddie didn't know where he could get any drugs after all, she threw them both out and took off. He didn't kidnap anyone; he didn't have a gun like she'd said. He told me that and I believed him. Why wouldn't I? There was no gun found. Eddie was never in his life seen with a gun.'

I wrote as fast as I could. I didn't dare interrupt.

'Patty explained to Eddie that a policeman had been to see her. She must have been terrified. Up until then, she figured her troubles were over. She'd done what she was instructed to do.'

'Instructed to do?'

'Instructed to get Eddie Baines into the Montevallo house before the bodies were discovered. The officer told her Eddie was a suspect, and he warned her and her family to say she'd been home with them the night of the murder. That was the first time Eddie heard he was officially a suspect, and now he assumed it was all over for him.'

'Who was this policeman who—'

'She said she didn't know. The Olschefskis said she'd made it up. I spoke to all the cops in New Caxton. No one from the police department said they questioned her, not until after Eddie was arrested. None of them said they'd been to her house.'

I leaned forward. 'So what you're saying . . .'

'Here's what I'm saying. Here's what I know. If a cop came to Patty's house, it was to be kept a secret.'

'How long had the police been suspecting him at that point?'

'They weren't. But Eddie fell apart, right there on the street, when Patty told him they were suspects. Panicked. He started begging, pleading with her, asking her not to lie. They were together the night of the murder. The whole night. People saw them together. He told her she'd get caught in the lie because, eventually, the police would find out about the next night – when they *were* at the Montevallo house, erasing the incriminating evidence Patty told Eddie someone had planted. So she started to panic too. Someone was walking toward them on the street and she started screaming. Screaming for help. Pushing at Eddie like he was attacking her. That's when Eddie really saw the handwriting on the wall.

'He ran. Ran into a house at the end of the street, the only house that was dark. No one was home. The door was unlocked. It was a safe residential neighborhood. Eddie grabbed a knife in the kitchen, ran into the pantry, and stabbed himself. He couldn't take what he knew was coming. Eddie Baines tried to kill himself and he made a damn good attempt at it, I'll tell you. This was a suicide attempt that was no simple cry for help. He plunged a huge butcher knife into his chest. Broke his sternum, but the sternum deflected the knife, caused it to slide sideways. Missed his heart. Right up until the very last time I saw him, he never stopped wishing he had succeeded in killing himself.'

Gorman sat back and held his hands out toward me. 'That's the situation I was dealing with. Complicated.'

'Very.'

I liked Gorman. He wanted to stick to the business at hand, no more. No ego that I could see. So why had he miscalculated? 'When you saw him, Mr Gorman, what's the first thing you asked him?'

'I told you, Dan.'

'Dan.'

'If he did it.'

'What did he say?'

He thought hard. Eddie obviously hadn't said yes or no. 'He told me it didn't matter whether he'd done it or not. That he would be the one to pay. *They chose me* is what he said.'

'In those words?'

'Yes.'

'Who chose him?'

'I'm not sure. I think he'd gotten it into his head that the whole town had picked him as the scapegoat. Totally paranoid. The man was mentally ill as far as I'm concerned. I humored him, sympathized with him. Then I told him none of it mattered because *I* knew he didn't do it. Explained to him there was no solid evidence to say he did. But he wasn't listening to me. He didn't care anymore about anything. He'd given up. Frankly, the guy seemed close to brain-dead. Sat right where you are now and never moved a muscle. I had to pull answers from him. Mostly, he'd give me a shrug or a nod. Of course, he was still in a very weak condition from trying his damnedest to kill himself. The surgery—'

'Did you ask him about the deathbed confession?'

'He made no confession. The cop on the scene interpreted Eddie's words as a confession, and that's what the prosecutor chose to believe. That was her whole case. Legally, a dying declaration waives the usual hearsay rules of evidence and is admissible even if the person lives – provided it can be proven that he believed he was dying when the declaration was made.'

'Was it proven?'

'Not as far as I'm concerned.'

'As far as the judges were concerned?'

'Yes.'

I put a big asterisk next to the line of notes I was taking. 'The cop didn't read him his rights at that point?'

'The cop insisted he wasn't under arrest. In the hospital, when he was being wheeled into surgery, that's when he was arrested and read his rights. When the surgeon said it never happened, the prosecutor did a number on him. Her argument was that he was running around like a chicken with his head cut off, in an emergency situation, and he hadn't had any sleep in a long time. She told him he missed it.'

'The nurses? Did they hear it?'

'The nurses said they were concentrating on keeping Eddie's vital signs stable. Said they weren't paying attention, so they could have missed it.'

'Dan?'

'What?'

'If Eddie didn't do it, who did? Who told his girlfriend to see to it that he was incriminated?'

He settled back deeper into his chair. 'My job in the case of Eddie Baines versus the state of Rhode Island was to show there was not sufficient evidence to convict this man of the murder of Connie, Peter, and Timothy Montevallo. That's exactly what I did. I don't care who *did* kill those people.'

I looked up from my notebook. 'You don't?'

'No. I mean, I hope whoever did it gets caught, of course. But I am not one of your fans, Mrs Burke. I am not—'

'Denise. You're not what?'

'I am not a true-crime aficionado. I hate crime, the real thing and your brand too.'

I never think about things like fans. When I looked into Daniel Gorman's eyes, I had to remind myself of his perception of me: as a celebrity of sorts. Owen had had that same perception, but he was used to celebrities. Maybe that's why I trusted Owen so willingly; he was one of us. Foolish me.

I said, 'What else besides the lack of evidence convinced you that Eddie didn't do it?'

'I didn't need anything else.'

'On a personal level, then. If you'd been a nonpartisan observer, what would have told you he was innocent?'

First, Dan Gorman looked down at his watch. Then he spoke. 'As an observer, I would have said Eddie Baines was surer than hell he was going to be found guilty, even though he didn't do it. He had no interest in fighting the charges because he knew it wouldn't do any good. He'd completely accepted his status as he saw it. He was on automatic from the time I saw him until he was convicted. If he'd done it, he'd have fought. That's what real killers do. Proclaim their innocence until the noose chokes off their voice.'

'I know.'

'I guess you would.'

'But isn't that what innocent people do who are framed?'

'No. Mostly they're too shocked or too furious to think straight. My job is to fight *for* them. In this case, I didn't think

I'd have to fight very hard. I was dead wrong. It'll never happen again.'

'Did you ever talk to Eddie after the trial?'

'Why would I? Filed the appeal and I was out of it. He drew a good lawyer for the appeal. The guy was sure he'd win it, too. Just like I did. And, like me, he didn't. He lost the appeal, and he threw in the towel.'

'Meaning?'

'He resigned. Despite our politically correct tough-on-crime climate, he announced that it was immoral to press a case against an innocent party. Imagine that. Fat lot of good his protest did. Eddie Baines was the chosen patsy, and whoever chose him knew he'd have a damn easy job of it. Eddie was a savvy fellow. More savvy than me, as it turned out. Knew the battle was lost before it began. Since he hadn't succeeded in killing himself, he looked forward to the state doing the job for him. Spending the rest of his life in jail was the same thing, as far as he was concerned. Didn't matter.'

I sat back and looked at him. Burned out. I said, 'I haven't read the transcripts yet, just the news accounts of the murder and the trial. And I've talked to a few people. It seems no one has ever brought up Brenda Montevallo's involvement with drugs.'

'So what?'

'She disappeared for years. She left her baby with her mother. She comes back from God knows where, her family gets wiped out, and there's not a shred of evidence as to who committed the crime. Sounds like Colombia to me, not Rhode Island.'

I said that with a bit of a smile. I wanted to get him off the track – the track he planned to stay on while he talked to me. It worked. Right then he came to life. His voice boomed. 'There was no connection between Brenda and the death of her child.'

I said very calmly, 'Who says?'

'No one. A hunch. She was pathetic. She was destroyed.'

'And she was beautiful, I understand.'

'What are you trying to say?'

I crossed my legs. I looked at a line scribbled in the margin of my notes. 'Dan, why didn't you call Eddie's sister as a witness? She told the police that the lavender polo shirt was hers. That Eddie had—'

'Part of my strategy that didn't work.'

'What was that strategy?'

'Not to dwell on bloody shirts. Not to dwell on anything, period. Do it fast.' He leaned forward. 'You don't understand, do you?'

'Understand what?'

'Never for a minute did I think there was a rat's chance in hell that Eddie would be found guilty. I recommended a bench trial. Three justices would require only facts. It wouldn't be necessary to go through the usual manipulations. I thought their decision would be based on the absence of evidence.'

'Then would you please hazard a guess about why the judges found him guilty?'

His lips set. 'They were success-oriented.'

'They were what?'

'Success-oriented. It was a high-profile case for them. There had been enormous pressure to solve it: to find the perpetrator, to punish him, and – for a while – to demonstrate the need for Rhode Island to adopt the death penalty. Political futures were on the line for all of them, right down to the cop on the beat. To the cop that took the so-called confession. The state's case against Eddie Baines was based on their own needs.'

There was nothing I could say to that. Daniel X. Gorman's eyes were suddenly very hard. He was angry, but he controlled his anger well. His lips were pressed so tightly together they were white. I had to say something to bring him back. I said, 'Somebody got to them.'

He leaned back in his chair. He was sagging again. 'Sounds like it, doesn't it? But that's not the story. They're little people. They want wins for their communities and, in turn, for the people who manage their appointments. Judges are judges in this state because they make their payments. New Caxton, Rhode Island, has nothing to do with Colombian drug lords and neither do the judges. They keep things real low-key. They don't want the Feds nosing around making fools of them. Life's short, you know. That's what you learn in this business. They've got their little niche and they owe it to one person: your friend. I don't owe him a goddamn thing, and that's why I'm stuck where I am.'

'What friend?'

'The good congressman.'

'When I asked your secretary for an appointment, I mentioned the good congressman's name and she responded immediately.'

'She wants her niche too.'

His gaze softened. He couldn't help it. He wasn't a bad guy, but he was trapped somewhere he didn't want to be, and he knew he wasn't about to be let out anytime soon. What he felt for Eddie Baines was empathy. I said, 'What was the worst thing they did?'

'Who's they?'

'The judges on the bench trying Eddie Baines.'

He never skipped a beat. 'They didn't allow the fucking time element into evidence. Excuse my language.'

Men don't use the F-word in the company of a woman unless they want to undermine her or, conversely, if they feel they can trust her. It's all in the tone. He was trusting me. 'What time element?'

'From the time of the killing – from before the time of the killing, all day Friday – we listed the witnesses who'd been with Eddie, or talked to him, or even seen him. He punched out of work at five. Gabbed with coworkers on the way to their cars. They were feeling good. The week was over. It was payday. They shared a six-pack in the parking lot. Eddie picked up his girlfriend at the factory where she worked. She'd hidden in a little corner somewhere. Her brothers were supposed to pick her up. The parents were killing themselves trying to get her to stop seeing Eddie, figured it would help if she didn't have use of a car. But she knew her way around, that one.

'They went to a 7-Eleven and picked up a Sara Lee coffee cake for his mother: dessert. They had dinner with her and Eddie's sister and the sister's fiancé. They ate at five-forty-five, left the house at seven. A neighbor dropped by while they were eating. The woman needed to borrow some half-and-half. Her husband was throwing a fit because she only had milk for his coffee.

'After dinner they went to buy gas. It's the only gas station in town. A lot of people go in and out to shoot the bull with the owner, bum a cigarette.'

'Frankie Gedzeniak's gas station.'

'That's right. They chatted with him for quite a while; Eddie and Frankie played ball together. Eddie and Patty hung out until after eight-thirty. While he was there, Eddie lent a friend ten dollars. Told the friend not to worry about it, he'd just been paid. The prosecutor claimed he was so free with his money because it wasn't his money, it was Connie Montevallo's. But the employees where Eddie worked can cash their pay checks right after they're paid. That's what he always did.

'Eddie bought a pack of cigarettes as they left. It's on the register tape. Recorded. The place is a bookie joint. Still, Gedzeniak was willing to incriminate himself, explain to the court why he had such a careful record. Judges wouldn't let me call him.'

'Why?'

'Irrelevant. There was no suppression hearing to determine whether questionable evidence was admissible. They just went ahead and suppressed at will.'

'I can't believe it.'

'That's the point. I couldn't either, not even while it was happening. From the time Eddie left work until after midnight when he went home to bed, witnesses saw him. The longest stretch where he wasn't seen by anyone . . . including Patty . . . was no more than fifteen minutes. You can stab three people to death in less than that, but ditching bloody clothes and cleaning up makes fifteen minutes unfeasible. And he was wearing the same clothes all evening. A lot of people told me that. Could he have taken the clothes off, committed the murder naked, cleaned up, and then put the same clothes back on? Yeah, right. Him and Lizzie Borden. Or maybe he wore a black sweatsuit over everything. But Eddie Baines wasn't planning to murder anyone. He just lived his life from minute to minute. And the minute came where he had to do something outlandish.'

'What was that?'

'Clean up the scene of a triple murder. He didn't see a choice. His girlfriend told them there had been evidence planted against him. He believed that to be true. He was desperate. To be charged with the murder meant his destruction, his family's destruction. He had to save them. So he did it. He went to the Montevallos with Patty twenty-four hours after the crime and helped her clean up the gore. Mostly, he stood there while she flooded the place.'

He took out his pen and played with it, stroked it while he thought about what he was trying to convince me to believe. 'They didn't let the time frame in, but they did let in the watch, and the watch belonged to the victim, not Eddie. I was not allowed to present the time frame, which would have demonstrated that it was impossible for Eddie to have committed this crime.'

I started to ask why, but he'd already told me why. The judges were success-oriented. An unsolved crime as violent as the killings in New Caxton that goes unpunished would make for a very definite lack of success.

'What about that watch?'

'Right. The watch. The prosecutor introduced it as evidence. Somewhere along the line, there was a major screwup. If evidence had been planted, if the prosecutor suspected the evidence was planted but didn't bother to act on her suspicions, then she might assume the watch was Eddie's. I'm not accusing anybody in particular of anything, but the watch was entered into evidence as belonging to Eddie. The watch was found on the kitchen floor – ripped off his wrist, they said, in the struggle with Connie. But the watch belonged to Petey. It was taken from Petey's wrist, tampered with, and left on the kitchen floor – I guess to look as though Eddie stole it and then dropped it, I don't know.'

'By "tampered with," you're talking about the hair in the watch-band. His.'

'Yeah.'

'Patty got one of Eddie's hairs and put it in the watch?'

He blinked. 'Patty? Of course not. The cops did that.'

'Which cops?'

'If I knew, I'd have done something.'

'Were witnesses called to say the watch wasn't Eddie's? That it was Petey's?'

'Sure. Some said the watch wasn't Eddie's – his friends – and some perjured themselves and said they didn't know whose watch it was.'

'Jesus. What about the sneaker print?'

'Wasn't Eddie's.'

'The kind of shoe he wore, his size.'

'Wasn't his.'

'Whose, then?'

'I wouldn't know.'

'If it wasn't his, someone went to a lot of trouble to find an identical sneaker and make the print. The cops?'

'Maybe. Patty had a shitload of stuff with her when she went in that house with Eddie. Cleaning supplies. But Patty took the fifth.'

I flipped through my notes. 'She brought the cleaning supplies when she and Eddie went to the Montevallos to clean up. Were they in a bag?'

'Big bag.'

'The sneaker might have been in there.'

I waited for him to respond. He didn't.

'So where's the bag of cleaning supplies that had a sneaker hidden under the paper towels? Where are the used paper towels?'

'She got rid of them. Someone got rid of them. Maybe her parents *ate* them, for Christ's sake. I couldn't get to her. She wasn't arrested. The prosecutor called her and she took the fifth.'

'But couldn't you have—'

He slammed his fist down on the desk. 'I *told* you I didn't read this whole goddamned thing right. I fucked up!'

His eyes went down to my hand. He said, 'We've got the same pen, except yours is the real thing and mine's a knockoff.'

My agent bought the green-enameled Montblanc for me – sent it to me along with the check from Tri-Star when they bought the rights to my first book. I told Dan Gorman mine was a knockoff, too, that I'd bought it at Wal-Mart.

He said, 'The judges decided on a conviction before their little show even began. They fully intended to secure their status.'

'Success-oriented.'

'Yeah.'

'What did you make of Officer Weinecke?'

He leaned far back into his chair. 'The Polish boy? The one who took Brenda's call?'

'Yes. Who's now the chief of police of New Caxton.'

'It has not been lost on me that the now-chief lives in what used to be the Hall townhouse. Nicest house in town. You get it with the job. Not bad for a guy imported to marry an unmarriageable daughter. Bastards. All of them.'

On my way home, I thought back to what Owen had said about Daniel X. Gorman. 'He's one of those guys who's stuck in a rut. And he was up against Gretchen Loeb. She's a pisser, let me tell you. Threw him off.'

'She was the prosecutor?'

'Yes.'

'You know her?'

'I know everyone in Rhode Island, Denise.'

'Do you know the attorney who handled the appeal?'

'Not well. Not the way I do Gretchen. Gretchen's been around. She and her husband are old friends of mine. The guy who handled the appeal was a good kid, but not cut out for any of this.'

I stared for a long time into the blank wall in my office, which I keep blank for when I need to think. I was thinking: Star athletes are pampered. Eddie was pampered in kind. But his father had died and he wanted to do right by his mother. She never pampered him, she only supported him. And when he was injured playing college football, no one pampered him. He got his degree on his own. He could fend for himself. Yes, the college paid for his last year, but that's not pampered, that's showing mercy to someone who deserved it. Because his father had just died, he had to support his mother. He came home. But there were no jobs for newly graduated, would-be teachers in Rhode Island. Luck of the draw. So he took a job in his father's old factory. By then, manufacturing jobs didn't pay enough to allow a worker any independence. Particularly one who was still part-time with no benefits. The factory was not a ladder up, the way it had been in his father's time. There was no *up* to go to. He was going nowhere. He snorted some cocaine to take the edge off.

Owen seemed to think doing time was what Eddie needed to stay out of worse trouble. But staying out of trouble was something Eddie had always done until he was accused of murdering three people, and there is no worse trouble than that.

24

I wrote a letter to Eddie Baines. I asked if I could come talk to him. He responded immediately.

Dear Mrs Burke,

I have received your letter. After I was in prison for a couple of years – once I finally came to my senses – I began to see what had happened. I never knew what happened to me up until a short time ago. I didn't know while it was happening. I didn't know while my mother was alive, when she was telling me she would see to it that people understood that I wouldn't kill our neighbors. Now I know she died trying. I am ashamed because I'd succumbed to self-pity.

Maybe you will uncover the truth. There is no way I can do that, so I am glad for the opportunity to speak with you if it will help. Anytime you can come, I will welcome your visit.

Sincerely yours,
Edward Baines

The letter woke me up. I'd heard many times that Eddie had been a smart kid, a good student, but I hadn't imagined an articulate man when I'd thought about him. That's because

I knew he was a black man. Eddie, never Edward. I was prejudiced. I'd created a stereotype in my head. I felt shame.

I called the warden's office. Normally, I have to do a lot of explaining to be allowed visitation privileges, since I am not family, not a counselor, not connected to the legal system. Louis has to vouch for me via the publisher's attorneys. It takes several weeks. Pride not being an issue with me anymore, I automatically started to mention Owen's name: Owen Allen Hall, the secret password. But I caught myself and blurted out instead, 'Charles Hall told me to tell you it would help me a lot if you could expedite matters.'

The warden at the Rhode Island State Penitentiary didn't say, Who? He said, very cheerily, 'As a nonfamily member, you can see the prisoner for one half hour. He's entitled to a visit from nonfamily for one half hour each month.' He made no mention of the regulation that nonfamily members had to be counselors or lawyers. The name Charles Hall overrode the regulation. I asked if Eddie had many visitors. He said, 'At first he did. Then just his mother. Then, no one. Typical.'

I said, 'How long since he's had a visitor?'

'I'd be glad to find out for you.'

I thanked him.

I've been to four prisons and I've spoken to four accused killers in the prisoners' visiting rooms: Sam Litton, the woman who killed her children, the lady poisoner, and the guy in Tennessee who ended up confessing. The first, my friend Sam, I believed to be innocent until he opened his mouth. After that experience, I approached the other three with the knowledge that I would most likely be confronting evil in human form. O.J. wouldn't see me; he saw no percentage in doing so. The others wanted one more person to proclaim their innocence to since there were no dream teams around.

I saw them not as mad, not as victims of a crazed moment,

not as innocent because of the miserable lives they'd claimed to have lived – just as plain evil. But Eddie Baines? How many people are convicted of murder who are actually innocent? I like to think, not too many. I didn't visit Eddie thinking he was innocent, the way I did Sam, or guilty, the way I did the child killer and the poisoner and the guy who confessed. I visited him to hear what he would tell me.

Whenever I sit down across from the subjects of my books – as well as across from those who, in the end, don't make the cut – the first thing they do is flash me a lovely smile. Sam Litton's smile told me on the spot that there had been, most definitely, a terrible mistake. It was the same smile he used in the *Bridgefield Press* newsroom and in the shop across the street from the paper where we'd go and pick up the coffee and pastry orders, the smile I got once when he asked to see pictures of my kids. After the smile, though, the words that I won't forget came out of his mouth: *I never hurt them, Denise*. There was no mistake from that moment on but that he was a murderer and he was evil.

Lorraine, the woman who shot her children, was still stiff from the surgery she'd had to repair the wound she'd inflicted on herself. But she'd tried to smile that smile at me and said, 'Someone killed my baby. I thank Jesus, on my knees – every night – for at least leaving me the other two.' The smile faded into a smirk. I wanted to ask her why she wasn't mad at Jesus for not saving the third one. Although she tried, she could not manufacture the look of someone who had suffered the loss of a child. The look of Louisa Longman. Lorraine managed something that was more like a grimace, like she'd just stubbed her toe.

The poisoner grinned from ear to ear and asked if I'd brought her anything. She weighed three hundred pounds, easy, and she was very short. She was referring to food. When I told her

I hadn't, the grin evaporated; her face just glazed over, and not until I told her I'd bring her something next time did she become animated again. She'd like a chocolate éclair. I brought her one as promised. I managed to restrain myself from spitting on it.

Eddie Baines didn't smile. It didn't matter to Eddie whether or not I liked him. He hadn't thought about charming me when he'd agreed to see me. He wasn't hoping I'd bring him food. He was from New Caxton. He wanted to see that his mother was honored as she deserved to be; he displayed the manners he'd been taught by his family. He picked up the handset and said, 'I'm sorry, ma'am, that you have to be in this place.'

I said, 'I've been in prisons before, Mr Baines.'

He said, 'Yes, I understand that.'

Eddie Baines was tall and slim. He seemed almost frail. Not my image of a football player. But everyone said he'd preferred basketball to football. New Caxton being a football town, he'd gone along with what he was told to do. Because he thrived on being taken care of? Or because he was taught to respect the opinions of those who were more knowledgeable than he? The former pro coach told him he was a football player, a damned good one, and he had to forget about basketball. So he did.

I asked, 'Who do you think killed the Montevallos, Mr Baines?'

He frowned. 'I don't know their names.'

I didn't show my surprise at his answer. I'd learned from watching Poppy in action. She only showed surprise when dramatic effect was necessary, as with, 'You didn't enjoy being on the run, Mr Litton? Had you considered ending your murder spree so that you wouldn't have to be on the run?'

I said, 'Who does know their names?'

'Brenda Montevallo knows. And Patty must know

something, because she's the one they used to get me to do it.'

Do it. Would he never learn? 'By do it, you mean—'

'Clean it up.'

His head went down. Then he looked back up at me with clear eyes. Clear eyes, but still such a massive naïveté about him. There *are* people like that: never doubt a person's word; can't judge others realistically; think everyone is trustworthy, has their best interests at heart. Maybe that happens when a child is loved too much.

Then he said, 'When I finally let myself think about all this, I came to see that the idea was for her to get me to leave my fingerprints, not get rid of something that had been planted against me. But then – when we got in the house – Patty went berserk. I mean, once she saw . . . I didn't believe Patty when she told me about what had happened. And when we were inside, I realized she'd never really believed it either. What we saw was so horrible . . .'

He put his hands to his head and leaned forward into them, as if the weight of the memory was impossible to support without help.

He said, 'She went crazy. She just attacked that house, turning on the water everywhere, throwing pail after pail all over the place. I did the same. I didn't want to be blamed for what I saw. I went crazy too. And all of a sudden there was a knock at the door. Patty and I just hung on to each other and stood there. We were paralyzed. But then whoever it was went away. We grabbed everything and ran. I kept saying to Patty that we had to go to the police. She kept saying, No, no. My car was under the highway. We got in and drove away.'

'Then what happened?'

'We got high.'

'And then?'

'And then there was nothing. Nothing. I kept drinking, and

I tried to get in touch with Patty. Now . . . I don't know. While I was on trial I remember thinking that we probably washed away the fingerprints that the real killers left. But then I came to understand that the people who did the killing would have been careful not to leave a trace. Would have known *how* not to leave a trace. They knew their business. We were sent there to incriminate ourselves.'

'Mr Baines, I can't understand how you could have been in that house and not . . . not fled within seconds, after seeing the bodies of that family. Your neighbors.'

He started to tremble. 'I couldn't leave Patty there alone. The bodies were right there in front of us. I just went along and did what I did because she was so crazy and because it kept me from looking at them. We turned all the faucets on. We filled up buckets and dumped water on the floor. I didn't want the bundle on the bed to be Timmy, but I knew it was.'

'Mr Baines.'

He breathed in deeply. 'Yes?'

'Did you and Patty, the night before, go into Mrs Montevallo's house not expecting to find anyone? Did you think they were out, at choir practice or somewhere? Did you go to steal money that might be there? And when you found them home, is that when Patty went crazy? Did she grab a knife and start stabbing them? And, if so, are you protecting her? Or did you go crazy, too? Did you stab them?'

Tears sprang to his eyes. He held my gaze but said nothing. He was unable to speak.

'You can either answer the questions, and we'll go on, or you can ignore the questions and we'll go on. I just felt you should know what's in my head.'

He said, 'I didn't kill the Montevallos, and neither did she. I didn't murder them, and I didn't go to the house to steal Mrs Montevallo's money. I'm not a murderer, and I'm not a thief.'

'Earlier, did you say that you don't remember what happened after you cleaned the Montevallo house?'

'I remember it. I told you there was *nothing* afterward. I meant my life was nothing. But I was sick. I mean, sick to my stomach. I couldn't eat, I couldn't sleep. I needed to be with Patty. I needed her to come to the police with me and tell them what we'd seen, what we'd done . . .'

'What you'd done?'

'We didn't kill them.'

'I'm sorry. Please go on.'

'I wanted to tell the police about some guy coming to see Patty and telling her to do what she did. But I couldn't get to her. When I finally did, it was too late. She had been turned against me, I could see that. After I was arrested, when the lawyer told me that the police found no evidence that she was with me at all, that there was no proof of what I was saying, I knew my word was no good. Her family's word was. If my father had been alive, it would have been different. But my mother was alone . . . a woman alone . . . my mother . . . her word was no good either. And someone got Patty this lawyer. A lawyer who works for a famous lawyer.'

'How did they find your sneaker print?'

'They didn't find any print of *my* sneaker. Those were my good sneakers. I only used them when I played basketball with the kids.'

'What kids?'

'The kids at the Providence Y. I'm supposed to be a teacher. It was a way to stay in shape.' He looked into my eyes right then. He'd showed me a tiny trace of the man he must once have been. The trace disappeared. 'If only Patty'd let me talk to her. My defender said Patty maybe brought a sneaker like mine with her and dipped it in blood and made a print on the wall. She didn't do that. Someone else did.'

'A cop?'

'Cops were the only ones they let in there, right? They said they found a watch that belonged to me, but the watch was Petey's. They put a hair in it. I'm sure you know. A "negroid" hair, is what the lady called it. That it was mine. But they messed up. Everyone knew it was Petey's watch. He'd won it at a singing competition. So then they got people to swear under oath that they couldn't be sure it was his watch when they knew all along it was. There were people in the courtroom who knew it was Petey's watch, Petey's aunts and uncles and cousins. I kept waiting for them to jump up and say, *Hey, that's our Petey's watch.* But they didn't. I knew it was his watch because I was there when he won it. I took my mother to the competition. That day she said to Mrs Montevallo that my dad wouldn't have missed it for anything, and neither would we. Mrs Montevallo kept telling Petey that the best football player that ever played in New Caxton had come to hear him sing. She hugged me because my being there meant so much to Petey. Petey showed me the watch after.' His voice became a whisper. 'The best . . .'

'What did Dan Gorman say when you told him about that watch?'

'I didn't tell him. I didn't see what good it would do. He realized during the trial that it wasn't my watch. I let him down, didn't I? I was selfish because I felt sorry for myself.'

There was nothing I could say to him. I watched as his shoulders came up. His back was suddenly straight. 'I didn't care then. I was selfish then. And I am so angry with myself. It wasn't my watch. People who knew me testified that I never wore a watch. I sat there listening in the courtroom, and I knew that because of the watch business I should have been set free. But I also knew I wouldn't be, no matter what. I didn't fight. I didn't fight because I didn't care. And I didn't care because there was something wrong with me at the time. There must have been, for me to let my mother down like that.' His hands had a little tremble in them. 'We don't wear watches. The judges knew.'

'We?'

'Athletes. Football players.'

For a moment, I thought maybe there was some truth to what Owen had said: Athletes have people to tell them what to do every minute of the day, so why wear a watch? If they want to know what time it is, just ask. But there was no truth there. It made no sense.

'Mr Baines, why don't athletes wear watches?'

'We break them if we forget to take them off. You know, if we wear them to scrimmage.'

My watch broke once. Skiing. I hit a bump and went head over heels. Later, I noticed my watch had stopped. 'Do you think Patty Olschefski put your hair into the watch?'

'No. I think someone else did. Afterward. One of the people who wanted me blamed for the killing.'

'Why were you chosen to be accused of this crime?'

He settled back into the slump. His eyes closed. He said, 'They knew I wouldn't fight back. I don't know how it is that some people can know things like that about a person. I guess maybe that's what they're paid to do: figure out what's in a person's head. When I came home from college, I had this plan. I'd be a teacher, I'd keep a lookout for my mother, I'd meet a local girl and fall in love, and I'd get married and have children and be a good father like my dad had been to me and my sister. I would show everyone that the Baines family would always be part of the town. My dad used to say how important it was to have strong roots and a strong family. The Baines family was important in New Caxton, he said. But what I couldn't see was that there *was* no Baines family in New Caxton anymore. Things got tough after my dad died. My uncles left. My cousins are all over the place. I wanted to put things back the way they were.

'But there was nothing there for me when I got home. My mother encouraged me to go off where someone needed a teacher. Or go back to school. Learn to be something else. But I couldn't leave her. My sister was planning to be married. Even she was going to move away. I had a fight with my sister once, told her she was taking the easy way. Now I see I needed my mother at that stage of my life, not the other way around. That's maybe what really kept me there. She was a rock, just like my dad. She did him proud. I wanted to do the same.

'And then I met Patty and her friends. One night I tried cocaine. Well, it made everything seem okay: the job I was working, my situation. I thought if I could just hold on until things improved, until I could teach school, everything would be fine. But, you know, maybe it was not as complicated as that. Maybe I just needed football. Maybe I didn't know how to exist without it.'

Someone had told Eddie Baines the same thing Owen told me.

Now Eddie began to ramble, turning things over in his head as he must have been doing for some time, trying to straighten out what had happened to him and how it had happened and why. I let him go on, analyzing why he was a failure, a loser, a blind man, a fool. Then, when I had five minutes left, it was my turn. If you know why a crime is committed, you'll find the path to the perpetrator. I asked him, 'Why were the Montevallos killed?'

He didn't skip a beat. It seemed part of his story of loss. He said, 'I guess Brenda didn't toe the line.'

'What line?'

'I don't know. I don't know what was going on with Brenda.

She was involved with something else, but I have no idea what. All I knew was that if you wanted five bucks' worth of cocaine and Brenda was in town, she'd have it on her.'

'She was a dealer?'

He shook his head. 'No. We'd been friends. She snorted coke and was glad to share it with her friends. Simple as that. Usually, she just gave it to me. Wouldn't take any money. Whatever Brenda was into, it wasn't drugs.'

'What was it?'

'I don't know, but I bet whoever got to Patty does. I wonder what he threatened her with to get her to do what she did. Worse than terrible. Her family sent her away, you know.'

'I know.'

'If I could have just talked to her, she would have told me.'

'Why do you think that?'

'Because we loved each other.'

I started putting papers together. 'I'm sorry about all you've been through, Mr Baines.'

'Don't be sorry for me. I deserved what happened. But my mother didn't. And my sister . . .'

A guard approached us.

I quelled my urge to say, No one deserves this who didn't kill somebody. There wasn't time for any more rambling. Instead, I asked, 'What about your sister?'

'Well, she'll never speak to me again. I don't blame her.'

'But you'd like to speak to her.'

'Yes.'

'What would you say to your sister?'

'She knows I didn't . . . Never mind. I would like to tell her I don't have anything to remember our mother by.'

'What would you like to have?'

'Anything. Anything she might have touched.'

'I'll see what I can do.'

The guard put his hand on Eddie's shoulder. He put his headset back into its cradle on the wall and turned toward his keepers.

The warden escorted me right to my car. He said, 'Last person to visit Eddie was a friend of his. His mother had to sign a form that he represented the family. Came regularly. But that last time he came, there was a little ruckus. Eddie refused to see him. Told his guards he wouldn't see visitors anymore.'

'A prisoner can do that?'

'Why not? We got the chaplain to talk to him, but he was adamant.'

'When was that?'

'Just over a year ago. The friend's name was Frankie Gedzeniak.'

I called Eddie's sister from Rhode Island. She said to me, 'Listen, I've got two little babies. I'm making a new life here. I'm a thousand miles away. If my mother had come with me, she'd be alive. But she had to stay by him.'

'Is your brother a killer?'

'No.'

'Then doesn't it stand to reason that she'd stay by him?'

She ignored that. 'Listen, he didn't kill the Montevallos. We all knew that. But he messed up his life. Eddie had everything. Everything except patience. Patience with himself. He couldn't have what he wanted when he wanted it, so he went bad. He messed up everyone's life: mine, my mother's, my husband's. Him and his cocaine and that wretched girl. He didn't give a damn about my mother, and she gave up everything for him. Now he has to pay the price.'

'But if he didn't kill the Montevallos, what price are you talking about?'

'The price for killing my mother.'

She burst into tears. I was glad. It forced her to shut up. While she cried I told her about my visit with her brother, everything he'd said. I told her, 'Your mother stood by him. That's what mothers do. I'm sure you understand that. If one child is in the weaker position . . . it doesn't matter why . . . that's the child you stick by. The other child feels abandoned, gets jealous, but a mother can only stretch herself so far.' I was talking through my hat, explaining the meaning of motherhood, but I kept right on going. 'What he said to me I can only interpret as huge remorse for the hell he caused you. But the reason he's in prison is because he couldn't live up to expectations people had for him. That's what he's being punished for. The town's hero got injured and his football career came to an end. He failed them. One of the last of New Caxton's black families went down. The people in that town have nothing. He was supposed to give them something, I don't know what: the past, maybe. Bring back the glory days. He failed them and he failed you. Well, isn't that too goddamned bad. You're all really pathetic.'

She started to say something but I didn't let her. I was on a roll.

'He doesn't want a hell of a lot, you know. He doesn't care if he ever gets out of prison. Why should he? What's he got? He didn't see me so that I could expose the truth. He has no faith in the truth. The truth will stay buried, is what he thinks. He saw me because he wanted one thing. One small thing.'

I paused. I made her wait. She said something, but her voice was too high and trembling for me to make it out. I repeated her brother's request. And then I apologized for yelling, for getting her so upset. After a few moments, she gained some control. 'All right. I'll send him something.'

'Thanks.'

She said, 'Yeah.'

I didn't go back to Alexandria, I went directly to my office. Didn't pick up Buddy first, didn't listen to my answering machine. I just sat down and started making sense out of all my notes, typing what they triggered onto my computer. I stared into my blank wall for a long time.

When I did get back to Alexandria, it was nine o'clock. I told the kids to lie if there was a phone call for me. They rose to the occasion, answering the phone with their best, most sullen hellos. I'd hear *Nope*. And again: *Nope*. Then they'd say *Sure* to what was, no doubt, 'Will you give her a message?' even though I'd told them I didn't even want messages. They can enjoy acting rude for only so long. After a few such calls, my son poked his head into the bedroom and said, 'Ma, what if Steven Spielberg calls?' I told him Mr Spielberg would call Myron, not me. Then my son said, 'Dad called. I guess he can give you his message when he gets home. So did Poppy. In case you wanted to know.'

My strategy only succeeded in holding Poppy back for two days. Then she came to the office and knocked on my door. She didn't let herself in. I let her in.

'Sorry to bother the *artiste*. But I'll never let you shut me out, so get used to it. That's what friends are for.'

'I was going to call you.'

'I know. But I got tired of waiting.'

'I went to see Eddie Baines. I've needed time to recover.'

'I hope you've recovered, because I'm dying to know if he did it.'

'Don't know.'

'Do too.'

'I don't.'

'C'mon. What do you think?'

'I think he's either innocent or a hell of an actor.'

'Is he another Sam Litton then?'

'No.'

She gave up. 'What will you do next?'

'Back to Rhode Island.'

'Well, at least you like it there. Don't ask me why.'

'Poppy, I miss being with Owen.'

'Listen, honey, can't you just fuck him?'

'No, Poppy, I can't. I don't want to. I miss sitting in his garden. Talking. His ingratiating behavior.'

She rolled her eyes. 'Denise, get over him. So it'll take awhile, so what. Owen was just more insanity in this insane double life you lead. You're a wife and mom, ya know? And you're a professional . . . an artist. I meant that when I called you an *artiste*. Really. I don't know how you do it.'

'A lot of women do it.'

'Impossible. Women have all these friggin' choices, but if you can't choose and you try to do more than one thing, you're screwed. You're the exception.'

'No, I'm not. First I took care of kids. Then wrote books.'

'You're still taking care of kids.'

'Nope. I'm just loving them.'

'If that's not taking care of them, I don't know what is.'

'Thanks, Poppy.'

She was suddenly sweeping out the door. Just before she shut it, she said, 'Move on, honeybunch.'

"Gordon? Who [illegible]
"[illegible] rather [illegible]
[illegible]

"[illegible] What [illegible]
[illegible]

[illegible]

[illegible] spreading between
[illegible]

[illegible]

[illegible]

"[illegible]

[illegible]

25

A linear move was to go from Dan Gorman, who defended Eddie Baines, to Gretchen Loeb, who prosecuted him. And then it would be time to track down Brenda Montevallo. I invited Poppy back to tell her I was moving on. She was welcome to come chat in my office.

First, she poured vodka on the rocks. She said, 'Will you have a problem talking to her? I mean, a former lover of Owen. I know you're still feeling—'

'Poppy, it was a long time ago, a weekend fling. Brenda wasn't really a lover, not in the way that—'

'Actually, I'm afraid I'm talking about Gretchen Loeb, not—' She stopped. She restarted. 'Sorry, I thought you knew.'

I rubbed at the *ping* that sounded in my forehead. 'How could I know such a thing?'

'Mark Loeb is Gretchen Loeb's husband.'

'Mark Loeb, the lobbyist?'

'Yeah.'

'You know, every goddamn woman Owen has ever laid eyes on, he's laid.'

'Not me.'

'Why not you, Poppy?'

'Not my type. Can't stand a man with a sense of humor.'

'So when are you going to find a nice dour fellow to settle down with?'

'Soon as I'm sure I've found him. But you know, sometimes I think there are only two guys I could stay with for more than three months. Prince Albert, but he's been dead for quite a while, and then that fellow who adores you.'

'I'm supposed to be flattered, right? But I don't think we're quite talking adoration here. Nick—'

She said, 'I wasn't referring to Nick.' She waved her hand toward Buddy, snoring on the sofa.

I laughed. 'I thought you couldn't stand Buddy.'

'I don't approve of his vile habits. Then again, all men have vile habits and I don't approve of any of them. But I can't help but be jealous of adoration.'

'What about his sense of humor? Buddy is really quite—'

'Denise. Enough of this. What now?'

I tossed my drink down. 'I spoke to Owen briefly. I wasn't calling him to ask if we could give it another try, even though he thought I was. I told him I was continuing with the book and was talking to people who knew him. I wanted him to be aware of that. He seemed resigned, so I was glad I did it. Closure and all that, right? I felt relieved. But while we talked, while I listened to the sound of his voice, I could feel my breasts starting to tingle with the desire to be touched by him. Can you imagine?'

'Of course I can. Did you tell him that?'

'No.'

'I would have. Shake him up a little.'

'I don't want to shake him up. Really, it has to be over, Poppy. I had a physical reaction, but I managed to maintain discipline.'

'Denise, I didn't tell you he screwed this Loeb woman to be nasty. I did it so you'd have a little extra ammunition when you go and pin her down. She's a hotshot, you know. Her husband, obviously, isn't just *any* lobbyist. You know the muscle he's got around here. The thing is, her imperious attitude will keep her from getting past where she is. Women aren't allowed to be imperious. She's the chief prosecutor for the state of Rhode Island, but she'll never be more. She won't be coming to Washington to join her husband.'

'How do you know that?'

'That's the rap I got on her from the fellow who knows. See, I had the decidedly indistinct pleasure of fucking *Mister* Loeb. And on that note, I'm off.'

She swung open my door and then turned to me, sitting there, speechless as usual at her grand exits. 'Oh, and yeah. There are a lot of people in Rhode Island who drive Chevy Novas. And a lot of them chose the color green we're looking for. I gave the names to the Rhode Island state police. Told them to get on the stick.'

She took a folder out of her tote and handed it to me. Then she left. I opened the folder and scanned the list. The names and addresses were in alphabetical order. The last one was Jerzy Weinecke.

Gretchen Loeb probably never noticed if her husband was sleeping around. She was too wildly in love with herself. Her hair and her makeup and her manicure were all fresh: professionally done before work. She had on a dark tartan coatdress, strong and professional but female. There was a tattered piece of paper attached to the file cabinet with a refrigerator magnet. It was a scorecard. It read 228-34. An extraordinary record, no question. Too extraordinary. She should have moved on. Poppy was right. But why am I surprised at that? Poppy never seems to be wrong. I had an extraordinary record myself, but I didn't post it; you use refrigerator magnets to post your children's *artwork* on the refrigerator.

She had a way of speaking: nonstop, relentlessly, her sentences never quite ending, never giving anyone else a shot at segueing in. Just the kind of arrogance that I am very good at disturbing. The kind that, when I have two drinks in me, I respond to with an argument ending in the word *cocksucker*.

She started with, 'Sit down, my God, excuse the mess, everything on my desk has got to be taken care of today—' She made a sweeping motion over the sloppy stacks of papers scattered in front of her while my hand was out; then she looked me up and down and took it. 'You know, Mrs Burke, I believe that—'

I forged my way. 'Denise. And I'll call you Gretchen, if that's all right.'

That stopped her for a second. 'Yes, well, fine. Denise. Denise, I am about the terribly time-consuming business of procuring justice for the people of Rhode Island, and so I have very little time, no time in fact, to do much of anything else, unlike yourself. I can't put what I do on hold for a week, say, and just take a break, go off on vacation, for example. Consequently—'

'Rhode Island has just one prosecutor, then? I know it's only five miles square, but—'

She held up her hand – 'Please' – and sat down. 'Don't take offense at what I say; I'm speaking in general terms; I don't mean you personally. You've taken offense and rightly. I have so little patience except when I'm doing what I'm supposed to be doing. But I was not exaggerating; I'm the best there is, and I take everything my jurisdiction has to offer. I intend to build an inventory which . . .'

I took the other tack. I let her babble, let her convince herself that she had the whatever-it-takes to make it to the Supreme Court. Poppy told me Gretchen Loeb was so universally disliked that even Owen would not bother trying to get her a judgeship. Her husband had already given up too, hotshot wheeler-dealer that he was.

Gretchen Loeb, like Richard Nixon, was a misanthrope; it took an incredible effort for her to appear nice. While she went on, I fumbled in my bag, paged through my notebook, fiddled with my pen, made it a point to look as though I was waiting for her to say something worthwhile. It wasn't until I tried to scrape off a nonexistent spot on my skirt with my fingernail that she finally noticed me not paying any attention to her.

Gretchen stopped talking. I looked up from my diddling around. Her lecture on the importance of her work compared with the frivolity of mine, and everyone else's too, had come to a grinding halt. I smiled at her. I said, 'Do you know who killed the Montevallos?'

Her upper body lurched forward. 'How dare you ask me that?'

Now I looked down at my pad and wrote something down. The first line of the Gettysburg Address.

She said, 'You're a sharpie, Denise, aren't you? A tactician. Well, hear this: Eddie Baines killed the Montevallos. And—'

'But if he did, surely he didn't act alone. Who—'

'Listen, that asshole Gorman has already told me you've decided Eddie didn't do it. All I know is—'

'Gorman is wrong. I haven't decided.'

'—this. He was the only defendant in the courtroom, and I argued successfully with little to support me. But apparently your only interest here lies in appealing to my sense of morality. Well, morality isn't one of my job requirements. In fact, such a virtue would—'

'Would prevent you from sending an innocent man to jail for the rest of his life and leaving a few guilty ones on the street killing more people. I assume they're out there killing more people, since they're pros.'

'Thought you said you hadn't decided about Eddie.'

'I haven't. I'm not saying he wasn't *involved*.'

'Hey now, shit platitudes like the ones you spout – with panache, I have to admit – may be a hit with the Neanderthals who get off on your books, but it's not going to get you anywhere with me. Eddie Baines was a bum. I don't take credit for that. I *am* taking credit for getting him convicted, though. My job is a lot easier when the accused is a bum. But he was also a murderer. And—'

'Just because you're a bum doesn't mean you necessarily advance to the position of killer. In fact, I think just the opposite is true, since—'

'A killer-slash-bum. Happens a lot, whether your pop psychology references agree or not. I see it every day.'

'Every day? That's a lot of killer-slash-bums.'

'A goddamn figure of speech.'

'The evidence, what little there was, didn't even place him on the scene, even though he admits he was there. The day *after* the murders were committed. He admitted that.'

'And wasn't that noble of him? Gorman isn't stupid. He let Eddie concoct that one because of the sneaker print. *His* sneaker, no question. We had a podiatrist testify.'

The podiatrist. A *bookie*, no doubt, I wanted to say, but I didn't. I had no idea of what she knew. 'Let's say someone stole his sneaker, dipped it in blood, made a print, and then cleaned it off and put it back in Eddie's house. Say the girlfriend managed that, saw to it that he did leave a print. Okay. So let's say he was on the scene. If he walked through there, he would have gotten rid of whatever he was wearing on his feet. Just like he'd gotten rid of the clothes he'd been wearing, according to the state's case. But he didn't. He hung on to the sneakers. Beats me why, but I'm also at a loss to know why those sneakers weren't full of gore. Even if he cleaned them as thoroughly as you'd have people believe, there still would have been traces of blood in the grooves.'

'Maybe he scrubbed them with a toothbrush. Bleached them. Who the hell cares how he managed it?'

'I have two teenage kids. You can't clean white sneakers no matter what you do to them. If grass stains stay, I assume blood stays. And if you take bleach to sneakers, they look it. They—'

'Ah, the old maternal instinct surfaces. You should have been there. You'd have loved the clichés spouting from Eddie's mother. *He is a good boy. He couldn't have done such a thing. He was with me*. Yeah, right. Once your uterus is put into gear, your brain cells become affected and don't function.'

'And if you choose that your uterus will not be put to its primary function, you become a sexist, apparently.' I got out of my chair, placed both my hands on her desk, and leaned into her face. 'Listen, how about we don't get personal here. The guy admitted he was on the scene. I do believe that. So did his mother, as a matter of fact. That's because he told her, just like he told me.'

'Sit down, for Christ's sake.' I did. 'Sure, sure, sure. He was coerced into entering a house where a triple murder had occurred, a particularly disgusting one. So it's twenty-four hours after these murders have been committed, and his girlfriend wants him to help her clean up this mess. Well, let me say that it was a mess, all right. I was there within an hour after the bodies were discovered. Seen the videotape?'

'Not yet.'

'You're in for a real treat there. To have seen it all in person, like I did – we're talking beyond gruesome. Except for the little boy, the bodies were white. Bloodless. The quilt kept most of his blood in. If Eddie Baines hadn't committed this crime, he wouldn't have been able to do any cleaning. He'd have been too busy retching. Needless to say, we didn't find any vomit.'

'Did you vomit when you examined your first crime scene?'

'No, but I—'

'I remember the day I looked into the back seat of a car where three children had been shot. I almost vomited. I didn't, because I had to do what I had to do. So did Eddie. He held back the vomit so he could save his life. In his mind, save his mother's. His sister's. His father's rep—'

'No. He killed them. Out of rage. Rage because Connie Montevallo didn't have enough money to satisfy him.'

'Rage? Did you talk about rage when you prosecuted him?'

'I didn't have to. I had more convincing evidence.'

'Convincing evidence? Where was the weapon? Where were the witnesses? Where were Eddie's Miranda—'

'There was plenty of—'

'Who was it who wanted Eddie Baines's sneaker print left on the scene? Maybe even his fingerprints?'

She leaned back in her chair, swiveled it to and fro. She crossed her legs. There came a swish. Then, one corner of her mouth turned up. She reminded me a little of Poppy, except Gretchen Loeb was disarmed by male charm and a hairy chest just like the rest of us. She said, 'You wanna go to lunch?' She didn't give me a chance to respond. 'The scenario you're toying with is a real stretch, let me tell you. It's downright comical, as a matter of fact. I'm going to take the time here to set you straight. So you won't look like a dunderhead. Owen told me every true-crime book needed a hero. I thought he was full of shit. But a hero – that's me, right? I'm the one who brought a violent and vicious killer to justice.'

Owen, it seems, had to lean on argument in addition to charm. I pasted what I hoped was a grateful smile on my face. I said, 'Lunch sounds good.'

She pressed down the button on her intercom and told her

secretary to cancel her lunch meeting. The secretary said, 'Do you want me to cancel your reservation?'

'No.'

Gretchen would probably run into the person she'd canceled at the last minute and she didn't give a god damn. Would enjoy running into whoever it was.

We went out and got into the back seat of her state car. She didn't have to tell the driver where to take her. She said to me, 'I don't read. For pleasure, I mean.'

'What do you do for pleasure then?'

'Work.'

'Me too. Fortunately for me, reading is part of my work. I read critically, though. Analytically. The classics, all the true crime, hot fiction. To see what other writers have done and are doing to turn people on. The bonus is, I get pleasure from it.'

'In other words, your work is just a matter of picking people's brains.' She laughed loudly and then sashayed from her horse laugh to serious words, no catching of breath, no heavy sighs. 'So here's how I know Eddie Baines did it. He was certainly strong enough to kill three weak people, didn't need help. He wanted to impress his girlfriend, scare the living shit out of her so she wouldn't leave him, something that would happen as soon as her parents got wind of the news that she was fucking around with a black guy—'

'They already knew.'

'Okay. Yeah. Patty's parents found out what she was about as soon as she started seeing Eddie. But they had to be shrewd if they wanted it to stop, so they bided their time.' Gretchen continued building her list all the way to the restaurant. She didn't consider that I already knew her arguments. Gretchen didn't know that heroes are supposed to have a certain sensitivity.

In the restaurant, a very elegant one, not the one with bullet holes in the wall, we ordered and we ate. While her mouth was full, it was time to press her buttons with the same line that pressed Dan Gorman's.

'Gretchen, what about the mother's drug connections?'

'What mother?'

'Timmy's mother. Brenda.'

'What drug connections?'

All I did was raise an eyebrow.

'Yeah, yeah, she snorted cocaine. Just like every overnight guest I've ever had to clean up after. So what.'

'I'm talking about her connection with Eddie.'

'What connection?'

'Brenda and Eddie grew up together. They were practically next-door neighbors. She was his source. He could count on her to have cocaine handy. But she wasn't a dealer. She just always had it. Now why was that? And when a patsy was required, who was it who knew Eddie would be . . .?'

'What the fuck are you talking about?'

'She was planning to go to California when the crime took place. But after the murders, she went back to Arizona instead. Went *back*. To what? To who? Maybe to someone who wanted to prevent her from going to California – or anywhere else. Who wanted her back.'

'I'm sorry, but I just—'

'The world is full of control freaks, you know? Men obsessed with women to the point where they'll kill them before they'll let anyone else have them.'

Gretchen's lips parted, but she thought this time before she spoke. Her eyes seemed to shine a bit. She'd decided to divert me. 'Owen didn't tell me you were here to do anything but chronicle a crime that is now over and done with. He didn't tell me you were going to be stirring up shit . . . Listen, you're a curiosity to Owen, you know?'

'That could be. But I know I've proven to be a curiosity to you. That's actually what I do. That's how I get people to tell the truth. We're getting near some kind of truth here, aren't we?'

I was accusing her of taking part in a cover-up. But she wasn't hearing. She couldn't get past trying to attack me with her intimate knowledge of Owen. She said, 'The good congressman was getting depressed. He was changing. That's because he was having more and more trouble finding women who aroused – shall we say? – his curiosity. He'd been through so many. He was really bored. On top of it, he's the last of the bachelors. His buddies keep talking about their children, not their girlfriends. He suddenly realizes he doesn't have children, and his girlfriends are getting too dull to be with. Then you came along. Got him out of his funk. And so—'

'And so I exploited him.'

She blinked. She took a little gold compact out of her bag, opened it, stared into the mirror, took out the puff, and started dabbing at her chin. My mother used to do that when she was out in public, nervous and with no immediate access to a drink. While she dabbed, Gretchen said, 'He's losing his grip. It's going to get him into trouble.' She laid the puff back into the compact and snapped it shut. 'Owen has a sex addiction. He's one of those men who needs a ration of pussy every three days or he'll have a migraine. Like, his sperm will start building up and building up and then he's got to fuck someone or the top of his head will blow off. Kind of a PMS thing. But the addiction has started subsiding a bit, so I've heard. Or maybe he's finally gotten over it and has begun masturbating alone instead of using women's bodies.'

She wasn't going to get a reaction from me, even though I was wishing I had a gun so I could shoot her.

She said, 'My husband sees him quite often. Owen's alone

a lot lately. Hey, don't get me wrong. I love Owen, but he's one of those people who's had a lot of fun, and his married friends are reaching an age where they're starting to have new kinds of fun and he's excluded because his friends can't deal with his little-girl dates. It's getting him all depressed. But, hell, are you really planning to do this book?'

'Why else am I here?'

'Owen wasn't sure, you know.'

There was nothing more that Gretchen was going to give me. I was not interested in shooting the breeze with her. I stuck my little notebook and pen into my bag. I made a signal for the waiter. I said, 'I appreciate all the time you've given me. But I've got a few stops to make.'

She knew I meant it.

In the car, on the way back to her office, she said, 'Can I ask you something?'

'Of course.'

'It seems to me that your book is going to be missing something. If you want a book to sell, you need sex, right?'

'Yes. I'll need sex.'

'The grandmother wasn't raped. This wasn't a sex crime.'

'Doesn't have to be rape. There's a black man and a white woman screwing in a cemetery in a little town with people all around them, people who don't miss a trick and who like to handle things themselves. Readers will get to be voyeurs' – I rolled on before she could break in – 'and this Brenda. She was promiscuous and she didn't have a job and she wasn't on welfare. But she had a nice car and she looked real good. And how did she pay for the plane tickets in and out of Rhode Island? There's only one way to manage that, isn't there? But she wasn't a hooker. There had to be a sugar daddy.'

'What are you seeing here that no one else saw?'

'That no one else wanted to see?'

'Yeah, sure.'

'I see what doesn't happen in small-town America. Maybe an entire family rubbed out because one member gets out of control. And then, instead of facing the truth, a scapegoat is ferreted out. People were annoyed with Eddie Baines. Serves him right. And since he was black, it would look like a race thing. Nothing unusual there. But it wasn't a race thing.'

'Did I say it was? I didn't play any race card. Hey, you're a writer. You get paid for an active imagination. Don't let it get away from you, though, or you'll make a real fool of yourself. Eddie Baines went nuts. That's all that happened. He lost it and he—'

'You tried to make it look like Eddie had a drug habit that turned him into a homicidal maniac.'

'Yeah, I tried and I succeeded, because it was true. We're all capable of blowing up if we mix the right illegal substances together and wash it down with a bottle of whiskey.'

'That's a nice theory. I'll quote that. But it won't stand up. Talk to Owen. He knows Eddie didn't do it. That's how this all started. He's the one who is convinced Eddie . . .'

'No he isn't. He doesn't give a shit about this case. He zeroed in on you because – I don't know – you're cute or something. He liked your ass. He wanted to get even with your husband. Who the hell knows? He had to be especially clever to hook you, that's all. Owen's off the deep end. And you'll be too, if you're not careful. You go around picking and choosing from all the fallout of the shit you're stirring up and sure, maybe you'll get a good book. But this was a drug crime, all right. Eddie Baines freaked out because he took too much of a good thing. There are no South American drug czars ordering a hit on three little people in New Caxton, Rhode Island.'

'I agree. It wasn't drugs. Brenda Montevallo was into

something else, something more complicated. Perhaps she paid a monumental price.'

'Well, that's imaginative, all right.'

'There is someone walking around out there who did an outstanding job of setting up Eddie Baines. And the town of New Caxton – excuse me, the people in it – came to believe what they wanted to believe. That they did the right thing. Well, fuck that.'

She smiled. 'So now you're back to square one, aren't you? You don't think Eddie did it and don't try to deny it.'

'I don't think he did it.'

She leaned toward me. 'If Eddie didn't do it, I hope someone comes forward with the evidence that shows who *did* do it. I *am* human, believe it or not. I'll be glad to be the one to try whoever killed the Montevallos if it wasn't Eddie. So I hope just such a hero comes along for you. But I don't want to be your hero. I was joking when I said I did. Heroes are losers.'

I drove down to New Caxton, feeling as though I was finally beginning to sort things out. I have an imagination, but I don't make things up. Geniuses like Richard Condon are the ones who do that. They deliberately and carefully prevaricate – tell lie after lie until the truth is revealed. I just happen to have this need to rub people's noses in the truth, because when I was a kid no one came to my rescue. In order to have come to my rescue, they would have had to admit that my mother was an alcoholic. Once, back in Connecticut, I went on a field trip to the Bronx Zoo with my son's second-grade class. A teenage girl in some other school's group was fooling around and she was leaning out of the monorail, not getting in, not getting out, and the doors closed on her head. I leaped up and tried to pull them apart. They wouldn't budge. The other adults in the car didn't move to help me. No one else responded. Just as I screamed for help, the doors opened and the girl was all right. So later, when I was talking to the other chaperones, I kept saying things like *If those doors had closed on her neck instead of her head, she'd have been decapitated.* They didn't respond to that either. They all stared past me just the way they'd stared past the girl when the doors shut on her. That night I told Nick about it, and he went and got a bottle of wine and a couple of glasses. He poured, and then he explained that the people turned to stone because they needed order. 'They won't admit that life is chaos, Denise.' I said, 'But life *is* chaos. There's no order.' And he said, 'That's why people read your books. You give people a crime, and they know that by the end of the book justice will reign. You are in the business of making order out of chaos to quell the masses.' He smiled. 'That's what I do too, you know.' I smiled back at him, not at his combination wisdom-slash-assurance, but because he'd explained why no one came to my rescue when I was eight years old and hadn't eaten for three days. People didn't want to admit to chaos. They wanted maternal instinct. Even Gretchen Loeb.

Now I was going to go against the formula. I was going to create chaos.

I drove to Frankie Gedzeniak's body shop. I filled up my rental car and asked him if I could talk to him. He said, 'Sure.'

As soon as we got into his office, he said, 'I know what you're doing here.'

'Here in your shop?'

'No. Here in New Caxton.'

'You were a friend of Eddie's.'

'Good friend. I was going to testify for him, and then they wouldn't let me.'

'You must be feeling bad about it.'

'Yeah. But there was nothing I could do.'

'There might be something you can do now.'

He leaned his hip against his desk and crossed his arms. 'What's that?'

'Can I ask you a question?'

'Why not?'

'Had any customers recently with front-end damage?'

'What's that got to do with anything?'

'You said I could ask you a question. Do you mind answering it?'

'I had someone with front-end damage. Yes.'

'Would you tell me the name of the owner of the car?'

'No.'

'Why not?'

'Because her husband's the chief of police.'

I hadn't wanted to hear that. I don't like chaos anymore than the next guy. 'Ever do any work on her car before?'

'Yeah.'

'Paint it?'

'You always paint a car when you fix the body.'

'Even in this town?'

'Well, usually.'

'Was it green before you painted it?'

His eyes darted from side to side.

I said, 'There's no one here but us.'

The telephone rang.

I asked him, 'Did you paint it blue?'

He didn't pick up the phone, and it kept on ringing. 'Would this really help Eddie?'

'Maybe.'

'It was green. I painted it blue. This second time she told me her husband thought red would be better.'

On the plane back to Washington, I kept thinking I had to tell Poppy that Jerzy Weinecke had tried to do to me what he'd done to Mike Longman. But I would wait. I didn't want anyone going into a panic. I needed things to remain calm until I could get to the one person whose name I kept staring at on my list. Brenda. Right then the Rhode Island cops were mentioning to the New Caxton chief of police that they were checking on Chevy Novas, his model, his year, his color. He wasn't about to go ramming into anybody any time soon.

Brenda had the answers. Maybe she *was* the answer. With everything I knew, I still had no hint as to why the Montevallos were killed. I couldn't forget the basics: Not who, why? Find out why. Why did Brenda Montevallo lose her family? Could *she* have killed her family for some diabolical reason? I underlined her name.

In Mike Longman's notes, he wrote that Brenda lived with Maximo Sostre, launderer, in Tucson, Arizona. The name was in the Tucson telephone book, One Pole Star Plaza.

I called Brenda. I got house staff with a Mexican accent. I asked to speak to Mrs Sostre. The woman asked me who was calling I said my name, she told me to please hold, I held, and then a minute later there was a click and I was holding dead air. Apparently, Brenda Montevallo was the only one Owen hadn't convinced to talk to me. I kind of wondered what she said if he ever got around to asking her why she never told him that Timmy was their child.

I called back twenty minutes later. Brenda answered the phone. She said, 'Wait a minute.' I heard a door close and when she came back, she was smoking, taking huge inhalations before answering my first few questions with one word – yes – followed by whooshing expulsions of smoke: Is your maiden name Montevallo? Did you once live in New Caxton, Rhode Island? Were you related to the Montevallo family killed in New Caxton?

I didn't have to ask her any more questions. She started

expelling whooshes of entire sentences without any prompting. 'Listen, I can't stand thinking about it.' She inhaled. 'I can't get into any more trouble.' She blew out smoke. 'They were all killed, you know, all of them.' She took another deep drag. 'I have another child. Here, with me.' She exhaled. 'I left her to go home.' Inhale. 'Now she's all I have left. I need to take care of her.' Exhale.

'I never knew you had another child.'

'No one knew.'

I asked her, 'Did Eddie Baines kill your family?'

She seemed to choke a little. Then she said, 'I made a mistake. See, I chose Timmy over my baby, my little girl. Before I could get attached to her, you know? But Timmy's gone now. See? I gotta hang up.'

I leapt. 'Who killed your little boy?'

She slammed the phone down.

I tried calling her again, several times over the next few days. The woman who answered told me each time that Mrs Sostre wasn't available. I left my number but she never returned my calls. I whined to Poppy about it. She said, 'A couple of Sam Litton's victims were found in Arizona, right?'

'Phoenix.'

'We must have talked to people there.'

'We did.'

'Call them. They'll get you a private investigator to find out any information you need.'

'I don't know. When I talked to her on the phone, she sounded like she was going to have a nervous breakdown. But I can tell she wants to talk. She wants to tell me what the hell she means when she says she chose one child over the other. She needs to get something off her chest, and I don't believe a private investigator will be the sort she wants to spill the beans to.'

'So what'll you do?'

'I do like the Southwest.'

'What the hell for? It's a desert.'

'You've never been curious about what it's like to be in a desert?'

'The only thing I'm curious about is why people commit crimes and how to catch them before they commit more crimes.'

'That's what I'm curious about too. So now I need to absorb the atmosphere surrounding Brenda Montevallo. Get a feel for her life. It'll make for a better book if I do.'

'You think she'll see you if you knock on her door?'

'Only one way to find out.'

I proceeded to cross everything off my calendar except Parents' Day at Friends School. I'd leave for Arizona after I put in my time. If the President's wife could squeeze that event into her schedule, so could I. Hillary Clinton called me, in fact, to see what I was wearing. Her wardrobe is planned for her, but once in a while she becomes a little distrustful of the experts and calls in the real thing, a couple of moms. I quoted my mother's what-to-wear-when-in-doubt advice. We chatted. I told her I was going to Arizona, and I had an order for an Arizona Suns T-shirt from my son and a pair of Navajo earrings from my daughter. I asked her if Chelsea would like either since her ears were pierced and her father took her to basketball games.

Hillary said, 'Um-m-m—'

'She'd like both, right?'

She laughed. 'I'll leave it to you. The only thing I know for sure that won't please Chelsea is a pair of gloves.' I laughed with her. The day after the first inauguration, several fashion columns reported that, at the ball, the First Lady had some sort of hanging things attached to the strap of her evening bag. I'd noticed the hanging things during the evening and smiled to myself. They were a pair of long white gloves that Chelsea had stripped from her arms after, no doubt, stamping her foot and saying, 'I hate these gloves. They're too tight! They feel like bandages wrapped around my arms. I won't wear them.' There are some mothers who would have given Chelsea a withering look that said *Wear them and shut up*. Instead, Hillary calmed her down, took them from her, and, since her evening bag was too small to stuff them into, tied them around the strap. She said to me, 'If I hadn't had long sleeves, I would have put them on me.' I told her she should have asked one of us with short sleeves to come to the rescue. She said. 'Oh, who cares what fashion editors say?'

On the morning of Parents' Day the kids had already been picked up in their van to prepare for whatever hurdles they were planning to put us through, and I waited for Nick. We'd go together, of all things. Part of a new strategy we'd developed to learn to make contact again. He was trying to please me; he arrived on time. 'So off we go then,' he said. 'All set to see the children play their guitars? Not that what they do is actually *playing*.' Our son had announced recently that he and his friends had formed a band called Pass Faith. They didn't let the fact that none of them could play a musical instrument bother them.

I said, 'I'm ready. Thank God these things are like Halloween and Christmas. Once a year.'

'Thank God,' he said too. 'And guess what?'

'What?'

'Your President and mine heard I was going, and he called me up and said, "Thanks a lot, you dirtbag." Now he has to go too.'

We laughed. And as we drove away, my thoughts went right

back to where they'd been – to Owen. I fantasized about a trip to Tucson with Owen meeting me there. I was giving my psyche one last vacation before I made it move on too.

26

Poppy said she felt like driving me to the airport.

I said, 'Sure.' I waited to see if she planned to tell me why.

When we got inside the airport lounge she said, 'I'm worried about you.'

'Why?'

'I think this Sostre person is a guy we almost arrested once named Kaplan.'

I thought she was joking. 'Maximo Sostre is an orthodox Jew from the diamond district of Manhattan?'

She laughed. 'Nope. He's a plain Jewish guy from Long Island who went bad. Max Kaplan, we think. We're not really sure that Señor Sostre is one and the same.'

'And what did Max Kaplan do?'

'Lots of things. He's a very creative and talented importer. He imported some kind of bottled papaya drink from the Caribbean. Or guava drink or something. But the juice was only fifty percent fruit. The other half was liquid heroin. Easily separated if you've got the right equipment, which Mr Kaplan had. In Miami, where else? Problem was, some poor slob of a freight handler at the Dade County airport was a little thirsty and helped himself to a Papaya Surprise out of a case. Lived about a minute and a half.'

'And you never caught Kaplan.'

'Nope. Just the boys in his lab. Hell of a lab. The kitchen in some Cuban family's condo. They got to eat out a lot. The equipment was top grade. We kept some of it for our own lab. Don't let on in some book of yours, either.'

'What makes you think Kaplan and Sostre could be the same person?'

'Simple. His description. Also, his chameleon qualities. We couldn't find a single thing on the Kaplan guy: a New York address but before that – nothing. Kaplan came out of thin air, alighted, and disappeared again. We have nothing on Sostre except he hangs out with some of the people Kaplan did and, like I said, fits his description. And there are a couple of things that point at parallel routes the two gentlemen took. We're just checking now. But you might have one hell of an operator on your hands.'

'Why should this particular operator take a shine to Brenda Montevallo?'

'Maybe you'll find out once you've spent a few days in the desert. I think your plane's probably here.'

We got off our bar stools and wandered to the gate. She said, 'So when you come back are you heading for Poland to track down Eddie's girlfriend?'

'You never know.'

'Don't. I have a confession to make. I tracked her down for you. Patty Olschefski lives in a town called Kielce, halfway between Warsaw and Cracow. In other words, nowhere.'

'You've never wanted to go to Poland either, I'll bet.'

'That's right. Same reason I won't go to Tucson. Another desert. Honest to God. You should see the pictures of this town. The front lawns have no grass.'

'What do they have?'

'Just dirt. And instead of garages, pigpens.'

'I suppose you found out other things in addition to the scarcity of grass seed.'

'Yeah, I did. She'll come home eventually. With her Polish husband and half a dozen kids. Unless, of course, it's never expedient for her to come home. And that probably depends on you.'

In Tucson, I checked into the Arizona Inn. It was a four-star hotel, but I still felt like I was back in Sacramento. The air was hot and so dry the inside of my nose hurt. I reminded myself to keep drinking a lot of water. A desert is a desert whether it's got a chichi hotel or not.

When I'd gone to the trial of my fish-fancier poisoner, I stayed at the one hotel in her hometown, fifteen minutes outside the city where her trial would take place. Within a short time, I knew everything about her, the history of her family, her husband and his family, and their ongoing war over her fish. I experienced similar gossip at the Arizona Inn from Mexican, Navajo, and cowboy staff with names like Rosa Sanchez, Cal Pru, and Jimmy Raintree.

By the time I had finished eating a room-service snack, I had talked to the concierge, the bellboy, the housekeeper, and the kids who brought up the food. I was friendly and chatty and handed out large tips. I found out what Brenda Montevallo did for a living. She was a mistress. Before that she'd worked in a dress shop. Now she belonged to a Mexican gentleman who was really an American. A rich one. Brenda used his name, but he'd never married her.

I drove by the address several times; according to Cal, the neighborhood was referred to as the Greenwich, Connecticut, or the Santa Barbara of Tucson depending on your geographical frame of reference as to which is the wealthiest spot on earth. All the houses looked like ancient Spanish missions. I walked along the narrow streets, and the only thing I could hear was the tinkling of little fountains coming from behind courtyard walls, a phenomenon one didn't find in the trailer parks of Sacramento. Then I saw her. She was with a uniformed nanny pushing a child in a stroller. A little girl around two years old. Born not too long before Brenda's last trip to New Caxton. When she chose Timmy. Before she could get attached to her newborn. My eyes began to sting.

Brenda Montevallo's real parents must have been attractive people. She wasn't bulky like all those women in big coats and sturdy shoes I'd seen my first day in New Caxton. She had never fitted in there, I realized, the minute I laid eyes on her. She was tall; she was slim; she had thick chestnut hair; she was quite elegant. Her mother must have jumped the fence. My mother's neighbor's cat was half-Siamese. It was black but it had the Siamese yowly voice and crossed blue eyes. A tube-shaped cat, not the roly-poly kind. Brenda made me think of that cat, half-patrician, half tom. The cat died in a fight with a weasel. Brenda looked like she'd die in a fight with a flea. She seemed to be in a fog. I wondered what he had her on.

Some women have a physical attraction they can't help, which can only work against them, an inherent sexiness that shows in the tilt of their chins, in the way they walk, in the way they look at you – or rather, in the way a man thinks they're looking at him. Bedroom eyes. I could see why she'd caught Owen's attention. And she'd caught the attention of the gentleman whose arm she hung on the second time I saw her. It was early evening. They were dressed to kill. She was exquisite; he looked like a guy from Long Island whose name was Kaplan. They walked across the street and through the gated wall of a courtyard, into an estate that probably wasn't much different from their own.

I phoned Poppy and kept her apprised. I told her what Brenda had meant about baby number two. She'd left Sostre, even though it meant she'd have to give up the new child. And now she was back with her, since her first child was no more.

Poppy said, 'Hold on here a minute. You're thinking Sostre killed the Montevallos to get Brenda back?'

'Maybe.'

'Then get the hell home.'

'It's just a theory.'

'Denise, I'm getting a tad worried here—'

'Listen, I'll keep you posted.'

I hung up. I was worried too, but I had things under control.

The next day I tried calling Brenda again. A woman answered. 'The Sostre residence.' This one didn't have an accent.

I asked to speak with Mrs Sostre and told her who I was before she could ask. She had me wait. A man took the call. I knew it was him. 'Who did you say was calling?' he asked.

'My name is Denise Burke. I spoke to Brenda a few days ago. I need to speak with her again.'

'She's not here. Perhaps you would like to talk to me instead.' I detected flirtation. He was playing with me.

I told him that would be fine, and he asked if we could get together rather than speak on the phone. He named a restaurant, which happened to be the one in the Arizona Inn. He knew where I was staying. He would meet me there at twelve-thirty the next day.

I made a list of what I would ask him and lost the list. I'd tell him about the book and then explain that I wanted my facts straight, which was why I'd hoped to speak with Brenda. Then I thought how much I'd like to ask, *Señor Sostre, do you know a guy named Max Kaplan?*

Sometimes I forget that what I do is far removed from a food column. That my interviews are not a matter of asking Robert Vaughn, the Man from U.N.C.L.E., the secret to his scrambled eggs. I ask questions of the kind Napoleon Solo tended to ask, but I would stay in bounds. What Poppy had told me about Max Kaplan was confidential. I didn't want to spook him.

The next morning, I got up and translated the notes I'd been taking into a kind of structured report. I finished just before eleven and decided to take a little sun before the duet with the father of Brenda's second child. I put on my bathing suit and was by the hotel pool lying on my back in a chaise, dehydrating all the Washington humidity out of my skin and thinking about raising myself and sliding into the water for a few minutes before going to my room to shower and get dressed, when there was a bang and a flash. A few sun worshipers never even bothered to turn over – just like the people in the monorail station when the girl's head got caught in the train doors. Most just sat up and one said, 'What was that?' I dashed toward the noise coming from just inside the hotel. Half the staff were screaming, and the other half was trying to keep people away from the entrance to the restaurant. A propane tank had exploded in a yard behind the kitchen.

The walls of the inn are thick and fireproof. The fire department had the burning grass and shrubs out in short order. Only one person was in back of the kitchen when the tank exploded. A busboy. He was killed. According to the buzz, he went out to check the tank because he thought he smelled something funny. An illegal immigrant, a conscientious fellow.

I became hysterical. Firemen in all their regalia stared at me standing there barefoot in the lounge outside the restaurant wearing a bathing suit. Someone wrapped me in a blanket and got me to my room. A woman in a blazer with the hotel's insignia on the pocket stayed with me until I calmed down. She kept apologizing for the accident.

There'd been a faulty valve on one of the propane tanks, just the way there'd been a faulty valve on the propane tank at

Rosie's father's coffee shop in New Caxton where I'd had my hot chocolate with melted Milky Way. There was a connection between Maximo Sostre and New Caxton. Someone had just died because Sostre decided it was time to sabotage another propane tank like the one at Stoshu's. I didn't think he'd feel any worse about the busboy than he did about the thirsty freight handler in the Miami airport. Or any worse than Charles did about Rosie's father. Mr Owzciak hadn't deserved what he'd gotten. They wanted to warn him. Control your daughter. They warned me, directly. How convenient that I was in Tucson. They couldn't very well blow up the kitchen of the Executive Office Building next door to the White House to warn Nick to control his wife.

Before I left on the next flight out of there, right after I walked through the remains of the hotel kitchen, which I couldn't resist doing, I sent an anonymous note to a correspondent, a rabble-rouser, at the *Arizona Sun*, telling him who blew up the restaurant at the Arizona Inn. I called Poppy from the phone on the plane because I had to tell her that Sostre might not be Max Kaplan, but he was just as dangerous. He wanted me to stop writing my book a hell of a lot more than Owen did.

As soon as she heard my voice, she wouldn't let me speak. She didn't need me to tell her what happened, she already knew. 'I have been trying and trying to reach you. Have you called Nick? He's a total wreck. He needs to know you're alive.'

'The explosion made the DC news already? It just happened a few hours ago.'

'All explosions count as breaking news. What's the matter with you? I'll call Nick. He's running all over the place.' She hung up on me.

Nick was at the DC airport. He grabbed my elbow and started

dragging me toward the doors. I told him I had to get my stuff; my notes were in my luggage. He said, 'Fuck the luggage. We'll have it sent.'

'It was only a warning. He'd never have hurt me. I'm famous. I'm married to—'

He let go my wrist but he turned and took me by my shoulders and drew my face up to his. 'Owen was far more famous. That didn't stop someone from killing his child, did it?'

'Whoever killed his child didn't know it was his child. Who told you about that?'

'Poppy told me. She's feeling damned guilty about encouraging this.'

This? 'Now hold on a minute. Owen wasn't meant to know. Someone told him who didn't understand—'

'Shut up, Denise, just shut up.'

'Nick, stay out of it. The guy in Arizona is in deep shit. He won't hurt me.'

'You've been blind. This is all too much. I had no idea you were entangled in something so dangerous. And I'll be damned if—'

That's when security came over and asked us to take our argument outside. I hoped the fellow wouldn't be around during the argument I planned on having with Poppy.

At home, I called Rosie. I asked her if the explosion at her uncle's restaurant had been investigated. She said, 'Of course not.' I asked her why not. She said, 'Listen, the explosion was to get me to stop trying to find out who Timmy's father was. But by then I already knew. After all, I'm a librarian. And I graduated cum laude.'

'But your father was badly injured.'

'Better him than me.'

'Oh, Rosie.'

'Sorry to offend.'

'Who did it?'

'The hand that feeds.'

I was right. Charles Hall and Max Kaplan had more than an employer-employee relationship. More like partners. Sostre must have called Charles to let him know I was in Tucson. Charles suggested a good way to scare me off, one that had worked before.

Once I'd hung up, Nick started in berating me all over again. The doorbell rang. Nick got it, and then I heard voices. He was talking to Poppy. I went into the living room. Poppy and Nick were deep in conversation. They both looked up. Poppy said, 'Denise, I tried to reach you after the explosion. Tried and tried. When I couldn't, I went to Nick, thinking he might have a way to get in touch in an emergency. I mean, with the kids and all. I had to tell him what was going on, and now I have to tell you.'

I said, 'I'll put on some coffee.'

We sat down at the kitchen table. Poppy was taking her coffee black, something she did only when she was wired so she could stay wired. It was not time to enjoy coffee, only drink it. She said, 'Max Kaplan is not only a former importer of tropical fruit drinks, he's been a lot of other guys too. He started out in the middleman business. He made illegal business legal. He went on to find a good position with the Gambinos, formerly of New York, now of the federal prison system. He escaped the net and struck out on his own as a salesman. He sold information so that someone could take over the Gambino gambling franchise once they went down. Michael Longman found out who that someone was. So did you. And I had to tell Nick about it, so he'd understand that we had to reach you and tell you to get the hell out of Tucson.

'From that sale he got the seed money to start his import business. After the fruit juice, he began a company that imported PVC plumbing pipes and parts from Mexico. Took advantage of NAFTA. The U.S. military was his chief customer, as if this country needed to import plumbing parts from anywhere. And this'll sound familiar, Denise. Before the liquid PVC material was poured into forms, it was mixed with liquid heroin. Then a chemical shop in San Diego melted the PVC down again and separated out the heroin. Same procedure as getting it out of papaya juice, though a few more steps are involved.

'As head of that company he called himself César Santiago. He went from César to Maximo, because when people said, '*Hola, César*,' he didn't answer right away. Needed something closer to home. When you work for the CIA, you always get assigned first names similar to your own. Or the same as your own. Isn't that interesting?'

She took a sip of coffee but held up her other hand so I wouldn't respond. 'Anyway, the new company was swallowed up in a sting about two years ago. His company and all its officers – I guess we can call them that – but not Max, were corraled. We almost got him. Slipped through our fingers and was gone.

'Santiago's base was Tucson. He went there to live. That's when he went from Santiago to Sostre. Brenda Montevallo had a job in a dress shop that fronted another one of his operations. Sostre had done Charles Hall that small favor. Sostre took notice of her. He was smitten. Maybe she'd bragged to him that she'd slept with a congressman. Turned him on. Who knows?'

'How did the FBI find out about the operation?'

'Someone blew the whistle on him. Someone inside wanted out, couldn't get out.'

'Oh, Poppy.'

'Oh, Poppy, what?'

'It must have been Brenda.'

Nick said, 'Why do you think that?'

'To get even with him.'

'For what?'

'For killing her family. Only if he got carted away could she be free of him.'

Nick said, 'What are you talking about?'

'He had the Montevallos killed so she'd understand where she belonged. With him.'

Poppy said, 'So the guy Brenda must have thought was her friend, the one who went with her back to New Caxton, probably spoke to Sostre as soon as he knew what she was about. Sostre told him to stay there but to make sure Brenda wasn't in her mother's house the evening of August fifth.'

Nick looked to Poppy. 'Can you tell me what the two of you are saying?'

'Denise has figured out who had the Montevallos killed.'

'Some guy kills his girlfriend's family and she goes back to him?'

I said, 'Nick, she went back to the only member of her family left. Sostre controls her through her second child. She doesn't want him to kill that one too.'

'The baby you saw?' His voice was shaking a little.

'How did you know that?'

'Poppy told me.'

'I told him everything,' Poppy said.

'Why?'

'Because you're my friend. Because there are people who obviously can't let this book be written, Denise. They mean to stop you.'

'I've got you to protect me, though, right?'

She'd steeled herself long enough. She banged her fist on the table. 'That's the real reason I told Nick. Because, no, goddamn it, I can't! It'll take a long time to find concrete stuff on Sostre. Meanwhile—'

I raised my voice too. 'Let me tell you both something. I've worked real hard. This book is going to *be* something. When it's finished, the Rhode Island police will have no choice but to reopen the investigation. Eddie will be out.'

Unlike Poppy, Nick remained composed. He would reason. He said, 'Let's go back to the beginning. If all this is true, if Sostre hired professional killers to murder the Montevallos, they wouldn't have needed to frame Eddie Baines. Hit men don't leave evidence behind, they don't get caught. It would have been irrational for Sostre to have them go through the trouble. There was nothing in it for him to do something so unnecessary. It would have been downright foolish—'

He stopped because he was distracted by the look passing between Poppy and me. I said it before she did. 'Charles Hall knew Brenda's family would be murdered. He was glad of it. It would keep Brenda from changing her mind about keeping their little secret. He—'

'What little secret?'

'Brenda's child – the one who was killed – was fathered by his brother.'

'His brother?'

'Yes.'

'Owen Hall.'

'Yes.'

'Owen told you that? Where, in bed?'

'Nick . . .'

'Never mind. Go on.'

'Charles saw to it that Eddie Baines would be blamed for the crime.'

'Why the hell would he do that?'

'He needed things closed up. Over and done with. In that town, you don't leave answers up in the air. You give people answers. You give them a neat ending, and then they can put their worries behind them. They don't want chaos.'

Poppy said, 'Rosie being the exception, and look where it got her.'

Nick made a motion of slicking back his hair without touching a single strand. A nervous habit. 'Okay, okay . . . No, wait . . . Listen, Denise, there's still no hero here. You said you couldn't have a good true-crime book without a hero.'

'There's a hero, all right.'

'Who?'

'Me.'

'Dear Lord.' He put his head in his hands.

Poppy said, 'Please drop it, Denise.'

'You're the FBI. I know you won't let anything happen to me. Your job is to protect people. So do your job.'

First Owen, then Poppy and Nick. Drop it, they all said. But there was one supporter who I knew wouldn't let me cave. I would go back to my little town in Connecticut, where life was once simple and where I'd been stifled until I met him. Not that he unstifled me. I did that myself. But he was there.

[illegible]

27

I went into the *Bridgefield Press* offices on a Sunday morning. The *Press* was closed, but my key was still on my key chain. Leo was there just as he'd always been, even as the locals rushed past the office on their way to one of the quaint churches lining Main Street, even while antiques hunters stalked the shops interspersed with the churches. He enjoyed the solitude of Sundays just as much as he enjoyed the little principality that he and I and Sam Litton had created around the big old oak desk when the office was buzzing.

He was sitting in Sam's chair. I said, 'What are you doing at that end of the desk?'

As if he were used to me walking in on him every Sunday, he simply answered, 'One day I decided I wanted to feel what Sam's angle on us had been. On you, to tell you the truth. You were right opposite him. I liked it. I never went back to my old position.'

'And why did you want to do that?'

Silly me. I thought he was going to say something like *Because I missed you.* He said, 'I thought maybe I could figure out why he didn't kill you. After all, your husband wasn't all that important. Not at that point.'

'Well, that's nice, Leo. And did you?'

'Yes. He was doing some banking. Just in case, some day, he might need you. Might need a softie to vouch for him.

Backfired, though, didn't it? Didn't know you were anything but.'

'Did you know I was anything but?'

'No, I didn't. Didn't get to see much more than the Connecticut rich-matron-with-nothing-better-to-do side.'

I went and sat down in the food column chair. 'Leo, I'd love to trade insults, but I've got the makings of something really extraordinary going on. There's this one problem, though. I thought maybe you could help.'

'What?'

'This time around, maybe someone *is* planning to kill me. That's what Nick thinks and he's a wreck. Poppy, too, and she's trying to wear me down. Well, actually, someone did try to kill me.'

I told him everything.

While I spoke, his eyes narrowed, but he never interrupted me. When I was finished, he said, 'I've got some interesting news for you, rather than the advice you're looking for.'

'What's that?'

'I'm afraid I talk through my hat, Denise. I'm really nothing but bluster. I enjoy hearing myself. I never expect people to listen to me . . . after all, they never have. I especially do not expect people to take my advice which I make up as I go along, all of it based on whim. I shit out advice is what I do, and frankly, I used to get a real kick out of you eating my shit. And with such *zeal*. So now you've got a genuine problem and guess what? My powers of ingenuity have fled. I have no answers. But as I said, I never did. You were hearing answers where there was only shit. Why don't you just call a cop, Denise? Tell the police your story.'

I have always been drawn to mean men. Or maybe Poppy's right. That there are no nice men. But Gretchen Loeb was a woman. A mean woman.

Gaping at Leo, feeling repulsed with myself, I said to him, 'The real question I'm asking here has to do with my not wanting to end up like you, a bored and boring stiff who finds himself with no friends except two people he doesn't really care about but who he's forced to share a desk with. Then it turns out one's a psycho and the other an unfulfilled, mad housewife incarnate. What the hell happened to you, Leo, to end up with us? You're not an idiot. You don't have rotten teeth and chronic bad breath. Tell me how to be a failure. Give me a lesson on being a flop so I can avoid it. You don't have to go to your resourceful ingenuity this time. Go to your personal history.'

He puffed out his meager chest and straightened his back. But almost instantly, his appalled look changed to affection and his eyes crinkled. Then he burst into a roar of laughter. 'Oh, little Denise, where the hell were you forty years ago?'

'Soon to be born.'

'Sit back down.'

I did.

'Dear girl, your lucky husband found a woman with guts. Of course, he wasn't quite clever enough to keep you from recognizing that you had them, was he?'

'Leo, you're making this up as you go, right?'

'No. I only make up advice. What I observe is real. But I have to admit I was always so glad you found sense in my pomposity. Made me feel less a fraud. Less a failure.'

'Leo—'

'You know, Denise, when you came in here one morning, right after we all found out that Sam had been arrested and you told me you were going to Florida, I almost vomited with envy. He sent me the same letter he sent you after all. The real reason I took his chair was to get a feel for his take on *me*. He saw us both as a couple of patsies. Back then, I filed the letter'

– he gestured toward the wastebasket – 'while you acted on it. Your husband was furious. He came to see me. *Talk to her*, he said. *Get her to—*'

'Nick came here?'

'Yes. He was totally distraught. Needed to speak to one of your friends. I was the only one he could think of.'

'He never took my friends seriously.'

'I was a *male* friend, you see. Men take men seriously. All your feminist baloney raised my consciousness, even if I never let on and have no intention of ever doing so. The professor said to me that every time someone asked him, *Say, did your wife know that serial killer?* he'd say, *No, of course not.* He couldn't stand it that you were part of something thrilling, so removed from what he was about.

'But I'm not saying the good professor was jealous. No, he was duty-bound. He's on old-fashioned fellow. How come you never managed to raise *his* consciousness?'

'I think it's rising as we speak.'

'No matter. At first, I thought he was jealous, but then I realized that he saw his Henry Higgins persona was no longer germane and he didn't know what his next move should be. He'd developed you from the eighteen-year-old you were when he met you to what he needed: someone to honor and cherish him all the days of his life. That's a good one. Suddenly, it wasn't working. He was in a panic. So I told him he'd given you wings and he'd better stop pulling all the windows down because you'd only break them. He slumped out of the office looking like hell.

'Then, the next day, you bounced in and told me you were going to Florida whether your husband liked it or not. You would do what you set your mind to doing. And, of course, I'd rattled off some crock of shit or other that you took as advice, and you went dancing out the door as if what I'd said inspired you. And I sat here – well, over *there* – immobile, a lump, a *flop* as you so correctly put it.'

I reached out to touch his hand, but he was too fast for me. He pulled it out of range. 'Listen, Leo, the advice you gave me – and it turned out to be anything but a crock of shit – you told me I'd need a hero to write a good crime book. I swear by that piece of advice.'

He smirked. 'Did I say that?'

'Yes.'

'Probably something I read in *The New York Times Book Review* that week.'

'Leo?'

'Yes, dear?'

'I'm in danger, aren't I? You're avoiding telling me that, right?'

He leaned forward into my face. 'Yes, I think it sounds like maybe you are. But so the hell am I. My ticker's been missing a few beats every so often. More and more often, lately. And I've got emphysema. And I owe some bookie a fortune. I'm in danger, too. Better you get killed doing what you're doing than the way I'm going to go. Your risk is pretty small, considering your connections. Considering that best friend of yours at the FBI and what your husband does for a living these days. Besides, you could walk out the door over there, stand on a sidewalk, and have the *Bridgefield Press* sign fall on your head, and then you're a kumquat in some nursing home like I'm going to be.'

He started playing with a paper clip. Then he began to whimper. I got up and went around behind his desk and put my arms around him. I said, 'I love you, dickhead.'

I held him so he could cry onto my shoulder instead of air.

When I left a few minutes later, he stayed there at the desk even though I'd invited him to come and have lunch with me.

I turned back at the doorway. I said, 'This is the second time you've told me to just go out and do what I wanted to do.'

He waved me off.

'But Leo, the last time you worried about me you had me read *Titus Andronicus*. Don't tell me you didn't know what you were saying. You wanted me to find out what happened to his daughter.'

'Yes, I did. And you didn't let it stop you.'

When I walked under it, the *Bridgefield Press* sign stayed put, too.

I went around the building to the parking lot, and as I got into my car I heard him calling to me. His skinny little head was poked out a back window. He called out, 'Where's your asinine dog? Finally get hit by a truck?'

The front door was ajar when I got home. I figured our cleaning woman had left it open. In the foyer, I dropped my stuff and took off my coat. Buddy's nose did not appear from around the corner of the hallway. I hung up my coat and realized he must have taken off. Leo's last words to me rang out, and now they weren't funny. The cleaning woman knew how to keep furniture glassy-looking; she was a firm believer in polishing with all the elbow grease she could muster. But she was ditsy. I went back to the door, threw it open and called Buddy. I went down the steps and looked up and down the street. I called him again. Nothing.

Well, I would get myself organized and then dial the pound. Dogs don't roam very long in Alexandria without getting picked up. Or hit by a truck.

I went back in the house and carried my things up to the bedroom. The comforter wasn't folded at the foot of the bed, it was all rolled up in a bundle and there was bright red ink under it, staining the bedspread. I didn't understand how the children thought they could spill red ink all over my bed and then try to hide it with the comforter. Or why our cleaning woman hadn't taken care of it.

I walked to the bed and put my hand out and touched the bundle. Then I saw the seeping slits. It wasn't ink, it was blood. I felt my insides rise up. Images of my children's faces danced in front of me. I ripped off the comforter. But it was only Buddy.

I choked back what was coming up from my stomach. I turned and ran down the stairs toward the front door. But I stopped in the foyer, picked up the phone, and called Nick. I told his secretary I had an emergency and I needed to speak to him. She would have known it was an emergency without my having to tell her. I'd never called him at the Executive Office Building. I only left messages. She said it would take a few minutes to get him, as he was in a meeting. I said, 'Fine. I'll wait.' Now she really knew it was an emergency.

Nick said, 'Denise?'

I could only get out, 'Come home,' and then I started choking again and crying, and he said, 'One of the children?' and I said, 'No.' I wanted to say, *But I thought so*. I couldn't get out anything else.

Nick said, 'I'll be right there. Hang on.'

28

The first thing Nick did was call Friends School. The children were fine. I told him I'd hired a guard to watch them. Then I tried to explain that the guards were only required to watch the house when the children were home. That made me start sobbing again. Nick called the security group and told them to watch the house twenty-four hours a day. As soon as he hung up, he got me to the sofa. He covered me with an afghan and then brought me a drink. He squatted down beside the chair, hugged my knees, and told me that he loved me. He told me how sorry he was that Buddy was gone. Then he got up, kissed my hand, and went and called the police. A cruiser pulled up right away. Nick showed them Buddy's body. They called the cleaning woman, who said she'd locked the door behind her. The officers thought we were crazy. They wondered aloud what we'd done to make an enemy who would do a thing like that.

Nick went down to the cellar, got a box, and put Buddy in it. He carried him out the back door into our yard. Then he called the cleaning woman again and asked her if she knew someone who could come and get our mattress. Her son came in a pickup truck. Nick asked him if he had a shovel in his truck and could we borrow it. Yes.

When the children arrived home, I told them what had happened but promised them they were safe. We all took turns digging a hole to bury Buddy. Then we went inside and we played cards for a long time, and then we took out family videos and watched Buddy in his favorite spot on the carpet ignoring Christmas gift openings and birthday parties, and then we watched him doing his favorite thing – running up and down the beach in Rhode Island.

I didn't go back to my office. Leo had been wrong. I couldn't write my book. I could eventually, if and when Max Kaplan was behind bars, which probably meant not until Charles Hall Enterprises was dismantled. With that, there'd be a new effort to flush out Max Kaplan because his name would pop up. Or maybe Brenda would kill him.

Poppy came around a couple of times. She and Nick were mollified. I'd stopped work.

I visited the K Street library. I felt calm there. I stayed several hours and just gazed out the window. The next day I went back. I went there every day. At first, I listened to music on my son's Walkman. Then I read a little – books, not newspapers. And then, on a Thursday, the day that had always been my library day, I got mugged. Or kidnapped, or whatever it was. That little episode I described to Poppy the day of Owen's memorial service.

I knew it had nothing to do with Kaplan. It wouldn't be worth it to him to hire three men to drive me to Baltimore and leave me there. True, he'd figured blowing up a restaurant hadn't been enough. But he had to know killing my dog was plenty. There was no need for further warnings. So it wasn't a warning, it wasn't anything. It was the *Bridgefield Press* sign falling on my head. I didn't tell Nick and I didn't tell Poppy because they were so settled. They wanted me safe. I would be. I stopped going to the library. I stayed home and redecorated the dining room.

And then the phone call came. It came around midnight,

not long after a pair of guests at the Willard Hotel notified the desk that they'd heard strange thumping noises in the next room. Nick got it. All he said was 'Hello,' and then he said nothing at all. Then, 'Yes, all right.' That singular moment, watching Nick begin to hang up the phone, pausing in the middle of the action, staring straight ahead and then casting his eyes toward me, signaled that someone was dead. A human being this time.

It was not one of the children; I would have known that just by the ring of the phone. Besides, they were up in their beds. It could not be the one sibling we had between us, Nick's sister. Nick would have taken on a strong and regal bearing as befitted the man in charge comforting his bereaved sap of a brother-in-law. Not Bill Clinton, or Nick would be rolling into some preordained and immediate action. It had to be a friend, his or mine, or someone we knew well. Please, God, I begged, not Poppy. I never prayed except when I wanted something not to be. He hung up. The phone rang again.

'Nick,' I whispered. 'Who?'

He was speaking into the phone, using one-syllable words. Asking how and when. Then he put the phone in its cradle. His eyes shifted toward me again, but he didn't say anything.

'Nick, please.'

His mouth moved. Nothing came out. He cleared his throat, and then he said, 'Owen Hall was just found dead in a hotel room.'

The phone rang again. Again, he picked up, listened for just a second, and said, 'I know.' He continued the conversation. It was his office, probably needing instructions. He wouldn't have to deal with me quite yet. The government came first. I went into the family room and turned on the TV. But I'd read Nick wrong. He was right there behind me. He'd hung up; the phone was ringing once more, but he was ignoring it. Owen was the

CNN breaking-news story. Breaking right then.

Congressman Owen Allen Hall, Democrat of Rhode Island, was found dead a short time ago in a room at the Willard Hotel, a luxury hotel just half a block from the White House. Found with him, alive, was an unidentified woman who expired in an ambulance on the way to the Georgetown Medical Center. First reports theorize that they may have died during sex games . . .

I didn't hear anymore because Nick was saying, 'Woman? What woman?' His eyes seemed to be bulging out of his head.

I said, 'Not me, Nick. I'm right here.'

Then I was freezing cold and I was shuddering. I got up and snapped off the television and went to my bedroom so I could get under the covers. The new covers. I listened as the phone rang and then stopped and then rang some more, the answering machine clicking in between. Nick stood in the bedroom door. That was when he chose to tell me that he'd sold the beach house. 'I sold it, Denise. We will never set foot in the state of Rhode Island again.' Then he was gone, doing what you do when you work for the government and a congressman is found dead with a dying prostitute.

Poppy reached me. She described how Owen died, told me about Chinese cords. Did her best to soothe me.

Nick didn't come back until the next day. The pompous Yale professor strode into the house. He remained stiff and sturdy throughout the oration – his version of Owen's death – right through to the question, 'Did he have you do that to him too, Denise?' Right through until I slapped him. I slapped him to shut him up, and I slapped him for his revenge – selling the beach house.

29

The day of Owen's memorial service, I arrive home in the early evening, plowed after drinking with Poppy. Nick is waiting for me. Outside the front door. He's watching for me. He comes down the steps, grabs my elbow, and says, 'We're taking a walk.' Before I can say anything, he spits out the words 'You were mugged.'

I can't believe Poppy told him. Must have called him the minute we said good-bye. I say, 'No, I wasn't. Not mugged. I was mistakenly kidnapped. No one pulled a gun, no one hit me, no one grabbed my purse, it was all a—' His face is turning red, his eyes starting to bulge. 'Nick, you're going to have a heart attack. The kids will be so embarrassed.'

Then he takes me in his arms, crushes me, and starts to babble. 'You're drunk. Denise, this isn't a joke. This whole fucking thing has got to stop. You know now that it's dangerous. You haven't come out and said it. I demand you say it. Then tell me it's over. You have to put a stop to it.'

I pulled myself out of his grip. Once, I tried to pull myself out of Owen's grip. I couldn't. Owen didn't let my wanting to be released influence his desire to keep me embraced.

'What is the matter with you? Of course I put a stop to it. Months ago. He's dead, Nick. He's dead.'

He yells. 'Are you mad? I'm talking about the book. Will you never be able to stop thinking about him?'

'Owen—'

'Nick! My name is Nick. Owen is dead. Dead!' And then he goes mad, flailing his arms, babbling away, insisting that he's Nick, my husband, and that Owen is dead.

I sober up on the spot. Nick Burke is throwing a fit in the middle of Alexandria. Jesus. I hug him. He hugs me back. We rest in each other's arms. 'I put the book aside. I really have, Nick, you know that. I had a scary episode, yes. It was very scary. But it's Washington we live in. More crime than in Palermo, remember? Someone thought I was somebody else. I didn't tell you about it because I knew it would make you frantic all over again. I sure was right about that. My God.'

He wills himself to calm down. 'All right, then. Obviously, you weren't hurt.'

'No, I wasn't. Just shook me up.'

'But you're all right.'

'Yes.'

'I have to go out tonight. To the White House. A bit more damage control. You're not lying to me, are you?'

'No, I'm not. I'm fine.'

'I meant about the book.'

'I want nothing to do with the book, Nick. I don't want to even think about it.' I mean it.

I head inside, and he goes to his car.

How ironic that Bill Clinton chooses to call on Nick to help protect Owen's reputation.

I go to my office and spend an hour sitting at my desk, staring into my blank wall. It stays blank. I go the next day too, earlier, unable to see anything but whiteness, no images arising for me to lose myself in. Then I'm there every morning, organizing papers, putting my notes into a file, ending my work on the book. I keep hearing Buddy's snore coming from the sofa. I look over, but he's not there. I continue to pack everything away. When I finish, I sit down in front of my blank wall once again and gaze into it. I think. And I realize who killed Buddy.

I go to the sofa and sink into the smell of my dog. I pick up a notebook. I start writing. I write the lead chapters of the book, and, unlike my other books, I don't begin with the discovery of a body. I start off with the words of the long-ago traveler – his impressions of New Caxton. Then I contrast that with a description of my own impressions of the lobby of the New Caxton Public Library: Aristotle, Venus de Milo, and the winged Hermes. I write about the soul of the place, a place that someone should airlift to the Smithsonian for tourists to gape at. The various pieces of the exhibit would have little cards that show the step-by-step creation of the town upon the departing footprints of the doomed Narraganset Indians.

I write about the farmers selling off their land; the industries moving in; the oppressed of the world granted a reprieve if they agree to work and live there, cheek by jowl between two vicious rivers; the trickle-down theory shown to be the voodoo economics that George Bush told us it was; the dissolution of the descendants of farmers, and the indentured factory workers descending into hell; and finally the hell that the Montevallos and Eddie Baines were dropped into as the man in charge tried to keep from ending up in ruins. The house of Charles Hall was going to tumble. There'd be no saving himself. It was Charles not Sostre who killed my dog; he almost had me, too. But I'm not afraid of him. I write and write until I'm worn out. Then I call Rosie.

Rosie tells me about the arrests in New Caxton, the closing down of her wire room. Using Mike Longman's information, the police are making their raids. She hasn't been arrested herself yet, but she's waiting. She is stoic; she imagines Charles Hall is not. You're right about that, Rosie. I ask her how the little brother of the founder of the library died a hundred years ago. She says, 'Supposedly, he fell down a flight of stairs. No one saw him fall. They just found him at the bottom of the stairs. His neck broken.' Back when I first entered the heavy outer door of the New Caxton library, I had discovered an omen, after all.

And she says, 'Jerry Weinecke is in trouble. He didn't report an accident he was involved in. Someone was killed. I don't know the details.'

I call Louisa Longman to tell her it looks like there will be an arrest in her son's death. I tell her I'll see to it that there is. She says, 'Mike was murdered, wasn't he?'

'Yes.'

'Why?'

'He was about to expose serious crimes.'

'Will his exposure come to light?'

'They are coming to light.'

'Will these exposures save lives?'

I think of Eddie Baines. 'Yes.'

'I'm glad of that. Mike's father, his brother and sister, will comfort themselves in knowing he didn't die in vain.'

'I'm sorry, Louisa.'

'I know you are.'

I considered telling her that the man who killed her son tried to kill me. On his own – to preserve his new and successful life. Without any direction from Charles Hall. I wanted to tell her, because right then I needed the sweet words of a kindly mother to surround me, to make me feel better, to give me the strength to hang tough, to keep on. But such an act was left to me to do for myself.

I turn the phone's ringer off. Now I do lie to Nick. I tell him – and Poppy too – that I am reorganizing my office and to leave me be. I am stoic just like Rosie. I'll be found out, but when I am I will let Nick and Poppy cope with that. And so, that day arrives. Nick comes to the door and I can't ignore him because he won't stop pounding. He's going to throw another fit.

I let him in. He looks around – he's never been to my office before – goes to the sofa, and sits down in Buddy's hair. Then he puts his head in his hands the way he had at the kitchen during the failed tough-love debacle. But this time he starts crying. The notion of men feeling free to cry is becoming cumbersome.

So I take another weeping man in my arms. I don't tell him I love him, since I am so hostile over his selling the beach house. But I don't call him a dickhead. I feel cold and I have no words of comfort. I say, 'I guess Bill fired you.'

I imagine I'm hoping to get him from crying and into a good fight, with him deriding me for cracking wise. But he doesn't get angry with me for joking at such an inappropriate time. He mumbles, 'She was a human being.'

I think he's talking about Buddy but know at the same time he can't be, because Buddy was a he and even Nick isn't that oblivious. I have no problem with the human being part – that seems exactly the way to think of Buddy. I ask, 'Do you want a Kleenex?'

'Yes. I'll get them.'

'You don't know where I keep my Kleenex.' I get up and get the box of tissues off the top of the file cabinet. On my way to him, Nick says, 'They identified her.'

'Who? Who are you talking about?'

'The woman who was with Owen. Poppy's coming over.'

'She is? What for? Why are we so interested in one of Owen's prostitutes? Why is Poppy?'

'Owen didn't take drugs, did he?'

'Of course not.'

'The hotel room where he died was full of drugs. His body was full of drugs.'

'So he had a lapse. He was going through a lot. And he paid.'

Nick says, 'That was exactly the plan, I guess. How it was supposed to look. And they all bought it. But that poor girl . . . she was entirely innocent.'

'Listen, Nick, I'm having a hard time understanding—'

He pulls me down next to him. I was standing there holding out the box of Kleenex. 'Poppy found out who she was. She wanted me to know so I'd stop denying that somebody besides Owen died. Poppy kept saying that if she knew, then I should know. Poppy found out who the woman was when she came upon the proof. The police couldn't find out, but Poppy did.'

'Proof.'

'Yes. The proof needed so you would believe what I have to tell you. I know you think your friend betrayed you, but she didn't see it that way. This was between me and her.'

'What do you want to tell me? I don't like this, Nick. Tell me what it is you're talking about. You're making no sense.'

Then he's crying all over again, mumbling 'Poppy will tell you. I can't.'

And Poppy's key is in the lock; she turns it, the door opens, and she's standing in the doorway, tall and strong as a tree.

The call girl who died with Owen was twenty-three years old and she was from a good family, but the reason she was a call girl was typical. She was an addict.

Poppy says, 'She has a two-year-old back in Des Moines who lives with her parents.'

I say, 'Why is it that drug addicts don't seem to know that abortion is legal?'

Poppy sits down next to Nick in the dog hairs. Nick says,

'Charles Hall hired some dregs to kill Buddy.'

'I know. I figured that out. Setting off a propane tank in Arizona didn't do the trick so he tried one more idea: Buddy. Worked. So what's your point?'

'Don't you see, Denise? Owen was killed.'

'Killed? You're saying that Charles hired these same dregs to kill Owen too? C'mon, now. He wouldn't have done such a thing. He'd lost control of Owen, of everything, but he wouldn't't—'

They are both gaping at me. Poppy says, 'It was Owen who was responsible for the kidnapping, Denise.'

'What kidnapping?'

'Yours.'

I look from her to Nick. I ask them if they're both out of their minds.

Poppy takes a little tape recorder out of the black leather tote. She plays me a tape. Two men are talking. They both have distorters screwed on the phone mouthpieces so it requires some effort to understand them. They are discussing picking up the 'target' at an address in DC. My office address.

'Poppy.'

She clicks off the tape.

'Denise, the call was made from two public phones at airports. Owen's is the deeper voice. The agent who gave it to me doesn't know it's Owen's. The guy was keeping tabs on Sostre. The second voice is Maximo Sostre. But I want you not to talk, only to listen so we can get this over with.' *Click.*

Owen is saying. *Not there. You'll have a dog to contend with.*

Sostre says, *Not me, you understand.*

Of course I understand. Don't play with me.

Sostre tells Owen that the dog will be no problem, but Owen says no. Owen says, *Not at her office. Somewhere else. She goes to a library on K Street on Thursdays. There's a Metro stop nearby.*

She'll be walking between the library and the station.

Then they discuss dates and choose the date that I was grabbed out on the street and taken to Baltimore.

Sostre begins to explain what they'll do to me so that Owen can be assured that it will look like an accident, but Owen cuts him short. He says, *I don't want to know your business.*

I get up and pace. Poppy says, 'Sit down, Denise.' Then she says it again, louder: 'Please.' She goes and gets my desk chair and wheels it over by the sofa, across the coffee table from Nick. I sit down.

Then she says, 'That's why Nick had to do it.'

I wait to hear what that's supposed to mean. She looks away. I say, 'I don't know what Nick did.'

Nick says, of all things, 'Sold the beach house.'

Poppy's face turns red. 'For Christ's sake, Nick, if you could tell me you can tell her. Do it.'

He makes a heaving sigh and takes in a deep breath. He stands up. He goes to the window. Whatever he has to say, he's going to do it with his back to me. But still he can't. He just stands there.

Poppy says, 'You want me to do it for you, Nick? You said you wanted to be the one to tell her. But if you can't, fine. Listen, Denise—'

He whirls around and shouts, 'It costs a freaking two million dollars to have a congressman killed. Won't *that* make a fine addition to your book!'

Poppy stares at him. 'Shit, Nick, you don't have to—'

He raises his hand. Then Nick lifts his head high. He has an announcement to make. We are about to hear from the oracle. 'It was self-defense!'

My ears are ringing. Little dots are forming in front of my eyes.

'Nick,' Poppy says, 'let me have a go.' She holds my eyes

with hers. Through the dots. 'Denise, I didn't want you to know. I couldn't bear for you to know what Owen was going to do to you. I was a wreck at the thought of you hearing such a thing. And I couldn't go anywhere with it. For me to make such an accusation . . . I mean, there's a margin of error with voice determination tests, you know? And no one's forgetting our reputation any too soon, either; the crime lab is . . . Listen, this would have taken . . . Never mind. I went to Nick with the tape. I thought he could do something. Go to his old friend. To Bill. Go right to the President with it. I never dreamed . . .' She drops her eyes. 'But now it's done.'

I feel myself go cold. I keep thinking I'm hallucinating. Stress and all. A delayed reaction over Buddy's death. But I hear Nick's voice; he's speaking again, and the calm in him is gone. 'I had to defend you from him, Denise. I told Poppy I would call Sostre. I let her think I was just going to threaten him. I convinced her that he would not do what Owen wanted him to do.' He swallows. 'But I lied to Poppy. That's not what I did. How would that have stopped Owen from trying someone else? I called Sostre and told him I had a tape of the conversation between Owen and him. I told him to kill Owen instead. He thought that was very funny. He laughed. I asked him how much. He told me. He said he was doing me a favor. That's how he put it. The two million was nothing. Would just cover his expenses. But he *liked* the idea. He'd a score or two to settle with Owen's brother, he told me. I was giving him an opportunity to get even with Charles Hall for fucking up. That's what he told me.'

Poppy interrupts. 'And here's what he meant by that. Charles arranged for the explosion in Arizona, not Sostre. But somehow Sostre was implicated.'

Nick says, 'He said to me, *I'll call off the present contract, of course*. Just like that. The contract that Owen had arranged with him' – he chokes up – 'to kill you.'

Then Nick falls to pieces again and I start to go to him, but Poppy pushes me back and then starts swatting at Nick like he's an annoying mosquito buzzing her. She says, 'Finish, finish.' He shakes his head. 'Tell her what made you tell me.'

'I can't.'

I try to see them between the dots that become more and more dense, blocking my line of vision. I feel like I'm watching a forbidden movie through a peephole. I'm paralyzed. Poppy stops hitting him. She controls herself. She tugs each sleeve over each cuff so they're even. She breathes in deeply. 'This is how Nick justified what he'd done, what allowed him to feel free to make a confession . . . to ease his burden: The timing.' She looks from her cuffs to me. 'When I left you today, as I was walking down the street, it hit me. I looked at the notes I'd just taken. You told me you thought you were mugged on a Thursday. On the tape, Owen told Sostre you'd go to the library on Thursdays. I called Nick and asked him the date he'd called Sostre. I looked at the calendar. It was a Thursday.

'Denise, Nick stopped your being killed just as it was about to happen. Sostre reached his hired creeps on their car phone just when they got off the highway at Camden Yards. With you in the back seat. There are these abandoned railroad tracks that lead into a tunnel right past—'

Now Nick tries one more time to be tough, He says, 'So you see I was right to do what I did. To defend you. *Because there was no time.* No time to think of another solution. There *was* no other solution. I told Poppy what I'd done. That I'd saved you. It's what she asked me to do, didn't you, Poppy? I wanted her to know just how well I'd performed.' His voice quavers. 'But that poor girl . . . that prostitute . . . who didn't . . . The dirty, goddamned bastards . . . the filthy bastards!'

The dots are now a thick cloud of gnats. The saliva in my

mouth dries up. There's a first time for everything. I faint. Slide off the chair onto the floor. I'm out for just a few seconds. I open my eyes. Nick and Poppy are both on their knees next to me.

'Don't speak,' Poppy says. 'Breathe.'

I say, 'Nick will get caught.'

'No he won't,' says Poppy Rice, chief of the FBI crime unit.

Nick has a glass of water, and he helps me onto the sofa. The sip of water makes me gag, and I double over, my head on my knees, the way you should do when you're about to faint. But I've already fainted. I don't know what you should do *after* you faint.

I say into my lap, 'Owen was worried about my dog protecting me. He never gave Nick a thought. And he didn't know his brother had already killed my dog. But my God, why?'

'Why what?' Poppy asks. 'Why Nick, or why Owen, or why what?'

'Nick has explained why he did what he did. But Owen can't. Why Owen?'

'Owen had to stop you from writing this book. That must be obvious.'

'Poppy, I'm asking *why* he had to stop me. I damned well know he *wanted* to stop me.'

Poppy takes my hand. I think she can't stand watching it tremble so violently. 'I thought you would be able to tell us the answer to that, Denise.'

They are both waiting for my explanation. They think I'm keeping some dark secret from them.

'I only know this. He told me he changed his mind about the book. That Eddie had done it after all. That he'd been right to see that Eddie was convicted. Well, I told him I knew he was lying. So he backed off. No, Eddie didn't do it, he said. He was compelled to protect Brenda, he said. From suffering more than she already had. Her family was dead. New Caxton's brand of loyalty and all that. He owed it to her to see she was not suspected by the police, because he'd had a . . . fling with her. But the real reason was because he'd found out the child who died was *his* child. And so he wanted the truth to come out and Brenda be damned. Free Eddie is what he wanted to do, he said. But that was a crock of shit, wasn't it? He didn't care about Eddie. He wanted revenge. Upon his brother, who knew he'd had a child. Revenge against his brother for not telling him he had a child. Because he found out he was the child's father only after the child was dead.' I swallow. The saliva is drying up again. 'Now it would be his brother's turn to hide in the organ pipes.'

Poppy and Nick think I'm delirious.

'Owen told me he had to do the job himself. Bring the real killers of the Montevallos to justice. But that isn't what he wanted. He wanted me to stop. Even though the book I was writing would bring his brother down. There would be his revenge, but Mike Longman would do that for him. That's who would get the job done, not me. So he meant it when he said he wanted me to stop, and when he couldn't stop me, he decided he had to kill me. There was something Owen didn't want me to find out. But guess what? I don't know what it was.'

None of us say anything. Because we all want to know the same thing. What that something was.

Poppy walks over to my file cabinet and leans against it. She gazes out the window at the view. She is finally thinking. When she's through thinking, she says, 'Something made Owen feel threatened. It could only have to do with his political career. But from what quarter? Those ying-yangs in New Caxton would keep on electing him even now, if you gave them the chance. They'd say, Yes, we'd just as soon be represented by

Congressman Hall even if he's dead. Something Strom Thurman's constituents will say when he finally keels over. They'll do anything to stay up on their perch at the top of the grapevine, gorging on the rotten grapes, telling themselves the grapes are delicious just the way your friend Leo told you they would. But if Charles Hall went down, they couldn't survive. And there would be only one person to blame. Owen. And then they would have to gain revenge for their fallen benefactor. For that reason, they would desert Owen.'

Nick says, 'No. Owen would be their only chance. When the upstart gets rid of the older brother, he's the new king. He would do right by them.'

'All right. So the threat would have had to come from within the system. If your book came out, the Congressional Ethics Committee would have to investigate Owen because he knew what his brother was about.'

I shake my head. 'It would be hard to prove that he had knowledge of an illegal operation. Charles would have seen to it that there was no traceable connection. But even if it were proven and Owen went to jail, those people would re-elect him again the minute he got out of jail. Poppy's right.'

Nick stands up. 'I don't care about any of this. About these idiot people . . . these criminals and drug addicts. I only care about you, Denise. And me. And *our* children. I don't want you to do this book. And believe me, I understand what that means. I've always understood that there was a person inside of you who could write her own ticket. I wanted to own that kind of strength so I could suck it up. You overcame a huge hurdle to accomplish all you have. I respect what you do. I'm in awe of you. I'm sorry that I've never said that either. I'm sorry I've never told the children that you're so extraordinary, that their mother is one in a million. Denise. I'm sorry. I *will* do that. I'll start doing that, I promise. But for now, although

Owen may be dead, you are still in danger. As long as this Sostre is alive.'

Ah, my big, brave college professor. I say, 'Nick, you're the one in bigger jeopardy here, aren't you? You want this to end because of what *you* did. But guess what? It'll hang over you whether I go ahead or not. Jesus, Nick, there had to be some other way.'

Poppy says, 'Shut up, both of you. Face it, Denise, there wasn't. But Nick, if you want to stop Denise you'll have to sell another two-million-dollar house and go back to the first contract. I can just hear this Sostre guy now: "First you want the congressman killed instead of your wife; now you want your wife killed after all. Make up your mind, Professor." That's probably—'

Nick shoots across the room toward Poppy. So do I. I throw myself between them. I have my palms planted against both their chests. I have to push with all my might. We're all shouting at one another, and then we hear the shouts and realize they're coming from us and we stop. We let our arms drop and we stand there. I say, 'Why don't we all have a drink? Poppy, break out your bottle. We'll toast Buddy. If I'd stopped writing this book when you said I should, he'd still be alive. The damage is done and there won't be any more. So face this: I'll be goddamned if I'm going to stop now. Sostre killed the Montevallos. I'm going to finish him, and I'm going to finish Charles Hall.'

When Nick and I get home, the front hall echoes. I think I hear my Buddy coming, always so glad to see me no matter what. But the noise of his paws fades away before he makes it around the corner. He's dead. And I finally let out all my grief over the loss of my dog. I cry for the rest of the day and all night and all the next day too. My kids don't go to school and

Nick doesn't go to his office. They stay in bed with me, and they bring me Wonder Bread casserole, and my son gets his guitar and plays for me. His dreams of having a successful band are progressing. He's already learned two chords.

30

I decide to visit the cemetery where Owen's ashes lie and where the Montevallos are buried too. I guess what I'm doing is looking for secrets, the ones that continue to elude me. 'Chalk it up,' Poppy says, before I leave. The theory that Owen just plain snapped was enough for her. Well, he snapped all right. But not because he became overwhelmed by all the events of his life weighing so heavily. I say to Poppy, 'It had to be more than his fear that he'd be ousted. I believe he could make it look like he wasn't part of his brother's life if he had to. I know there's more that he couldn't afford to be known.' Poppy says, 'All I know is, revenge is never sweet. There's always a hidden cost. He paid it.'

'Will Nick?'

'That wasn't revenge. It was—'

'Yeah, I know. Surrogate self-defense.'

'And how about we throw in a little temporary insanity?'

Something draws me to the cemetery. Poppy keeps trying to talk me out of it, harping at me to drop it. And when I tell her I am going to visit Owen's grave she says, 'I keep begging you to get on with your life, Denise, but if you're not ready to do that yet, fine.'

I end up telling her I am going there to end my mourning. I'll mourn all of them and be done with it. I need to mourn my lover, or at least the man who'd been my lover until he snapped, and the three people I came to know only after they'd been murdered, and Mike Longman, and my dog, too.

I park my car by the gate, where there is an arched wrought-iron sign that says THE HALL-ALLEN MEMORIAL CEMETERY. It is not named after any saint. I've found out the names of the three martyrs that the cemetery next to Connie Montevallo's house was named after: Saints Barbara, Monica, and Margaret of someplace, I forget where. Except they are no longer saints. When Vatican II got rid of certain saints who were actually mythological characters, they also canceled out those young maids who starved themselves for Christ rather than be defiled, i.e., married. Anorexia and bulimia have been around for a long time.

I gather up the two little bunches of flowers I brought, and I get out and walk to the gatehouse. The guard gives me directions to the Montevallo's graves. I don't ask where the Halls are buried. I can see some sort of mausoleum at the highest point ahead of me and know I'll find Owen there.

I walk up a gravel path to the top of the hillside. On either side of me are huge oaks and maples, and scattered about them are clumps of mountain laurel and sprinkles of wild flowers. I know that if I go on down the other side of the hill beyond the cemetery, I'll come to Owen's house and the vast tract of land where he and Charles grew up in a mansion, now disappeared, where Owen tried to find protection and refuge from his brother amid a fort of organ pipes.

When I reach the hilltop and turn, I feel I've seen the remarkable view before. I have: through the eyes of my traveler, who had gazed down in wonder and satisfaction. The two rivers are not blue, they're greenish-brown with pollution, but lovely and meandering all the same. The island he referred to as a jewel is gone, eaten away by floods, no doubt. And not only are there no longer any native craft, there isn't any other kind of craft either – boating on open sewers isn't something anyone would feel moved to do. Instead of the farmland that the traveler had envisioned, instead of the quaint little port at the rivers' convergence, there are the rows of beaten factories.

The town, in the tradition of the old countries across the sea in Poland and Italy and West Africa, chose this beautiful hillside to lay their dead to rest, in dignity and beauty, something that eluded them while they were alive. Who needs a park? I'm sure the mayor said.

As I walk along clutching my bouquets, I can't help but look for the graves of miscarried fetuses. There are several.

Under a white birch tree, I find four little rectangular granite blocks all in a row, each with a name: Peter Mauro Montevallo, Concetta Donato Montevallo, Peter Mauro Montevallo, Jr., and Timothy Peter Montevallo. Under the names, their dates of birth and death, those of the last three identical. I feel a chill. I break up one of the bouquets and lay a few flowers on each stone. I convey a message to Connie, Petey, and Timmy. I tell them their killers will be caught.

At the top of the hill is the marble vault where the early Hall forefathers have all been moved, now kept company by an urn containing the ashes of the latest Hall to die. The vault looks like a little imitation Greek temple. It's hideous. The letters carved into the marble are huge: HALL. And then there is a quote: *I love the name of honour more than I fear death.* My guess, Julius Caesar. Owen's grandfather's choice is surely more prophetic than he ever imagined it would be. I think of the photo of Cornelius Ryan's grave, so elegant, so moving, so lacking in such narcissism.

I can't figure out where to put my second bunch of flowers.

Word travels fast in New Caxton, and while I stand there, gazing again at the traveler's vista, clutching the flowers, I can see Rosie coming in the gate below, and I watch her trudge up the hill. She is a slim woman, but she carries her miserable life on her shoulders and she is bent.

Off to the side of the Halls' tomb is a marble bench, and when she reaches the top of the hill she goes directly to that. Neither of us speak, and I wonder if she will even look at me. But she does, and gestures for me to join her. The bench is a shinier, cleaner white than the mausoleum. It's new. Owen's name is carved in big Roman letters. We sit. I lay the flowers next to me. She says, 'I've been indicted.' I tell her I've heard. 'I don't care,' she says, and then, 'I was his girlfriend too, once.'

I don't say, *Who the hell wasn't?* But I wonder if it's really true or just another one of what must be so many longings, never to be fulfilled.

She says, 'When I was a teenager. He was at college and I was the hometown girl he anointed as the one to be screwed on his vacations. At the time, I believed what he told me. That he loved me.'

A breeze comes up. The leaves of the birch flutter in the breeze. 'Rosie, I'm sorry.'

'Thanks.' She folds her hands in her lap and lifts her face to the breeze. Her hair has grown back, her pulled-back pony tail as dirty as before. The breeze doesn't move it. 'So, anyway,' she says, 'I got pregnant.'

My body turns toward her. We are sitting about as far apart as we can get on that little bench. She faces me. 'Through the intercession of Charles, my parents sent me to live with one of the Hall cousins in Vermont. Owen was not to know. I had to promise that.

'When I went into labor, I was rendered unconscious, the baby was dragged out of me, and then it was taken away. That's what happened to me in a guest bedroom in a beautiful old house in Vermont. I was told my baby would go to a good well-to-do family in Boston, would have every advantage, would be happy.' She closes her eyes. 'All lies.'

I repeat, 'Lies.'

'When I gained consciousness I asked to hold the baby. I didn't even know if it was a boy or a girl. The people the Halls hired to take care of me told me it was better if I didn't know, that I should make believe it never happened and that way I would forget all about it.' She laughs. 'But twenty years later, I tracked the baby down.' She laughs again.

I've gone back to gazing, but now I look at her. There is no smile on her face. The laugh was a strangle. She says, 'Took me no time at all, once I made the decision. I'm not just a librarian, you know. I'm a damned good one. I have a graduate degree. Isn't that a riot?' Her voice keeps choking. It's the most horrible sound.

'I tracked my baby right back to New Caxton, where the Halls figured it belonged. Forget advantages. Forget about any chance for happiness. When the Montevallos were dead, when Timmy was gone, I thought Owen should know that Timmy was his child, and then later I decided he should know about his other baby, too. The one he had with me.'

Now she turns to me. 'So, Denise, guess who adopted our baby?'

She waits for an answer. I think it best to take her question seriously, to answer her calmly because she seems very close to coming apart. 'I couldn't know the answer to that, Rosie. The only person I know here is you, really. I feel like I knew the Montevallos, but they're dead.'

'That's right,' she says. 'They are, but you're on the right track. The baby was adopted by Connie and Chick Montevallo.'

I think, *Petey*. But no, Petey was too old.

'When they found out their son was so terribly disabled they wished for another baby. But Connie couldn't get pregnant. All the same, their wish came true. My baby arrived on the scene with perfect timing. A girl. A baby girl. Lovely.'

I want her to go away so I can lie down. Lie down on that bench with my face against the cool marble, my face against Owen's name to keep me from fainting for the second time in my life.

'I killed Owen, Denise.'

Her words mix with the little black gnats that I force from coming together into a black cloud the way they did before. When I fainted in my office. I take deep breaths.

'I told him. I decided he should know that he'd fucked so many women in his life that his son's mother was his daughter. That his daughter's son was his son. That his daughter was my daughter, too. His son, my grandson, his grandson, our grandson. I'm a mother and a grandmother and I've never changed a goddamn diaper in my goddamn life.'

She keeps right on going because there's no way I'm capable of stopping her.

'Then I told him he couldn't turn things around after all, the way they tell us revenge will. He couldn't gain revenge for Timmy by getting you to show that Brenda was in some way responsible for her son's death so that she'd be punished. Because Brenda was his child, just as Timmy had been.'

I don't know if she has come across the space to me or if I've moved or if we both have, but she is holding on to me and I to her and she talks into my shoulder, crying and crying. 'He did what I knew he would. Called me ugly and miserable, told me I was a convenient little piece of ass and now I was a hag. He shouted at me that I was crazy, a crazy whore, and then he broke down. I knew he'd do that. He'd have to. Because he wasn't evil, he was just . . . I don't know. Whatever it is that his brother and the citizens of New Caxton made him. I got to put my arms around him one more time. And when he calmed down, he seemed very strange. But of course what I told him would make anyone strange. I didn't know he'd go and kill himself. He killed himself because he knew I'd tell you. About incest. Incest is mentioned in the Bible. It's an abomination. He would be through. That would be the end. He would have nothing. Like me.'

I say, 'Rosie, Owen didn't kill himself. It was an accident. You mustn't blame yourself.'

'He made it look that way. He took the drugs on purpose to kill himself. I drove him to it. Oh my God, I loved him so much.'

Rosie shrinks into a mound of grief and weeping. She becomes the definition of weeping, different from Leo and Nick's version of crying, so heavy and heaving, each wrenching sob louder and longer than the last. She shrinks and shrinks. Her whole body has turned to tears. It takes a long time before she can stop. I encourage her not to stop. I just keep hugging her tighter and tighter so she won't shrink away. Cry, cry, cry, Rosie, because what you did almost killed me.

It has helped me to be hugged just a little while back, even though my own tears were shed for a dog. So I hold on to her for dear life, and over and over I keep saying that it was an accident. Maybe, eventually, she'll believe it. But the truth is, I'm glad she won't. More of a cushion to protect Nick.

When I feel her body begin to take some sort of firmness again, when there is no more crying left in her, she pulls back from me. She has one last thing to say. 'Denise, I'd been wanting to tell him since that first day you came to the library. I waited until I knew it would be too late for him to stop you.' And then she lets out a long low wail. She screams into the silent cemetery, 'I didn't mean for him to kill himself. I didn't. I wanted to be the one to punish him. Why didn't I kill him myself, with my own hands?'

I get hold of her. I get her to stop. I say again, 'It was an accident.'

31

The Rhode Island justice system determined that Eddie Baines was entitled to a new trial: There had been prosecutorial misconduct (Gretchen Loeb coerced the officer who found Eddie wounded to say that Eddie's words to him constituted a dying declaration); judicial misconduct (the judges not allowing into evidence Gorman's time frame); distortions (the watch); tampered evidence (the polo shirt); and expert testimony that was inexpert (the sneaker – the podiatrist had lost his license to practice medicine years earlier because of alcoholism-related incidents, though he continued to maintain that practice since his patients were the residents of New Caxton, where loyalty counts).

In the middle of the new trial, things came to a grinding halt. Police Chief Jerzy Weinecke figured it would help him get a lighter sentence in his own trial for the murder of Michael Longman if he turned state's evidence against Charles Hall. So he admitted that he took orders from Charles to suppress evidence that would have shown the murders of the Montevallos were committed by someone other than Eddie Baines; after Weinecke ruled out the possibility of a husband committing the crime, he had turned to the possibility that Brenda maybe had a jealous boyfriend but had put a halt to that line of inquiry at Charles's request.

Halfway through his new trial, the case was thrown out and Eddie was released.

Indictments were brought against Gretchen Loeb, her two assistants, the New Caxton chief of police, the police officer who declared Eddie's words to be a dying declaration, and all three justices who had tried Eddie; the charges ranged from conspiracy to obstruct justice to perjury in Eddie's wrongful conviction.

Gretchen Loeb went on record to say it wasn't her fault that the police fabricated evidence. 'If I can't believe the police, who am I supposed to believe?'

With all that, I decide to check in with Dan Gorman. I experience a little déjà vu. There are messed-up people in his waiting room, and the secretary ignores me once again. He has to come and let me in. And he still doesn't 'care' about who really killed the Montevallos. He clarifies that: 'I may have to defend them.' And he says, 'There's overwhelming evidence that Gretchen Loeb knowingly used false evidence. She violated every ethical canon as well as breaking the law.' He pauses, then says, 'I'll tell you this.' I figure he's going to say something about how he was right about the success-oriented judges, brag that he was right about Eddie's innocence, but I've got him wrong. He's made of sterner stuff. 'In a free society,' he says, 'there must be a line between strenuous prosecution and official misconduct, between advocacy and bias, between justice and injustice. A lot of people crossed that line here. Big-time.'

I tell him I guess he'll get the judgeship he so coveted. I say, 'When you do, I'll send you a real Montblanc.'

He says, 'I knew yours was real.'

I interview the judge who handed down the indictments. He says to me, 'We're beginning to lose track of due process in the pursuit of truth. In this country, rush to judgment is becoming a rush to death row. Neither is going to happen on my watch.'

Rosie's weeping confession in the cemetery gives my book its ending: Owen killed himself because the people of New Caxton would not vote for a man who practiced incest, no matter that he didn't know he was guilty of such a thing at the time it happened. Though I use Rosie, I remind her of the other grandchild she has, who is with Brenda in Tucson.

Patty Olschefski's parents bring her back from Poland to testify at Eddie's new trial. She identifies Jerzy Weinecke as the cop who told her to lie. She tells reporters that Charles Hall was the one who told her there was incriminating evidence against her and Eddie left in the Montevallos' house. The reporters ask her if she would be willing to testify to that in court too. She says yes. But she won't get the chance, because a little earlier that morning Charles threw a chair out of his massive office window and then chased it.

He left a note. He wanted it known that Jerzy Weinecke acted on his own. Was only supposed to scare Mike Longman. As for the busboy in the Tucson restaurant, that was unfortunate. *Unfortunate* was the word he used in the note. He didn't mention sending Weinecke after me. I'd been right. Weinecke was on his own when he tried to kill me. Now that I can't shock Nick or Poppy anymore than I have, I am about to drop a note about that to the prosecutor assigned to represent the state of Rhode Island against Jerzy Weinecke.

When Eddie is a free man, he doesn't go back to New Caxton. There is no home for him there. Instead, his sister insists he come and live with her family until he's back on his feet. When I'd asked Eddie's sister to send Eddie something of their mother to him, she sent him their mother's wedding ring.

No one has been charged with the murder of the Montevallos. God only knows where Maximo Sostre is or what his new name is. But the ones he hired to kill them are now dead. Poppy assures me of this. Someone did a little singing, and once the FBI knew their identity they waited for a golden opportunity to have a few agents act in self-defense when the killers tried shooting their way out of a hidey-hole. Cost the FBI a lot of their slush fund to get that job done. Poppy said, 'Actually, Denise, we don't call it the slush fund in public, in case that might bother some senator. We call it the surveillance fund.'

I keep thinking that Sostre will surface to tell about the contract arranged with him by Nick. But of course, if he does that, the only way out of the penitentiary he'll find himself in will be a walk down death row. Poppy says there is no way he can prove such a thing happened anyway. I say to her, 'You think he poses a threat to me?'

She says, 'Nah. He knows what it takes to survive. He's erased everything behind him already.'

The book is a success. It's being made into a 'major motion picture.' I read the script. It's truly horrific. Denzel Washington – who else? – will play Eddie. He'll be terrific. There is a big publishing party. I invite Leo. I don't think he'll come, but he does. He's in a wheelchair pushed by a health aide. He says, 'I am able to walk, but if I do, I'm not able to breathe.' He has a greyhound on a leash. 'Couldn't win a race. I saved him from death by lethal injection. Only for you, Denise.' He hands me the leash.

Myron's nose is bent out of shape at the dog. Steals attention from the Rolex he's presented me with.

Louis just broke up with Waltraut, so he is not his usual

jovial self at the party until Leo arrives with the dog. By the end of the party, Louis and Leo are in the middle of some sort of laugh-a-minute conversation as if they've known each other all their lives.

With the movie money, I buy a new beach house, not in Rhode Island. Rhode Island's too far from Washington. When Clinton's out of office, I'm staying put. I like it here. The beach house is in St Mary's-by-the-Sea in Delaware. Denzel, the greyhound, loves the kids. He lets them run down the beach with him.

Poppy.

My best friend, Poppy, is at present, celibate. When she had to go to New York to investigate the larceny case, the cardinal assigned his own investigator to work with her, a Jesuit who is a lawyer and holds a PhD in theology from Columbia. He and Poppy fell in love. Kind of explained some of her decisions concerning me. Also, she couldn't tell me about it because she promised him she wouldn't. She said that when I confessed to her about Owen when we had coffee in Alexandria, it killed her not to get my advice about this crush she was developing on the priest. Then she said she realized I was her friend before he was her intended, and so they told me, together, about their being crazy in love. He is willing to relinquish his vows for her, but he won't break them. It will take two or three years for him to leave the priesthood before he can marry Poppy.

He said to me, 'I've never had a flock to watch over. Now I will: Poppy.'

Poppy confided to me, 'Not having sex is very sexy. I look at some painting, or I go to a play, and I become aroused. I have all kinds of erotic dreams. Once the two of us were at a bar and I was sucking beer out of a bottle because the glass they brought me was dirty – priests out on dates can't go to nice bars. Anyway,

I was jabbering away about something and suddenly I noticed how intensely he was staring at me. His eyes had gotten really dark and there was smoke coming out of the top of his head, honest to God. He tried to break the gaze between us but he couldn't. Neither could I. I broke into a sweat. I had an orgasm. I almost bit the neck off the beer bottle. When it was over, he called the waiter and ordered us two glasses of ice.'

Nick.

My husband and I should maybe consider celibacy. We aren't doing very well. He doesn't want to stay when Clinton's term ends. He wants to run away, as far as possible. He's been talking about the University of Edinburgh. The children can spend their junior year there, he says. Sounds like my son's plans for the band.

I tell Poppy about how we will probably split up after all. Poppy says, 'Leave Nick and I'll marry him instead of the priest. I mean it. I've come to realize that the reason I've had such an aversion to men is that I just don't understand them. I cannot tell you the shock I felt when Nick told me what he'd done. So now I know what I want in a man: one who will kill for me. Not many of those around. I settled for *I'll leave the priesthood for you*, because the other's such a long shot.'

I manage not to tell her to just shut up for once. I don't, because it's always been her way. Her manner of solace.

So I say to her, 'Just because he'd kill for me doesn't mean he'd kill for *anybody*.'

She smiles. 'You're okay now, Denise, aren't you?'

'Yes,' I lie.

I tell Nick I am flying to Texas to talk to an ax murderer, every true-crime reader's favorite kind of killer, and that I'll be gone a couple of weeks. I have to be there that long since I'll be looking to see if a hero exists. I'll be busy, might not be able to call. He squares his shoulders and says nothing. In Houston, when I open my suitcase, I find a little note he's slipped in. It says, *Hope all goes smoothly. While you're away, you will not be a shadow. You have never been a shadow.*

That is the best he can do in his present condition. I am busy, but I call him.

Closer

Kit Craig

'When you're a mother, you're a mother all your life. You don't stop being a mother just because they do disgusting things and you don't stop when you find out what they are doing. It isn't what they do. It's who they are to you.'

What do you do when you discover your son is a ritual killer? Respectable, overweight, middle-aged Stella Zax feels that she has no choice but to kill her aberrant child. Then she summons an eager young reporter to her prison cell to explain why. She chose Theo Slate, she says, because he reminds her of her dead son. Whatever her reasons for confiding in him, Theo knows that this is a chance of a lifetime.

But then disturbing things start to happen. Someone wants to get close to Theo. Far too close for comfort . . .

Praise for Kit Craig's previous Headline thrillers:

'Absolutely spell-binding' *Washington Post*

'A tightly wound psycho-thriller written with terrifying understatement . . . riveting and menacing' *Newsweek*

'Genuinely frightening, throbbing with menace and horror . . . outstanding' *Publishers Weekly*

0 7472 4938 5

HEADLINE FEATURE

Render up the Body

Marianne Wesson

Cinda Hayes no longer believes in the legal system the way she used to. She's left her job as Chief Prosecutor of the Sex Crimes Unit in the DA's office to become Director of the Boulder County Rape Crisis Center. But she hasn't been long in her new position when she finds herself agreeing to defend a death row murderer – who's also been accused of rape.

Though Cinda abhors the crimes he's committed she abhors the death penalty more. And her client Jason Smiley's claims of innocence are so persuasive that she starts to wonder if he is the victim of a gross miscarriage of justice. But the more she becomes involved in his case the more the rest of her life starts to go awry . . .

'An excellent debut' *The Sunday Times*

'A very fine achievement' *Independent*

'The story is gripping throughout, with a shocking final twist. This is a remarkable debut' *Sunday Telegraph*

0 7472 5769 8

HEADLINE FEATURE